I0675425

Enemy Lines

Book Two | Secrets of the Blue and Gray

Vanessa Lind

Enemy Lines

Book Two in the Secrets of the Blue and Gray series

Featuring women spies in the American Civil War

Inspired by the spellbinding adventures of female Civil War spies, a sweeping epic of women whose courage and resilience helped turn the tide of war

March 1863. As the Civil War rages on, Union spy Hattie Logan makes a harrowing escape from Libby Prison. Now she's determined to track down double agent Luke Blackstone and make him pay for betraying her and the man she loves. Her desire for vengeance takes her to Tennessee, where she teams up with fiery and unpredictable Pauline Carlton, an actress turned spy.

With the help of a Nashville prostitute, Hattie uncovers a treacherous plot involving Blackstone and one of the South's meanest guerrilla fighters. But John Elliott, the handsome soldier who oversees her spying, doesn't believe her. Only when Pauline is captured and Hattie defies him does the lieutenant relent. Forging an uneasy truce, Hattie goes with him behind enemy lines. Now she must decide how far she'll go to get her revenge.

Drawn in part from real hidden histories, this moving story of friendship, love, and courage will capture your heart.

EBook ISBN 978-1-940320-21-2

Print ISBN 978-1-940320-19-9

Contents

Chapter One

March 5, 1863

Hattie Logan ached for the sky. She missed the wispy pink clouds of sunrise, the bulging gray-blue underbellies of rain clouds, the towering black thunderheads that portended a storm. In her cell at Richmond's Libby Prison, there wasn't a single window, and so with each passing day, she painted pictures of these skies in her mind, lest she forget.

A week had passed since her arrival at Libby from Castle Thunder, another Richmond prison where the Confederates held deserters, Union spies, and other miscreants. This was one of the Rebs' newer prisons, opened only a year ago. Like Castle Thunder, it had originally been a warehouse. But while Castle Thunder had previously been a tobacco warehouse, groceries had been stored at Libby, and the faint odor of onions and spices hung over Hattie's cell.

The longer the War of the Rebellion dragged on—nearly two years now—the more prisons the Rebels needed. Libby mostly housed Yankee officers taken as prisoners of war. Hattie was the only woman here, and as far as she knew, the only spy. Being the only woman was the bigger problem, for it meant she was stuck off by herself in this windowless room, which she suspected had been a closet during the grocery days.

Captain Alexander, the Castle Thunder warden who'd forced Hattie's transfer here, must have known she'd be isolated, and that suited his desire to punish her. But Hattie had been isolated much of her life. People in the Indiana town where she'd grown up had despised her family. The other children had shunned her, and she'd gotten used to being alone.

The biggest hardship she faced now, far worse even than the lack of windows, was that she'd been separated from Thom Welton, the man she'd come to love. On assignment with the Pinkerton Agency in Richmond, she'd posed as Thom's wife. They'd spied together, and they'd been arrested together. As far as Hattie knew, Thom was still locked up at Castle Thunder, and she feared for his life. Every night, she fell asleep remembering his gentle brown eyes and the warmth of his lips pressed to hers.

Captain Alexander claimed he'd transferred Hattie so Thom would get a fair trial. But she knew his trial wouldn't be fair. The Rebels had trusted Thom to carry messages across enemy lines. Having discovered he was a Union spy, they wanted to make an example of him.

A rat skittered across the floor of Hattie's cell, interrupting her thoughts. She reached under her pallet and grabbed a shard from a dinner plate she'd broken with the rat in mind. She raised the jagged piece of stoneware over her head, then hurled it at the creature. The pottery hit the floor and splintered into dozens of pieces. Unscathed, the rat glanced at Hattie, not with fear but with what she took as a smug sort of knowing. Then it disappeared into a gap between the floor and the wall.

Luke Blackstone had gazed at her in that same way, Hattie thought, right before he'd betrayed her and Thom.

She gathered up the splintered stoneware, then crouched beside her pallet and tucked the pieces beneath it. Next time, she'd sneak closer to her target. It wouldn't be easy, but she'd find a way. Determined. That's what Miss Whitcomb had called Hattie, back when Hattie was enrolled in her Ladygrace School for Girls in Indianapolis. The headmistress hadn't always meant it as a compliment, and Hattie was quite certain she had never imagined her pupil's determination being trained on a rat.

Footsteps sounded on the wood-planked floor. Keys rattled, and Hattie's cell door swung open, revealing Erasmus Ross, a slight man with thinning, neatly combed hair parted to one side. As usual, he had a revolver holstered on each hip. Next to the larger of the guns, he kept a bowie knife. His eyes, dark and deep-set, always struck Hattie as menacing.

"What's the commotion, Miss Logan?" he asked in his Carolina drawl.

Hattie pushed herself to a standing position and looked Ross squarely in the eye, which was easy enough since he stood only a few inches taller than her. "This cell is crawling with rats. Why is nothing being done about it?"

Ross's thin lips turned at the corners. "This ain't no hotel."

"The rats are unacceptable. I insist on speaking with Lieutenant Turner about another cell."

Sneering, Ross fingered his knife. "You want moved in with the men like you was at first? I'm sure they'd enjoy that."

Ross liked to remind her how she'd posed as a male prisoner, Hatfield Logan, during her transfer to Libby. Dressed as a man, she'd hoped to avoid a spy's punishment, which at worst would be hanging.

But Hattie's time as Hatfield had been short-lived. After only a few days at Libby. Ross had seen through her disguise, and Lieutenant Turner, the warden, had had her moved into solitary confinement. Male prisoners were at least allowed to congregate in common areas. Some had even managed to escape.

Hattie was certain no one suffered more than she did in this dark, rat-infested hole. "I need to be able to sleep without worrying a rat will run across my face," she said.

Ross laughed. "Good luck with that."

She drew herself up, hands on her hips. "I demand to see Lieutenant Turner."

Ross's fingers went from his knife to his revolver. "The lieutenant's got his hands full," he said, stroking the pistol's grip. "Prisoners coming in by the wagonload. Seems to me you Yanks are having a rough go of it these days."

Hattie stomped her foot, a reflex picked up from years of watching her mother use it to get her way. "Your assessment means nothing."

His lips turned in a jeering smile. "Not even if it involves Thomas Welton?"

"You have news of Thom?" she asked. She touched the watch she wore on a chain beneath her bodice, which he'd given her the last time they spoke.

"Oh, but I'm sure it means nothing, coming from me. And here I'd arranged for a visitor. I shall have to—"

"A visitor!" Hattie clasped her hands at her chest. Maybe Miss Warne, her supervisor from Pinkertons, had made her way to Richmond. Maybe she and Allen Pinkerton had gotten Hattie and Thom released in a prisoner exchange.

Ross shrugged, reaching for the door. "Since you're so out of sorts, I'll advise her to come another day."

She rushed toward him, not caring how desperate she seemed. "Bring the visitor now, Mr. Ross. I beg you."

He cocked his head. "You're nothing if not mercurial, Miss Logan. But then most of the fairer sex are."

"I won't say another word about the rats," she said. "Only bring my visitor, please."

His gaze narrowed, his dark eyes boring into hers. Then he turned on his heel and strode out the door, shutting it with a thud. The keys clanked in the lock, and his footsteps receded.

She sank to her pallet. Erasmus Ross was pompous and gnat-brained. She shouldn't have let him get the best of her. She knew better. When a man had the upper hand, the only way to turn the tables was to play to his expectations. She'd failed at that with Luke Blackstone, and she was determined not to make that mistake again.

She lay back, resting her head on the bundled dress that served as her pillow. She closed her eyes, replaying for the thousandth time the goodbyes she'd exchanged with Thom back at Castle Thunder. How he'd squeezed her hand and told her that whatever happened, she should remember his love.

Did Ross truly have news of Thom, or was he only taunting her? If the news was real, she desperately hoped it was of Thom's release. Maybe Mr. Pinkerton had gone all the way to the top, prevailing on President Lincoln to intervene on Hattie and Thom's behalf. Or maybe by some miracle Thom had escaped Castle Thunder despite his ill health. He was clever, and under normal circumstances, strong and resolute.

She rolled to one side, facing the wall. She was strong and resolute too. She'd find a way out of here. And when she did, she'd find a way to get Thom Welton out of prison. Together, they'd go after Luke Blackstone and make him pay for his betrayal.

Inside the wall, she heard the scampering of rats' feet. There must be a whole family living here, she thought. A whole colony.

There'd been a rat living in the walls at Mrs. Sullivan's boardinghouse, too, back in Washington. Or maybe it had been a mouse. She and her best friend, Anne, who'd been rooming with her at the time, never saw the creature, but every time they heard its scampering feet, Anne shrieked and begged Hattie to kill it. But it was impossible to kill what she couldn't see, and besides, Hattie had been generally disinclined toward killing. But now, considering how these rats taunted her, she believed she could kill a whole army of them.

She missed Anne. She hoped she was happy back in Indiana, nursing her younger brother who'd been wounded at Manassas. In the last letter Anne sent before Hattie went to Richmond with Thom, she had seemed almost giddy—an unusual state for her—because a handsome Union lieutenant she'd met in Washington was courting her.

Anne was diligent about reading the news, hoping to learn the whereabouts of her older brother, Richard, who'd been separated from their younger brother at Manassas. Had she read of Thom's arrest? Did she know Hattie had been with him? For her friend's sake, Hattie hoped not. It would only give Anne more to worry over, especially if she had any inkling of the conditions Hattie and Thom suffered.

Footsteps sounded again in the hallway. No doubt it was Ross, returning to goad Hattie into saying something else she'd regret.

Behind the thudding footfalls, softer, lighter footsteps pattered. Hattie sat up straight. A rattle of keys, and the door swung open.

Ross ushered in a woman wearing a black silk skirt, hooped in the Southern fashion, with a high white lace collar and silver buttons down the front of her bodice. Over one arm, she carried a basket.

"Persistent, this one," Ross said. "Wouldn't take no for an answer."

The stranger moved gracefully toward Hattie, her skirt swinging gently, and held out her free hand. "Elizabeth Van Lew," she said. "A pleasure to meet you."

"Miss Van Lew!" Hattie clasped her hand, feeling the strength in her dainty fingers. She glanced toward Ross, expecting him to lean against the wall, where he could keep tabs on the visit. Instead, he backed out the door, which clicked shut as he latched it behind him. Then his footsteps retreated.

"I'm sorry not to have come sooner," Elizabeth Van Lew said, speaking with a gentle Southern accent. "How wicked of Captain Alexander to have sent you to a prison with no proper facilities for women."

Hattie felt momentarily tongue-tied. Thom had spoken highly of Elizabeth Van Lew, noting how brave and clever she was to stay in Richmond while making no secret of her abolitionist convictions. According to Thom, Elizabeth was a spy, too, passing Rebel secrets to Union officials, though she hardly looked the part. Standing several inches shorter than Hattie, who was none too tall herself, she had a thin face punctuated by high cheekbones and a sharp nose. Straw-colored hair curled at her forehead, the bulk of it pulled into a loose chignon. Hattie guessed her age to be around forty. A spinster, Hattie recalled Thom saying, unmarried and unashamed of it.

"I'm so glad you've come," Hattie said, recovering her senses. "I can't believe Mr. Ross allowed you in." Absurdly, she looked around the cell as if a chair might have materialized so she could offer it to her visitor. "I wish there were somewhere to sit."

The older woman waved a hand as if to shoo away the thought. "I've stood in many a cell and come away none the worse for it."

"Thom—Mr. Welton, I mean—told me you—" Hattie glanced at the closed door. "Do you think it's safe to speak freely?" she asked in a low voice.

Elizabeth edged closer, and Hattie smelled the scent of jasmine on her skin. "Best to talk quietly. Too many guards, too much chance of someone listening through the walls. It's better at night, I've been told, but I wouldn't be safe on Richmond's streets then."

Envisioning Mr. Ross on the other side of the wall, ear pressed close and listening, Hattie whispered, "Thom told me about how you visit Union prisoners. When his health took a turn, I went to your house on Church Hill, hoping you could direct me to a trustworthy physician. But there was a Rebel officer headed to your doorstep. He told me he was delivering a summons, and I feared the worst for you."

Elizabeth batted her hand in the air. "That summons was only an accusation that I'd been trading in Union currency. The charges could not be proven. I've had closer calls, believe me."

"I wish I'd been able to see you then," Hattie said. "If I'd had your help summoning a doctor, none of this would have happened."

Elizabeth's eyes narrowed. "A surgeon turned you in?"

"Luke Blackstone," Hattie said, her voice filled with contempt.

"The snake," Elizabeth said. "No wonder he's run off to Tennessee."

Tennessee. Hattie had never been there, but she would go to the ends of the earth to track down Blackstone if that's what it took. "I hope Mr. Pinkerton's on Blackstone's trail," she said.

"I wouldn't know," Elizabeth said. "I've no association with Mr. Pinkerton. I work with friends here in Richmond. We do what we can to aid the Union cause. We're Southerners, but that doesn't change our respect for the Union or our disgust over the despicable institution of slavery."

She lifted the lid of her basket and removed a cloth-wrapped bundle that smelled delightfully of ginger, along with a small leather-bound volume. She pressed the bundle into Hattie's hands. "Nourishment," she said. "For body and spirit. The ginger cakes are from a recipe I've used many times in my work." Her eyes sparkled. "You know the old saying. The quickest way to a man's heart is through his stomach. Many a guard has let me in to see a prisoner after I offered a batch of my ginger cakes."

Hattie smiled as she took the bundle, the cakes still warm from the oven. "Thank you," she said. "The food is horrid here. Some days, I think they've cooked up rats in the porridge. There's an ample supply, to be sure."

Elizabeth's brow knitted. "I've spoken to Lieutenant Turner about that. I was hoping the situation with the food—and the rats—had improved. I shall have to speak to him again."

Then she offered Hattie the book. "Until conditions improve, this should provide some distraction."

"*Wuthering Heights*," Hattie read from the cover. Holding in her hand an escape to windswept moors an ocean away, she felt her eyes well with tears. "I've heard it's delightful."

Outside the door, footsteps approached. A key rattled in the lock, and the door swung open. "Time's up," Ross said. "This little visit is over."

Elizabeth closed the lid to her basket, holding Hattie's gaze in her sharp blue eyes. "Read the book with *care,*" she said with a wink. "And with *feeling*. You'll find it a wondrous *escape.*"

Miss Van Lew followed Ross through the doorway, her skirts swinging side to side. Then the latch clicked and the key turned in the lock, leaving Hattie alone once more.

Chapter Two

March 6, 1863

Hattie lay awake, nibbling on ginger cakes and, in the flickering lantern light, devouring the book Elizabeth gave her. Emily Bronte's skillful hand transported her from the filthy prison to the wild moors where Catherine Earnshaw fell under the spell of dark and disarmingly handsome Heathcliff.

Several chapters in, a rat crept toward Hattie, enticed by a crumb of ginger cake. She kicked at it and continued reading.

It was after midnight when she noticed the first pinprick. She ran her thumb over the page. Yes, a pin had made the hole. She flipped back through the pages, running her fingers over every line as if she were a blind person reading braille. Then she flipped forward, finding more pinpricks. So this was why Elizabeth had urged her to read the volume with *care*.

Hattie had first come across a pinpricked message while working with Anne in Allen Pinkerton's mailroom, where they secretly opened letters brought by Thom and other Pinkerton couriers. Pinpricking was a rudimentary form of coding. She preferred the challenge of untangling a route cipher or a message coded with a

Viginère's square. But for Elizabeth's purpose, pinpricking was a good choice, easy enough to decipher but not so obvious that a guard thumbing through the book would notice it.

The pinpricks appeared in a pattern, one every thirteenth page. When Hattie was certain she'd found them all, she went back and read the words in order:

an escape is planned trust the dark man

Escape. She closed the book and tucked it under her pallet, her mind spinning with possibilities. Back at Castle Thunder, when she'd shared a cell with other women, she'd heard of escape attempts, some successful and some not. In one memorable ploy, a prisoner had escaped by faking his own death. If she could break free from Libby, she could work on getting Thom released from Castle Thunder, Hattie thought as she drifted to sleep.

When she woke the next morning, she had to blink several times before she realized that the glorious sunrise that had filled her mind was only a fragment of a dream. In reality, only the dreary wooden walls of her cell greeted her.

She rose from her pallet. At her basin, she splashed dirty water on her face. Maybe today a guard would finally bring a pitcher of fresh water. She unbundled the dress that had been her pillow, a green frock that had once been her favorite. One of only two dresses she'd smuggled into Libby, it was now smudged in several places and grimy all around the hem from dragging in the dirt.

She slipped the soiled green dress over her petticoat, then bundled the navy dress she'd worn yesterday and placed it at the head of her pallet, ready to serve as her pillow that night. When a guard brought her breakfast porridge, she was seated on her pallet, back against the uneven planks of the wall, nose deep in *Wuthering Heights*. She kept reading as she spooned the watery gruel into her mouth. Wrapped in the passions of the orphaned Heathcliff and Catherine, she scarcely noticed its bland taste.

When the same guard brought her noonday meal, Hattie was still entranced by the book. Ignoring the small, dry square of cornbread and mealy sweet potato, she kept reading. In the story, Catherine was now long dead, though not forgotten by Heathcliff, and the tale had turned toward Heathcliff's daughter and Catherine's son.

A rat crept toward the untouched meal. Hattie shouted at the rat, and it scuttled away, vanishing through a hole. Then she choked down her lunch, knowing she needed the nourishment.

Later in the afternoon, when another guard came to escort her on her daily walkabout, she had just finished reading. Someone in authority—Hattie doubted it was Erasmus Ross—had taken to heart her pleas for much-needed exercise. These excursions, though brief and limited to the confines of the prison, at least gave her a chance to stretch her legs.

She enjoyed seeing other prisoners, too, even if they weren't allowed to converse. On the top two floors, the men occupied a total of nine rooms, and though these spaces were far larger than Hattie's tiny closet, they were jammed with men who slept head-to-toe over every square inch of the floor. As in her quarters, the ceilings were low and the ventilation nonexistent, so the air smelled of unwashed bodies and sickness. The interior walls, like those of Hattie's cell, were made of wooden planks, but Libby's exterior walls were brick.

And the men had windows—barred windows, but at least they could see out. As Hattie walked the floors with the guard, she could glimpse the winding James River and the canvas tents dotting Belle Isle, yet another Confederate prison. She was aware of the men staring, curious as ever about the woman confined in their midst. But her thoughts were on Heathcliff. He'd been thrust from the only home he'd ever known, estranged from nearly everyone he'd taken for family.

Hattie understood how this must have felt. The day before Captain Alexander transferred Hattie out of Castle Thunder, he'd thrust on her a letter from her father, a Secesh sympathizer and a key player in supplying grain to the South. He had sufficient clout with Confederate officials to get her released, and yet he'd disowned her.

This shouldn't have come as a surprise, Hattie reminded herself. For years, she and her brother, George, had made no secret of their opposition to slavery, which their parents very much supported. In fact, if their mother had gotten her way, she'd have raised her children on her own father's Louisiana plantation—or rather, his slaves would have raised them.

Still, Hattie was shocked to learn her parents had cut her off entirely. Would they have done the same to George? They abhorred his having gone off to fight for the Union, but Hattie thought they might miss him. She certainly did.

She imagined reuniting with George and introducing him to Thom, their lives intersecting after the war. Her brother would like Thom, she knew. Aside from the Rebels he'd duped, everyone liked Thom.

But that was all well in the future. First, she needed to get out of Libby. *An escape is planned. Trust the dark man.*

She hadn't a clue who that might be, but she soon found out. Instead of the scrawny, pimple-faced soldier who usually delivered her evening meal, a tall, square-shouldered man with skin dark as ebony brought her cornbread and sweet potato. He was handsome and neatly dressed though she noticed there was straw stuck to his boots.

He set her tin plate on the upended crate that served as her table, then nodded at the copy of *Wuthering Heights* on her pallet. "Enjoying your book?" he asked.

She nodded. "Very much."

"Reading surely does make for a great..." He paused, searching her face as if to make sure he had her attention. "...A great escape. Get yourself caught up in a book, and afore you know it, it's gotten real...late."

She believed she caught his drift. "Then I expect I'll be up late tonight."

His lips turned in a smile. "Glad to hear it, Miss Logan."

He slipped from her cell then, leaving her to her dinner. Hattie recalled what Elizabeth said about there being too many guards in the daytime. That must have been why he'd mentioned staying up late.

After downing the cornbread and sweet potato, Hattie allowed herself another of Elizabeth's ginger cakes from the bundle she'd wrapped in her bonnet, hoping to protect them from the rats. She savored every bite, sweet and pungent with ginger. Then she lay down on her pallet, fully clothed, right down to her button-up boots.

Would the escape be tonight? How would it happen? What should she do to get ready? She had little to bring with her, only the bundled dress beneath her head and the book, plus the two remaining ginger cakes—she figured she'd need those for sustenance.

An hour passed, then two. Hattie thumbed through Bronte's novel, rereading some of her favorite passages, but the words barely registered. A single thought coursed through her mind. *Escape. She was going to escape.*

Her eyes grew weary, and she finally snuffed out the lamp. She told herself she should try to sleep, that she'd wake when the guard returned, and in the meantime, she should rest up for whatever challenges lay ahead.

She dozed off with the ticking of Thom's watch for comfort. The next she knew, footsteps had startled her awake. Two sets of footsteps, she realized. Approaching her door, they slowed.

Sitting up straight, she grabbed the bundled dress that served as her pillow and, from her nightstand, the bonnet and book. The rapping on her door was so light, she might have mistaken it for the scrambling of an overzealous rodent.

Then she heard the sound of a key sliding into the lock, and the door creaked open, revealing the silhouettes of two men. The one holding the lantern she recognized as the guard who'd brought her dinner. The other, large and hulking, she couldn't see well.

"There's someone's been askin' to see you, Miss Logan," the guard said quietly.

Hattie let go of the meager belongings she'd prepared for her escape. She struck a match, the sulfur smell stinging her nose. As she lit her lantern, the second man strode into its light. He was tall and so solid he seemed almost square, with wide shoulders and a firm jaw. His beard was cut close, and he had the sort of plain, broad face that inspired trust. But it was his eyes that most struck her, colored a pale, familiar hue. The blue of Anne's eyes.

"Richard!" Hattie rose from her pallet.

The guard shushed her. "Five minutes," he whispered. "That's all you've got to talk. Can't guarantee no more than that." He backed through the door, closing it behind him.

Richard Duncan strode toward her. "They said there was a woman here," he said, keeping his voice low. "Some even said they saw you, but I didn't believe it, not till Miss Van Lew paid a visit and told me so herself. Today, I made a point of being nearby when you went round on your walk. I said to myself, why, that's Anne's good friend Hattie."

"It's me, all right," she whispered. She gazed up at his broad face and pale eyes, so much like Anne's that she wanted to hug him. But remembering how jealous his fiancée could be, she only held out her hand.

He grasped it, then planted a kiss on either cheek. "Seeing you, it feels almost like Anne herself's here. Though I'm awful glad she's not."

She let go of his hand. "Me too. She's been desperate for news of you. Back in Washington, we used to check the casualty lists every day."

He shook his head. "After the Rebs captured me, they wouldn't allow any letters. Last week, they brought me to Libby. The fellows here tell me we're supposed to be able to send letters out, but the warden says that's only after I've shown good behavior. I guess that means not trying to mow down a regiment of Rebs, like what got me captured in the first place."

"You know about Henry?" Hattie said, thinking of Anne and Richard's younger brother.

Richard glanced away, then looked back at her. "Got shot up pretty bad at Manassas. That's the last I saw of him."

"Oh, but he's safe," Hattie said. "Last September, we found him at the Patent Office in Washington. Only it's the Indiana Hospital now. One of the doctors wanted to cut off his arm, but a lady doctor came and—"

He raised an eyebrow. "A lady doctor?"

"Yes," Hattie said, recalling the forthright woman dressed in bloomers. "She told Henry not to let them amputate, that he should tell the surgeon he'd track him down with his gun if he took that arm. And the surgeon left him alone."

With his thumb and forefinger, Richard stroked his beard. "I'll be. And Anne? I hope she's not...not..." His voice faltered.

Hattie rushed to reassure him. "Anne's not in prison. She left Washington early in the year, escorting Henry home. I got a letter from her just before I left for Richmond. She's doing fine."

He shook his head. "I know Father said it would be perfectly safe, but I had my doubts about the two of you going East to work for Mr. Pinkerton."

"It was safe when we were just in the mailroom. But after Anne left, I took another assignment. It was..." Hattie's voice trailed off. How could she explain that playing the courier's wife had been both exhilarating and terrifying?

"It was important work for the cause," she said. "But mistakes were made." She couldn't admit aloud that one of these mistakes, a big one, had been her own. "And here I am. But Elizabeth has led me to believe that there's a means of escape. And the dark man—"

Richard smiled. "You mean Robert Ford."

She blushed. "I didn't know his name. The message was about a dark man, so that's how I thought of him."

"Robert's a prisoner too. Fought with the Union, captured at Shenandoah. The warden put him in charge of the horses here, so he's able to get around more than most of us. Miss Van Lew arranged for him to bring me here tonight. And yes, there's an escape planned. Some of the men have been chiseling a tunnel. Started months ago, I'm told. They go at the work every night, digging from the basement. Three nights ago, they reached the street. If all goes as planned, a number of us will attempt an escape soon."

"I'm ready," Hattie said eagerly. "You need only send someone to get me."

Again Richard stroked his beard. "It's not that easy, Hattie. There are a lot of men who've worked long and hard for this. A few were with my regiment, which is why they've included me in their scheme. I don't know that they'd take kindly to a woman leaving here in the same manner as they do."

She fisted her hands on her hips. "Tell them that if given the chance, I'd chisel right along with the rest of them."

"It's not that, Hattie. An escape is dangerous. The tunnel is narrow and dark. It's the rainy season, so it could fill with water. And that's not to mention the danger once the manhunt begins."

She grabbed hold of his sleeve. "You can't leave me here, Richard. Anne would never forgive you."

He nodded slowly. "I know that. But you have to understand, it's not entirely up to me."

Tears welled in her eyes. She swiped them away with the back of her hand. This was no time for crying.

She mustered her confidence. "Tell them I'm a spy for the Union. I can handle myself in a tunnel, and I can make my way back to Washington. And when I get there, I'll go right back to spying. If we're going to win this war, our generals need every bit of information we can find.

Chapter Three

March 9, 1863

A day passed, then two. No sign of Robert Ford, no word from Richard. Hattie grew increasingly restless. On one of her walks, she thought she spotted Richard in the middle of a group of men on the second floor, but as her gaze settled on him, the man turned his face away, and she realized she was mistaken.

Was he intentionally avoiding her? No, she told herself. Richard was a good man. He loved his sister, and he knew how close she and Hattie were. Hattie only hoped he could persuade the other men that she was more than capable of escaping through their tunnel.

By the third day, her hope had dwindled. That night, she ate the last ginger cake, the one she'd been saving to sustain her en route to the north. There was no sense letting the rats get it. If the men refused her, she'd find another way to get out, she told herself. But she also knew that if this scheme was successful, the warden would surely tighten security.

She bedded down for the night, keeping her dress on as she had the last two nights. Tonight, her pallet seemed especially hard and cold. Sleep had never come easily in this place, her mind spinning in all sorts of unhelpful directions whenever she lay in the dark. Tonight, questions of what would become of her weighed heavily on her mind.

Erasmus Ross insisted she would stand trial for spying. If she did, she couldn't very well say she'd had no association with the Pinkerton Detective Agency. Not after fellow spy Lucy Hamilton had implicated both Hattie and Thom to save her own skin.

The Rebels were losing patience with spies. Uniformed army scouts were tolerated—both sides used them to gather intelligence. But spies in civilian dress were another matter. Months earlier, the Rebels had arrested thirteen Union spies in Tennessee, the last state to secede. The men were soldiers who'd dressed in civilian clothes to gain access to Southern railroads, which they then sabotaged. Six of these men had been tried and hung for their spying. The others had been transferred to Castle Thunder, where they'd languished for months before finally being released in a prisoner exchange.

After Dr. Blackstone gave them all up, Lucy had been released in an exchange too. But that was only after she'd betrayed Hattie and Thom. No matter how brutal the interrogations, Hattie would never compromise her fellow spies to save herself. Neither would Thom. Thom, with his warm smile and soulful eyes.

She thought of the first time she'd seen him, swinging a bag of mail onto the mailroom table. He'd gazed one by one at the mailroom girls until his eyes fell on her. No matter how often she told herself that his attentions were a means to end, she'd found herself falling under his spell. When their supervisor, Kate Warne, had chosen Lucy for an assignment in Baltimore, playing Thom's sister and sharing his house, Hattie was hard-pressed to hide her envy. But in the end, Hattie had gotten the best assignment of all, playing Thom's wife.

Hattie drifted off to sleep with visions of the future she and Thom had dreamed of after the war ended, as a real husband and wife. She woke abruptly to a lantern's glow, inches from her pallet. Its dim glow lit the dark face of Robert Ford.

"Colonel Duncan sent me," he whispered. "It's time."

She sat up, heart pounding, then snatched up her bundled dress and the novel Elizabeth had left her. "I'm ready," she whispered.

He shook his head. "Cain't take nothing with you, Miss Logan. That tunnel's too narrow."

She let the dress fall to the floor. But she couldn't leave the book with its pinpricked message. "Can you dispose of this?" she asked Mr. Ford.

Giving a curt nod, he took the book from her outstretched hand and slipped it into his coat pocket. Without another word, he turned and slipped through her cell's doorway, motioning for her to follow. They padded down the hallway, Hattie lifting her skirt to silence its rustling. In the dark, she followed the bobbing light of Robert's lantern, trying to match his light tread by stepping only on the balls of her feet.

They passed the warden's office. Then Mr. Ford turned to the right and led her through the kitchen. To Hattie's surprise, the door was unlocked. Apparently, there was no concern about prisoners raiding the pantry for extra helpings of the detested cornbread and sweet potatoes.

Robert Ford led her around a hulking shape that she assumed was a stove. As they approached the exit, a rat darted across the floor. As it ran beneath her lifted skirt, its tail brushed against her ankles.

She squeaked the start of a scream. Mr. Ford turned and pressed his hand over her mouth, shaking his head in warning.

She nodded, and he retracted his hand. They crept from the kitchen and down another hallway toward what Hattie judged was the east end of the building. Stopping in front of a door, Mr. Ford took a key from his pocket and slipped it noiselessly into the lock. He turned the key, twisted the knob, then returned the key to his pocket and gestured for her to enter.

Inside this room, the metallic odor of blood and the sickly sweet smell of ether greeted her. These smells she recognized from having visited Richard and Anne's younger brother, Henry, at Indiana Hospital in Washington. In the circle of light cast by Robert Ford's lantern, she spotted glass-doored cabinets filled with bottles containing pills and tinctures.

Mr. Ford led her to a far corner of the room. Crouching, he tugged a metal ring, opening a hinged hatch in the floor. "There's a ladder, Miss Logan," he said. "Watch your step going down."

"You go first," she said, remembering what Richard had said about him being a prisoner too. "I'll follow."

He shook his head. "I've got others to see out first."

He held the lantern over the gaping square of darkness. Near the top, she could barely make out a single wooden dowel that she took for the first rung of the ladder. Gathering her skirts, she knelt at the edge of the opening and thrust a foot inside, feeling around in the dark until her foot found purchase on the ladder.

"Thank you," she whispered to Mr. Ford. Then she swung her other foot around and lowered herself onto the ladder. Holding to the top rung, she stepped tentatively downward.

Above, the hatch closed with a thud as she went hand over hand into darkness blacker than any she'd ever known, the smell dank and musty, overlain with the odor of sewer gas. At the bottom of the ladder was what she perceived to be sand. She stood stock-still, trying to get her bearings.

At first, she saw nothing, heard nothing. She turned slowly, rousing her senses to detect which direction she should go. At what she judged to be three-quarters of the way around, she felt air that was more chilled than the rest. She took one tentative step in that direction, then another and another. In case she needed to return to the ladder, she counted her steps as she went though she didn't know what good that would do. If she retreated the way she'd come, she'd risk giving up the whole operation.

In the sand, the scuttling of the rats was faint but discernible. She shuddered, recalling how Erasmus Ross had bragged of locking up an unruly prisoner in one of four cells erected in the cellar for that purpose. Rat Hell, Ross called it.

She felt her way toward the source of the chill air. Reaching a stone wall, she felt her way along it, the sand shifting under her feet.

Ahead, a disembodied voice spoke. "Is that you, Hattie?"

"Richard?" she said, shuffling toward the voice.

She sensed his presence just before running smack into him. He grabbed her shoulder, steadying her. "Thank God," he said. "I was about to give up."

"Where are the others?" she asked.

"Gone through already," he said. "We've barely got time to get through ourselves before daybreak."

"It's that late?" she asked, having given no thought to the time when Mr. Ford had come for her.

"Or early," he said. "Depending on your perspective."

She felt the warmth of his large hand clasping hers. Gently, he tugged her forward. "Feel that?" he said, pressing her hand to a jagged stone edge. "It's where we enter the tunnel. Fifty feet or so, and we'll be on the other side. It will be tight in there. Don't let yourself panic."

She'd never been fond of enclosed spaces. "You go first," she said. "I'll follow."

"No," he said. "You've seen my size. I'm not sure I'll fit. But I'm sure as hell going to try."

"If you get stuck and I'm behind you, I can shimmy back out and go for help."

"That's kind of you, Hattie. But we can't risk anyone going back. If I die in that tunnel, at least I'll know I was close to freedom. Now you'd best get going."

She bent toward the space where she'd felt the opening, but he pulled her back. "You've got to undress."

She pulled back, shocked. "And go through naked?"

"The men did, yes. As I said, the tunnel's narrow. Clothes only increase the chance you'll get stuck. You're small enough, you can keep your chemise on, I suppose. But no more than that."

"But on the other side..." Dashing through Richmond's streets in her chemise wasn't exactly a way to avoid undue attention.

"That's why we've got to get this done before daybreak. The tunnel goes under the street. You'll come up in a yard next to a storehouse. There's clothing inside, and the men who went before us should have broken into it by now. Ready?"

"Yes." She turned, an unnecessary precaution in the darkness, and unbuttoned her bodice. She slipped out of it, then unfastened her waistband and stepped out of her skirt. In the cold, she stood in her chemise and a single petticoat, goosebumps rising on her skin.

"What about my boots?" she asked.

"Leave them," he said. "There are no handholds, so you'll have to push yourself through from behind, and your boots will help."

She tossed her clothes into the darkness. "All right. I'm ready."

He clasped her hand. "Fifty feet, and then you'll be free."

"And you'll be right behind me."

"Yes. But if anything happens to me, I'm counting on you to get word to Anne and my parents and Lavina."

"Nothing's going to happen to you."

He let go of her hand. She poked her head through the opening and squeezed inside. The earth pressed cold all around her. In addition to the smell of wet dirt, the sewer gas odor was even stronger here. She dug the toes of her boots into the dirt and shimmied forward. *Fifty feet,* she told herself. *Fifty feet to freedom.*

She elbowed forward, then pushed again with her toes, feeling more like a salamander than a human. Behind her, she heard strained breathing, and she knew Richard had crawled in behind her. As little room as she had, she couldn't imagine how his broad shoulders fit.

She inched ahead, the tunnel seeming to close around her. Panic rose in her throat, her heart pounding.

Stay calm, she told herself. *There can't be more than thirty more feet to go.*

She belly-crawled forward. *Thom*, she reminded herself. She had to get out so she could help Thom escape.

She turned her head, lips brushing the dirt, and pushed forward. Her petticoat caught on what she took for a rock. Why hadn't she taken it off?

Panic rose in her throat. She shoved herself forward and heard her petticoat rip. If the end of this blasted tunnel didn't show itself soon, she really would be naked by the time she got there.

Twenty feet, she told herself, though she had no way of knowing whether this estimate was at all accurate.

She inched ahead. *Ten feet.*

At last, she felt a blast of fresh air and saw a patch of near-light. Freedom. She shimmied toward the opening. When her fingers touched grass, she shoved again with her feet. Her head free of the tunnel, she breathed deep. Filling her lungs, she felt giddy. It was dark here, too, but the eastern sky had lightened to a deep midnight blue.

She crawled out, never having felt so glad to be standing on her own two feet. Brushing dirt from her underclothes, she heard footfalls in a slow march. *Sentries*, she thought. *Guarding the prison entrance.*

She knelt at the edge of the tunnel's opening. "Richard?" she whispered loudly. "Are you there?"

She listened closely but heard nothing. "Richard," she repeated, bending so her ear was directly over the hole.

"Stuck," he said in a strained voice.

She reached her arm into the tunnel. "Grab my hand."

She wiggled her fingers but felt nothing.

"Can't," he said faintly.

She flattened herself to the ground, edging closer to the opening and thrusting her arm as deep as she could into the hole. Waving her hand about, she brushed Richard's fingers. "Grab on," she said, wriggling so close she feared she might fall headlong into the tunnel.

He gripped her hand. She tugged with all her might, but he remained stuck.

"No...no use," he sputtered. "Get...get help. Haze...Hazel Mae. Cot...cottage...across from the church."

She squeezed his hand. "I'll have someone here in a flash. Meantime, do your best to relax."

There was no answer.

She pushed to her hands and knees. Eying the eastern sky, she brushed dirt from her undergarments and from Thom's watch. Ahead, she saw the storehouse Richard had mentioned. She ran toward it though she knew there was no time for clothes. Back pressed against the storehouse wall, she edged around to where she could see the church, across the street to the northwest. She'd noticed it before, looking out from the prison windows on her daily walks.

She caught her breath, then looked up and down the street. Except for the sentry guarding the prison entrance, it was deserted. When he turned to march the other way, she walked briskly across the street. In the dark and from a distance, she hoped her soiled, torn petticoat would pass for a dress.

She strode up 21st Street, head held high as if she were wearing an elegant gown. She turned left on Main Street, then made her way to 20th, where the dark shape of the church came into view. Across the street was the cottage Richard told her to go to. In the dark, it looked hardly bigger than her prison cell. From behind the curtains, a dim light glowed.

Turning, she saw that she was still within view of the sentry. Again, she waited till he turned, then dashed across the street. But this time, her foot twisted, caught on a cobblestone. As she stumbled, she held out her hands, catching herself before her face smacked into the road.

Her ankle throbbing, she lay prone on the cobblestones. She had to get out of the road. She wasn't sure she could stand on her own, and even if she somehow managed to get to her feet, limping would only attract attention.

Better to crawl, she decided, and hope that if the sentry spotted her, he'd mistake her for a drunken soldier and leave her alone. And so she set out on hands and knees toward the cottage. Reaching the yard, she grabbed hold of a tree's low limb and hoisted herself to stand, balancing on her good foot. She edged toward the far side of the trunk, and when the coast was clear, she hobbled toward the cottage.

Reaching the door, she rapped three times, sharply but softly. Almost immediately, the door opened, revealing a stout, older woman with dark, shining eyes and coffee-colored skin. She wore a blue calico morning dress, and a wave of dark hair peeked out from beneath the red kerchief tied around her head.

"Hazel Mae?" Hattie asked. "There's someone who needs help."

She nodded. "The men said there might be a woman comin' behind. Told 'em I'd believe it when I saw with my own eyes." She chuckled. "Guess you've made a believer of me, child." Grabbing her by the arm, Hazel Mae pulled her inside, then shut the door.

At the sudden movement, the pain in Hattie's ankle intensified, and she winced. "The tunnel." She wobbled, and Hazel Mae tightened her grip on her arm. "My friend. He's...stuck."

"Looks to me like that ain't your only worry," Hazel Mae said. "You done hurt yourself."

"It's only a twisted ankle," Hattie said.

"Or a broke one. Let's get you off it. Lean on me, and don't put no weight on it if you can help it."

Leaning into Hazel Mae's plump form, Hattie limped around a flowered curtain that hung from the ceiling, covering a back corner of the room. There, Hazel Mae eased her onto a cot. It was a relief to get her weight off the ankle though it still throbbed.

Hazel Mae unfolded a quilt and tucked it around Hattie. "I'm goin' to fetch help," she said. "For your friend. Meantime, you just lie here an' rest."

Head on the pillow, Hattie was vaguely aware of her petticoat and boots on Hazel Mae's clean sheets. Struggling to sit, she reached for her petticoat. "Dirty," she said, feeling woozy.

With a firm hand, Hazel Mae pushed her back onto the pillow. "Don't you worry none about that. Close those pretty eyes and try to get some rest while I find someone to go after your friend."

Hattie didn't want to rest. She wanted to see Richard free, and she wanted to get far, far away from the prison. But her exertions had spent all her energy, and the door had scarcely latched behind Hazel Mae before she'd fallen deep into sleep.

Chapter Four

March 10, 1863

The sound of pounding at the door startled Hattie awake. Opening her eyes, she squinted at the hazy light streaming through a small window above where she lay. But her cell had no window, she thought, momentarily confused.

"Open up!" a man's voice called from beyond the door.

She blinked, orienting herself to the cottage where she'd found refuge following her escape. The flowered curtain, hiding her cot. Hazel Mae's cot.

The doorknob rattled. "Open up, I say!"

The curtain pulled back, revealing Hazel Mae's round, dark face. "Stay put, child. I'll handle this."

Her face disappeared behind the curtain, and Hattie heard the tapping of Hazel Mae's cane as she shuffled to the door. This puzzled Hattie. Last night, Hazel Mae had seemed able-bodied despite her age.

"Hold your horses," Hazel Mae called out. Then Hattie heard her unlatch the door. "What you up to, rousin' an old woman at this hour of the mornin'?"

"Some prisoners broke out last night," the man said. "You seen anyone sneaking around this way?"

"Oh Lord, oh Lord," Hazel Mae wailed. "Raise up your wall of protection 'round this old woman. Don't let them men come after me."

Hattie heard a shuffling of feet, and she imagined the man's discomfort at Hazel Mae's display of emotion. "They ain't armed," the man said. "So far as we know. You catch any sign of them, you come straight over and tell the warden, you hear?"

"I surely will, sir, same as I come right over an' told him how one of you guards was catcallin' ladies on the boardwalk. Weren't proper, that. And I been meanin' to tell him 'bout another that looks to me like he's been in the whisky."

The sentry cleared his throat. "Don't be worrying yourself over us guards. It's them escaped prisoners you'd best set your sights on."

"Oh, I will. Surely I will. The least thing out of place, I'll come tell."

The man grunted, evidently indicating the interview was over, for the next thing Hattie heard was Hazel Mae latching the door, then crossing the tiny room.

Hazel Mae drew back the curtain, then moved nimbly toward the cot. Having abandoned the cane, she smiled broadly, but her knitted brow betrayed concern. "How's that ankle, child? Think you can get yourself movin'?"

Hattie pushed herself to a sitting position. Gingerly, she swung one leg and then the other over the side of the cot. Her right ankle throbbed. "I hope so. What about Richard? Is he all right?"

Shaking her head, Hazel Mae sat down beside Hattie. "Lord Almighty, it weren't easy gettin' that man unstuck. Built like a grizzly, he is. But I got some help, and we took turns tuggin' his arms till we got him free."

"Where's he now?"

"Long gone. Barely made it outta town before sunup. He didn't want to leave you, but I tole him you ain't in no shape to make a run for it just now. I tole him we'd look after you till that ankle improves you can make your way north." She brushed a curl from Hattie's forehead. "You sweet on him, child?"

She shook her head. "He's my friend's brother, and he's engaged to be married. And I've got...a sweetheart."

"Won't he be glad to see you home safe," Hazel Mae said.

And I him, Hattie thought.

Hazel Mae reached around the end of the cot and produced a faded carpetbag, frayed at the corners. She set it on the cot beside Hattie. "This showed up on my back steps last week. I'm guessin' it come from Miss Lizzie."

"Miss Lizzie?" Hattie asked.

"Miss Van Lew. I clean up at her house on Church Hill. My niece Mary, she got me the position. Weren't so safe here for a free Negro once the South started fighting. Mostly it's the men they concern themselves with, scared they'll take up arms, but Mary looks after me all the same, and Miss Lizzie too. She's the one that freed Mary and sent her north to get herself educated. Now she's back, helping Miss Lizzie with her secret work."

"Her secret work," Hattie repeated. "You mean your niece spies too?"

Hazel Mae laughed. "Lord, yes. She's a keen one, that girl. For a while there, she got hired on with Lavinia Davis."

"The confederate president's wife," Hattie said.

"That very one. Got her some choice secrets to pass along from there, I tell you what. White folks might be scared of our men, but they ain't the least bit worried 'bout us womenfolk moppin' their floors and tendin' their babies and listenin' all the while." She shook her head. "Almost criminal, how easy they're hoodwinked. Miss Lizzie got me this house so's I could keep an eye on things over at the prison. Just act like you don't know nothin' 'bout nothin', she tole me, and it will all be fine."

"As you did with that guard at the door," Hattie said. "You'd do well on stage, Hazel Mae."

"Can't imagine they'd ever allow for a colored woman up on stage," she said. "Anyhow, the next man that comes by here might not be fooled so easy. Anybody force his way in, he's bound to find you." She opened the carpetbag and withdrew a folded bundle of clothes. "Miss Lizzie tole me there might be a woman breakin' free. That's why she had this left here, I reckon."

She set the bundle in Hattie's lap. As she unfolded it, a chill ran through her. "These look like mourning clothes," she said, holding up the black silk dress and veil, along with a pair of black gloves.

Hazel Mae nodded. "That makes sense. Last time I cleaned for Miss Lizzie, she said she'd come 'round if there was a prison break. Next day, she said, watch for a funeral at the church across the road. 'Round ten in the morning, she said."

"You think she wants me to put on these morning clothes and go to the funeral?"

"Reckon so," Hazel Mae said. "Best get into that dress. Pert near nine-thirty already."

Hattie looked down at her soiled, torn petticoat. "I'll get it dirty."

"Don't matter, child. Ain't no one gonna be lookin' up your skirt."

Hattie pushed herself from the cot. Balancing on her left leg, she pulled the dress over her head. Hazel Mae stood and helped her fasten it, tightening her corset and then securing the buttons. "Near perfect fit," she said, patting Hattie's waist. "Ain't much gets past Miss Lizzie."

Hattie set the veil on her head, arranging the black tuille about her face. Hazel Mae brought some hairpins, and Hattie secured her hair beneath the veil so none of it showed. "Do you think anyone will recognize me?"

"Doubt it," Hazel Mae said. "Could be any grievin' woman under all that black."

Hattie stepped forward, wincing at the pain in her right ankle. Hazel Mae grabbed hold of her arm. "Wait there," she said. Crossing the room, she retrieved the cane and brought it to Hattie.

"I can't take this," she said. "You need it."

Hazel Mae laughed. "Not as much as I let on. Them guards is used to seein' me with a cane, but I got a walkin' stick I'll use till I get me another."

Aided by the cane, Hattie started toward the door.

Hazel Mae touched her elbow. "Not that way, child. Them guards'll have a heyday if they see you comin' out my front door. And it ain't like you can scoot away fast."

She gestured toward a narrow door that Hattie had taken for a closet. Hazel Mae opened the door, and at first, all Hattie saw were a mop, broom, and dustpan. Then Hazel Mae reached inside and undid two latches at the back of the closet. She pushed against the wood, and Hattie saw that the wood was hinged, opening into the backyard.

"Those two big lilac trees, they'll give you cover," Hazel Mae said. "When you're sure no one's looking, go 'round the back of that storehouse to Main Street. From there, you can go straight to the church."

Hattie took her hand, solid and warm. "I can never repay your kindness."

Hazel Mae patted her hand. "Ain't no need. Miss Lizzie tole me you've been spyin' for the Union. Just get back north and get this war won so all us colored folks can live free."

Letting go of her hand, Hattie ducked into the broom closet. Squeezing sideways, she passed through the back opening into the open air. Beyond the door, the lilac bushes grew large and close, their tangled branches offering a measure of protection.

Breathing in the damp air, Hattie shivered. She looked to the left and then to the right. The gray skies drizzled rain, the few people on the street huddling under umbrellas.

As briskly as she could, Hattie hobbled through Hazel Mae's tiny backyard to the alley. Turning right, she continued past a large storehouse next door, hugging tight to the building in case a passerby happened to glance down the alley.

At Main Street, she stepped back a moment, waiting for a carriage to pass before she turned onto the street. Pain shot from her ankle, causing her to pause. The carriage driver glanced in her direction, then continued down the street.

She hobbled along the path, crossing at 21st street and then turning south toward the church. Ahead, she could see the west end of Libby Prison. Twice the usual contingent of guards marched back and forth, patrolling the entrance. *Closing the barn doors after the horses are out,* Hattie thought, and she was glad for the black veil hiding her smile.

On the uneven path, she slowed her pace, using the cane for balance. Hearing the clatter of wheels on the cobblestones, she looked up and saw the carriage that had passed her was now pulling up alongside the church.

As she approached, the church doors opened and four men emerged from the sanctuary, carrying a coffin. They maneuvered it down the steps. As they descended, the carriage driver, wearing a black top hat and long black coat, hopped from his perch. He flung open the back doors of the carriage, and the men slid the coffin inside.

Behind the funeral carriage, a second carriage pulled up. The driver jumped down and opened the side door. Dipping his head, he gestured for her to approach.

She nodded, then hobbled toward the open door. Anyone looking would take her for an elderly mourner, she hoped, too lost in grief to bother with a cloak or umbrella. She took the coachman's extended hand and, placing her cane ahead of her on the carriage step, hoisted herself up.

The driver shut the door as she sat on the padded seat. The air was cool, but at least she was out of the rain—and off her feet.

Sniffling, she brushed droplets of rain from her sleeves, bodice, and skirt. Water dripped from her hem, forming little puddles on the carriage floor.

As the horses began to trot behind the funeral carriage, she peeled off her wet gloves. With her fisted hand, she wiped away the condensation that had formed on the carriage window. Through the blur of rain, she looked out on the military hospital on Chimborazo Hill. As the carriage progressed on its route, she saw Ricketts Landing on the banks of the James River.

Both carriages turned east. In a moment of panic, she realized that they were traveling Old Stage Road. She'd gone down this road months ago to an ill-fated meeting with Luke Blackstone. She'd gotten what she came for, information that confirmed Blackstone's illegal dealings with Hattie's father. But the tables turned when Pinkerton spy Lucy Hamilton took it upon herself to bring a doctor to tend to Thom, who'd been faring poorly. The doctor she fetched was Blackstone. Realizing Hattie must be a spy, he'd had tipped off Rebel authorities, and they'd arrested Lucy, Thom, and Hattie.

Now Hattie gripped the edge of her seat. What if this funeral ruse turned out to be a plot to deliver her into the hands of her enemies? She pressed her face to the window, looking out on the landscape, wondering whether she should throw herself from the carriage if Blackstone's house came into view. A risky venture, especially with her bad ankle, but she shuddered to think of the alternative.

The carriage slowed and then stopped in front of a heavily wooded patch of ground. Through the window, she watched as the driver of the funeral carriage went around to the back doors. Two men in oilcloth coats emerged from the woods. Each gripping a handle, they slid the coffin out. Hoisting it up and onto their shoulders, they strode toward the trees. Between branches, Hattie saw a few gravestones.

The coffin might not contain an actual corpse, she realized. The person inside might be another escaped inmate, brought here to begin his trek north.

She set her hand on the door's handle, thinking that this might be where she was to get out too. But then her carriage jolted forward, the horses trotting around the funeral coach that was stopped in front of them.

After about a quarter-mile, Hattie's carriage slowed again. Thankfully, it was not in front of Luke Blackstone's cottage. The coachman hopped down and came round to open the door. He helped Hattie out, and she hobbled with her cane toward the gate in the white picket fence. The coachman hurried ahead to open it for her. As she passed through the gate, he tipped his hat to her, then closed the gate behind her. Light rain fell as she continued up the walk, mindful of the wet flagstones.

The cottage door opened, and a plump, dark-haired woman, a white apron over her red calico dress, ushered Hattie inside.

"You look soaked to the bone," the woman said. "I'm Abby. And you must be Hattie. I've been expecting you."

Here in the warmth, Hattie felt the damp cold of her dress more acutely, and she feared her teeth would begin to chatter. "Thank you," she said with some effort.

"Let's get you warmed up." Abby, who Hattie took to be in her thirties, steered her toward the parlor where a fire blazed in the hearth.

Hattie sank into the overstuffed chair nearest the fire. "So warm," she murmured. Then she remembered her clothes. "Oh, but I'm getting your nice chair all wet."

Abby waved a hand in the air, dismissing Hattie's concern. "The chair will dry. But you'd best get out of that dress before you catch your death."

Hattie sneezed. "I hope I haven't already."

Abby shook her head. "Miss Lizzie should've sent a cloak along with the dress. But she's had a lot on her mind lately, what with trying to get her brother excused from military service."

"Oh," Hattie said. Her head felt light, and she swayed a little. "I didn't know..." her voice trailed off.

"Let me help." Abby peeled off Hattie's wet gloves, then began unbuttoning the wet black silk of her bodice as if Hattie were a child. "You needn't worry about anyone seeing you. The men have come and gone already."

"The...men?" She felt suddenly confused. The funeral. The fire. This stranger...what was her name? Gabby? No, Abby. That was it. Abby.

"The men who escaped the prison with you." Abby undid Hattie's last button. "Over a hundred in all, I'm told."

"A hundred," Hattie repeated. She couldn't fathom so many men passing through the tunnel, which now felt fuzzy and distant. She wondered whether she'd actually gone through it or whether the cold, dark journey had been part of some grotesque nightmare.

Slowly, she pulled her arms from her sleeves. Abby undid her waistband, and she stepped out of her skirt.

"Your petticoat is soaked through," Abby said. "Off with it."

Hattie wriggled out of the wet garment. Underneath, her linen chemise and her stockings were damp too. For the first time, she noticed her boots, caked with mud, and the tracks she'd left coming into the parlor. Her foray in the tunnel, wriggling through the dirt, must have been real after all.

"Sit," Abby said.

The command didn't immediately register at first, not until Abby pressed lightly on Hattie's shoulder to make the point. Hattie closed her eyes. "The fire," she said. "It's delightful."

Abby reached for a colorful quilt folded over an arm of the sofa. "Get those boots off," she said, handing Hattie the quilt. "Your chemise and stockings too. You can cover up with this. I'll fetch a nightdress."

Slowly, Hattie bent and unbuttoned her boots, her fingers aching. Then she pulled her chemise over her head and removed her tattered stockings. Then she sat a moment, exhausted from the effort, not caring that she was as naked as the day she was born. Despite the warmth from the hearth, goosebumps prickled her skin. She wrapped the quilt around herself and pulled her knees to her chest, huddling in its warmth.

Abby bustled back into the room, a white nightdress slung over her arm. "You don't look well," she said, handing Hattie the nightdress.

"I'm just...chilled," Hattie said. "And my ankle's hurt. I...slipped last night, crossing the street."

The effort of moving her legs and arms overwhelmed her, and so Abby helped her on with the nightdress.

"Off to bed with you." Taking Hattie's arm, Abby pulled her gently up from the chair.

"But the fire." Hattie gazed at it longingly. "It's such a comfort."

"It won't be a bit of comfort if the guards come knocking and find you huddled here on the sofa."

"Would they have reason to look for me here?" Hattie asked, hanging onto Abby's arm as she limped from the parlor.

"I hope not," Abby said. "But one never knows." She opened a door to a small, tidy bedroom. The only furnishings were a mirrored armoire and a bed covered in a pale blue coverlet. A patch of gray light shone through the gauzy curtains that covered a tiny window.

"This house is far enough from town that it generally escapes notice," Abby added. "But if half as many prisoners escaped as we were planning—"

"You helped plan the escape?" Hattie asked.

Laughing, Abby lifted the coverlet. "There's more than meets the eye to this plump little hen. Not that the guards would ever suspect it. Sized me up as harmless, they did. And I suppose I am, except for the letters I passed to the prisoners through Mr. Ford, detailing the plan of escape, plus arranging things so those who got out found safe passage out of Richmond."

Hattie climbed into bed. "It sounds as if you did everything but dig the tunnel."

"There was a fair amount of coordination required," Abby said, smoothing the covers over her. "But Mr. Ford was an excellent partner, and it's quite satisfying to have set so many on the path to freedom. May God see us through to victory and do away with the wretched institution of slavery once and for all."

Hattie wondered how this unassuming Southern woman had arrived at views so similar to hers. But she had a more pressing question. "You're safe here? No one suspects your involvement in the escape?"

"Not that I know of. Not yet. But that could change. I'll need to get to Washington. So will you, as soon as you're well enough for the journey. Now get some rest."

Hattie didn't have to be told twice.

~ ~ ~

When Hattie woke, it was to the warm smell of broth. Flickering lamplight lit the room. Abby sat at her bedside, holding a steaming mug. "Wasn't easy, procuring a chicken. But you've slept the day away, and I've had plenty of time to make a nice broth from the scrawny thing."

Pressing her hands to the mattress, Hattie pushed herself to a sitting position, then took the mug in her hands. "Thank you." She closed her eyes and breathed in the vapors. "You have no idea how long it's been since I've been offered anything so delightful."

Abby plumped the pillows, arranging them at the headboard so Hattie could lean into them as she sipped the broth. It warmed her throat, easing the scratchiness that had settled there.

"How's that ankle?" It wasn't Abby who asked but another woman, her voice familiar.

Hattie turned in the direction of the voice. "Miss Van Lew!" she said.

Elizabeth Van Lew stepped from the shadows. Worry creased her forehead. "I was overcome with terror when I'd heard you'd been hurt. Thank heavens Abby's scheme to bring you here was successful."

"Hazel Mae did exactly as we asked," Abby said.

"The funeral was brilliant," Hattie said. "Erasmus Ross himself wouldn't have recognized me in those mourning clothes."

"The cane was a nice touch," Elizabeth said, "though I'm sorry you needed it. I hope you haven't broken that ankle."

Hattie wiggled the toes of her right foot. "I don't think it's broken. Just badly sprained."

"And she's got a touch of the grippe," Abby said.

Elizabeth frowned. "We'd best send for a doctor."

Hattie's reaction was swift. "No doctor."

Elizabeth touched her forehead. "But you've got a fever. No wonder, with conditions as they are at the prison. And if you intend to complete your escape, that ankle must be examined."

"I'll be fine," Hattie said. "I'm rested, and I can use the cane till the ankle heals."

"We can't stage a funeral all the way to Washington," Abby said. "You'll have to go as the others did, through the woods."

"Then I'll use a walking stick," Hattie said. "I can have a doctor check the ankle after I get to Washington. You said you'll need to be leaving, Abby. I need to leave too. My husband..." Her voice trailed off. Thom wasn't her husband, of course. She'd only come to think of him that way.

Elizabeth and Abby exchanged glances.

Hattie tightened her grip on the mug. "I'm no use to Thom here. When I get to Washington, I'll go to Mr. Lincoln if I have to, to get him out of Castle Thunder."

Elizabeth set her hand on Hattie's arm. "There's something you need to know, dear. I'm afraid I'm the bearer of bad news." Her face clouded, and tears welled in her eyes.

Hattie leaned forward, the tiny room with its mirrored armoire and dark corners seeming to fade from view. "Has some harm come to Thom?"

Glancing at Elizabeth, Abby pressed her hand to Hattie's shoulder as if to steady her. Elizabeth's grip on Hattie's arm tightened.

"I was informed yesterday. After a swift and most certainly unfair trial, Thomas Welton was executed."

The mug slid from Hattie's hands, the broth's wet stain spreading over the coverlet. "It can't be," Hattie said.

"I wish it were otherwise," Elizabeth murmured. "I hated to tell you, but if you'd found out—"

A wail rose from Hattie's throat, filling the tiny room. Hugging her arms to her chest, she rocked forward and back, forward and back. "No!" she cried. In her vision, there was no Elizabeth, no Abby, no pale blue coverlet, only Thom's gentle brown eyes filled with love for her.

"Not him. Not my Thom."

Chapter Five

March 13, 1863

In Hattie's grief, the days that followed blended into one long nightmare. She refused nourishment, refused even water. Abby seemed to her a ghost, gliding in and out of the room, trying to convince her to eat and drink.

As Hattie drifted in and out of sleep, her thoughts were a feverish montage of happy memories of Thom's smile, his touch, and his kisses overlain with the horrors of their arrest and imprisonment. In her darkest moments, she sensed the ugly presence of the man who'd betrayed them. In her agitated mind, she bargained with Dr. Blackstone as if he were the devil himself, begging him to take her and spare Thom. Without Thom in the world, the ticking of his watch felt like both a comfort and a curse.

On the third morning, Hattie woke to a burst of light. The curtains had been thrust open, and sunshine beamed through the small window. She propped herself on her elbows, squinting at the stranger who stepped away from the window.

"That's better," the stranger said, striding briskly toward the bed. "Now I can get a proper look at you."

As Hattie's eyes adjusted, she saw the stranger was a woman, her hair held back with a slender black headband and falling in ringlets to her shoulders. But she wasn't dressed at all like a woman, her crisp white shirt tucked into a skirt that fell only to her knees. Beneath that, she wore trousers.

She set a black leather bag on the bed next to Hattie. "Dr. Edith Greenfield," she said, extending a hand.

Hattie blinked, wondering how this person could have materialized from the haze of her grief.

Dr. Greenfield cocked her head, studying Hattie's face. "Some pallor. A sallowness of the cheeks." She lifted Hattie's right eyelid and leaned close, her handsome face filling Hattie's vision as she examined her eye. "Pupil responsive to light."

Hattie squirmed away from her, fascinated and repelled all at once. "You're the doctor who told my friend's brother not to let them saw off his arm.

The doctor reached for Hattie's wrist, pressing her fingers to take her pulse, her touch warm and firm. "A soldier should always question an offhand opinion from a man whose livelihood comes from sawing off limbs." She let go of Hattie's wrist. "Eighty-five. Elevated, but then you do seem a bit agitated."

Hattie sat up straight. "Of course I'm agitated. I don't want a doctor. I want to be left alone."

"Ah, but Miss Green refuses to leave you, even though she's risking her life to care for you. As am I, I might add."

Hattie softened, overcome by a wave of regret. "I don't know why you'd bother."

Dr. Greenfield went around to the end of the bed. "Because your life's not worth saving, you mean?" She lifted the coverlet, exposing Hattie's feet. "Because you think your life's over anyhow, now that you've lost your one true love?"

Hattie folded her arms at her chest. "I don't care to discuss any of that with the likes of you."

"With the likes of me, is it?" The doctor sighed, cradling Hattie's ankle in her hands. "You should know, Miss Logan, that I've gone to a fair amount of trouble to get here. It's rather hazardous, you know. I've got a doctor's clearance, but that's not especially easy to come by, and it's supposed to be used only for severest cases. The Rebels only let me through because their own doctors are few and far between these days, and when a mother's boy is dying, she cares little about whose side I'm on."

"I care," Hattie said indignantly. "Very much. If not for Dr. Blackstone—"

Dr. Greenfield looked up at her, eyes blazing. "What of Dr. Blackstone?"

Hattie hesitated, sizing up how much she should trust Edith Greenfield. "In my work with Pinkerton's, I discovered Dr. Blackstone's association with certain Northern traitors." She chose not to say that one of those traitors was her own father. "I visited him, hoping to glean details about their operation while giving the false impression that I sided with the Rebels. That went well enough until an associate sought Dr. Blackstone's services on Thom Welton's behalf. The doctor recognized me, and the jig was up."

Edith Greenfield's expression darkened. "Then he must be a double agent. The worst kind of traitor, if you ask me, entering the fray wherever he stands to profit."

Like Father, Hattie thought. "I hold Luke Blackstone responsible for Thom's death." It was the first time she'd said this out loud.

Dr. Greenfield took a strip of folded cloth from her bag and began wrapping it snugly around Hattie's swollen ankle. "From what I understand, Blackstone has no regard for his doctor's oath. I treated a Virginia man recently who was beside himself, thinking he'd contracted yellow fever. He confessed he'd been part of a plot orchestrated by Dr. Blackstone to gather up clothes and bedding from patients in Bermuda who'd died of yellow fever, then transport trunks full of these tainted goods to auction in Washington. Not fully informed of the risk, the man had looked inside one of the trunks. When Blackstone found out, he dismissed him from the plot, calling him a fool and telling him the trunk he'd opened contained enough miasma to kill anyone within sixty yards."

Hattie had no difficulty imagining Luke Blackstone's involvement in such a plot. "Were you able to save the man?"

Tying off the cloth at Hattie's ankle, Dr. Greenfield nodded. "Fortunately, his illness wasn't the fever. The symptoms are quite distinct. Spike in temperature, vomiting, pain. A yellow hue to the skin, and bleeding from the orifices."

"What about the auctioned trunk? Did the people who bought it sicken and die?"

"Thankfully, my patient had enough integrity to convince the auction house to withdraw the trunk from sale once he'd learned of the plot. What became of it after that, he didn't know. But he told me the next time yellow fever breaks out in Bermuda, he thinks the good doctor will try again."

"Despicable," Hattie said. "Can't Blackstone be arrested and charged?"

"Not without evidence. When his hireling told me his story, I alerted the authorities. But I refused to give them the man's name." She tucked in the ends of the cloth. "I won't compromise a patient's safety, no matter which side he's on. But if it helps the Union cause, I'm happy to share whatever I learn in the course of my work."

"You mean you're a spy, like Luke Blackstone?"

"I'm no double agent," Edith said sharply. "I care only for the Union cause. And as I said, I would never betray a patient's trust."

"But who do you report to?" Hattie said. "I've never heard of any doctors working for Mr. Pinkerton."

"General Sharpe," Edith said. "Though soon I'll be leaving for Tennessee, where in addition to running a hospital I hope to pass along information that will be useful to our soldiers."

Tennessee. Hattie straightened, recalling what Elizabeth had said during her visit to Libby Prison. "I'm told Luke Blackstone's in Tennessee."

Dr. Greenfield's lips pressed in a thin smile. "I do hope so. It would be such a pleasure to lay a trap for him." She cocked her head slightly, studying Hattie. "This talk of Blackstone has perked you up. I hope that means you've decided that wasting away is hardly the best way to honor a person you love. If you've got half the spunk I've heard you've got, you'll get back to spying as soon as you're able. I never knew Mr. Welton, but I suspect that's what he'd have wanted you to do too."

The doctor closed her bag. "I must be going. I took quite a chance coming here, and I need to get back before my Confederate escorts discover I'm not holed up at the farmhouse where they left me to tend to a child with the measles. No one but Elizabeth could have convinced me to risk coming here. She can be quite persuasive."

"She's amazing," Hattie said.

"No more lying abed now." Dr. Greenfield lifted her bag from the bed. "Abby says you had a fever when you arrived, but it's gone now, and you've got good color. Your heart and lungs are fine. Your ankle is sprained but not broken. With a walking stick, you'll get around well enough. That's good. From what Abby tells me, the two of you will need to leave here by week's end."

Hattie took the strange woman doctor's words to heart. Dying was no way to honor Thom's memory. Better to live with purpose, to see Luke Blackburn exposed and punished as a double agent, so he could never again betray a patient or plot to infect innocent people with yellow fever, not to mention conniving with her father to aid the Rebels.

Later that day, when Abby brought soup and water, Hattie ate and drank. She got out of bed and tested her ankle by walking around the room. It wasn't exactly sturdy, but between the support Dr. Greenfield's wrapping provided and the walking stick Abby brought her, she agreed with the doctor's assessment. She was ready to leave.

When she'd returned to the bed, Abby sat beside her. "Richmond is crawling with Rebel soldiers charged with hunting down escaped prisoners along with anyone who aided and abetted them," Abby said. "They've closed in around Richmond and down the Peninsula. Elizabeth sent a note saying we need to leave soon. She recommends heading for Kelly's Ford."

Hattie shook her head. "I have no idea where that is, but I trust Miss Van Lew's judgment."

"As well you should. She's gotten word that Pennsylvania's 16th Cavalry is planning to cross the Rappahannock near there in hopes of attacking Fitzhugh Lee's troops. The rebels control the area between Richmond and Culpeper. But if we can get past Culpeper, we should be able to intercept the 16th at the Rappahannock." Abby's face darkened. "Problem is, the Rebs are on the lookout for you especially."

"They're embarrassed to have let a woman escape?" Hattie asked.

"Quite. Elizabeth says they're looking for me too. I was at the prison quite a lot, and now I'm not. So they've gotten suspicious. Thank heavens for Robert Ford. Elizabeth says he hasn't given anyone up, not even when Turner had him tied to a barrel and lashed within an inch of his life."

Hattie's hands flew to her mouth. "How awful."

Abby nodded. "Elizabeth vows she'll get him out of there. And if anyone can accomplish that, it's her."

She got up and went to the armoire. From inside, she pulled out two worn haversacks. Handing one to Hattie, she sat back down on the bed. Hattie reached inside the canvas bag and pulled out its contents. A cotton frock coat, gray with brass buttons, ripped at one of the armholes. A battered gray cap. A pair of wool trousers, frayed at the hems, and a pair of wool socks.

"A rebel uniform." She looked up at Abby. "We're to dress as men?"

Abby reached into her own haversack and pulled out a gray cap, which she set on her head, giving it a jaunty tip to one side. "I think we can pull it off, don't you?"

Hattie shook her head. "I tried dressing as a man when I got transferred from Castle Thunder to Libby. A woman named Loretta Velazquez helped with my disguise. She'd been arrested for impersonating a soldier."

"On the Rebels' side?"

Hattie nodded. "They're not so desperate for soldiers that they'd allow women to fight, no matter their loyalty to the South."

"If she helped you, she couldn't have been overly loyal."

Hattie shrugged. "I truly don't know. With Loreta, it was hard sorting fact from fiction. But you're right. She helped me, and so did one of the guards at Castle Thunder." She paused, recalling Jake's kind eyes and the way he'd called her *lass*. "That's how I was able to make the transfer to Libby as Hatfield Logan. The idea was that if I could circulate among the men instead of being the only woman imprisoned there, I'd have a better chance of breaking free. I would've, too, except that Erasmus Ross found me out."

Abby frowned. "Elizabeth says Ross is on our side."

"I know she does. But he's a mean one, and I'd have a hard time trusting him myself. When he discovered my disguise, he seemed to take it personally, a woman pulling one over on him, and from then on, he treated me more harshly than was called for."

Abby patted her leg. "Thank heavens we got you out of there." From her pocket, she withdrew two slips of paper and handed one to Hattie. "And with any luck, this is your ticket to true freedom.

"A pass," Hattie said, studying the paper. *GUARDS AND PICKETS*, read the printed letters, followed by the handwritten name *Ryan Murphy*. On the next line, the printed word *TO* was followed by the handwritten words *Culpeper Courthouse*. Underneath was a scribbled signature above the printed word *Provost*.

Abby held up her pass, identical except for the name *Patrick Murphy*. "I guess this makes us brothers," she said.

For the first time in days, Hattie smiled. Thom would have been proud. *This is only the start,* she promised him. *I won't give up till Blackstone's made to pay.*

Abby slipped her pass into her haversack, and Hattie did the same. "Assuming we make it to Culpeper, we'll have to go from there to Kelly's Ford on foot. It's ten miles. Think you can manage it?"

"I'm certain of it."

~ ~ ~

Two days later, Hattie and Abby were aboard a train that was chugging away from Richmond. They left from the same station where Hattie had arrived with Thom, eager to prove herself as a spy, posing as his wife. At the time, she'd planned to spend only a few days in Virginia, delivering letters with Thom and gathering information to take back North.

How differently things had turned out, first with Thom's acute rheumatism and then, more dramatically, with their arrest. And now Thom was gone.

Hattie blinked hard, banishing her tears. She set her face with a look of shell-shocked indifference. She didn't have to rely on her acting abilities. In the crowded train car, nearly every man's face wore the same beleaguered look.

Beside her, Abby pulled her soldier's cap low on her forehead and tipped her head down, as if trying to sleep. Hattie did the same. Ahead of their departure, they'd agreed that this was the best way to conduct themselves on the train.

Head bobbing, eyes closed, Hattie felt far from relaxed. The carriage ride into Richmond from the safe house had frayed her nerves. They'd ridden with the shades drawn, but Hattie sensed when they were passing Libby Prison and Castle Thunder. *Thom*, she wanted to cry out. She would not think of his execution. She'd think of their last moments together, touching fingers through the bars of his cell. *Save yourself*, he'd said. And *I love you.*

Across from where Abby and Hattie sat feigning sleep, a Confederate soldier told a ribald joke about a Union officer's meeting with the devil. The punch line drew chuckles from his comrades.

They're no more than boys, Hattie reminded herself, boys who lived with fear in their hearts. That they'd die in battle. That if their slaves were freed, the fragile world they'd known, the elegant plantations built on the backs of their slaves, would crumble. She knew such boys, knew their plantations. Her mother had grown up on one, deep in the South, and she'd pined so hard for that way of life that Hattie doubted she'd enjoyed even a single moment of happiness once she'd left.

Abby nudged Hattie's leg. Hattie opened one eye and saw the officer who'd told the joke standing over them, arms folded at his chest. Tall and broad-shouldered, he looked to be in his mid-twenties, with orange hair and a bristly mustache. "Sit up!" he commanded. "Slumping like that, you're a disgrace to your uniforms."

Hattie straightened, and Abby followed suit. Abby kept her eyes on Hattie, who'd decided as they'd prepared for the journey that she'd do the talking for the two of them whenever possible. Abby had many talents, but disguising her voice wasn't one of them.

"Yes, sir!" Hattie said, deepening her voice. She locked eyes with the officer.

Abby bobbed her head in agreement.

The officer shoved Abby's shoulder. "What's the matter, boy? Cat got your tongue?"

"My brother stutters," Hattie said.

"I – I – I," Abby said.

The officer slapped her across the face. "Spit it out."

Hattie stood, and her hand went to her hip as if she carried a pistol beneath her coat. "I jes' told you," she said defiantly. "My brother cain't talk right."

"He'd best learn," the officer snapped. Then he turned on his heel and retreated to the group he'd been sitting with.

Hattie stayed standing, feet braced against the movement of the train, and kept her eyes on him until he broke his stare and turned his back to her. He made some low remark about dimwitted boys, and the soldiers around him laughed.

Abby tugged the ragged hem of Hattie's coat, and she sat. "Imbecile," she said under her breath.

Abby dropped her head to her hands, shaking it a little in what Hattie took as a warning to retreat. But she kept her own head up, gazing out the window at the fields and farmhouses they passed.

The rest of the ride went without incident. Finally, the conductor came through, announcing the Culpeper station and checking the passes of the soldiers getting off. To Hattie's dismay, the red-headed officer was among them. The train entered the town from the east, passing a tent camp enclosed by a white picket fence. Beyond the camp were small, modest homes. Then a large stone courthouse came into view.

The train chugged to a stop in front of a small wooden station with a tin roof. Watching until the officer and his associates got off, Hattie and Abby shuffled forward and descended the steps.

Hattie tugged on her cap so that it covered her eyes. The day was bright and the sun felt warm through her coat, though a brisk wind was blowing. "Glad to get out of there," she said in a low voice.

"Now to get out of here," Abby whispered, "before anyone notices these are infantry uniforms, not cavalry."

They clomped along the road, Abby imitating the gait Hattie had shown her, more man's swagger than lady's glide. They strode at a steady clip, though not so fast as to draw attention. Hattie's ankle began to ache. She'd decided against a walking stick, fearing it would raise questions of why an injured soldier was headed to one of the more hotly contested parts of Virginia. Hunger gnawed at her stomach, and her throat felt dry, but this was no place to stop, with soldiers from Fitzhugh Lee's cavalry regiment milling all around.

The farther they got from the town's center and the courthouse Lee used as his command center, the fewer soldiers they saw. That meant less chance of them being stopped and questioned over what two infantry soldiers were doing in these parts, but it also meant they stood out to those residing in the area. Fortunately, there seemed little activity in the houses here, and they passed only two civilians, a woman and a man. Soldiers must be quartering in this part of town, Hattie thought. According to Abby, Culpeper had seen more than its share of battles.

They'd just passed the last house, heading north on the road that led to the Rappahannock, when they heard horse's hooves behind them. Abby started to turn, but Hattie nudged her. "Look straight ahead," she said. "And keep walking."

A Rebel picket rode up beside them. Reining in his horse, he called to them. "You boys with the 3rd Virginia?"

"Yes, sir!" Hattie answered, her eyes fixed straight ahead as they continued walking.

Without a word, the picket turned his horse and, judging from the hoofbeats, began trotting back toward town.

"That was easy," Abby said.

"Too easy," Hattie said. She grabbed Abby's hand, tugging her toward a thicket of laurel. Ducking beneath branches, she heard hoofbeats, not of one horse but several. "He's bringing reinforcements," she said. "Run!"

She pressed into the woods, stooping beneath branches, skirting around tree trunks. Close behind, she heard Abby's panting breaths. Her foot caught in a depression in the ground, and her ankle wobbled. Steadying herself, she ran on, ignoring the pain.

They forged on through the woods. On the other side was the road, skirting an open field that Hattie judged to be a half-mile wide.

"Is that the same road we were on?" Abby asked.

"I think so," Hattie said, catching her breath. "It must loop around."

Sure enough, they heard the pounding of horses' hooves in the distance.

Abby started for the trees. Hattie grabbed her arm. "That's the first place they'll look." She pointed toward the edge of the field ahead. "The gully!"

She grabbed Abby's hand and they ran, Hattie putting as little weight as possible on her injured ankle.

They reached the gully. It must be an irrigation ditch, Hattie thought, veering as it did away from the road and through the field.

"We can't possibly—" Abby gasped.

"We'll crawl on our bellies," Hattie said, flinging herself into the shallow ditch. "It's the only way."

She scooched forward through the dirt as she had in the tunnel. At least here, vegetation kept her being mired in mud, and feeling the wind on her back, she had no sense of claustrophobia.

Behind her, the sound of Abby's breaths grew more distant. "Keep going!" Hattie hissed.

"I...can't," Abby said weakly.

"You can. Dig your toes in. Clutch the ground with your fingers and pull."

Hattie propelled herself several more yards, then stopped. She didn't dare raise herself to look, but from the sound of Abby's breathing, she'd closed the distance between them.

Holding her head to one side, Hattie resumed her belly crawl through the field. The gully seemed endless. Even with the wind, she grew hot and sweaty.

She lifted her head slightly and saw a patch of pines ahead. "Just a little farther," she said, uncertain whether Abby could hear.

At last, the gully came to an end. Still, Hattie kept crawling, staying low to the ground until she was certain the pines would conceal her. Then she pushed up from the ground, breathing the piney scent as she leaned against the trunk of a tree, its bark rough against her back.

She smiled, seeing Abby crawl toward her from the grove's edge, scuttling on her elbows like a crab.

"I knew you could do it," Hattie said.

Abby pulled herself up to sit as Hattie did, leaning against the trunk of a nearby pine. She breathed hard, gulping air. "Now what?"

"Now we wait till we're sure they're gone."

Abby closed her eyes, her head tipped back against the tree trunk. "It'll be dark before long. I was hoping we'd be at Kelly's Ford by then. What if the Union cavalry has already crossed?"

"If they have, they must be laying low. Otherwise, there'd be Rebels charging in from every direction." Hattie reached in her haversack for a piece of the hardtack they'd brought along. "I'd offer to break you off a chunk," she told Abby. "But I'd surely lose a tooth in the process."

Abby reached into her haversack and withdrew a similar hunk of hardtack. Turning it over in her hand, she said, "Are we sure it's actually food? It seems more like a slab of wood." Tentatively, she nibbled at a corner. "Tastes like one too."

Hattie clamped her teeth over one edge of the hardtack and tried to soften it with her tongue. At last, she chomped off a morsel. Gulping water from her canteen, she washed it down.

"You'd best go easy on the water," Abby said. "At least till we reach the river."

Nodding, Hattie capped the canteen and returned it to her haversack, then leaned back against the tree. The front of her was covered in dirt, and her ankle hurt. But the muscle aches and the sniffles she'd suffered when she'd first escaped Libby were gone, and she reveled in the open air all around.

She and Abby considered moving on after dark but decided to bed down where they were. "Too many pickets in these parts," Hattie said. "If they've gotten the slightest whiff of the Union's plans, the patrols will be heavy. After dark, they're far more likely to shoot and ask questions later."

They laid out their bedrolls on a cushion of dropped needles at the base of a tall pine. After the sun went down, the night turned bitterly cold, the trees only partially shielding them from the north wind.

Overhead, stars popped out one by one, showing themselves in the velvet sky. "The Milky Way." Hands behind her head, Abby craned forward to see. "The first time I saw it, I couldn't believe the sky could hold so many stars."

"My brother and I used to lie back in the grass on summer nights and look at the stars," Hattie said. "He knew all the constellations. I hope wherever he is now, he can see them tonight."

"He's a soldier?" Abby asked.

"Yes," Hattie said. "But I haven't heard from him for a long time. A soldier from his regiment told me he ended up in Canada, spying for the National Detective Police."

"My brothers are fighting on the Confederate side," Abby said. "All three of them."

"How can that be, when you've risked so much to help the Union?"

"We grew up in Richmond, but my mother's people were from Boston. She wanted me to have a good education, and she couldn't find a school down here that would educate girls in anything but manners and finding a husband. So she sent me north when I was ten to live with her sister and attend school in Boston. I got the schooling she'd wanted and then some. I'd gone back to Richmond to visit when the war broke out. My first impulse was to rush back north to help the Union cause. Then my mother introduced me to Miss Lizzie, and she persuaded me that I could do far more good if I stayed where I was and joined her network."

"And so you have," Hattie said. "Look at all of us that you helped break free from prison. Those men will go back to fighting."

"And you'll go back to spying," Abby said.

"How do you know?"

"There's a fire in your eyes. I saw it when that officer confronted you on the train, and when that Rebel picket rode up. You won't be happy until you're back at it."

And until I've got Blackstone in my sights, Hattie thought. "What about you? What will you do once we cross the river?"

Abby shrugged. "Find my way back to Boston. I've got friends there, and my mother's people. I'm sure they'll be able to steer me to something useful."

"You could spy too," Hattie said.

"Me?" Abby laughed. "I haven't the nerve, no more than I'd have the nerve to take up arms and kill a man. But I'm glad for those who do. Only..." Her voice trailed off.

"Only what?"

She sighed. "I want the Union to win, of course. At the same time, I'm afraid of what that victory will bring. People like my brothers won't ever get over it. There's been so much resentment drummed up, so much fear of what will happen when the Negroes are freed."

"I hadn't thought of that," Hattie said.

Abby hugged her arms to her chest, and Hattie saw she was shivering. "Of more immediate concern is how we'll get through the night without freezing," Abby said. "I don't suppose we dare make a fire."

"Even small fires make smoke," Hattie said. "You don't want to wake up looking down the barrel of a Confederate pistol, do you? We're better off huddling close."

"It's not proper," Abby said.

"I don't see that anyone will mind," Hattie said. "You're not much good to me frozen." Reaching for Abby's waist, she edged toward her, pressing her front to Abby's back. Cocooned in this way, the two of them slept in fits and starts until the day finally dawned, streaking the eastern sky orange.

Hattie nudged Abby, who was snoring lightly. "Rise and shine," she said. "Today we make the Rappahannock."

They left the pine grove. At the edge of the field, they saw no pickets along the road, they scampered across the grass in a quarter of the time it had taken to crawl. Then they headed north along the road, keeping a steady pace as the rising sun lit their faces from the side.

An hour passed, and then another. Though the road remained mostly deserted, they stayed along its edge, darting in and out of the woods wherever they were able, stopping only occasionally to gulp water from their canteens and gnaw on bits of hardtack.

It was late afternoon by the time the river came into view. For a dividing line between enemy armies, Hattie was struck by how slow and unassuming it seemed, though it did look swollen by winter rains.

Gazing through the trees, she spied Rebel soldiers patrolling its banks. As best she could from a distance, she counted them.

"Twenty men, it looks like to me," she said.

"But it looks like only fifteen are armed," Abby said. "The rest are holding the horses."

"That's fifteen more pistols than we've got," Hattie said.

"And if I'm not mistaken, they've got sabers too."

"Those buildings—that must be where they're quartered." Hattie pointed to what looked like an abandoned mill and manufacturing facility of some sort.

"Fabulous," Abby said. "They've got a roof over their heads, and we spend another night in the woods with no fire to warm us."

"Maybe not the whole night," Hattie said. "If the Union forces are advancing, we might be able to tell their position after dark. If they're close, it might be worth risking trying to shelter in that shack near the riverbank."

"The one that looks like an ice house?" Abby looked skeptical. "What if there are Rebel soldiers inside?"

"We'll say Fitzhugh Lee sent us as scouts," Hattie said.

"Infantry scouting for the cavalry?" Abby said.

"If it's dark, they might not notice our uniforms," Hattie said. "Or maybe the shack will be empty."

"We could just stay in the woods," Abby said. "Let the federal soldiers take us as prisoners."

"Or shoot us," Hattie said grimly. "If we can hide in that shack, we'd have a lot better chance of trading these uniforms for our skirts. As women, we're at least less likely to be killed."

Leaning against a tree trunk, Abby edged toward the ground. "Any way you look at it, it's going to be a long night. And what if the federals don't advance at all?"

Hattie sank beside her. "Then we make a new plan," she said, having no idea what that might be.

~ ~ ~

Hattie woke to a moonlit sky. Abby's head resting on her shoulder. Horse's hooves pounded the road. Craning her neck, Hattie could see the horse galloping away from the river.

She shook Abby awake. "A sentry's left the Rappahannock for Culpeper. He must have some sort of news to deliver to Fitzhugh Lee."

Abby stretched her arms. "In the middle of the night?"

Hattie stood, straining to see around the trees. "Meaning it's important news."

Abby stood too. "See those campfires on the far side of the river? They can't be more than three miles away."

Hattie smiled. "The Union's readying for an advance. Let's see if we can conceal ourselves before the battle begins."

"I have my doubts," Abby said, but she followed Hattie to the edge of the woods. Despite the late hour, a light shone in the mill building. Hattie started across a clearing toward the river, Abby at her heels.

As they crept past the mill, Hattie heard laughter from inside, followed by the strains of a song she'd heard in Richmond, "Flight of the Doodles." After what seemed an eternity, she and Abby reached the icehouse.

Hattie pulled on the door, but it didn't give. She braced her feet and tried again. This time, the door swung open. Inside, she and Abby flattened themselves against the wall, listening for any evidence of soldiers. Hearing no one, Hattie crept through the darkness to the center of the floor, feeling around the edges of a trap door in the ground. The air escaping from around the door was cool but not frigid.

"If there's ice, it can't be much," she said. "So at least we won't freeze."

Beside her, Abby shivered. "What I wouldn't give for a fire."

At one side of the trap door was a waist-high stack of hay bales. Next to these, sacks of grain were piled to a similar height. "At least we can bunk off the ground," she said.

Abby climbed atop the hay bales while Hattie arranged the grain sacks so that she was cocooned within them.

"What do we do when it's time for the horses to be fed?" Abby asked.

"With any luck, the Federals will advance before then," Hattie said.

~ ~ ~

Fortunately, the Federals did advance before feeding time. Hattie woke to the sound of rifles firing. She scrambled from the stack of feed bags and cracked open the icehouse door. Pressing one eye to the opening, she saw that the eastern sky was just beginning to lighten. Torches flickered in the darkness, held by Rebel soldiers as their comrades fired over the river. She heard the splashing of men fording the Rappahannock and the barking of commands on the near side of the river and also, she judged, from where the splashing was.

She closed the door and leaned back against it. "The Federals," she said.

"Thank God," Abby said.

As daybreak came, there was little to distinguish it inside the icehouse, where the only light came from gaps between some of the boards. In hushed silence, Hattie and Abby listened to the sounds of the battle around them. Horses' hooves pounded from the direction of Culpeper Road. Rebel reinforcements, Hattie thought, summoned by the sentry they'd heard leaving in the middle of the night. She wondered if the general's nephew Fitzhugh Lee was among them.

As the battle sounds continued, Abby and Hattie took turns cracking the door and peering out. It seemed at first that the Rebels were pushing the Federals back across the river. But by midmorning, the Union was crossing in numbers too great for the Rebels to turn away even with the reinforcements from Culpeper.

The Federal forces advanced in waves, horses and men fording the swollen river. "The Union men must number in the hundreds," Hattie said.

"Maybe even the thousands," Abby said, flashing a smile.

Still, the casualties gave Hattie pause. In Washington, she'd seen plenty of wounded soldiers being carted to the hospitals. But it was another thing entirely to look out from the crack in the door and glimpse a man falling from his horse, struck by an enemy sharpshooter. Fellow soldiers retrieved some of the wounded, but in the heat of battle, others remained where they'd fallen, their blood staining the ground as life left them. Whether the fallen men were Rebel or Federal, Hattie found herself whispering prayers for their souls and then looking away. *That could be George,* she thought, hoping he was safe in Canada as she'd been told.

War's an ugly business, she recalled Thom saying. A pang of sorrow struck, and she touched her bodice where his watch hung, its steady ticking offering a small measure of comfort.

A wall of Union soldiers advanced, the icehouse walls shaking as their horses thrummed the ground. As Hattie watched through the crack in the door, the last of the Rebel soldiers retreated.

"They're about gone," she told Abby. But as she was about to shut the door, she saw that the Rebel commander, who'd been forced from his horse, was fleeing toward the icehouse.

She shut the door, heart pounding. "Quick!" she urged. "Into the rafters."

Wide-eyed, Abby scrambled to the top of the baled hay and hoisted herself into the rafters. Climbing to the top of the grain sacks, Hattie did the same. Balancing on a rafter, she edged toward the roofline, crouching low.

A moment later, the icehouse door opened. Squinting into the light, Hattie saw the commander. He looked no older than twenty-five, small in build and with a mustache that drooped at the corners of his mouth.

He gazed around the icehouse. Fearing he, too, might try to conceal himself in the rafters, Hattie held her breath. Then he shut the door and settled himself to one side of the hay, almost directly beneath Abby, whose leg was lit by a sliver of light.

Hattie closed her eyes, willing her breaths to be shallow and measured. *Don't look up. Don't look up.* She repeated the words like an incantation.

Eventually, the sounds of battle retreated in the direction of the farmhouses Hattie and Abby had passed along the Culpeper Road. The Confederate officer rose from where he'd been crouching and edged toward the door. As he opened it, his saber flashed in the sunlight. Then he was gone.

Hattie and Abby remained in the rafters a while longer, not daring even to speak. Finally, hearing only the muffled sounds of artillery fire in the distance, Hattie said, "I think it's safe now."

"I couldn't have lasted much longer," Abby said as she climbed down. "Got a charley horse worse than any I've ever had."

Hattie began unbuttoning her gray jacket. "Time to shed these and put on our skirts."

"But the Rebels could be back," Abby said.

Hattie shook her head. "Not with so many of our cavalry on their tails. This is Union territory now."

"I hope you're right," Abby said, unfastening her trousers.

Hattie tossed aside her gray cap and wriggled out of her jacket. "Me too."

They stuffed their uniforms behind the grain sacks and dressed as women again. Then they stepped from the icehouse, their faces streaked with dirt and their hair unkempt. They made a wide circle around the casualties, some wearing gray and others blue, then headed for a smoldering campfire outside the mill building.

"Over there," Hattie said, pointing to a haphazard woodpile at one end of the building.

They each retrieved an armful of wood to stoke the fire. Soon, it was a comforting blaze, and they stretched their hands toward it, warming them.

"The Federals might mistake us for Rebel women," Abby said.

"They might," Hattie said, feeling the delightful warmth creep up her fingers. "But they wouldn't shoot a woman."

Abby raised an eyebrow. "Your faith is commendable."

The afternoon dragged into evening. The sounds of battle, punctuated by booms of artillery, continued retreating to the northwest.

"The Federals are pushing back Lee," Hattie said.

Abby eyed the darkening sky. "You think it's safe to sleep here?"

"I don't see why not. But first, I'd sure like to find something more palatable than hardtack to eat.

Rummaging in the mill building, they found a skillet, a half-barrel of salt pork, and a stash of sweet potatoes plus a few squares of cornbread that must have been left from yesterday's supper. They tucked sweet potatoes along the fire's edge.

Balancing the skillet on a large burning log, they heated a slab of salt pork. As it sizzled, Hattie's mouth watered, and all the more so after she lifted the skillet from the fire using a folded horse blanket as a hot pad, cut the pork in half, and bit into her share. She left the sweet potatoes for Abby, having had her fill of them while in prison.

As the day waned, the sounds of battle diminished. "The fighting must be over," Abby said. "Maybe we should catch up with the Union soldiers before it's completely dark and make ourselves known."

Hattie mopped up the last of the skillet's grease with a square of cornbread. "It might be more prudent to wait till morning and make sure the line holds."

"Why wouldn't it?" Abby said. "From what we saw, the Federal forces outnumbered Lee's three to one."

"Such odds haven't always turned in our favor." Hattie cocked her head. "Hear that?"

Abby turned toward the sound. "Horses. Headed this way."

Hattie grabbed her arm and tugged her toward the river. "We've got to get across."

"But those soldiers waded up to their chests this morning. And that water's got to be cold," Abby said.

"If Lee's gotten the advantage and the Union's in retreat, we can't stay here." Lifting her skirt, Hattie waded into the river, icy water swirling around her ankles. "It's not so bad," she said as much to convince herself as Abby, who remained on shore.

"What about the current?" Abby called to her.

Now up to her knees in the water, Hattie could barely make out her words, loud as the horses were, coming from behind her. Turning, she saw a wall of blue thundering toward the river. As the first line of mounted horses plunged into the water, Hattie lost sight of Abby. She waved her arms at the advancing cavalrymen, hoping to keep from being trampled.

The rider nearest her, an older man with graying sideburns and haggard eyes, pulled his reins, slowing his horse. He blinked hard. "What the hell?" he said.

"Federal!" Hattie yelled. Her brain addled with cold, this was all she could offer by way of explanation.

Looking puzzled, the cavalryman scooted back from his saddle, then stretched his hand to her. Grabbing hold, Hattie reached for the saddle horn with her free hand and hoisted herself onto the horse.

~ ~ ~

In the Union camp on the north side of the Rappahannock, a weary soldier led Hattie to a tent, then handed her a dry dress. She had no idea where he'd gotten it—perhaps from a camp follower or a nurse along one of the rear lines. In any event, she was grateful for it.

He left her to change out of her wet clothes, and then another soldier came for her. "General wants a word with you," he said.

She followed him into the night, past tethered horses and men bedded down for the night beside campfires. She hoped Abby was here somewhere, but she saw no sign of her. Reaching the steps of a white clapboard church, the soldier led her up the stairs. Inside, several of the wooden pews lay in pieces. Hacked up for firewood, she thought, and though this seemed a desecration, she wondered if it was any more so than the sermons that might have been preached from the church's pulpit, advocating for the institution of slavery.

A man with light-colored hair and a thin goatee sat at a makeshift desk, a plank balanced on the ends of two pews. Aside from his receding hairline, his appearance was that of a man too young to be a general, and yet that was how the soldier escorting her addressed him.

Looking up from the note he was writing, General Averell stood and gestured for Hattie to take a nearby chair. She sat, and so did he, hands folded on the plank. In the flickering candlelight, he studied her with sharp but tired eyes. "Your name," he said.

She sat straight, shoulders back. "Hattie Logan, recently escaped from Libby Prison."

He cocked an eyebrow, studying her. "The Rebs hold women at Libby?"

"Just me, sir. I was among the last of the group who recently escaped," she said. Not for the first time, she thought of Richard, wondering whether he had found his way to safety.

General Averell leaned back. "Held for what offense?"

"Spying, sir. At Allen Pinkerton's direction."

He fingered his goatee. "Mr. Pinkerton will confirm this?"

"Absolutely. He was working to free us."

"Us?"

"Thom Welton and myself, sir."

"Ah, yes. Welton. Unfortunate, how that turned out."

Hattie's eyes blurred, and she wiped away a tear with the back of her hand. "Thom wanted me to break free if I could. I'm glad I managed it, and I'm grateful to whichever of your soldiers it was that brought me here."

He sighed. "An act of gallantry that won't be sufficient to redeem the day, I'm afraid. Already there's grumbling that we retreated instead of advancing to Culpeper's Courthouse. But the Rebels had guns in a permanent emplacement, covered by earthworks. Not much our artillery could do against that. The quality of our ammunition was miserable, and we'd nearly exhausted it. What choice did I have but to withdraw?"

In the candlelight, his face looked so young and earnest that she felt compelled to reassure him. "I'm certain you had the best interests of your men at heart."

"I appreciate your confidence, Miss Logan, whether or not I've earned it. Now, what am I to do with you?"

"I need to get back to Washington, sir. To let Mr. Pinkerton know I've made it out."

"I can see to that." He scribbled a note.

"And I was traveling with a friend, Abigail Rice. I lost sight of her at the river. Can you tell me if she's here?"

"So far as I know, you're the only woman for miles around, Miss Logan."

"Perhaps she's in a nearby camp?"

"There are more than two thousand cavalrymen under my command, Miss Logan, give or take a few dozen who were taken captive in today's battle or...otherwise diminished. But if there's a woman among my men, I expect I'll hear about it sooner or later. In the meantime, you should ready yourself for departure, Miss Logan. This is noplace for you to linger."

Her soldier-escort returned her to the tent where she'd hung her clothes to dry. She bedded down on a pallet there, feeling guilty that she was taking up an entire tent when soldiers were sleeping under the stars.

She hoped Abby had found shelter too. She didn't want to think of the other possibilities, that she'd gotten swept into the river or that she'd run from the advancing soldiers and was back among Rebel troops.

Chapter Six

March 18, 1863

The general wasted no time. The next morning, a soldier came to take Hattie to Morrisville Station. Ignoring her pleas that she be allowed to stay until she could find out what had become of Abby, he had her put aboard a train to Washington.

Arriving at her destination, she felt the city was at once familiar and altogether changed. Weeks ago, she'd left here with Thom, buoyed by hope and possibilities. Now all that was gone. All except for her chance to see the man who'd betrayed them brought to justice.

Alone and without so much as a change of clothes, she had to think of what to do next. By day's end, she'd need to find somewhere to sleep. When she'd agreed to spy as the courier's wife, she'd given up her room at Mrs. Sullivan's boardinghouse. But first, she wanted to see if she could find Miss Warne, the Pinkerton operative who'd assigned her to spy as Thom Welton's wife.

Mr. Pinkerton had closed the mailroom where Hattie and her friend Anne had worked, opening Rebel correspondence. By the time Hattie left Washington, he had moved the agency's headquarters from Washington back to Chicago. But as far as she knew, the government still had a contract with Mr. Pinkerton. The last time she'd seen Miss Warne, she'd been operating out of a small, inconspicuous house in one of Washington's residential neighborhoods.

The place wasn't far from the train station, so Hattie set out walking. As she approached the white frame house, her steps slowed. Miss Warne knew about the letter Hattie had intercepted, implicating Luke Blackstone in a grain smuggling scheme with Hattie's father. And she must surely know by now that it was their Pinkerton associate Lucy Hamilton who'd given up Hattie and Thom after their arrest.

But did Miss Warne also blame Hattie for Thom's death, as Hattie herself did when she was feeling low? She should have disguised herself before meeting with Blackstone. She should have tried harder to get to Elizabeth Van Lew, who could have recommended a trusted doctor instead of Blackstone. She should have found a way to break Thom out of prison before her transfer to Libby.

Hattie shook her head. Thom wouldn't have wanted her second-guessing herself, and she had to believe Miss Warne wouldn't either. Hattie mounted the steps to the little house and rapped on the wooden door.

The snub-nosed woman who came to the door was short and squat, her gray hair knotted at her neck. Her blue eyes looked Hattie up and down. "You've come about a room?"

"I've come to speak with Miss Warne."

The older woman squinted at her. "Who?"

"Miss Warne. Kate Warne."

"Never heard of her."

"But she was here the month before last."

The woman set her fisted hand on her hip. "And now it's me here, isn't it? With rooms that need letting. If that's not what you're after, I can't stand here chatting all day."

"Sorry," Hattie said. "I don't suppose you know—"

The door shut in her face.

Hattie turned and went quickly down the steps. She stood on the path, surveying the homes all around. If Miss Warne was still in the city, Hattie had no way of knowing where to find her. And she might not be here at all.

To the west, the sun was sinking in the sky. Late afternoon and Hattie had no plan. She started back toward the city's center. Ahead she saw the spires of the Smithsonian's Castle. On impulse, she veered east toward the Patent Office, where she and Richard's sister Anne had gone often to visit Anne's younger brother, Henry, while he was recuperating from his war injuries in the makeshift hospital there.

Anne had taken Henry back to Indiana right after Christmas, but she'd said she planned to return to Washington. That was unlikely now that Pinkerton's mailroom had closed, but there was a small chance she'd come back. If so, she was the person Hattie most wanted to see.

Anne had relatives in Washington, the Trents. If Anne were here, they'd surely know. But if Hattie showed up at their door after such an extended absence, Anne's Aunt Patty and Uncle Joe would pepper her with questions she wasn't ready to answer. Instead, she decided to seek out Anne's cousin Julia at the Patent Office Hospital where she volunteered with the Sanitary Commission.

The Patent Office building was enormous, four stories high and fronted with massive columns. Lifting her skirt to her ankles, Hattie climbed the steps and entered through the brass-handled doors. Inside, she stood a moment, watching the bustle of activity in the hallway. As she'd caught herself doing often since learning of Thom's death, she turned the thin ring he'd given her, part of their ruse as husband and wife, round and round on her finger.

It wouldn't do to wear the ring in front of Julia, she realized, so she slipped it off and put it in her pocket. Then she wound her way among cots of bandaged soldiers in the Patent Office's alcoves. A few of the healthier men called out to her. One asked if she'd stop and take down a letter he could send home. Another wanted her to sit and talk with him for a while.

Much as Hattie hated to, she ignored these pleas. The day was waning, and if she was to have any chance at all of finding Julia Trent here, she needed to keep moving. She checked the first floor and then the second and third. No sign of Julia.

Feeling discouraged, she climbed the stairs to the fourth floor, where masonry arches held up a roof dotted with skylights that let in the last of the day's light. In the second alcove Hattie checked, she found Julia rolling strips of fabric into bandages. She wore a plain dark dress, as was required of all female volunteers and nurses. Her brown hair was pulled back from her face, and her lips were turned in a frown as if she was weary of the work.

But when she looked up and saw Hattie, Julia's eyes lit up, and she smiled with the vivacity Hattie remembered. She dropped the bandage she was rolling and ran to Hattie, arms wide to embrace her. The warmth of her hug brought tears to Hattie's eyes.

"Wherever have you been?" Julia exclaimed. Stepping back, she took her in from head to toe. "They certainly haven't been feeding you well, wherever it was."

Hattie looked down at her dress, hanging loose about her waist. "It will take some time to explain," she said, unsure whether she should fabricate a story or take Julia into her confidence.

Julia took her arm and steered her toward the stairs. "I know just the place where we can talk."

"I wouldn't want to keep you from your work," Hattie said.

"You won't," Julia said as they started down the stairs. "I've had about all I can stand for today. And believe me, there will be more bandages to roll tomorrow. And more dressings to change and more letters to write and more hands to hold."

"It's good, what you do here," Hattie said.

"Thanks," Julia said. "Sometimes it feels like no one notices. But that's not the point, is it?"

From the third-floor landing, Julia led her down a long hallway. Past an alcove, she turned a knob and nudged Hattie inside a tiny room that, judging from the rolled bandages and bed sheets and blankets, had been converted into a supply closet. The only light came from a small square window at the far end of the little room.

"This is where we nurses go when we need to get away," Julia said. "It all gets to be too much sometimes. The blood, the screams, the sawing of limbs."

Hattie shuddered. "I don't know how you stand it."

Julia turned over two empty crates. "Not the finest seating, but it serves in a pinch."

Hattie eased herself onto one upturned crate, and Julia sat on the other. "It feels wonderful to get off my feet," Hattie said.

"Same." Lifting the hem of her dress, Julia rubbed her right ankle. "I never knew how exhausting it could be to stand all day." Smoothing her skirt, she tilted her head and eyed Hattie. "Papa and I attended a show at Grover's last month. I expected to see you there, taking tickets. But you were gone."

Julia had pointed Hattie to the job at Grover's National Theatre after Mr. Pinkerton's mailroom closed. Hattie had enjoyed the theatre work, but after an actor accosted her, she hadn't been especially sorry to leave. "It was only a temporary position."

Julia looked at her quizzically. "Then why aren't you back home in Indiana?"

Hattie drew a deep breath. Julia was only sixteen, but she'd grown up quite a lot with the work she did at the hospital. And it could be useful to have a confidante in Washington. "I'm not welcome at home. My parents are Secesh sympathizers. They've disowned me."

"How awful." Julia squeezed her hand. "And how unreasonable, when all you ever did was open mail for Mr. Pinkerton."

"That wasn't all I did," Hattie said. "But if I explain, you must promise never to tell a soul."

Julia's eyes shone. "I can keep a secret, I promise."

Hattie studied her face, young and earnest. "Not even your parents can know."

Julia shook her head. "I won't say a word."

"Good." Hattie drew another deep breath. "The Pinkerton Agency sent me to Richmond to gather information for the Union."

Julia's eyes widened. "As a spy?"

Hattie nodded. "In the company of one of Mr. Pinkerton's couriers. I posed as his wife. But he fell ill. One of our associates summoned a doctor, unaware of his Southern sympathies. Unfortunately, I'd paid him a visit to glean information on a traitorous scheme he was engaged in. When he found out that I and my associates were with the Federals, he turned us in. All three of us were imprisoned in Richmond."

Julia gasped. "You've come here from prison?"

"In a roundabout way, yes. You may have read in the papers. There was a break at Richmond's Libby Prison."

"Yes. Papa talked of nothing else the day the item appeared in the paper. Over a hundred of our boys escaped. But there was no mention of you."

"My being there at all was a fluke. Women aren't generally held at Libby. And I don't suppose anyone there was eager to admit that a woman had bested their guards by escaping." Hattie clapped her hand to her mouth, then released it. "Oh, but I've not mentioned the best part. Your cousin Richard was there at Libby. He's helped me escape."

"He's alive?" Julia's eyes widened. "I can't wait to tell Father and Mother."

Hattie touched her arm. "You'll have to wait, Julia. Till word gets to them some other way. I trust Richard has made his way north, but we got separated after leaving the tunnel, so I don't know exactly where he is now. And your parents can't know that I've said a word about him, or that could compromise me going forward."

"Right. Because you're a spy." Julia shook her head. "I can't believe I know someone who's an actual spy, much less someone who escaped from a Rebel prison. It's so exciting. I don't see how you can keep it a secret."

"A necessary secret," Hattie said. "It's best if people forget me altogether. My...our arrest was publicized, but I was known there as Mrs. Welton. Now I've got some scores to settle. But I don't mind your knowing since you've vowed to keep my secret. But I'd like to tell Anne. She's got such a good head on her shoulders, and I could use her help. I don't suppose she's back in Washington?"

"Oh my!" Julia's eyes danced. "But of course, you wouldn't have heard. Anne's gotten married."

Hattie thought she must have misheard. "Married?"

"To that handsome officer who joined us for dinner on Christmas Eve."

"Franklin Stone?" Hattie knew Anne was entranced by the charming lieutenant, though it seemed to Hattie from the one time they'd met that Lieutenant Stone was in the habit of charming whichever lady paid him the most attention.

"It was Papa's doing, you know, inviting him to dinner. And he's from Indiana, too, remember? He rode home on the same train as Anne and Henry, and I imagine he and Anne had a good deal of time to talk. Apparently, he spent most of his leave with her. By the time he was set to go back into battle, they'd gotten engaged. He returned to the front, but his injury gave him more problems than he'd expected, and he was discharged on medical grounds. Anne sent word last week that they'd gone ahead and married."

Hattie reeled with this news. Her sensible, logical friend—how could Anne have married a man she'd known only a few months? "I...I'm speechless," she said.

"It did come as a surprise, but he's so handsome, and Anne's so accomplished. It's not hard to see how they'd be drawn to one another."

Hattie fell silent. So much for Anne returning to Washington.

Julia studied her. "Have you only gotten to Washington today?"

Hattie nodded dumbly.

"Where are you staying?"

"I – I don't know. I gave up my room at Mrs. Sullivan's when I left for Richmond." Hattie stood, trying to thread together a series of next steps. "I've got a little money put away from when I was working." *Very little,* she thought. "If I hurry, I can make the bank before it closes and find a hotel room."

Julia popped up from where she sat. "Nonsense. You'll come home with me."

"But your parents—I can't just appear out of nowhere."

"They know you and Anne worked in Mr. Pinkerton's mailroom. We'll just say that after your position at Grover's ended, you did some additional work for Mr. Pinkerton out of town."

Hattie raised an eyebrow. "And if they ask whether I was spying?"

Julia looped her arm through Hattie's. "Then we change the subject," she said, with all the confidence of a sixteen-year-old whose limited experience kept her blissfully unaware of life's potential pitfalls.

~ ~ ~

Seated in the Trents' dining room, Hattie decided that however often Julia had to change the subject—she'd already done so twice—it was worth the trouble if only to enjoy a real meal in a warm room among friends whose lives were blessedly calm, even in wartime. She had to remind herself to take small bites—thank you, Miss Whitcomb—and not wolf down each course as it was set before her. Chicken soup, pear and mayonnaise salad, Beef Wellington—she'd nearly forgotten such delicacies existed, much less imagined ever indulging in them again.

So far, Julia's diversions had been effective, steering the conversation away from Hattie. Her father, who everyone called the Judge, was easily persuaded to expound on his thoughts as to which mistakes had kept the North from quickly ending the war. Her mother could be likewise distracted on the subject of Washington gossip, especially regarding Mary Lincoln, Mrs. Trent being one of the First Lady's few defenders. In addition, Julia's younger brothers, Samuel and Halsey, were inclined to antics that caused the adults to abandon whatever they'd been discussing and bring them in line.

By the time the servants came around with dessert, Hattie was so full she thought she might burst, even though she'd prudently left a few bites of each delicacy on her plate so as not to seem overly ravenous. But the scents of cinnamon and nutmeg steaming from the apple pie proved too much to resist, and she accepted a thin slice, savoring each warm bite on her tongue.

"Now that you're back, Hattie, I do hope you'll stay in Washington a while," Mrs. Trent said. "I'm sure Julia would welcome a companion now that Anne's taken up a whole new life back in Indiana."

"Married!" The judge exclaimed, wiping a crumb of crust from his mustache. "I should bill out my services as a matchmaker, bringing those two together."

His wife shook her head. "It was love, not your doing, Joe. Anyhow, Hattie, I want you to know you're welcome to stay here as long as you like. Consider this your home away from home."

Hattie pushed aside her dessert plate, having savored as much of the pie as she dared. "Thank you kindly, Mrs. Trent. I can't tell you how helpful it is to have a bed to sleep in while I determine what to do next."

"If I know Allan Pinkerton, he'll have you off on some adventure within the week," the Judge said.

Julia jumped up, pushing back her chair. "Hattie, you look tired enough to lay your head on the table and sleep. If we may be excused, Mother, I'll show Hattie to her room."

"Of course, dear. You do look a bit peaked, Hattie. And underfed. Whatever you've been off doing—"

Julia bent to kiss her cheek. "Good night, Mother." She pecked her father's cheek too. "Good night, Father."

Hattie dipped her head to each of them in turn. "I can never repay your hospitality. Thank you both."

Mrs. Trent beamed. "Our pleasure entirely, dear. Now off to bed with you."

~ ~ ~

When Hattie woke the next morning, her first thought was that she must be dreaming, so warm and comfortable was her bed. Sunlight streamed through the lace curtains, making her wonder how long she'd slept. She could've lain there all day, luxuriating in the clean sheets and freshly washed chemise Julia had insisted she wear.

But a plan had begun taking shape in Hattie's mind last night, and she wanted to see where it would lead. She stretched her arms, then rose from the bed and stretched again, reveling in the feeling of the plush rug beneath her toes. She hoped Abby had found her way to comfortable circumstances too. If only there was some way to find out.

Laid across the arm of the upholstered chair beside the bed, the frock Hattie had worn yesterday—and the day before—looked out of place, wrinkled and smudged with dirt. But the dress was all she had, so she'd have to make do.

She fastened her corset and pulled her stockings, which like the dress had seen better days. As she reached for the dress, there was a rapping at the door.

"It's Julia. Are you decent?"

"Close enough," Hattie said.

Julia came in, shutting the door behind her. She had two frocks slung over her arm, one a pale green-gray trimmed with bright blue ribbons, the other a brown and purple paisley print.

"You can't get by with only one outfit," Julia said. She fanned each dress over the rumpled covers of Hattie's bed. "These morning dresses aren't the finest, but then you don't want to attract attention, do you, so there's no need for hoops. And you look to be about my size, so I'm guessing they'll fit."

"I can't rob your closet," Hattie said.

"Mother buys me way too many clothes," Julia said. "I've hardly worn either of these. If I never wear them again, I doubt she'd notice."

"She'll notice if I came downstairs wearing one of them," Hattie said.

"Not this morning, she won't. She's already gone off to some fundraising event for the soldiers."

Hattie fingered the soft, supple fabric of the brown and purple print. "I have to admit, I'm a bit tired of that old dress. It reminds me of things I'd rather forget."

"Then you should burn it," Julia said resolutely. "Before she left, Mother asked me to find out whether you'd prefer breakfast brought to your room or whether you'd prefer to join me in the breakfast room. Charles has come by, and he'd like to say hello if you're up for it."

Hattie caught her eye. "You've said nothing to him about the specifics of my...situation?"

"Not a word," Julia said. "He knows only that you're back in the city after several weeks' absence and that until you find other accommodations, Mother has offered our guestroom."

"Good." Hattie considered her options. Julia's older brother was sharp and inquisitive. By breakfasting in her room, she could avoid his probing into how she'd spent the past few weeks. But as an Army surgeon, he might have helpful information to share. "I'll be down as soon as I'm dressed," she said.

"Very well." Leaving the dresses, Julia went to the door, then turned. "Oh, and you'll find a few other necessaries in the top dresser drawer. They're old but suitable. If you don't claim them, they'll get torn up for bandages."

She left before Hattie could thank her. Checking the dresser, she found a fresh camisole, stockings, bonnet, and even a cinched purse. She chose the brown and purple paisley frock—the drabber the better, she thought, recalling Miss Warne's plain garb. As she dressed, she was especially glad for the bath one of the servants had drawn for her last night. Clean clothes, clean skin.

She tucked the watch and its chain inside her bodice. "For you, Thom," she whispered. "I'll set things right."

Though her attire was simple, she felt almost elegant as she went downstairs to the breakfast room. Sunlight streamed from the big east window, illuminating the table. Charles rose as she entered, blinking in the sunlight. A handsome man, square-chinned and dark-haired, he must be a distraction to some of Dorothea Dix's army hospital nurses who didn't know he was engaged to be married to a woman he adored.

"What a delight to see you, Hattie," he exclaimed.

"Likewise." She flashed a smile, then slid into the empty chair beside him, the seat upholstered in cornflower blue, and a servant rushed to help her scoot the chair close to the table. "Where are the boys?" she asked.

"They've gone upstairs with their tutor," Julia said from across the table.

"Quite reluctantly, I'm afraid," Charles said. "Father had an early meeting at the Treasury, and Mother is off to some function or other."

"A ladies' tea," Julia said. "To celebrate the arrival of spring."

"Has spring arrived?" Charles said. "You could have fooled me, the way the wind's blowing today."

A servant filled the bone china cup at Hattie's place with what smelled like real coffee. A single sip affirmed that the coffee was genuine, a welcome change from the bland chicory beverage served in Virginia.

She turned to Charles, still holding the cup, a comfort in her hands. "You must be incredibly busy with all the casualties," Hattie said.

He shrugged. "It could be worse, I suppose."

"Charles thinks the war will drag on at least through the end of the year." Julia reached for an orange from a bowl in the middle of the table. "I'd be happy to see it end tomorrow."

Charles passed Hattie a basket. Lifting the cloth, she delighted at the smell of fresh-baked buttermilk biscuits. She set one, large and warm, on her breakfast plate, though she could've eaten every biscuit in the basket if given the chance.

"I understand Mr. Pinkerton sent you out of town," Charles said. "Chicago, I suppose?"

She let his supposition rest. "Mr. Pinkerton removed himself from assisting the army after General McClellan stepped down. So there has been less for his employees to do in this city."

Charles frowned, offering the butter dish. "That leaves Lafayette Baker's National Detective Police. I've heard little good about his leadership."

Hattie kept her eyes on her biscuit as she buttered it, not wanting to seem too eager for information. "I understand there's now another man in charge of gathering intelligence for our troops. A General Sharpe?" If General Sharpe was sending Edith Greenfield to Tennessee, perhaps Hattie could convince him to send her too.

Charles sipped his coffee, then leaned back in his chair. "That's right. Sharpe's been put in charge of military intelligence. A new post, but he's already got a well-oiled operation from what I hear."

Julia sliced into her orange, and the sweet, citrusy scent of it wafted over the table. "Sounds to me like a lot of men stepping over each other trying to get the same job done."

"I suppose it is," Charles said. "But it's the Army's first stab at organizing intelligence efforts, and it seems they've chosen to try out several approaches all at once, hoping one of them sticks. It would be a stretch to say any of the men in charge truly knows what he's doing. Pinkerton's a cooper who stumbled into detective work. Baker conned his way in. And Sharpe got his post because he's fluent in French."

"But we're not fighting the French," Julia said.

"No, but Sharpe was asked to translate a book that detailed France's secret service operation. When he completed the task, the commander who'd assigned asked if he'd draw up a plan for organizing a secret service operation for our boys. Before he knew it, he was in charge of a brand new Bureau of Military Intelligence. It's only been up and running a few weeks, but I understand there's already been some useful information relayed about Rebel lines along the Rappahannock, some of it coming directly from Sharpe's scouting. This week, in fact, I'm told he personally identified the points where General Averell's troops could best cross the river. Reports are vague, but as I understand it, Averell made some substantial gains before retreating."

Kelly's Ford. Hattie suppressed any hint of recognition as she swallowed the last delectable bite of the buttery biscuit. "How commendable. I expect General Sharpe is operating out of the War Department building as Mr. Pinkerton did?"

Charles shook his head. "He's stationed in the field, which no doubt aids the accuracy of his work. Aquia Landing, I believe. He's also got a division intercepting and reading Rebel correspondence there."

"But that's what you and Anne did for Mr. Pinkerton," Julia exclaimed. "Perhaps General Sharpe will take you on."

Charles studied Hattie. "You're not staying on with Pinkerton's?"

She shifted in her seat. Julia meant well, but she seemed not to realize that sharing even a seemingly innocuous tidbit about Hattie's situation opened her to questions she'd rather not answer. "I'm considering my options," she said vaguely.

He pushed back from the table. "Just stay away from Lafayette Baker," he said. "For a man who's supposed to be on our side, he seems to be involved in a number of underhanded dealings."

"I surely will," Hattie said. She'd had her own run-in with Baker a few months back, trying to ascertain whether her brother was spying for him in Canada. While she was alone with Baker in his office, he had tried to demonstrate his technique for searching a woman by reaching for her bodice. It wasn't an incident she was eager to repeat. Her meeting with General Sharpe, if she could manage to get one, was bound to go better.

Chapter Seven

March 19, 1863

After a stop at the bank to withdraw a portion of her meager savings, Hattie hired a carriage to take her to the wharf district. There she joined a line to board a packet steamer bound for Aquia Landing.

Though the run was commercial, a soldier was checking each passenger's credentials as they boarded. The only official-looking document Hattie had with her was the pass one of General Averell's men had issued in case she was questioned during her ride from the Rappahannock to Washington.

Slipping the pass to the soldier, she caught his eye and smiled. Returning the smile, he gave the paper a cursory glance, then handed it back and waved her on board.

Part of her wanted to sit close to where she'd sat when she'd traveled down the Potomac with Thom on the first leg of their journey to Richmond. But her sorrow felt too raw, and she chose instead to sit at the opposite end of the steamer. It wouldn't do to let her emotions get the best of her.

Even walking the streets of Washington had been difficult. Too many places reminded her of Thom. The War Department, where he used to come and go with his letters, bantering with all Pinkerton's mailroom girls but paying special attention to Hattie. The street leading from the Trents' house toward Mrs. Sullivan's boardinghouse, where Thom had walked her home last Christmas Eve. The Willard Hotel, where he'd asked her to dinner.

Time would heal the hurt. That's what people said when you lost someone you loved. But when a wrong needed to be set right, there was no waiting on time.

Hattie fidgeted her fingers in her lap, winding them around the strings of Julia's purse. Julia had meant it all as a gift, she knew, and Hattie was grateful for it. But she didn't like feeling beholden, and she vowed that at the first opportunity, she'd repay the kindness.

Opening the purse strings, she reached inside and took out the gold wedding band she'd worn as the courier's wife. She turned it around in her hand, then slipped it on her finger as Thom had done when they'd first set off for Richmond. *Know always that no matter what anyone says, you are my one true wife.*

The journey down the Potomac went faster than Hattie remembered, perhaps because she spent so much time going over various scenarios that might play out at Aquia Landing. Commercial packet boat service was limited due to the war. She'd only have a few hours to find General Sharpe and, if he'd see her, to make her request.

When she got off at the landing, she turned toward the broad encampment that was the Union headquarters for the region. Even more than on the steamer, she felt conspicuous, one woman among hundreds and hundreds of men. She held her head high and looked forward as if she knew precisely where she was going. She'd heard that some officers' wives joined encampments for a few days or even weeks at a time. If Hattie managed to look the part, with the bearing of someone who had every right to be there, she hoped she wouldn't be stopped.

Still, heads turned as she passed, walking with only a slight limp from her ankle injury toward the military compound. She did her best to ignore the stares, bestow a smile now and then to show her friendly intent,

The operations here appeared more massive by far than General Averell's encampment north of the Rappahannock. The military compound smelled of mud and manure, and she was able to deduce fairly quickly where the officers' headquarters were. As she turned that way, she saw that off to one side, beneath a grove of pines, there was a cluster of tents that seemed quieter than the rest, with only a few men milling around. A hospital, maybe. Or, if she was lucky, the headquarters of General Sharpe's Bureau of Military Intelligence.

She marched purposefully toward the tents. As she approached the largest one, thinking it might be the general's office, a soldier grabbed her by the arm.

"Lost, young lady?" He tightened his grip on her. "I'll show you out."

She stood firm, resisting his attempt to turn her back. "I need to speak with General Sharpe."

The soldier grinned, showing a gap between his front teeth. "Do you, now?"

She drew herself up as best she could with him holding onto her arm. "I've got important information."

"See those folks over there?" With his free hand, he gestured toward a line of people outside the farthest tent. All were men, many dressed in civilian clothes. From what Hattie could tell at a distance, several were dark-skinned, either Negroes or Indians, and at least two wore gray Rebel uniforms. "Those are the sort of people the general relies on for information. Prisoners. Deserters. Secesh who've gotten tired of not eating and are coming over to our side, or maybe they're only pretending to. Scouts the Rebels consider too lowly or stupid to spy." The soldier stepped back, still holding onto her arm. "You're none of that."

Her eyes flashed. "I've worked for Mr. Pinkerton."

"That won't get you far with the general, I assure you."

"And I crossed the Rappahannock with General Averell's troops."

This got her traction. "Tell you what. You come with me over to the intake tent, and I'll take your statement."

"No." She shook free of his grasp. "I need to speak directly with General Sharpe."

He reached for her, but she ducked away. Ahead, on the boardwalk leading to the large tent she wanted to enter, she spotted a man of some rank, judging from his epaulets. Lifting her skirts to her ankles, she ran toward him. "General!" she called.

The man turned. His sandy brown hair was balding, and his mustache extended to his jawline, giving the impression of a frown. The corners of his hazel eyes drooped, giving him the look of a loyal hound dog.

"General Sharpe," she said as she caught up with him. Catching her breath, she extended her hand. "General Averell sent me." This wasn't exactly true, but it wasn't entirely false either.

The soldier who'd grabbed her arm joined them. "Sir, I told her—"

"Averell, you say?" the general interrupted. "You're a fairer sight than most of his soldiers, I'll give you that."

Hattie locked eyes with him. "A doctor who treated me recently suggested I see you. Edith Greenfield."

His face lit with recognition. "Ah, Dr. Greenfield. Well then, I'll hear you out, Miss—"

"Logan. Hattie Logan," she said.

He started at the mention of her name. "Logan," he repeated. "You were in Richmond. One of Pinkerton's people. Only you went by another name."

"Welton," she said.

He stroked his mustache. "Welton. Right. I'm glad you escaped his fate. Come with me, Miss Logan."

She followed him into the big wall tent and sat as he indicated, on a wooden folding chair next to his desk. Papers in tidy stacks covered the desktop. At the top of one stack, she noted a hand-drawn map. At the top of another, she saw handwritten notes with yesterday's date. Another stack was labeled "monthly report."

General Sharpe sat behind his desk and folded his hands. "What can I do for you, Miss Logan?"

She sat up straight, shoulders back, chin up, the way she'd learned at finishing school. "The question would more properly be what can I do for you."

His down-drooping eyes took on a keen edge. "You're no longer in the service of Mr. Pinkerton?"

"No, sir. Not since the Richmond assignment."

He took up a pencil and turned it end to end in his hand. "There was talk of trying to get you out. But you seem to have managed that on your own."

"I had help," she said. "The Libby Prison break. A woman from Church Hill made sure I knew of the plans."

"Elizabeth Van Lew?"

"Yes," she said. "You're aware of her work?"

"I've been made aware, yes. She has a rather elaborate network in Richmond. My scouts have connected with her, and the information she gathers is being funneled to this bureau." He waved his hand over the stacks of papers on the desk. "We interrogate Rebel deserters and prisoners. We have scouts behind enemy lines, and we've broken the enemy's signal codes, so wherever we've got men in position to read their flagging, we're able to pass along their messages."

"An impressive operation," Hattie said.

"The key is timeliness," General Sharpe said. "Until recently, accurate information seemed to come in only when it was too late to use it."

This must be a jab at Mr. Pinkerton's work, Hattie thought. But perhaps it had merit. The Pinkerton detectives, herself included, knew little about military operations.

"I'm told you rode personally to scout the Rappahannock for General Averell's advance this week," she said.

"I did. I wanted to ensure the accuracy of our reports on where our soldiers could cross with the least Confederate resistance."

"At Kelly's Ford."

His gaze bore into her. "You're well informed, Miss Logan."

"I was there, along with Abigail Rice, who helped me after I escaped Libby. General Averell's men got me across the river. And Abby, too, I hope. I lost track of her."

He shuffled through a stack of papers, then extracted one. "According to this report, the Rebels are keen on capturing Miss Rice. They want her prosecuted as a spy." He set down the paper. "But I've seen nothing about you, Miss Logan."

"I'm not surprised," she said. "I shouldn't have been transferred to Libby in the first place, and I expect the warden there won't own up to my escaping. But Abby...do you know if she's safe?"

"I've heard nothing. But don't despair, Miss Logan. General Averell is still regrouping after the battle at Kelly's Ford. She may have ended up in another part of his camp. It's a large operation."

"She's well worth trying to locate," Hattie said. "As I mentioned, she helped orchestrate the prison break. Afterward, she took me in, then summoned Dr. Greenfield to attend to an ankle injury I'd suffered during the escape. I was in a despondent state after learning that Mr. Welton had..." Her voice caught in her throat.

The general's eyes softened. "You were close with him."

"Yes," she said, her voice barely more than a whisper. She swiped at the tears that welled in her eyes, angry at displaying her emotions when she'd intended to show only strength. She squared her shoulders and met the general's gaze. "When Dr. Greenfield learned I'd been a spy, she took me into her confidence, saying that when she went doctoring behind enemy lines, she gathered information and passed it on to you. She mentioned going to Tennessee. I want to offer my services there if you'll have me."

He leaned back in his chair. "If you're willing to scout for us, there's no need to travel so far. If you've learned anything at all with Pinkerton, we can find a role for you here. In fact, one of my top aides, John Babcock, came to me from Pinkerton. Babcock's the one who initially conceived of a secret service department to coordinate the gathering of military intelligence."

She twisted the gold band on her finger. "I want an assignment in Tennessee, like Dr. Greenfield."

"Dr. Greenfield's assignment is one of necessity. Her unusual manner of dress, shall we say, makes her unpopular with the Army's medical branch, which from what I hear is already highly skeptical of female doctors. She's going to Tennessee because they don't want her here."

"But she'll spy for you there."

"Not for me. This bureau serves the Army of the Potomac. But I've advised the Army of the Cumberland that they'd be wise to avail themselves of her services."

Color rose to Hattie's face. If she was going to prove her worth, she should have started by gathering the basic facts about Sharpe's operation. "Then I'd like you to recommend me to the Army of the Cumberland too. I can decode documents written with route ciphers and Viginiere's. And Mr. Welton taught me much about gathering information without arousing suspicions."

Sharpe tapped a finger on his desk. "What about your family, Miss Logan? What do they think of you risking your life to do espionage work?"

She drew a deep breath. There'd been a time when she'd tried to hide her family ties. She found them shameful, and she'd believed they would get in her way. But Miss Warne had convinced her otherwise.

"My father is a Secesh sympathizer who smuggles grain to the South. My mother comes from a Louisiana plantation and hates anything to do with the North. They've disowned me." It helped, somehow, to say this last part out loud, a simple, indisputable fact.

The line of the general's lips seemed to harden, and she wondered if she'd admitted too much. "We play the cards we're dealt," he said. "A family with Southern sympathies can be useful in gaining Rebel trust, provided you keep control over how much you reveal. What about your husband?"

She must have looked confused because he added quickly. "You wear a wedding band, and yet you answer to Miss Logan."

She touched the ring, embarrassed at having made another error. "I wore it in my role as courier's wife," she said. "I must admit I felt sentimental on the ride over here, and I slipped it on."

"You must be careful, Miss Logan. Small oversights can have large consequences."

"Yes, General Sharpe." She slipped the ring from her finger and returned it to her purse, her optimism fading.

He reached for a quill. "You haven't said why you insist on Tennessee."

"I'm told the man who betrayed Mr. Welton and me is there. Dr. Luke Blackstone. He was working both sides in Richmond, and I'm told he's now in Tennessee, where he'll be less recognized. I'd like to make sure he harms no one else."

The general's gaze sharpened. "Blackstone. We've had reports that he tried to trigger a yellow fever epidemic in the North."

Hattie nodded. "Dr. Greenfield told me of that plot. I don't doubt that he'll try again."

General Sharpe reached for two blank sheets of paper. On each, he scribbled a note. Then he looked up at Hattie.

"General Rosecrans has been whipping the intelligence division of the Army of the Cumberland into shape. Scouts, spies, newspapers, signal intercepts, deserters, prisoners, and civilian refugees—he gathers information from all those sources, much as we do here. He's got a man in Nashville, Colonel Truesdail, who runs a police operation for him there." Sharpe folded one of the papers, then offered it to Hattie. "Here's a note to him, recommending you."

Hope swelled inside her. "Thank you, sir."

He folded the second paper, then handed it to her. "Give this to John Babcock. He's running interrogations here—you'll know the tent by the line of people outside. He'll make sure you've got the papers and funds you'll need to get to Nashville."

She stood, clutching the papers in her hand. "I appreciate your kindness, sir."

The general stood too. "It isn't kindness, Miss Logan. I expect results."

"I'll do my best to produce them, sir." She started out of the tent.

"One more thing, Miss Logan," he said.

She turned. "Yes, General Sharpe?"

"I recommend a change of appearance." He gestured vaguely at her. "Hair, clothes, something of that nature. If you run into this Blackstone fellow, you don't want him recognizing you straightaway. And think of a new name for your pass. The Rebels may not be saying publicly that you escaped, but you can be sure they're looking for you."

Chapter Eight

March 26, 1863

A week after her meeting with General Sharpe, Hattie rode the train into Indianapolis. Nearly two years had passed since she'd left the city. So much had changed, events both good and bad that had left their mark on her. She'd acquired skills she'd never dreamed of learning. She'd endured conditions worse than any she'd ever imagined. And she'd come to understand that she could accept her Indiana upbringing but not be shackled by it, making possible this visit to her home state on her way to Tennessee.

The train pulled to a stop in front of the massive brick station building where the various railroad lines that crisscrossed the city came together. From the window, Hattie saw more soldiers milling around than she had when she'd left back in 1861, and more civilians too. She rose from her seat, holding her carpetbag close as she entered the flow of passengers exiting the train car.

"Help with that, miss?" asked a young soldier behind her.

"Thank you, but I'm fine," she said. He was likely trustworthy, but she'd been warned that with quick wartime growth, crime was on the rise here. Aside from any belongings her parents may have hung onto, the bag contained all her earthly possessions.

A small crowd had gathered in front of the train, family and friends who rushed forward to greet passengers as they got off. Hattie watched her feet as she stepped from the train car, mindful of the ankle that felt a bit wobbly after the hours she'd spent sitting down.

When she reached the platform, she looked up to see Anne pressing toward her, tall and pretty in a cream-colored morning dress with a pink floral print. Arms outstretched, she drew Hattie into a tight embrace, then held her at arm's length.

"You can't imagine how thrilled I was to get your telegram!" she said. "You're truly a sight for sore eyes. But I scarcely recognized you with your hair darkened and bobbed."

"A change was in order," Hattie said. "And you've got a glow about you, Mrs. Stone. Marriage must agree with you. You can't imagine my surprise when Julia told me that you and the handsome lieutenant had tied the knot."

Anne blushed. "It was sudden, wasn't it? But one thing led to another and, well, it's wartime." She gestured for a man Hattie recognized as the family's coachman to take Hattie's bag. Then she linked arms with Hattie, and they started through the station, the air thick with the smell of coal smoke.

Turning toward the exit, they passed a stack of pine boxes. "Coffins?" Hattie asked.

Anne nodded. "Soldiers making their final trip home," she said grimly.

It saddened Hattie to think of all the grieving families who would meet trains carrying their loved ones in these boxes. And the stacked coffins, she knew, represented only a fraction of the war dead, with many bodies left where they'd fallen.

"You must be glad Franklin doesn't have to go back to the battlefield," she said as they exited the station into brilliant sunlight.

"He'd go back in a heartbeat if they'd allow it," Anne said. "He gets so frustrated, being stuck at home while others are fighting. He's gone back to practicing law, so at least he's got that to occupy him."

"That and a new wife," Hattie teased.

They reached the carriage, one of the finer ones parked outside the station. The coachman helped them inside, and the horses trotted off.

"How's Henry?" Hattie asked. "Julia wanted me to be sure to ask after him." Henry was the reason Anne had returned to Indianapolis in the first place, escorting her younger brother home after an injury landed him in the Patent Office Hospital. While he was recuperating, Julia had taken quite a liking to her cousin.

"Henry's getting on well enough, though he's in no shape to return to battle, which suits Mama and me fine. And Richard—can you believe we finally got a telegram from him after all this time? It arrived the same day as yours, and it said just as little, only that he'd been taken prisoner and was out now and safe and would send a letter soon."

"Thank goodness," Hattie said. "I've been hoping he'd gotten out all right."

"You knew he was in prison?"

Hattie nodded. "Did you read in the papers about Thom Welton being arrested in Richmond?"

Anne nodded. "So tragic. Clearly, the Rebels meant to make an example of him."

"And there was mention of his wife being arrested too?"

"Yes," Anne said. "But what does this have to do with Richard being in prison?"

"That woman—Thom's wife—that was me."

"His wife?" Anne exclaimed. "Arrested in Richmond? I thought you were working at Grover's Theatre after Mr. Pinkerton closed up his mailroom operations."

"I was. But the box office manager came back, and Miss Warne asked if I'd go South. With Thom, as it turned out." Seeing the shocked look on Anne's face, she hastily added, "It was all very proper."

Anne reached for her hand. "You cared for him, didn't you? Oh, Hattie. I'm so sorry at how it turned out."

Hattie nodded, tears welling in her eyes. "When we got to Richmond, Thom's rheumatism got much worse. I made his deliveries, then tracked down a man Miss Warne had asked me to locate, a man who was helping smuggle grain to the South."

She paused, considering whether she should mention her father's involvement. She decided against it. "The man was a doctor," she continued. "Because we'd been gone so long, Miss Warne came to Richmond to ask after us, and she brought Lucy Hamilton with her. Lucy took it upon herself to fetch a doctor for Thom, and she returned with the man I'd met with."

"Oh no." Anne clapped her hand to her mouth, then released it.

"He recognized me, of course, and he knew at once that I wasn't aligned with the South as I'd pretended. Knowing I'd played him for a fool, extracting information that would be valuable to the North, he turned all three of us over to the authorities."

"Lucy too?" Anne asked.

Hattie nodded. "She didn't do well in prison. She implicated Thom and me, and in return, the warden released her in a prisoner exchange. Then he ordered me transferred to Libby Prison to separate me from Thom. There were no other women there. They put me in a cell all alone with no company but the rats, and I was half-mad with worry over Thom."

"How awful," Anne said.

Hattie straightened, reminding herself she needed to be strong. "Thankfully, there's a remarkable woman in Richmond, with deep family roots there, who's allowed to visit Union prisoners. Turns out she's also a spy for the Union. She passed word to me of an escape some prisoners were planning, and to my great surprise, Richard was among them."

Anne pressed her hands to her bosom. "Our Richard! And Henry feared he'd been killed at Manassas."

"He was only wounded," Hattie said. "The Rebs took him prisoner, and he recovered. Happily, he ended up at Libby Prison. If not for him, I'd likely still be there. Some of the other prisoners didn't want a woman escaping through the tunnel they'd dug."

Anne laughed. "Afraid you'd muddy your dress, were they?"

Hattie smiled. "Richard insisted I be given a chance. The night of the escape, he waited around till the very end to see that I got out. Then he insisted on me going ahead of him. The tunnel wasn't exactly spacious. Large as he is, Richard got wedged near the exit. I ran for help, but he insisted I not linger to see that they got him out. I've been worried about what became of him. Getting through to the North is a lot easier said than done, I assure you."

"I can't begin to imagine," Anne said. "The papers said over a hundred Union men escaped Libby Prison that night."

"And one Union woman," Hattie said.

"Wait till I tell Mother," Anne said.

Hattie shook her head. "The details need to stay between you and me. The fewer people who know that Mrs. Thom Welton was actually Hattie Logan, the better. That way, I can go back to spying."

"After all you've been through, you're going back to spying for Mr. Pinkerton?"

She shook her head. "Not Mr. Pinkerton. He's moved his operations out of Washington. But there's a new Bureau of Military Intelligence, and the general heading it up is the one who sent me out here."

Anne's face darkened. "To spy in Indianapolis?"

"Not here, silly. I only stopped to see you. I'm headed for Nashville."

"But that's occupied territory. It's bound to be a hotbed of Rebel activity."

"Exactly," Hattie said. "That's the point."

"And you'll be working for the Bureau of Military Intelligence?"

"Not directly. The general has recommended me to a local effort."

"That's quite vague, Miss Logan," Anne teased.

"As it must be," Hattie said. "For your good and mine." Out the window, she saw the Duncans' big three-story house come into view. But the carriage rolled past it.

Surprise must have registered on Hattie's face as Anne hastened to explain. "Father set up Franklin and me in a little house nearby. It's not elegant, but it's a start until Franklin gets established in his law practice."

"He's not joining your father's firm?"

Anne shook her head. "They don't see eye to eye on certain things."

Hattie waited for her to explain, but she looked away.

"Here we are," Anne said a bit too brightly as the carriage slowed and then stopped in front of a small, two-story white clapboard house. "Home sweet home."

Though they were only a few blocks from the Duncan home, the houses in this neighborhood were far more modest. In the yard next door to Anne's, several children were playing a game of hoops.

Hattie and Anne left the carriage, and Hattie followed Anne through a gate in the low picket fence and up the flagstone walk, the coachman coming behind with her bag. Purple and white crocuses bloomed along with the path, and a light breeze carried the earthy, wet smell of spring.

Anne swung open the front door. "As I said, it's not much. But Franklin prefers it to living with my parents."

Hattie followed her inside, wondering how anyone would not want to stay with the Duncans, who along with the Trents were among the most hospitable people she knew. Their hospitality even extended to fugitive slaves escaping north to freedom, as Hattie had inadvertently discovered one day while visiting Anne's family.

"Where shall I put the bag, Mrs. Stone?" the coachman asked.

"The back bedroom," she said, gesturing toward the stairs. "Thank you."

"Oh, but I couldn't impose," Hattie said. If it had been Anne's mother inviting her to stay overnight, she'd have gladly accepted the offer, but that was in a big house with servants. Here the quarters felt cramped, and she sensed that when Franklin got home, the house would feel even smaller. "I understand there's a Ladies' Home set up in Indianapolis now. I can sleep there tonight before I go on to Nashville."

"I won't hear of it," Anne said. "My dearest friend in all the world sleeping with strangers. "Besides, the Ladies' Home is for soldiers' families. Have a seat in the parlor. I'll put on tea."

Hattie shook her head. "I'll not have you waiting on me," she said.

Anne sighed. "You are a stubborn one. Well, I for one can do with some tea." Motioning for Hattie to follow, she proceeded to the kitchen. Directly behind the parlor, it was small but tidy. In the light that streamed through a single window, the floor gleamed and the painted cupboards shone white. Anne had always been a bundle of energy, which she now apparently directed toward housekeeping.

"Do you ever miss Washington?" Hattie asked.

"Every day," Anne said, putting a kettle on to boil. "I know we were only opening letters, but it felt good to be doing something purposeful. And we were right in the thick of things."

"From the looks of it, there's a good deal going on here in Indianapolis," Hattie said. "Far more than when we left. Plenty of ways to help with the war effort."

"Franklin prefers I stay home." Anne pressed her hands to her skirt, and her gaze flitted briefly to the window. "We're expecting."

Hattie threw her arms around her friend, pulling her into a hug. "That's marvelous."

"It is, isn't it?" Anne said, as if the thought hadn't occurred to her before. "Mother's thrilled, of course. Her first grandchild."

Hattie's emotions went in several directions at once. With Thom, she'd imagined a life after the war, one that vaguely involved a home and children, and she felt sad knowing this dream was lost to her now. But she also felt a keen sense of purpose and excitement over what might transpire once she got to Nashville. And seeing the confines of Anne's new life, these prospects also made her feel guilty somehow.

She reached for Anne's hand and gave it a quick squeeze. "So much has changed for the both of us."

Anne nodded briskly. The kettle whistled, and as she turned toward it, Hattie thought she saw her wipe away a tear.

~ ~ ~

As Hattie expected, Franklin Stone took up a good deal of room in the small house. He wasn't a large man like Anne's brother Richard, but he had the same commanding presence she remembered from when she and Anne had first met him at the Trents. Even without his lieutenant's uniform, he was handsome as ever, with dark, penetrating eyes that had so captivated Anne that night. But the smile he'd flashed so readily then seemed rare now, Hattie observed as the three of them sat down at a round dining table to a supper of stewed chicken and potatoes.

"Anne tells me you're just passing through on your way to Nashville," Franklin said, slicing into a chunk of chicken. "Do you have family there?"

Hattie swallowed a bite of the stringy meat. Cooking wasn't Anne's strong suit, but why would it be? She'd grown up with servants to do the cooking, and even at the Washington boarding house, Mrs. Sullivan had prepared their meals. "I'll be seeing acquaintances in Nashville," she said.

"Quite a lot of war activity in Tennessee these days." Franklin lifted a forkful of meat. "It's less apt to be misdirected there than in the East."

"The Army of the Potomac seems to be finding its direction at last," Hattie said.

"I wasn't speaking of the military leadership," Franklin said. "It's the motivation of the troops that concerns me now that Lincoln has made such a grave error."

Shifting in her seat, Anne reached for a serving dish and offered it to her husband. "More potatoes, darling? You must be starved, working late as you did."

"Lincoln's error—surely you don't mean his freeing the slaves?" Hattie said.

Franklin's eyes bore into hers. "That's precisely what I mean. Our boys signed on to save the Union, not to let the darkies take over."

Anne set her hand on his. "Let's not get into this over supper."

Hattie saw her discomfort, but she couldn't let the remark stand. "Allowing fellow human beings the freedoms we all enjoy is more than enough reason to fight. Have you spent any time on a plantation?"

Franklin set down his fork. "You sound as if you're one of those radical abolitionists."

"And what if I am?" Hattie said.

He shook his head. "They'll run this nation into the ground."

"Franklin's a Peace Democrat," Anne said. "He just wants the Union restored."

Dabbing his mouth with his napkin, Franklin pushed back from the table, still glaring at Hattie. "There's a good number of us here in the West, and we intend to make our point however we must. So while you're in these parts, I suggest keeping your radical views to yourself."

~ ~ ~

Hattie left the next morning. Before leaving, she sensed an awkwardness between her and Anne that she'd never known before.

Last night, after Franklin went off to some sort of meeting, Anne had launched into a defense of him and his views. He was in nearly constant pain, she said, and it had nearly killed him to be sent home from the battlefront when his fellow soldiers were still off fighting. And did it matter if he was a Peace Democrat when she and her family were abolitionists? The war would end soon enough, and then all that would be behind them.

Hattie disagreed, but for the first time, she didn't feel she could speak her mind with Anne. She'd chosen Franklin. She was having his baby. It didn't feel right for Hattie to question those choices now. Anne was strong. She'd make the best of things. And maybe she was right. Maybe when the war was over, no one would care whether Union soldiers had fought to end slavery or to bring the South back into its fold.

Dropping Hattie at the station, Anne took both her hands and squeezed them. "You'll do well for the cause," she said. "Just don't be taking chances. You've gotten in enough trouble as it is."

Securing Anne's promise to convey her best to her family, especially Richard when he came home, Hattie boarded a spur line train. La Conner, the town she'd grown up in, was only a short ride away. No one would care if she reached Nashville a bit later than expected.

The idea of visiting the place she'd once vowed to forget had flitted back and forth in her mind on the train ride from Washington to Indianapolis. At first, she'd dismissed it. But the more she considered it, the more it made sense. Rejection—or rather, the fear of rejection—was what had made her foreswear her hometown, she realized. But with their letter rejecting her as their daughter, her parents had actually taken the sting out of it.

By the time the train pulled to a stop at La Conner's tiny station, Hattie was feeling almost nostalgic about her hometown. The dusty streets she'd walked to school, the general store where Mr. Thompson sometimes slipped her a peppermint candy, the wide sky overhead—these memories felt almost comforting. What she preferred to forget was the taunting of children whose parents resented her father for the prices he charged at his grain elevators and the discomfort she'd felt in a house where love seemed as distant as the faraway ocean.

She left her bag with the stationmaster, telling him she'd be leaving on the next train. Then she started down Main Street. Passing the greengrocer, the surgeon's office, the bank, and her father's big grain elevators that cast long shadows over the town, she had the odd sensation that everything was both the same and different. What had changed, she realized, was her. Having escaped this place, she no longer felt as if it was bearing down on her, hemming her in. She was free of its hold.

Along the path, passersby glanced her way, then looked away. Mr. Chilton, her father's banker, nodded as he passed, but he did not slow his pace, and she doubted he recognized her. Mrs. Chagnon, the elderly woman who used to come to the house to teach her piano, tipped her head in Hattie's direction. But like the banker, she offered no greeting.

Ahead, her parents' massive house came into view, three stories tall and with grounds that took up an entire town block. In the backyard, the big maples and oaks were leafless, their branches scraping the sky like witches' brooms.

Hoping not to lose her nerve, Hattie strode briskly toward the front door, passing the trellises on either side of the walk that at this time of year sported only thorns. She climbed the steps to the veranda with a porch swing that no one ever used. Hattie's mother was adamant about not mixing with the townspeople, and sitting out of doors, in full view of the street, would have made the Logans seem common.

Facing the paneled oak door, Hattie lifted and lowered the heavy brass knocker. She waited a moment, worrying her fingers together as she watched a robin tug a worm from the brown lawn. In her mind, she'd rehearsed over and over what she'd say to her parents. That she'd gotten free, no thanks to them. That she'd gotten their message loud and clear. That she'd not come to argue, only to learn if they knew where she might find George. It was a long shot, she knew, but she had to try.

The door swung open, revealing Sallie Higgins. A maid's cap covered a portion of her thinning gray hair, and her shoulders were a bit more stooped than when Hattie had last seen her. "Miss Logan?" she asked warily.

Hattie touched her cropped and dyed hair. "Yes. It's me, Sallie."

"You're the last person I expected to see." The servant glanced furtively to either side, clearly nervous.

"I won't stay long. I only want a word with Father." Hattie's father was aloof and preoccupied, but his unhappiness hadn't turned him mean like her mother.

"I'm afraid he's been called out of town, miss. On business."

Business to benefit the enemy, Hattie thought. She hesitated. "Perhaps I could speak with Mother then?"

"She's gone to tea at Mrs. Clancy's."

"At Mrs. Clancy's?" Hattie tried to square the image of her mother in the ordinary parlor of an ordinary townswoman. "Whatever for?"

"I wouldn't know, miss." Sallie's mouth formed a grim line, suggesting she knew full well and she disapproved.

Hattie's shoulders relaxed. She hadn't realized how stiffly she'd been holding them, ready for a confrontation. "I don't suppose there's been word from George?"

"I should think not after the send-off they gave him." Sallie shook her head. "Not my place to say, miss, but if my own son were alive, I wouldn't have written him off like that, no matter which side he went off to fight with. Your brother always was a good lad.

I suppose he forgave them. A letter came from him not a fortnight ago."

"A letter!" Hattie could have hugged her. A letter meant George was alive. "Where did it come from? What did it say?"

"I haven't a clue. Nothing was said about it, not around me, leastways."

Buoyed by this news, Hattie felt suddenly inspired. "May I come in?"

"I don't know that it would be wise, miss. There was certainly a good deal said about you a few weeks back, and not much of it kind, I'm afraid. If the missus found out I'd let you in, there'd be hell to pay, excuse the expression."

Outside on the street, a pair of horses clopped by, pulling a buggy. "I wouldn't want you to get into trouble, Sallie. What if you were to run an errand? To the grocer, perhaps. Then I could go around to the back and let myself in. No one would be the wiser."

Sallie looked doubtful. "Then I'd be in hot water for leaving the backdoor unlocked."

"For all Mother knows, I've still got a key," Hattie said. "And in all likelihood, she'll never know I was here, which is more than I can say if we keep standing here at the door, in full sight of everyone passing by."

Sallie's forehead tightened, accentuating her worry lines. "You make a good point, miss."

Hattie smiled warmly. Sallie had always been a good sort. "I'll stroll around the corner. You go out. I'll wait till I'm sure no one's looking, then let myself in the back."

"You'll have to make sure you lock up when you leave," Sallie said firmly. "You know how the missus likes things secure."

She shut the door. Hattie turned and went down the steps. A letter from George. If she could find it, she'd know where he was.

Feeling lighter than she had in days, she strolled toward the corner. A songbird warbled in a sycamore as she passed, the buds on the branches swollen with the promise of spring. The faint odor of manure, pungent but not entirely unpleasant, wafted from a nearby pasture. Her mother had always complained of the smell of livestock in La Conner, not that it did her any good.

Hattie walked around the wrought iron fence toward the back alley. Glancing back, she spotted Sallie headed in the direction of the greengrocer. Hattie turned into the alley, then went quickly up the back walk, passing the kitchen garden, bare except for a patch of rosemary that had somehow made it through the winter.

Relieved to find that Sallie had indeed unlocked the back door, she turned the knob, slipped inside, and closed the door behind her. In the kitchen, warm air enveloped her, smelling of roast beef.

She stepped back, surprised to see a servant rolling out pie crust. Sallie hadn't mentioned anyone else in the house. Hattie didn't recognize the woman, but that wasn't unusual. Her mother was not an easy woman to please, and except for Sallie, her household staff came and went almost with the seasons.

"Hello," Hattie said, hoping not to startle the woman.

The woman looked up, nodded slightly, then gave the crust a quarter-turn and went back to her rolling. Hattie relaxed. Sallie must have warned her someone would be coming in the back.

Hattie proceeded through the kitchen and up the back stairs, which led to the servants' quarters in the attic. She exited the stairwell into a second-floor hallway. She'd forgotten how dark it was in this part of the house, the bedroom doors shut and the curtains drawn.

Going down the hallway, she paused in front of her mother's bedroom door. Then she turned the brass knob, cool to the touch, and let herself in. Only rarely had she ever been allowed in this room, summoned when her mother had taken to bed with one of her headaches.

Now she went past the canopied bed with its rosebud coverlet to the dressing table. Quickly, she pulled open each drawer and inspected its contents. Hairbrushes, face powder, rouge. Tonics and tinctures. Mirrors and tweezers. Perfumes. But she saw no letter.

She repeated the process with the chest of drawers. *Don't touch that* was a phrase she'd heard time and again from her mother. Yet here she was, peering under Lydia Logan's folded stockings and chemises. It made her almost giddy.

Finding nothing of interest, she proceeded to her father's room, which smelled of mustache wax and shoe polish. There was less to look through here, and oddly, she felt more as if she was intruding. She'd always tried harder to earn her father's affection, not that her efforts had yielded much in the way of results, except for a few distant memories from her earliest years, when he used to lift her on his shoulders and carry her around town as if showing her off.

She checked his dresser drawers and armoire but found no letter. She was getting nervous, wishing she'd asked Sallie when her mother had left for Mrs. Clancy's and when she was expected back. She'd come to La Conner expecting a confrontation. Now that she'd dodged it, she wanted only to find George's letter and duck away without seeing either of her parents.

It wasn't the hurt from them disowning her that bothered her, or so she told herself. It was just the unpleasantness of feeling again how she'd been a disappointment to them from the start. Her parents were cruel, unhappy people. Circumstances must have made them so, but Hattie wasn't certain exactly what those circumstances had been, other than her mother's resentment at having been removed from the easy life at her father's Louisiana plantation. Likely she'd never know.

There was one place left to look, an unlikely spot. As Hattie padded down the hall toward the turret, she felt her spirits lifting, the way they had when she was young and the turret library had been her refuge in an otherwise unhappy home. Opening the door, she felt the same thrill as she had then, knowing that within this space, any number of other worlds awaited her. All she had to do was choose a book, open its cover, and begin reading.

The library was exactly as she remembered, Sallie's lemon polish only faintly masking the musty smell that pervaded there. As far as Hattie knew, Sallie was the only person besides her and George who went into the library. Her mother thought books were foolish, and the only books Hattie's father showed interest in were the big ledgers where his accounts were kept.

Hattie could imagine wanting to burn George's letter, but her father might have wanted to keep it. He had always shown more affection for George than his wife had, though it had frustrated him no end that George had no interest in learning the grain business. If he'd wanted to stash away George's letter, the library would be the perfect spot.

Stepping to the nearest shelf, Hattie ran her fingers along the spines of the books. She'd always felt a warm familiarity with these volumes, taking comfort in simply knowing they were there. Dickens, Bronte, Plutarch, Descartes, Shakespeare. Some she'd read over and over. Others were still waiting to be discovered.

One time, she'd asked her father where all these books had come from. He'd only grunted and said, "My father was a fool for books." It was the only thing he'd ever told Hattie about his own father, who'd died before she was born. But there must have been some sort of affection between them, she thought. Otherwise, why keep the books? Or maybe it was simply because a house the size of the Logans' was expected to have a library. The turret room was well suited for it, and her grandfather's collection would have been an easy way to fill it.

Gazing up and down the shelves, she had no idea where to start looking. If Sallie were less meticulous in her work, there might have been a space cleared of dust where a book had been removed, a letter inserted between its pages, and then the book replaced. But like the rest of the house, the turret was spotless. In Mrs. Logan's service, Sallie spent half her days dusting.

Hattie fingered a small volume of Shakespeare from a collection of all his plays, each book covered identically in blue cloth. *Hamlet.*

She pulled the volume from the shelf. Not so long ago, while enrolled at the Ladygrace School for Girls, she'd played Hamlet. It had been an easy part to learn because she'd read the play over and over when she was young.

Revenge his foul and unnatural murder. As she held the book in her hands, this was the line that came to her. Fitting, she thought, since she was on her way to Nashville in hopes of tracking down Luke Blackstone to get revenge for Thom's death, which truly was a murder in her eyes.

She was flipping through the pages on the off chance a letter was hidden between them when she heard footsteps. She slipped the book into her purse, then turned.

In the library's entrance stood her mother. She'd aged significantly since Hattie had last seen her, wrinkles radiating from her lips, the skin of her thin neck wattled like a turkey's. But her dark eyes bore into Hattie's as they always had. "You are an intruder here," she said sharply. "Get out."

There'd been a time when Hattie would have cowered at a rebuke like this, trying to make herself small and unnoticed. But in the last year, she'd gained control of such feelings. When a spy made herself unnoticed, it was a conscious and orchestrated act, not an emotional response.

Instead, Hattie stood tall, locking eyes with the woman in the doorway. "Hello, Mother," she said. The words she'd rehearsed eluded her. Her mother had the advantage of surprise, and she was skilled at taking advantage wherever possible.

Lydia Logan stepped toward her. "Your father and I have made it quite clear. You are no daughter of ours. I shall have the constable summoned if you don't leave here immediately."

Hattie suppressed the impulse to laugh out loud. She'd faced down rats and prison officials. She'd crawled through a tunnel to freedom. She'd crossed over enemy lines in the heat of battle. And her mother thought she'd be swayed by the prospect of a constable's coming?

"That won't be necessary, Mother. Tell me where George is, and I'll leave."

Her mother fisted her hands at her waist. "I've no more use for that boy than I have for you."

"I don't care who you do or don't have use for. I want to know where my brother is."

"I haven't the slightest idea."

Hattie stepped toward her. "Yes, you do. You got a letter."

Her mother's lips curled in a thin, tight smile. "And you didn't. Well, well. I'm sure if George wants you to know where he is, he'll find a way to get word to you."

Hattie leaned in, color rising in her cheeks. "You know as well as I that the only way he could get word to me is through you."

"Because you're a spy for those damned Yankees," her mother spat.

"Those damned Yankees," Hattie said evenly, "are your neighbors."

"Not all of them," her mother said. "Not by a long shot. If you were half the spy you think you are, you'd know that."

Hattie smiled. "So that's why you've suddenly got friends in this town. That's why you were invited to Mrs. Clancy's for tea. There's a band of Copperhead ladies here, plotting to aid the Rebels."

"Peace Democrats, that's what we are. This war is an abomination, and so is President Lincoln. Setting the darkies free. It's madness."

"It's justice," Hattie said. "Not that you'd ever recognize that."

Her mother folded her arms at her chest. "I've had enough of your impudence."

"And I've had enough of yours." Pushing past her, Hattie went through the doorway.

Her mother turned, eyes flashing. "There are people who kill Yankee spies, you know."

"So I'm told," Hattie said, and she slammed the door behind her.

Chapter Nine

March 28, 1863

More even than Washington and Richmond, Nashville was a city changed by war. Hattie had visited there once when she was young, in the company of her mother, who at the time had proclaimed Nashville the gayest, most prosperous city north of New Orleans. Rising from a rock overlooking the Cumberland River, the Capitol building had cost over a million dollars to build, a figure that had much impressed Hattie's mother.

In addition to the commerce carried out on the river, goods came and went from the city via eight stone turnpikes and three sets of railroad tracks. Over the Cumberland River was a magnificent suspension bridge. Of special interest to Lydia Logan had been the palatial mansions surrounded by expansive lawns and grand trees. Hattie remembered dashing carriages and brightly arrayed riding parties mounted on fine horses as well as the dozens of mercantiles where her mother had shopped.

What Hattie saw entering Nashville today was altogether different. Tennessee had been the last state to join the Confederacy, but farmers in the eastern part of the state had stayed loyal to the

Union. A year ago, the Federals, led by General Rosecrans, had regained control of Nashville in the state's midsection. The streets now were far dirtier than Hattie remembered, and as the train chugged alongside one of the city's turnpikes, she saw where a trench had been dug across the road, a deterrent, she supposed, to Rebel forces intent on retaking the city. From the hill where her mother had once admired Nashville's mansions, a cannon was poised ominously over the town. In addition, Hattie noticed that many of Nashville's elegant churches and colleges had been turned into military hospitals. She wondered if Dr. Greenfield was working at one of them.

The train pulled into the station, and Hattie disembarked. As expected, lots of soldiers wearing Union blue were milling around, but unlike many of the military men in Washington, they seemed bored and without purpose. She hired a buggy to take her to the City Hotel, where General Sharpe's assistant had included a night's lodging in her travel plans. She had no idea where she'd stay after that.

Arriving at the hotel, she saw that although it was new, it appeared to have fallen on hard times. Several of the tiles in the lobby were cracked, and a dark spot on the wood floor suggested a fire had somehow been lit there. She hastened to her room and then, without so much as opening her bag, proceeded to the Army Police Headquarters, per her instructions.

The place was bustling with activity. Several disreputable-looking ladies were huddled in a corner, laughing as they directed ribald remarks at the young soldiers guarding them. At one desk, a clerk was jotting down quantities of what Hattie assumed was contraband—bottles of quinine and other medication that had likely been intercepted.

At another desk, an officer jotted notes while an older woman dressed in black complained loudly about soldiers shooting off their guns in the town's suburbs. "Occupied or not, we should be free to walk about the streets in broad daylight without fear of being shot," the woman said.

The officer yawned. "We'll look into it," he said.

Hattie approached the only clerk who was available, a pimple-faced young soldier. She presented the note she'd been given. "General Sharpe sent me. I'm to see Colonel Truesdail."

"General Sharpe's with the Army of the Potomac," the lad objected. "We ain't got no business with them."

"I should think you do," Hattie said, "assuming the intent is to win this war. Is the colonel in?"

Color rose in the clerk's face. She supposed he wasn't used to a woman speaking so plainly. "I'll see," he said.

She grabbed his arm and thrust General Sharpe's note of introduction into his hand. "Show him this, please."

The soldier retreated to a back room. Hattie waited near his desk, clutching her purse and amusing herself by making mental notes of the facial features of each person in the room, tallying three pointed chins, two sets of hooded eyelids, and a very pronounced case of protruding ears. When she tired of this amusement, she took the small blue volume of Hamlet from her purse. Perched beside the empty desk, she began to read. If the young soldier had meant to discourage her by making her wait, he'd soon learn that such tactics didn't work with her.

She was starting the third scene of Act One when the clerk finally returned. "The colonel will see you now, Miss Logan," he said in a tone far more respectful than he'd used before.

Hattie tucked the book under her arm and followed him into the back room. The uniformed man behind the desk looked up from his work. He had a long face, a sharp nose, deep-set eyes, and dark hair that curved gently over his high forehead.

He stood to greet her, then motioned for her to sit. He dismissed the young soldier, asking him to fetch Lieutenant Elliott. Then he sat back down in his chair.

Realizing she was still holding the book, Hattie hastily tucked it in her purse, which she set in her lap. "Thank you for seeing me, Colonel Truesdail. I imagine you're busy."

Offering a wry smile, he swept his hand over the papers strewn on his desk. "Busy doesn't begin to describe it. We've got violent rebels, smugglers, and spies. More camp followers than you can shake a stick at. Grifters who think nothing of fleecing the army." He shuffled through a pile of papers. "Oh, and here's a complaint about a secesh sympathizer who is displaying a leg bone on her mantle. Purportedly, it came from a Union soldier,"

"I've come to help, sir," she said. "At General Sharpe's recommendation. As he wrote in his note, I've had some experience as an operative with the Pinkerton Agency."

"So why are you not looking to Allen Pinkerton for work now?"

"There were some...unfortunate circumstances involving my last assignment. And as I'm sure you know, Mr. Pinkerton's operations have shifted with the change in command at the Potomac."

Truesdail leaned back in his chair. "It's not that I'm opposed to taking on a woman, Miss Logan. I oversee a large contingent of spies and scouts, and there are a few women among them. I've got an agent at every hotel in Nashville. I've got military mail agents on trains. I've got offices in Cairo and Corinth. My people infiltrate smuggling rings, seize contraband, and capture Union deserters. They also gather a good deal of intelligence that we pass along to Major General Rosecrans. He's a methodical man, determined to rout Bragg's Confederates from Tennessee. He's had us systematize our compiling of information from newspapers, signal intercepts, deserters, and prisoners. We rely heavily on our spies and scouts to sort fact from fiction. There are a good number of duplicitous individuals out there."

Smoothing her skirt, Hattie kept her eyes fixed on him. "I'm well aware of that."

There was a rap on the door.

"Come in," the colonel said.

The door swung open, and the clerk ushered in a tall, dark-eyed, uniformed man. His expression was serious but not stern, and he had none of the notable features Hattie had spotted among the throng at the front of the headquarters. Indeed, his face was remarkably handsome and well-proportioned, yet he seemed to have none of the conceit Hattie had observed in other good-looking men.

"Lieutenant Elliott, we have a new recruit," Colonel Truesdail said. "Hattie Logan."

Hattie allowed a brief smile, pleased that the colonel had decided to take her on. "Actually, I'd prefer to go by Hattie Thomas, sir," she said. When General Sharpe had suggested she take a new name, it only made sense to use Thom's given name.

The lieutenant smiled, showing white teeth as evenly proportioned as the rest of his features. "A woman with secrets," he said. "You'll fit right in here."

"I was thinking you could place her with the actress. What's her name again?" The colonel rubbed his thumb and fingers together as if that might help him remember.

"Pauline Carlton," Lieutenant Elliott said.

"That's right," the colonel said. "Carlton."

Elliott frowned slightly. "I don't suppose you have any acting experience, do you, Miss Thomas?"

"She's been reading Hamlet," Truesdail said. "That must count for something."

How observant, Hattie thought, noting the title of her book before she stashed it in her purse. "Actually, I played Hamlet in a school production."

"You mean you played Ophelia," Elliott said

"No. I played Hamlet. It was an all-girls school, so some of us had to play the male parts."

The colonel groaned. "Not another woman dressing like a man. I swear, if I have to deal with one more female who's put on a man's uniform with the idea of following her husband or brother or beau into battle, I'll lose my mind."

"You're not looking to do that, are you, Miss Thomas?" Elliott asked.

"Only if it helps the cause," Hattie said.

"I for one would prefer you kept your skirts about you," Truesdail said.

Elliott gazed at her so intently that she nearly looked away. "Do you understand what you'd be getting into here, Miss Thomas?"

Hattie squared her shoulders. "I was a Pinkerton operative. In Washington and Richmond."

"It's different here in the Southwest," Elliott said.

"A nest of vipers," the colonel said grimly. "And at some point, we may need to send you behind enemy lines. The danger may be substantial. Not just from the uniformed Rebels but also from guerrillas that terrorize roadways in the less populated areas. In case you haven't noticed, there's some wild country in these parts. Not the sort of places where a woman would want to find herself in a compromised position. And if the Confederates learn you're a Union spy, it could be the end of you. They don't hesitate to shoot spies. Or hang them."

Hattie pushed the thought of Thom's execution from her mind. "Our soldiers make huge sacrifices day in and day out. If it serves my country, I'll do all a woman should do and all a man dares to do."

From the lieutenant's tight smile, she couldn't tell if he was impressed or amused. "Very well, Miss Thomas. We'll start you out with Miss Carlton and see where that takes us."

~ ~ ~

Hattie went back to the City Hotel to collect her belongings. As compensation for her detective duties, Lieutenant Elliott, who was to be her immediate supervisor, told her she would receive a modest salary plus accommodations at the house where Pauline Carlton boarded.

When she proceeded to the front desk to explain that she'd found a room elsewhere, she saw there was a commotion in the lobby. Soldiers were escorting a well-dressed man and woman toward the front door.

Taking Hattie's key, the balding man behind the desk smiled grimly. "Those two won't be needing their rooms no more either," he said, nodding at the couple who were apparently under arrest.

"What have they done?" Hattie asked.

Looking at her over the top of his wire-rimmed spectacles, the man leaned across the desk. "A smuggling scheme, that's what I heard. Colonel Truesdail and his men, they've been on the case. Seems a druggist in Louisville has been selling large quantities of medicinals to a certain lady who carries them south. A thousand ounces of quinine and two hundred pounds of opium, to be exact."

That sounded like exactly the sort of operation Luke Blackstone would be involved in. "Is that them?" Hattie asked, nodding toward the apprehended couple. "The druggist and the smuggler?"

The clerk shook his head. "No, them two's already in jail, along with a few of their associates. Those two there are..." He scanned the guestbook. "A Dr. Dubois and a Mrs. M.E. Trident. Aiding and abetting the whole operation, that's what I'm told."

At the door, the soldiers made their exit, suspects in tow. "There must be someone masterminding the whole operation," Hattie said, thinking of Blackburn.

The clerk shrugged. "Probably so. Smugglers and spies all over this city."

"How unsettling," Hattie said.

Drawing back, the clerk shuffled through a stack of papers and handed her a receipt for her stay. "I don't know where you're headed next, ma'am, but if it's anywhere around these parts, I suggest you be careful. There's quite a lot of unrest here. Divided loyalties and all that. Me, I try to stay out of the fray."

"A wise choice," Hattie said.

Leaving the hotel, she hired a buggy to take her to the address Lieutenant Elliott had provided for the boarding house where she'd be staying. As the driver set off, she thought about what had transpired at the hotel and what the clerk had told her. A doctor had been arrested, and she wouldn't be surprised if other doctors were involved in the same scheme. According to Dr. Greenfield, Dr. Luke Blackburn was in the area. For a duplicitous surgeon who'd attempted to infect unsuspecting civilians with yellow fever, assisting in the smuggling of quinine and opium to aid Rebel troops would be child's play.

She resolved to speak to Lieutenant Elliott about it at her first opportunity. At the very least, she needed to make sure he knew Blackburn was likely in the region and the harm he could do. With any luck, she'd also be able to convince the lieutenant to let her interview the doctor and the lady she'd seen arrested at the hotel. Or perhaps she should broach the idea with Pauline Carlton first. The lieutenant had said Pauline could show her the ropes. She'd been spying for the Army of the Cumberland police for some months now, posing as a Secesh sympathizer. Maybe she'd even crossed paths with Blackburn.

The buggy stopped in front of a white clapboard house with brown shutters. It was half the size of the boarding house where Hattie had roomed with Anne in Washington, but it looked well-kept, with a tidy front yard. The driver helped her out of her seat and carried her bag to the door. She paid him, and he left.

Crocuses were blooming in beds near the porch, and daffodils opened like trumpets, proclaiming the arrival of spring. Hattie rapped on the front door. She waited, and when there was no response, she was going to knock again. Just then, the door opened partway, revealing a wizened old woman in a black dress. Her shoulders were hunched, and though her gray hair was pulled back in a bun, wisps of it fell about her face. As the old woman looked her visitor up and down, Hattie noted an icy determination in her blue eyes.

"Mrs. Fletcher?" Hattie said in a Southern accent she'd learned from her mother. "I've come from Richmond. I understand you have rooms to let."

The woman opened the door a bit wider. "And who told you that?"

"Miss Pauline Carlton," she said. "I'm with the theatre, same as her."

"That's a far might better than the alternative," the woman said.

"Sorry?" Hattie said, not catching her drift.

The landlady motioned for her to come in. Bag in hand, Hattie stepped onto the braided rug in the entry.

Mrs. Fletcher shut the door. "The soldiers," she said. It took a moment for Hattie to catch her drift. "They'll be sending soldiers any day now, sure as shooting. Injured Yanks, and they'll be expecting me to take care of 'em. Can you imagine?"

"How awful," Hattie said. "It must be quite distressing, living under Federal occupation."

Grim-faced, the landlady shook her head. "If you was smart, you'd hightail it back to Richmond."

Hattie fingered the handle of her bag. "I do miss the South," she said. "But an actress must go where opportunity calls."

Mrs. Fletcher cocked her head. "Never thought too highly of the theatre myself. What's the point in all that pretending? But Pauline, she's a right good sort. Makes no bones about her feelings concerning the Yanks." Mrs. Fletcher leaned close. "Keeps a pistol, you know. She showed it to me once. Says she's just waiting for the right Yankee officer to shoot, and she don't care what they do to her after that."

Hattie drew back. "Oh my. She is quite...fearless." Instinctively, she felt herself falling into a role. Pauline would play the brazen one, and she'd play the genteel Southern belle.

"We need more like her. Give the Yanks a run for their money. Come along." She started toward the stairs. "I'll show you to your room."

Hattie followed her up the narrow stairs and down an equally narrow hallway with two doors on either side. Mrs. Fletcher opened the last door on the right, revealing a room almost as narrow as the hallway. In it were a pair of beds covered with patchwork quilts, one against each long wall. One was unmade, the bedding in a tangle. Frocks and bonnets hung on hooks about the room. Tacked on the walls were playbills from various shows. "Kiss in the Dark," "Rake's Progress," "All the World's a Stage."

"This Pauline's room," Hattie said.

"Right you are," said Mrs. Fletcher. "Said she's the one sent you, didn't you? On account of you joining her at the theatre. That bed on the left is yours."

"But I should think Pauline would..." Hattie's voice trailed off. Was this what Lieutenant Elliott had in mind? "I didn't realize we'd be sharing a room."

Mrs. Fletcher drew herself up. "Well, it's what I've got. Take it or leave it."

Hattie hesitated. If she went back to the lieutenant requesting other accommodations, he'd think her a fragile sort. "Fine," she said.

From the funds the lieutenant had provided, she doled out a week's rent, and Mrs. Fletcher informed her of the mealtimes. "I don't cotton to tardiness," she said with a schoolmarm's resolve. "Eat on time, or you don't eat at all."

After the landlady left, Hattie looked around the room, trying to decide what to do with her things. All the hooks on the wall were full, as were the armoire and the dresser. She'd brought only morning dresses, but she couldn't very well leave them folded up in her bag. She laid them out on the narrow bed. Assessing the wrinkles, she decided to venture downstairs and ask Mrs. Fletcher about ironing.

She'd hoped Mrs. Fletcher might take on the task herself, but she only directed Hattie to where she could find the iron and ironing board. "None of us got help like we used to," she muttered. "Darkies raising Cain all over the city. Mark my words, no good will come of it."

Hattie was no stranger to an iron, having used one to reseal opened mail in Mr. Pinkerton's mailroom. But playing the part of a Southern belle, she asked Mrs. Fletcher's help in getting started. It felt soothing, actually, moving the hot iron back and forth across her dresses, the fabric warm and compliant. And at this time of year, Mrs. Fletcher's kitchen was nowhere near as hot as the mailroom had been, though Hattie did have to do a good deal of commiserating with the landlady's seemingly endless complaints about the Yanks.

When she'd finished her ironing, Hattie brought her dresses back upstairs. Lieutenant Elliott had promised to send a courier to alert Pauline that Hattie would be joining her. Surely she wouldn't begrudge her for hanging up her clothes.

With this in mind, Hattie doubled up Pauline's dresses on the side of the room where her bed was, then hung her own clothes on the less cluttered side. She considered going to the theatre to meet with Pauline, but she wasn't sure how the subject of her joining the theatrical company was to be broached.

Besides, Hattie was hungry and tired. So instead of venturing out, she went downstairs for supper, taking care to make sure she was seated at the table five minutes before the appointed time. The meal was a paltry one, beans and potatoes in a sort of stew. At the table, the landlady led a running commentary about the outrageous price of foodstuffs. "Onions scarcer than greenbacks," she complained. "Five dollars a bushel for potatoes, every last one of 'em old as sin. Not a vegetable to be found at any price, and with what wood costs these days, a woodpile might as well be a gold mine."

Hattie joined the other boarders in nodding and murmuring agreement, fairly certain they all must share the landlady's views to some extent, or they'd have been booted out long ago.

She recalled what Anne had once said about a spy's deceptions being wearisome. It did wear on a person, doing and saying things that went against your beliefs. Hattie had managed it in Richmond, but she'd had Thom to confide in, to be herself with.

~ ~ ~

Hattie fell asleep that night thinking of Anne, who was adjusting to a hasty marriage, a pregnancy she hadn't anticipated, and a husband whose political leanings were far different from her own. She wished she could be closer, to help Anne through what must be a difficult time. As soon as she got her bearings here in Nashville, she vowed to write to her.

Some hours later, Hattie woke to a lantern's hiss.

"Hell's bells." A woman she presumed was Pauline was staring down at her. She wore a red gown printed in a dizzying herringbone pattern. The lantern's glow illuminated her high cheekbones and her dark hair. "Elliott warned me about you, and here you are."

Warned her? What was that supposed to mean? Hattie raised herself on her elbows, feeling groggy. "Shouldn't we be a bit more...quiet?" she suggested. "So as not to wake the other boarders?"

Pauline waved her arm with a dramatic flourish. "Those old biddies can't hear a thing. Every one of them snores like a freight train."

Hattie sat up properly, swinging her legs over the side of the bed. Leaning against the wall, she pulled the quilt around her shoulders. "What did Lieutenant Elliott tell you exactly?"

Her dark eyes flashing, Pauline plunked the lantern down on the dresser with so much force that Hattie thought for a moment the glass might break. "Oh, not so much. Just that I'm to get you on at the theatre, however I'm supposed to do that. And that you're to help my work though I doubt you know the first thing about it. Let's get one thing clear from the start, shall we? I don't need your help. I don't need anyone's help. And I certainly don't need a roommate."

Hattie pulled the quilt tighter as if it might shield her from Pauline's anger. "I didn't know we'd be sharing a room. Lieutenant Elliott said nothing about that."

"Of course he didn't." Pauline began unfastening her bodice. "He's got more on his mind than your sleeping arrangements. Or mine, apparently."

"I'll go see him in the morning," Hattie said. "Tell him—"

Pauline whirled around, her bodice gaping in the front. "You will not. I don't want him thinking I can't take charge of you."

Hattie sat up straighter, locking eyes with Pauline. "I don't need anyone taking charge of me. I've done this work before, with the Pinkerton Agency."

"Then you should've stayed there," Pauline said.

"I wish I had," Hattie spat, not wanting to let Pauline have the last word.

Chapter Ten

March 29, 1863

As it turned out, Pauline Carlton snored as loudly as any of the old biddies she disdained. Between that and the trouncing she'd doled out, Hattie slept fitfully, filled with dread at the prospect of having to deal with Pauline again when she woke. Whether her roommate liked it or not, Hattie intended to alert Lieutenant Elliott that this arrangement was not going to work.

At some point, she must have finally fallen into a deep sleep. When she woke, the curtains were open and light filled the room. Already dressed, Pauline sat on her own bed with what looked like a script in her lap.

"Well, aren't you the sleepyhead," she said pleasantly, affecting a Kentucky drawl. "I thought I might be forced to roll you over to the theatre in a cart."

Hattie blinked, wondering if this was the same woman who'd berated her last night. She had the same high cheekbones, black hair, and dark eyes. The red dress she'd worn hung on a hook beside her bed.

Hattie glanced at the hooks on her own wall, half-expecting Pauline to have thrown her clothes to the floor in a fit of rage. But they hung where she'd left them, tidy and unwrinkled.

"Cat got your tongue?" Pauline prodded. "That won't do for an actress, you know."

"Just...not at my best in the morning," Hattie said.

"We all do our best work at *night*," Pauline said. "Otherwise, we'd never make it in the theatre."

She must be acting, Hattie realized. The other boarders were awake, moving about in the hall, where they could surely overhear Pauline's loud voice. Last night—had that been an act, too, on Pauline's part? It had felt plenty real, but Hattie supposed it might have been a show designed for some purpose she had yet to discern.

At this point, Hattie had no choice but to play along. At breakfast, Pauline was polite and charming. Mrs. Fletcher, along with the other boarders, seemed to hang on her every word. She talked about her role in "The Seven Sisters," playing Pluella.

"My friend here has arrived at the most *fortuitous* time," she said. "We've got a cast member out sick, and I'm quite certain you can fill in, can't you, Hattie?"

Hattie said she'd do her best provided the manager agreed to take her on. There was general agreement around the table about the benefits of the theatre being open again now that gas was available for the stage lights.

Then the conversation turned to what Hattie expected would be recurring subjects around Mrs. Fletcher's table. The first was what should be done about the Negroes coming into Nashville since the Union had taken control. The other concerned the commanding general's recent edict that any person attempting to cross Nashville's pickets without a valid pass risked being shot as a spy.

When breakfast was over, Hattie left with Pauline for the theatre. On the way, Pauline chatted so cordially that Hattie began to wonder whether she'd dreamed her roommate's anger last night.

Pauline said she'd been raised at a trading post in the northern reaches of Michigan, where her father—of Spanish origins, she claimed—and her mother, who was French, had allowed her to run wild and free. As Pauline told it, she'd cavorted with the local Indians, who called her "Laughing Breeze."

As at the breakfast table, Hattie noted Pauline's flair for storytelling. She couldn't tell how much was true and how much was embellishment.

"I expect you'll have your own tales to share, once you've gotten settled in," Pauline said. But for the moment, she didn't seem especially interested in hearing them.

~ ~ ~

Allen's New Theatre occupied a small space in the heart of Nashville. Its capacity was half of Grover's Theatre in Washington, where Hattie had briefly worked in the box office before going to Richmond. Pauline led her around to the backdoor at Allen's. Inside, a small, oily-faced man with a trim mustache stood beside an open trunk, making tallies on a notepad.

"Linens must've grown legs and walked away," he muttered to no one in particular.

"Mr. Randolph, I've brought an actress to play the role of Nanine," Pauline said. "A friend who's come from the East Coast. Hattie, this is Mr. Randolph, the manager."

Looking up from his scribbles, Mr. Randolph squinted at Hattie. "Nanine, you say? I thought I'd filled that role."

"You did," Pauline said. "But she recently fell ill."

As if appealing to some higher authority, Mr. Randolph glanced upward to where the catwalks and pulleys disappeared into the darkness. "Can there not be one production without some sort of trouble?"

"At least this trouble has been providentially answered," Pauline said. "Miss Thomas can play Nanine's part. And if you find her suitable, she can likely stay on a bit with the stock company. You're short-casted for *The Seven Sisters*, you know."

Randolph shook his head. "It's a miracle we managed any productions at all."

Pauline patted his arm. "You fill the seats every night. While the war's on, they'll keep filling. What else are restless townspeople to do to get their minds off their troubles?"

"And I'll be happy to assist in whatever way I can," Hattie said. "Beginning with the upcoming production and carrying forward as you see fit."

He nodded absently. "If Miss Carlton says we need you, I suppose we do. Fill her in on the specifics, please, Miss Carlton."

"Very well," Pauline said. "And should we come across any linens lying about, I'll be sure to alert you."

As Mr. Randolph returned his attention to the trunk, Pauline searched backstage for an extra script. Finding none, she entrusted Hattie with her copy. Printed in large capital letters on the front page was the play's title, CAMILLE. "Rehearsal begins in an hour," Pauline said. "Nanine makes a brief appearance in each act."

"I'll be ready," Hattie said.

A fellow actor came in then, and Pauline turned away from Hattie to strike up a conversation with him about a recent article in a local paper calling for more morality in theatre productions. Pauline called the article nauseating and dull.

Having been introduced to the cast member but rather pointedly excluded from their conversation, Hattie excused herself. Holding the script to her chest, she proceeded to a seat in the auditorium's front row so she could peruse the script for Nanine's lines.

Fortunately, she was already familiar with the plot. When she was fifteen, she'd found the book from which the script had been drawn, *The Lady of the Camellias* by Alexander Dumas, in her parents' library. Reading it, she'd been moved to tears by the tragedy of the young courtesan who'd died alone to save the honor of the man she loved. Now she'd seen enough of the world and a woman's role in it to feel annoyed at Dumas for punishing his heroine when all she'd wanted was a chance at real love.

In the play, Nanine was Camille's maid. Hattie saw that most of what she'd need to remember were Nanine's entrances and exits. Her only lines would be "Yes, madam" in the scene where Nanine first appeared, and "He'll not get in now" in the second act when Camille told Nanine to bolt the door. In the final scene, finding her mistress dead from consumption, Nanine said, "Oh no! It can't be!"

Once Hattie had learned her lines and cues, her mind wandered to the particulars of her current situation. She had no idea what to make of Pauline's mercurial ways, upbraiding her last night and then treating her politely, if not warmly, today. She should be grateful, she knew, for Pauline's getting her on at the theatre since Lieutenant Elliott had wanted that.

But Hattie couldn't see how playing a minor role in Camille would be of any use to the Army Police, or how it might help her track down Luke Blackstone. The drama that had played out in the City Hotel lobby yesterday was of greater interest, as a plot involving one doctor might well lead to another.

~ ~ ~

The show opened three nights later. Pauline played a courtesan who served as a foil to Camille, the largest role of any female stock company actor. She proved a tarty counterpart to the more delicate star of the show. Judging from her flushed face at the curtain call, the performance exhilarated her.

Even though her part was small, Hattie was pleased with how she'd played it. In the final scene, as Nanine grieved her dead mistress, she'd felt as if she was crying for Thom, tapping into a deep well of tears.

When the audience had dispersed and the cast members were milling around backstage, Pauline pulled Hattie aside. Under the gaslights, her red rouged cheeks and lips looked almost comically harsh. She lifted her cordial glass of brandy in a toast. "Well done tonight."

Coming from Pauline, this praise felt effusive. "You were magnificent in your role," Hattie said.

"I do rather well as a tart, don't I?" Pauline took hold of her sleeve, pulling her close. "You're ready for your next role, Miss Thomas, playing a loyal Secesh. On the final night of this run, during the curtain call, you will step forward and raise a toast to Jefferson Davis and the Southern Confederacy."

Hattie drew back. "Toast the Confederacy? I can't do that."

"If you're to succeed at extracting valuable information from sympathizers, you first have to prove yourself one of them."

"I've convinced Mrs. Fletcher."

Pauline laughed. "Mrs. Fletcher is not nearly so discerning as the people whose trust you need to earn. You need to make a bold statement that will be remembered."

"Is that what you did?"

"No, but I've been at this for nearly six months, and I've gone to considerable lengths to slowly earn people's trust."

In six months, Blackstone would likely be long gone, Hattie thought. "But isn't rooming with you enough to establish my reputation as a Secesh sympathizer?"

"Not these days. Too many spies milling around. People are guarded, suspicious. Unless you do something dramatic to prove yourself, no amount of friendship will convince Confederate supporters that a stranger is on their side."

"But look at all the Union soldiers who came tonight. I can't imagine how they'd react."

With a grand sweep of her hand, Pauline waved off her concern. "Don't kid yourself. There were plenty of Secesh supporters here tonight too. Besides, it's just a simple toast. I'll make sure the word gets around. You'll want a packed house."

Something about Pauline's smug smile made Hattie feel as if she was setting her up for disaster. As a spy, Hattie knew she had to feign southern sympathies. But there was a huge difference between private commiserating over the Union's faults and the sort of public display Pauline was proposing.

The ruse could easily backfire. But Hattie also had a desire, carried over from her childhood, of trying to please no matter the cost. And if toasting the Confederacy got her closer to Luke Blackstone, she was all in.

She grabbed an empty glass that someone had set down on top of a props barrel. Raising it, she said, "To a full house on the final night."

Pauline clinked glasses with Hattie. "That's the spirit," she said, a flash of mischief in her dark eyes.

~ ~ ~

In the days that followed, Pauline said nothing more of the plan she'd proposed. In fact, she said little at all to Hattie, resuming the coolness she'd shown her at the start. It had been almost easier dealing with her mother, Hattie realized. Lydia Logan was at least predictable in her disdain.

In the room Hattie shared with Pauline, she felt again as if she were an intruder. One night, when she left her boots near the door next to Pauline's, her roommate pointedly moved them to Hattie's side of the room. Another night, when Hattie lay on her narrow cot, reading a book, Pauline snuffed out the light abruptly as if there was no one else in the room.

But Pauline was following through on her promise to make sure word of Hattie's upcoming toast got around. At breakfast one morning, she shielded her mouth with her hand and whispered in the landlady's ear. The old woman cackled. Gazing at Hattie, Mrs. Fletcher's expression shifted to one that approximated admiration. Then she passed her an extra biscuit, a sure sign of approval.

The morning of the final performance dawned bright and clear, with a hint of humidity in the air. The hours that followed seemed interminable. Hattie had rehearsed the toast in her head until she could say it in her sleep. She still wasn't entirely sure what Pauline was setting her up for, but if she was to play the part of a Secesh, she intended to give it her all, toasting with the verve that would make her Southern mother proud.

To take her mind off the stunt, Hattie spent the day exploring the city and making discreet inquiries about Luke Blackstone. Surgeons were always in short supply, and if an out-of-state doctor feigning Union sympathies offered his services here, he'd likely be welcomed at any number of hospitals, especially if he was a shrewd operator like Blackstone.

But as Hattie soon discovered, there were a lot of hospitals in Nashville. The Nashville Female Academy, the First Presbyterian Church, the Western Military Institute, even a carriage factory—all had been converted into wartime hospitals. She stopped at each of these places on the pretext of searching for her wounded brother. As at the hospitals in Washington, it was hard to pass by so many men in need of comfort, and she had to remind herself to keep her focus. If Blackstone was tending to Union soldiers, there was no telling the harm he might be inflicting on them.

Not all the patients she saw had been wounded in battle. Some suffered from dysentery or diseases like scarlet fever. At Hospital No. 15, the patients all suffered from venereal diseases, some contracted from prostitutes at the city's Smokey Row. The male nurse in charge there turned Hattie away, saying it was no place for a lady. From what she glimpsed of one of the patients, covered head to toe in a horrific syphilitic rash, he had a point. Around Mrs. Fletcher's table, she'd heard talk of Nashville officials moving "frail ladies" from Smokey Row to Louisville in hopes of slowing the spread of syphilis. Hattie couldn't help but wonder what people in Louisville thought of that plan.

Exiting the hospital through a different door than she'd come in, Hattie spotted a gallows. She drew a sharp breath, the sight a reminder of how her beloved Thom had gone to his death.

Deciding she was done with hospitals for the day, she headed for home.

Back at the boarding house, Hattie picked at her supper of potatoes and spring greens. Judging from Mrs. Fletcher's wry smile and approving nod, the old woman understood the source of her anxiety, which Hattie hoped she mistook for excitement.

At the theatre, she donned her maid's costume amid a flurry of activity which, as she knew from her stint at Grover's Theatre in Washington, preceded every final performance, as the traveling actors geared up to end one engagement and move on to the next.

Mr. Randolph bustled about with uncharacteristic giddiness. When Hattie peeked from behind the curtains at the auditorium, she understood why. The house was packed. No other night had been so well-attended. Hattie knew the real reason so many had come. Pauline's ploy with Mrs. Fletcher had succeeded, the old woman telegraphing all around town word of what would happen at the curtain call.

Hattie retreated backstage as the orchestra began tuning up, creating the usual cacophony of sounds. A call boy dashed from dressing room to dressing room, alerting actors that the show was about to begin. Then the prompter rang his bell, and the curtain rose on a Paris drawing room.

Immersed in the story's world, Hattie focused on her cues. Her senses seemed heightened, the emotions of the drama especially intense tonight. The audience seemed to feel this, too, sighing and gasping with more than the usual intensity.

Before Hattie knew it, the closing scene had arrived. With Camille on her deathbed, Hattie sobbed in what she thought must be a cathartic release. Then the curtains closed to thunderous applause. When they opened again, the crowd was on its feet.

The cast took their usual bows in front of the footlights. At Hattie's side, Pauline shoved a goblet in her hand.

"Now," she hissed as the applause died back.

You have a role. Play it true, Hattie told herself. Someone splashed liquid from a decanter into the goblet, and she stepped forward, raising it high.

"Here's to Jefferson Davis and the Southern Confederacy," she proclaimed. "May the South ever retain her honor and her rights."

A hush fell over the room, seeming to resound off the theatre's walls. As Hattie looked over the audience, she could only dimly see the faces. Most registered shock, though on a few, she saw smiles.

She lowered the goblet, her hand quivering. Shouts of approval, along with some booing, quickly reached a crescendo that thundered the auditorium.

Onstage, Hattie's fellow performers stepped away from her. Mr. Randolph rushed from the wings. "Whatever do you mean by such conduct?" he demanded.

Having no suitable answer, Hattie only smiled. Holding her head high, she bowed slightly. As she straightened, intent on making her retreat, she glimpsed the silhouette of a man leaning against the auditorium wall a few rows up from the orchestra, arms folded across his chest and his head tilted slightly to one side. He wore a black waistcoat and vest atop lighter colored trousers. In the dim light, it was hard to tell for certain, but he looked fair-skinned, with sandy-colored hair.

What struck Hattie was the way the man looked at her, with a sort of bemusement that hinted at recognition. She fled the stage, the cast giving her a wide berth. Backstage, she proceeded to the dressing room she shared with Pauline. Eager to get away, she slammed the door shut.

At the dressing table sat Pauline, who'd managed to slip from the stage without Hattie noticing. With a lopsided grin, Pauline raised her hand, mirroring Hattie's toast. "Here's to your new Secesh friends. May they yield rich rewards."

She lowered her hand, her gaze fixed on Hattie. "I was going to laud your courage, but from the looks of you, it has fizzled away."

Hattie glanced at her face in the mirror, as pale as if she'd seen a ghost. As if she'd seen the man she'd come here to find.

But she wasn't about to share that suspicion with Pauline, who knew nothing of her real reason for coming to Nashville. "It was all a bit unnerving," she said instead.

Pauline rose from the dressing table and crossed the room. Standing inches from Hattie, she said, "You haven't the nerve for it, you'd best get out while the getting's good."

Chapter Eleven

April 9, 1863

The morning after her toast to the Confederacy, Hattie woke nearly as exhausted as when she'd gone to bed. She'd had trouble sleeping, plagued by images of the man she'd seen leaning against the wall at Allen's Theatre.

She was certain he was Luke Blackstone. Had he recognized her?

Her appearance was changed, her hair dyed and bobbed, her frame slimmer than before due to weeks of near-starvation on prison rations. But a man as crafty as Blackstone would have a keen eye, and she felt panicked at the thought that he'd recognized her, a possibility she hadn't thought of when she'd accepted Pauline's challenge.

Now, having drawn attention to herself so openly, she risked Blackstone's scrutiny when she'd wanted to take him by surprise. If he exposed her as a Union spy, she'd be no good to Truesdail or Elliott or anyone else.

When Hattie joined the other boarders for breakfast, Mrs. Fletcher was beaming. "Did right well for yourself last night, I hear," the landlady said.

"She caused quite a stir," Pauline said. In a pink and brown morning dress, she looked resplendent, Hattie's blue ombre frock shabby by comparison. "To Jeff Davis," Pauline said, raising her spoon and then plunging it into her soft-boiled egg. These days in Nashville, eggs were a rare treat, and Hattie suspected Mrs. Fletcher had served them in celebration of last night's toast.

The landlady smiled wryly as Hattie took up her spoon. "I'm told there were a good number in attendance," she said.

"The house was packed," Pauline said. "You should've heard the applause. No doubt there will be a fine write-up in the papers."

Hattie spooned a morsel of her egg. "Good. Everyone in town will know where I stand."

"Including that meddlesome Yank Captain Truesdail," Mrs. Fletcher said, filling Hattie's cup with chickory coffee.

At least if the papers reported this incident, it would be under her assumed name of Thomas, not Logan, Hattie thought. But she feared Luke Blackstone would know her anyway.

She shouldn't jump to conclusions, she reminded herself as she spooned bite after bite of the warm, creamy egg. The lighting was bad. The man could have been anyone. And she didn't even know for sure that Blackstone was in Tennessee.

She knew one thing for certain. She couldn't afford to let fear get the best of her, not if she intended to do what she'd set out to, making herself as useful to the Union as possible. And if Blackstone had gotten the upper hand by recognizing her, she'd have to turn the tables by finding and exposing him. But she'd need to have her ducks in a row. If no one yet suspected where Blackstone's true sympathies lay, he could simply accuse her of lying, and it would be her word against his.

She downed the last warm bite of egg. "Delicious," she said.

"Don't get used to it." Mrs. Fletcher removed her empty egg cup. "Eggs are thirty cents a dozen and going up by the day. Why, only yesterday some young man from out of town threatened to stab a farmer at the market if he didn't hand over his cartload of eggs."

Complaints about the Yanks, who were blamed for every injustice in Nashville, went around the table.

With her free hand, Mrs. Fletcher withdrew a folded paper from her apron pocket and placed it on the table in front of Hattie. "This came for you this morning while I was making breakfast."

Across the table, Pauline cocked her head and smiled. "An admirer, perhaps? I'm sure you've a few after your performance last night."

Hattie unfolded the note. Penned in the theater manager's slanted script, it read:

MISS THOMAS:
It is my unpleasant duty to inform you that, by order of the management, your services will no longer be needed at Allen's Theatre.

H. B. Randolph
Stage Manager for Mr. Theodore Allen, Proprietor

Slowly, Hattie refolded the paper.

"Don't be coy," Pauline said. "Who's it from?"

"Mr. Randolph," Hattie said. "Apparently the theatre management doesn't share my sympathies."

"Oh, they do," Pauline said. "It just doesn't look good for the theatre, allowing a known Southern sympathizer onstage while the Yanks run the town."

This had been Pauline's plan all along, Hattie realized—to get her run off from the theatre. She locked eyes with her roommate. "I suppose a person might have foreseen that."

Pauline pushed her chair back from the table. "Foresight is in rather short supply these days. Don't you agree, Mrs. Fletcher?"

The landlady nodded vigorously, her double chin jiggling. "So it is."

Hattie fisted her hands in her lap. Pauline wanted rid of her, that much was clear.

Loud pounding sounded at the front door. "Open up," a man's gruff voice said. "Army police."

"Sure and they've come for you," Mrs. Fletcher said with a nod to Hattie.

Hattie shot another look at Pauline, who stood beside the table. Had she not bothered to inform Lieutenant Elliott and Colonel Truesdail of her scheme?

Pauline's dark eyes danced. "The police won't abide a traitor in their midst."

Hattie shoved back from the table, her chair scraping the floor. She tossed her crumpled napkin on the table. "Very well," she said, never taking her eyes off Pauline. "Let them in, Mrs. Fletcher. I'm ready."

~ ~ ~

Riding in the police wagon, Hattie felt as if a weight was pressing against her chest, making it hard to breathe. "Where are you taking me?" she asked the stout, balding officer who rode with her in the wagon.

"Ain't for me to say. If it was, I'd be taking you straight to the gallows."

Hattie sat up straighter. "I shouldn't fear death if that's what it comes to."

He shook his head. "Wildcats, you Southern women, and wily ones at that."

Hattie rode on in silence. She hoped she wasn't in the custody of some low-level official. If she was to have a chance at explaining, she needed to speak directly with Lieutenant Elliott and Colonel Truesdail.

To her great relief, the wagon eventually came to in front of the Army Police Headquarters. Now she just had to convince Colonel Truesdail that it was Pauline who'd acted wrongly, not her. Surely he'd understand that if she were a double agent, she'd never have made such a bold toast. Then again, maybe he wouldn't. Pauline could have told Truesdail anything she wanted. She certainly wasn't beyond making things up.

The stout officer marched her into the station, which as before was crowded with an assortment of ne'er-do-wells. Among them were three scruffy-looking men in gray uniforms, a smudge-faced boy who couldn't have been more than twelve, and two women who, judging by their plunging necklines and painted lips, had come from Smokey Row.

Hattie's escort transferred her to a slight, freckled officer who didn't look a day older than her. Yet despite his size, the officer's grip on her arm was surprisingly strong.

"I demand to see Colonel Truesdail," Hattie said. "This is all a misunderstanding."

The young man's eyes narrowed. "Is it, now?"

He steered her to a closed door at the end of the hall. *Lieutenant Elliott* read a small placard affixed to the door. Hattie's shoulders relaxed. At least she was getting an audience with someone who should understand her situation.

The officer rapped twice on the door. "Enter!" the man inside barked.

The officer swung the door open. "Miss Hattie Thomas," he announced. "Charged with treason."

At the desk sat Lieutenant John Elliott. In a chair to one side of the desk sat Colonel Truesdail. Both wore stern expressions. Neither rose as they normally would upon a lady's entrance. Traitors did not warrant such courtesies, Hattie surmised.

The younger man saluted his superiors. "Shall I bring the shackles?"

"Not just yet, thank you," Elliott said.

The officer backed out of the room, closing the door firmly behind him.

Colonel Truesdail pounded his fist on the desk. "By Jove, it was capitally done," he said.

Hattie let go of the breath she'd been holding. Lieutenant Elliott rose from his seat and pulled a chair from the far corner of the room, then motioned for her to sit "You've acquitted yourself famously, Miss Thomas."

She sat, clasping her hands in her lap. "So you understand it was all a ruse? I feared Pauline hadn't alerted you."

"She didn't need to," the lieutenant said. "There was talk of nothing else on the streets of Nashville yesterday."

The colonel rose from his chair. "Your purpose was easy enough to discern, Miss Thomas," he said. "And your plan was brilliant."

Pleased as she was with this praise, Hattie didn't feel right taking credit. "The toast was Pauline's idea."

Truesdail patted her shoulder in what she took as a fatherly gesture. "Either way, it must have taken some courage to carry it out. As I said last time you were here, I'm not inclined to trust women. But for you and Miss Carlton, I'll make an exception. There will be no question now of Secesh sympathizers trusting you with their secrets."

Hattie shifted in her chair. "Unfortunately, a note came this morning from the theatre's manager. I'm no longer welcome there. So I won't be able to—"

"Lieutenant Elliott will come up with another plan," the colonel said, interrupting her. "Won't you, John?"

Elliott smiled. "Between Miss Logan—I mean, Miss Thomas—and myself, I expect we can find another way to make use of her talents."

He believed in her, Hattie thought. Until that moment, she hadn't realized how she'd missed having someone believe in her the way Thom had, and before him, Anne.

The colonel stood. "If your plans involve any further public displays, just make certain our officers are properly informed. We don't want any unfortunate misunderstandings."

He left the office, closing the door behind him. Hattie straightened, meeting the lieutenant's gaze, which she found oddly unsettling in its intensity. "Unfortunate misunderstandings," she said, repeating the last words of the colonel's warning. "Does that mean Pauline failed to tell you about her scheme?"

Hands folded on his desk, Elliott leaned forward. "Pauline must have thought no one but the two of you should know."

"The two of us and half the town," Hattie said. "She wanted the house packed."

His smile faded. "Is it the danger that concerned you? That a half-drunk soldier, angered at your pronouncement, might have fired off a shot at the stage?"

"It's not that," Hattie said. "As I told you, I'm quite willing to sacrifice as much or more as our soldiers do."

He tipped his head slightly, a pose that might have been struck among friends. "And it's my job to ensure you never make such a sacrifice."

"Because I'm a woman," she said.

"Because other brave women have lost their lives for lack of prudence." His expression shifted, his gaze turning so intense that she felt as if he could see into her soul. This was personal for him, she thought. One of those brave women had been someone he cared about deeply.

"I intend to be prudent. I've endured...some difficulties before, and I don't intend to do so again if I can help it."

He opened his mouth as if to speak, and she feared he'd inquire into the nature of those difficulties. Then, just as quickly, he seemed to reconsider. Leaning back in his chair, he said, "You got along well at the theatre?"

She nodded. "Until last night." Something in the way he listened, as if she were the only person who mattered, made her feel as if she could confide in him. "But I wonder about Pauline."

His brow furrowed. "She's mistrusted there?"

"She's well-liked. The mistrust, I fear, is between her and me. She resents my placement with her, and I suspect at least part of her aim in suggesting the toast was to rid herself of the burden of my presence."

Lieutenant Elliott rubbed the back of his neck. "Pauline is a complicated individual. I know she can be blunt, perhaps even unfair in her assessments. But there's much you can learn from her too."

"I should think I could learn from her without the two of us sharing a room," Hattie said.

He lay a finger on his chin, seeming to consider what she'd said. After a moment's silence, he spoke. "This isn't the best time to make a change. Not when you're so much in the spotlight. Mrs. Fletcher's affinity for the South is well-known around town. We need to leave you rooming there provided you have sufficient tolerance for it."

"Of course I do," she said. "It's Pauline who may lack the tolerance."

"You needn't concern yourself with that, Hattie." His familiarity, using her given name, both encouraged and unnerved her. "Of more immediate concern is how we make the best use of you. Among the Secesh, I mean."

Now was her chance. "I'd like permission to speak with the prisoners recently arrested at the City Hotel for smuggling quinine and opium behind enemy lines."

He looked puzzled. "Why them?"

She pressed her lips together, deciding how much to say. "I witnessed their arrest at the City Hotel. I suspect they're part of a larger scheme."

"Indeed." Drumming his fingers on his desk, he seemed to be waiting for her to say more.

"Surely Colonel Truesdail wants to get to the bottom of this smuggling ring and expose the profiteers"

He eyed her sharply. "The colonel is keenly interested in bringing to justice any traitors in our midst, including those who smuggle quinine. Reselling it in the south, they make an astronomical profit, especially here in the West where fevers are killing nearly as many men as guns do. But smugglers can be remarkably elusive."

"I can gain the confidence of the woman I saw at the hotel," Hattie said, recalling the fear she'd seen in the woman's face. "Especially when she learns of my bold assertion of support for the South."

"Perhaps," he said.

"I shall," she said, avowing more confidence than she felt.

He tipped his chin. "You are nothing if not determined, Hattie Logan."

"Thomas," she corrected.

He cleared his throat. "Yes." He leaned forward, rifling through a stack of papers. Withdrawing one, he held it up, scanning it. "Here's the report of the arrests you mentioned. City Hotel, three weeks ago. Mrs. M.E. Trident and Dr. Charles DuBois."

"That's them," Hattie said. "The hotel's clerk told me."

He nodded. "Their associates appear to be Mrs. John Trainor, arrested in Louisville and brought here under charges that she has aided her husband in extensive smuggling operations. A Union cavalryman was also apprehended, charged with aiding the Trainors, plus another two men from this city. Also a Louisville druggist who has admitted to selling Mrs. Trainor one thousand ounces of quinine and two hundred pounds of opium. Quite the extensive network of fraud and treason, if the evidence bears out."

In her head, Hattie ran numbers she'd heard on the value of quinine. "So this ring stands to make nearly $200,000 on the quinine alone." *A sum large enough to attract the likes of Blackstone*, she thought. "I'd like to try to extract confessions from the women involved," she said.

"As would we. But it won't be easy."

"I understand. But it's all a matter of trust," she said, hoping to convince herself as much as him.

He set the paper aside. "These prisoners may be transferred soon to Alton Prison in Illinois."

She stood, locking eyes with him. "All the more reason for me to begin investigations immediately."

Flattening his hands on his desk, he met her gaze. "Investigations require a plan," he said. "Or does the Pinkerton Agency not care about orderly pursuits?"

She squared her shoulders. "I assure you my pursuit will be orderly, Lieutenant Elliott."

"Not just orderly, Miss Thomas. Your pursuit will be conducted according to my exact instructions." He scribbled an address on a slip of paper, then thrust it at her. "You will begin by seeking out Mrs. Felicia Ford, president of the Soldiers' Aid Society. I suspect she'll have ties to the women in this scheme. Gain her trust and the trust of her Society associates. Then we'll talk about you visiting Mrs. Trident in prison."

"That's all well and good, Lieutenant. But it will take too much time. As you said, the prisoners may be transferred any day."

He shrugged. "So be it. There's plenty of nefarious activity to be investigated in this city."

Activity that doesn't involve Blackstone, Hattie inwardly fumed. "Very well, Lieutenant Elliott," she said, slipping the address into her purse. "I will approach Mrs. Ford and return to you soon. Very soon."

"I'll look forward to it," Elliott said, though his tone, so friendly earlier, now suggested otherwise. "In the meantime, make sure you don't arouse any suspicions. When you leave here, complain far and wide to all who'll listen about how sorely you were treated by officials here."

"I've been told I have a knack for complaints," she said coolly.

"And don't get yourself in over your head," he said.

He didn't trust her, she realized. No matter how handsome his features, no matter how sincere his concern, she could see he was an obstacle she'd have to work around.

Chapter Twelve

April 10, 1863

S till bristling over how her meeting with Lieutenant Elliott had ended, Hattie ventured out the next day to meet Felicia Ford. The lieutenant's handsome face and warm manner could not offset the fact that he'd purposely set up an obstacle intended to discourage her.

On her way to meet the leader of the Soldiers' Aid Society, Hattie experienced the same dual reaction she'd gotten at the theatre, admiration from some and disgust from others. The admiration would serve her well with the Society ladies. But she still resented delaying her prison visit.

Felicia Ford lived in a stately mansion with a double porch, a second-floor balcony, and a trio of dormers protruding from the mansard roof. It was in a neighborhood of equally fine homes near St. Cloud Hill, which before the war had been an idyllic picnic area. After Rosecrans took Nashville last year, Union soldiers had felled the hill's ancient oaks and installed fortifications to protect the city from Confederate attempts to retake it. The scarred hill was an eyesore now, the landscape yet another casualty of war.

Hattie rang the bell at the Ford house. The Negro girl who came to the door couldn't have been more than fourteen. Barely glancing at Hattie, she let her in, then told her to wait in the foyer while she relayed her name and the purpose of her visit to Mrs. Ford.

Eyes downcast, the girl returned a moment later. "Follow me," she mumbled. Hattie hated to think what sort of treatment she might suffer here. Because Mr. Lincoln's January 1 proclamation had emancipated only Confederate slaves, the girl might have fared better in the South.

The Ford home was decorated in opulent style. Along a hallway edged with wide mahogany molding hung gilt-edged portraits of unsmiling men and women. One of them, Hattie assumed, must be Felicia Ford. The servant led her into the parlor. The walls were a deep shade of burgundy, and each window contained an upper pane of stained glass in ornate floral designs.

On the marble fireplace mantel were a variety of knickknacks, mostly porcelain figurines. In addition to the horsehair sofa and fainting couch, there were two chairs upholstered in gold satin and accented with blue pillows. Each chair featured a domed covering of latticework that gave the impression of a carriage top.

From one of these chairs rose a short, plump woman who looked to be in her forties. Atop her round face, her thinning hair appeared to have been dyed black. It was styled in the latest fashion, a frizzled mess of kinks attained by setting small curlers close to the scalp and sleeping on them overnight. Though she wore a walking dress, it was anything but plain, fashioned of a fine fabric printed in aqua and tangerine. Instead of a breastpin, she wore a large white muslin bow with lace-trimmed ends, giving her a rather ministerial appearance.

"You must be Mrs. Ford." Crossing the room to where the woman stood, Hattie held out her hand. "I'm Hattie Thomas. I've recently come here from Richmond and was advised that I must make your acquaintance straightaway if I intend to make myself useful toward the victory our valiant soldiers deserve."

Mrs. Ford clasped her small, warm hand over Hattie's. "You've come to the right place." To the servant, who stood in the doorway studying her feet, she said curtly, "You will leave us now, Sarah. See to the shelling of those beans for supper."

The girl stepped back and closed the parlor door. Mrs. Ford shook her head. "Such a trial dealing with the darkies these days, thanks to Old Father Abraham," she muttered. Then her face brightened, her thin lips forming a smile that revealed teeth that reminded Hattie of white kernels of corn. "But where are my manners? Sit, sit, Miss Thomas."

Bobbing and ducking, Hattie maneuvered into one of the half-covered chairs. "Thank you for seeing me, Mrs. Ford. I'm sure you're busy."

"Please, call me Felicia," she said. "And the pleasure is entirely mine. You're the talk of the town, Miss Thomas, after that toast you made last night. Nashville needs more women like you, refusing to cower to our oppressors."

"I did receive quite the upbraiding from the Army Police this morning," Hattie said. "But I took care to ensure that none saw me come here."

"And what if they did?" Felicia sputtered. "I'd stand up to them, same as you."

"But it wouldn't do for them to banish you from Nashville, what with all the relief work you do for the soldiers. And for prisoners, too, I presume."

"Someone has to look out for our poor boys, fighting their hearts out for our rights. If only they'd been able to keep that scallywag Rosecrans from taking Nashville." She shook her head. "Ah, but we all have our crosses to bear."

"I should like very much to do my part if your Society will have me."

Felicia slapped her palms on her thighs. "Have you? You will be an inspiration to us all, my dear. Come Tuesday next, three o'clock, and we'll give you a proper introduction to our work." She pushed up from her chair and strode toward the fireplace. On the mantel, she reached behind a row of figurines depicting children at play, extracting what looked like a long, white stick.

Gripping it on one end, Felicia pointed the other end at Hattie. "Like you, the women of the Soldiers' Aid Society are deeply committed to the cause." She smiled, flashing her corn-kernel teeth. "You might say we make no bones about it."

Hattie drew back, realizing that what Felicia was holding out to her was not a stick but a bone. "I see."

Felicia seemed not to notice her flinching. "This, my dear, is the leg bone of a Union soldier. We use it to open our Society's meetings. Grip the bone, placing your hand above mine."

Hattie did as she was told, making a silent apology to the Union soldier to whom the leg had belonged. Felicia took a scrap of paper from her pocket. Pressing it to her bosom, she launched into an oratory. "In this time of trial, when the best blood of the sons of the South is freely shed in defense of our liberty and independence, it is the peculiar duty of our sex to minister to the needs of those martyred to our Holy cause. Would that we could do more to demonstrate our sympathy for those who peril their lives in our defense. We stand ready to make any sacrifices that duty requires."

"Bravo!" Hattie said with as much enthusiasm as she could muster.

Felicia held the paper out so Hattie could see the words written there. "These are the words that unite us. You'll need to commit them to memory, so you can repeat them on Tuesday along with the other ladies."

She cleared her throat, then read earnestly from the paper:
Fold away all your bright-tinted dresses
Turn the key on your jewels today,
And the wealth of your tendril-like tresses

Braid back, in a serious way.
No more trifling in the boudoir or bower,
But come with your soul in your faces
To meet the stern needs of the hour!

"Quite stirring," Hattie managed to say. "And to think you pronounce this while gripping a wretched Yank's bone."

Felicia nodded vigorously. "I daresay there's no secret society with a more stirring ritual."

"I hadn't realized the group was secret," Hattie said, wishing she could let go of the bone.

Felicia's eyes twinkled. "Our hospital volunteers function quite openly. But behind the scenes, we have, shall we say, other projects. Now, let's see how quickly you can commit our vow to memory."

As they stood gripping the bone, Felicia concealed the poem from Hattie's view and recited the lines one at a time, instructing Hattie to repeat them. Hattie had never been so grateful for her quick memory, ending the ordeal in short order by making a stage-worthy recitation of the drivel.

"Splendid!" Felicia said. "Now you'll fit right in." As she returned the bone to the mantel and the paper to her pocket, Hattie noted how the poem's admonishments seemed not to apply to Felicia, clad as she was in a bright dress and wearing a sparkling emerald ring, not to mention her coiffed hair and powdered face that suggested a fair amount of time spent in the boudoir.

"I feel more than prepared to meet the stern needs of the hour," Hattie said, hoping to bring a swift end to this interview. "I shall look forward to gathering with like-minded women next Tuesday."

Felicia clasped her hands under her chin. "The ladies will be thrilled indeed at a new participant they can *wholly* trust. Sadly, our ranks more often diminish than increase. So many have fled to the South, and who can blame them, with the horrid machinations of Colonel Truesdail and his ilk. Not I, though. I shall remain here in Nashville and see through the liberation of our beloved Tennessee."

Hattie clasped her hand. "How fortunate to come upon another true daughter of the South, loyal to the finish. We must watch out for one another. Why, only a few weeks ago, as I was leaving the City Hotel, I saw Truesdail's men strong-arming two unfortunate souls accused of smuggling, one of them a woman."

Felicia shook her head. "That would be Mildred Trident. So very unfortunate."

Hattie let go of her hand, taking care not to show undue interest. "The poor soul. I do hope they haven't kept her in prison."

Felicia's brow furrowed. "I'm afraid they have. Last I heard, she was being held at the fortifications near the Capitol. Fort Johnson, the Yanks call it, but you won't hear that from me. I despise Andrew Johnson as much as I do Colonel Truesdail."

Hattie cocked her head. "A prison, up there on the hill?"

"Not a proper prison. But there are soldiers and sentinels all around, and they've scarcely allowed poor Mildred any freedoms at all. I'm told they intend to extract a confession under threat of sending her off to some prison in Illinois. And her with three children at home and a husband off fighting who knows where! Thank heavens her sister is here to care for the little ones."

"And I suppose her crime is no greater than mine, expressing her allegiance to the South."

"That's crime enough these days, to be certain. But Mildred had taken on, shall we say, a special assignment. She feared her husband would suffer a fever while fighting along the Mississippi, where the swamps are dreadful, I hear, and there's such a pestilence. Naturally, she wanted him to have quinine at the ready, and so she had to procure it, and she did so in quantities large enough to attract attention. If it weren't for those horrible blockades, none of us would have to worry about such things. But we must meet the stern needs of the hour!"

"I suffered some time in prison myself for a similar offense," Hattie said.

Felicia clapped her hand to her mouth. "Oh my. And yet you dared to defy the Yankees with your toast."

"In my experience, suffering leads to either fear or defiance. I choose defiance. I wish there were a way for me to share some encouragement—perhaps even some advice—with Mildred Trident."

"I wish the same. But you'd never get past the Capitol hill sentinels."

"There may be ways." Hattie offered a sly grin. "Perhaps by Tuesday next, I'll have a report to share with your ladies."

~ ~ ~

Hattie didn't relish the idea of returning to Felicia Ford's house on Tuesday, but at least she'd gained some useful information about the prisoner she hoped to interview. Waiting for Lieutenant Elliott's blessing seemed foolish.

Seeing no reason not to at least scout out the possibilities at the prison, she spent half her week's wages on a pound of butter at the market on her way home from the Ford mansion. Back at the boarding house, she cajoled Mrs. Fletcher into making tarts with the butter, using the rhubarb growing near her back steps and sweetened with the sugar and raisins she'd been hoarding. The tarts were for a friend who was in a bad way, Hattie told the landlady. A friend of the Confederacy, which coupled with Hattie's new-found status among the Secesh in Nashville was enough to convince Mrs. Fletcher to get straight to work on the project.

There was enough butter for three tarts, and after supper that night, Mrs. Fletcher brought one of them to the table. Setting out three small plates, she cut the tart into several pieces, setting one before each boarder and keeping one for herself.

"What a treat," Pauline said. She'd chatted amiably throughout the meal, filling them in on the goings-on at the theatre as a new troupe arrived to stage a production of *The Secret*. Lifting a piece of the tart on her fork, she said, "In celebration of our friend Hattie, who dares to reveal her true feelings from the stage."

Pressing her fork through the flaky crust and tender filling, Hattie smiled. Whether Pauline celebrated Hattie going along with her plan or whether she celebrated Hattie's absence from the theatre, Hattie preferred her approval to the alterative.

"Hattie's toast was the talk of the market today," Mrs. Fletcher said as she dove into her portion of the tart. "That and the men who were marched about the city in women's nightcaps."

On her fork, Hattie lifted a bite of pie to her mouth, relishing the warm mix of cinnamon, cloves, and butter on her tongue. Whatever her sympathies, Mrs. Fletcher was indeed a good cook. "In women's nightcaps?" she asked.

"That's right," Pauline said. "General Rosecrans is fed up with his Yanks surrendering to the Confederates in hopes they'll be paroled and sent home. He had his quartermasters procure a supply of ladies' nightcaps, then ordered the deserters paraded through town while wearing them."

"Cowards," Mrs. Fletcher said between bites of tart. "Near fifty of them, from what I seen, marched from the Capitol under heavy guard."

"The general would be better off calling for a truce," Hattie said. "That would stop desertions for good."

"Can't come soon enough," Mrs. Fletcher said darkly. "Today I was informed that because I've got a vacant room, I should expect a wounded Yank to be quartered here any day now. If they expect me to wait on him hand and foot, they've got another thing coming."

~ ~ ~

The next morning, Hattie bundled the two remaining tarts in a tea towel and packed them in one of Mrs. Fletcher's shopping baskets. Leaving the house, she took an omnibus to Capitol Hill. The driver stopped in front of the Capitol building, a regal limestone structure with tall columns and capitals, topped by a cupola from which a light shone at night.

The basket handle over her arm, Hattie bypassed the building, strolling instead along the path that skirted the palisades, earthworks, barricades, and artillery that Union forces had added to protect the structure, transforming the area into what they now called Fort Andrew Johnson, after the governor Lincoln had appointed after Federal troops took the city.

Hattie hoped her purposeful, confident stride would buy her some time while she assessed the situation. If any of the Union soldiers and officers recognized her from her toast to Jefferson Davis and the Confederacy, she would have a hard time getting in. Thankfully, she'd seen only a few Union officers in the audience that night. At the same time, she couldn't very well approach a sentry proclaiming herself on assignment with the Army Police. If word of that got back to Lieutenant Elliott, she'd be put on the next train out of Nashville.

She eyed the men guarding the entrance. She knew from her own time in prison that the older guards tended to be more lenient than the younger ones, especially if approached near the end of a shift, which was why she'd waited till late afternoon to make her visit.

She decided on a sentry who looked perhaps ten years older than her. From the idle way his deep-set eyes scanned the fort's perimeter, she suspected he was bored. Perhaps after yesterday's debacle with the soldiers in nightcaps, this was proving to be just another dull watch.

She hoped he was also hungry. "Excuse me, sir," she said, making her approach. "Might I have a moment with Mrs. Mildred Trident?"

Landing on her, his idle gaze sharpened. "This ain't a hotel, lady."

She ignored his remark. "I understand she's being held on serious charges," she said. "But Mildred is my cousin, and we're quite close." She paused as if collecting her thoughts, hoping the quiver in her voice would have the desired effect. "I've come all the way from Louisville to see her."

The guard snorted. "You won't be springing anyone free from here if that's what you're thinking. There's three of us guards to every one of them prisoners."

Hattie was beginning to wish she hadn't chosen this guard. At least he hadn't said Mildred Trident had been transferred out of Nashville. "I have no such intentions, I assure you. I've taken an oath of loyalty to the United States. I only want to cheer my cousin."

"Only cheer, huh? Then what's in the basket?"

She pulled back the cloth and thrust the basket close enough for him to smell the cinnamon wafting from it. "I managed to procure some fresh butter to bake her a tart."

With a stubby finger, he nudged one of the pies. "Might be you've baked a weapon into it," he said. "A knife, maybe."

"You're welcome to check," Hattie said.

The man thrust his grubby hand into one tart, then the other. Withdrawing it, he licked the rhubarb filling from his fingers. "Fair enough," he said.

"You may as well have one now that you've spoiled them," Hattie said. "Besides, Mildred has never been a big eater."

"A waif, from the looks of her," the sentry said, still eying the tarts.

"If you'll show me where to find her, I'd be most grateful. And should anyone ask, I won't let on that you let me in."

The guard looked side to side. He waited until an officer at the far end of the palisade rounded the corner, then tugged Hattie through the entrance and into a large courtyard where small groups of prisoners congregated.

"She's in that far stall over there." The guard nodded across the courtyard to a row of stalls. Hattie counted six pallets in each except the last one, which held only one pallet. "She don't come out much. You stick along the fence, now, and don't dally. Anyone asks, say you came in another way."

"Thank you." She lifted one of the mangled tarts from her basket and set it in his outstretched hand. "I won't forget your kindness."

Greedily, he shoved the tart in his mouth. She started along the fence, taking care to stay in the shadows, concealing her basket as best she could. One of the men in the courtyard spotted her, but he glanced her way for only a moment, then turned back to his conversation.

These prisoners must be officers, she thought, allowed the privilege of mingling in the open air. She hoped they realized how lucky they had it here. Compared to the men at Libby, they looked well-fed.

But as Hattie discovered on reaching her stall, Mildred Trident wasn't faring as well. The last time Hattie had seen her, during the City Hotel arrest, Mildred had held her head high. Now she sat on her cot, shoulders slumped, worrying her slender hands in her lap.

"Mrs. Trident?" Hattie asked softly, not wanting to startle her.

Mildred looked up. In some ways, she looked only a few years older than Hattie, but dark circles under her eyes and her ashen complexion made her seem older. "You've come to take me away?" she asked, her voice trembling.

Hattie shook her head. "I've only come for a visit. And I've brought you this." She turned back the tea towel, exposing the last of the tarts, and thrust the basket forward.

Mildred stood, a bit unsteady on her feet, and peered at the contents. "But...who are you?"

Coming forward, Hattie took her arm. "Your Louisville cousin." She raised her eyebrows, holding Mildred's gaze.

Wariness shone in her eyes. "I know no one in Louisville."

Hattie steered her back to the cot. "Let's sit a spell, and I'll explain," she said quietly. "Assuming there's no one close enough to hear."

Mildred shook her head, her dark, tangled curls bobbing at her shoulders. Knowing how disheveled she'd become during her incarceration at Libby, Hattie felt a pang of pity for the woman, smuggler or not.

Her sympathies heightened as Mildred's eyes brimmed with tears. "Sometimes it feels as if the whole world's forgotten me. And in a way, I wish they would, if only so the Yanks won't send me to Illinois as they've been threatening to."

Hattie reached for Mildred's hand, her fingers cold despite the warmth of this sunny April day. "I understand. I was taken prisoner myself not so long ago."

Mildred swiped at her tears. "I don't mean to be such a baby about it. It's just that my children..." She straightened, and her eyes narrowed. "They've sent you to get me to talk, haven't they?" She fisted a hand in her lap. "But I won't do it. I won't."

"No. It was Felicia Ford who told me where I could find you."

Mildred's countenance darkened, and her eyes flashed. "Why hasn't Mrs. Ford come herself? Her, or any of the Soldiers' Aid ladies? Fine for them to recruit me for their little project. But when things go awry, they're nowhere to be found. They knew how desperate I was to get quinine to my husband. I don't give a whit one way or the other who prevails in this war. I just want him home safe and sound."

The prisoner's plain garb, lack of adornment, and dirty fingernails weren't entirely due to her present circumstances, Hattie realized. Felicia's Society ladies had helped recruit a lower-class woman to do the dirty work of smuggling, with enough difference in status to keep themselves from the scrutiny of Truesdail's Army Police. She should have expected as much from women who desecrated an enemy's bones.

Hattie fished the tart from the basket and handed it to Mildred, hoping to recover her trust. "I only recently met Mrs. Ford, and I've not attended any of the Society's gatherings. I'm rather new to the city, having come here after running into some trouble out East. I was in the City Hotel lobby at the time of your arrest. Naturally, my sympathies were roused, and I recalled how a woman visited me while I was incarcerated, a kindness I shall never forget. Mrs. Ford told me where I might find you, but she mentioned nothing about the ladies having recruited you."

Mildred eyed the tart. "Of course she didn't."

Hattie pressed the little pie into her hands. "Go ahead. Have some."

Mildred cradled the tart as if it were a little bird. "I shouldn't eat it all myself."

Hattie laughed. "This is hardly a time to concern yourself with manners. When I was in prison, I'd have done almost anything for a morsel of decent food."

Delicately, Mildred plucked a piece of the tart's crust, then popped it in her mouth. She closed her eyes briefly. "It tastes like home," she said.

"You'll be home before you know it," Hattie said.

Mildred fingered the tart. "Not if they send me to Illinois. And I wouldn't mind so much, really I wouldn't, if not for my children. The oldest is only six. I know my sister does what she can, looking after them, but she's scarcely more than a child herself, and she has little experience with young ones. How they're managing to eat at all, I don't know. She came to see me last week, leaving the children with a neighbor. The guard wouldn't let her in, but he relayed her message that little Frederick is ill with the measles. I've heard nothing since." She looked up at Hattie, the tart momentarily forgotten.

"Surely she's sent for the doctor by now," Hattie said.

Mildred laughed sharply. "And paid him with what? I was supposed to be paid for what I done. Good money, they said." She shook her head. "I should've known they'd abandon me if anything went wrong."

Hattie's disgust sharpened. It was nothing new, privileged people toying with those of lesser circumstances. She'd seen it enough from her parents. But it still irked her. Mildred likely didn't care about states' rights or the peculiar institution of slavery. She was just trying to hold her family together.

"I knew a doctor in Richmond," Hattie said. "Luke Blackstone. I believe he's in Nashville now. His sympathies lie with the South. If I can locate him, perhaps he'd look in on your boy."

Mildred laughed sharply. "Luke Blackstone? That's who Dr. DuBois said would help us out if we got in a jam. As you can see, that hasn't happened."

Hattie's heart quickened. Blackstone was involved in this smuggling scheme, just as she'd suspected. She had to tread carefully, choosing her words with care. She put her hand to her chest, a gesture of surprise. "I thought Dr. Blackstone was more reliable than that. If you know where I can find him, I'll go to him and plead your case."

Mildred swallowed the last bite of the tart, then licked her fingers. "I have no idea where he is. Dr. DuBois said he's a stealthy one. I'm afraid all that's reliable are my prayers. That Frederick gets better. That my dear husband survives. That my sister can somehow keep feeding the children. That I'm not sent to Alton."

"Let us hope your prayers are answered," Hattie said, offering the tea towel from the basket.

Mildred dabbed a crumb from her chin, then returned the towel. "You're so kind to have come today. And I don't even know your name."

Hattie folded the towel and put it away. "It's best that way." She rose from the cot, the basket's handle over her arm. "All hope is not lost. There are ways out of even the most trying circumstances."

Before Mildred could ask how she knew this, Hattie slipped away.

Chapter Thirteen

April 26, 1863

*D*earest Anne,

 I've thought of you often during these weeks in Nashville. How I miss you! I've taken a room with an actress, Pauline Carlton. She can be a troublesome sort, and she made no bones about not wanting me here, but our mutual employer insisted on it. As you know who that is, I will say no more. You and I know full well how readily a letter can fall into unintended hands

 At any rate, Pauline and I seem to have reached an understanding of sorts, if not exactly a friendship. My duties at present are not entirely to my liking, and as you can well imagine, knowing my affinity for the theatre, I admit to some envy at her position, which I briefly shared after coming to this city.

 Like Washington, Nashville is crawling with soldiers, most of whom seem not to know what to do with themselves. Sentiments here run rather heavily in favor of the South, and the general mood is sullen owing to the Union occupation. It is not hard to see why President Lincoln has insisted Tennessee be protected, and

Nashville in particular held. The Confederates hold positions in the southern and western parts of the state, with guerillas terrorizing East Tennessee, and there are constant fears among the Federals that General Bragg will try to retake Nashville for the Confederacy. That would be quite the feather in his cap, giving the Rebels control of five railroad lines and the Cumberland River, not to mention the state's capitol.

I hope you are duly impressed with my attention to the particulars of this war, at least here in Tennessee. What choice do I have, without you here to offer me information?

I hope you and Franklin are well, bound by the joyful prospect of your family's expansion. Write when you get a chance. I am eager beyond measure for word from you.

Fondly,

Hattie

There was more Hattie might have written to her friend—about her toast and subsequent notoriety among Secesh sympathizers, about Felicia Ford and the Soldiers' Aid Society, about the charming but infuriating Lieutenant Elliott, about her secret visit to the prison, about how she fell asleep each night thinking of Thom Welton.

But as she and Anne both knew from opening letters in Pinkerton's mailroom, wartime correspondence was anything but private. Although her letter would be sent and received within Union territory, Hattie wasn't sure she trusted Anne's husband, engaged as he was in Copperhead activities. She wouldn't put it past him to read her mail.

Hattie folded the letter and slipped it in an envelope, which she sealed and addressed in her slanted hand, perfected at the Ladygrace School for Girls, where she and Anne had become friends. How distant and carefree her schooldays now seemed, when her greatest worry was the society girls mocking her.

On the other side of their narrow room, Pauline snored lightly. In addition to her theatrical work, which kept her up late, Colonel Truesdail had assigned her to keep watch on an elderly banker suspected of aiding the Confederates. Pauline complained about the assignment, saying that the old man, a regular at the theatre, was dull as dirt, boring her with tales of his youthful exploits in Alabama. He lived so much in the past that Pauline doubted he could do much harm in the present, but Truesdail insisted she persist.

Hattie was quick to point out that she'd prefer a banker over the social circles of Felicia Ford and her ilk. But she also knew that Kate Warne, her Pinkerton's supervisor, had inserted herself in Washington social circles so she could glean information, and Hattie had never heard her complain.

Still, Secesh sympathizers were few and far between in Washington. Here, Hattie felt awash in them, with no one but Pauline to turn to when she wanted to express her true feelings about the course of the war. She found the Society ladies by turns dull and infuriating, with the usual complaints about "contraband" Negroes and exorbitant prices.

In her time at the Society, Hattie had found little of substance to pass along to Lieutenant Elliott. The ladies whispered of smuggling quinine and opium, and one had even gone so far as to propose stuffing packets of the medicinals into the belly of a dead mule. From her prison visit, Hattie knew the ladies recruited lower-class women like Mildred Trident for their treasonous enterprises, but she couldn't very well share that information with Elliott since he'd expressly forbade her from going to the prison.

She thought of Mildred now and then, along with her ailing child. She didn't feel at all the same about her as she did about Blackstone, Mildred being a pawn in a game that Blackstone oversaw for his own gain. Whenever Hattie went about town, she kept an eye out for the doctor. She made inquiries whenever she had an opportunity, though she did so vaguely, not mentioning

Blackstone by name. Speaking of him with Mildred had been relatively safe—he'd clearly washed his hands of those who'd been arrested. But if she was right about him having recognized her at the theatre, she didn't want word of her inquiries getting back to him.

Another unfortunate aspect of her involvement with the Soldier's Aid Society was that she'd had to stop checking Nashville's hospitals for Blackstone. The ladies made regular visits to Confederate soldiers in local hospitals, and Hattie didn't want to run into any of them there.

It wasn't long before Felicia proposed Hattie start making hospital visits too. She'd sent her out with a dour-faced woman named Sarah to visit Rebel soldiers in Nashville's Hospital No. 14, housed at the five-story Nashville Female Academy. Hattie felt the same desperation there as she had in Washington City, where she'd gone with Anne to visit her wounded brother, Henry, in the Patent Office Hospital. So many soldiers with so many needs, and too few people to care for them. In many cases, little could be done other than trying to make them comfortable.

Sarah had assured Hattie that conditions had improved at Hospital No. 14 since January when casualties from the Battle of Murfreesboro had filled nearly all the hospital's 500 beds. "Thirty dead every day," Sarah said grimly. "Dying in the aisles, they were, praying and calling out for wives, children, fathers, mothers in homes they'd never see again."

Even now, Hospital No. 14 was chaotic. Hattie was loath to go back there. Sarah insisted Hattie ignore every plea from a Union soldier, even for something as simple as a sip of water, deferring instead to the Confederate wounded housed in the basement. With Sarah looking on, she could not make the sort of inquiries of the soldiers that might yield useful information for the Army Police.

Now, as she descended the boarding house stairs to post her letter to Anne, Hattie resolved that at the next Society meeting, she would tell Felicia she wanted to make hospital visits on her own. That way she could at least converse with Rebel soldiers without being watched over like a schoolgirl.

Breakfast was long over, and Hattie would have passed by the kitchen without a second thought had she not heard the crash of glass from beyond the closed door, followed by a sharp cry from Mrs. Fletcher.

Thinking the landlady might be hurt, Hattie pushed through the door. Mrs. Fletcher was kneeling on the floor. Scattered around her were thin shards of blue glass. Looking closely, Hattie saw a white powder covering the area.

"Is everything all right?" Hattie asked.

The landlady startled, turning her head and pressing her hand to her heart. "Land's sakes, child. You gave me a fright. Fetch the dustpan, would you? And the broom from behind the door."

Slipping Anne's letter into her pocket, Hattie did as she was asked, holding out the dustpan as Mrs. Fletcher swept up the glass and powder. Hattie was starting for the dustbin to dispense of the mess when the landlady grabbed the dustpan from her hand.

"Might be salvaged," she muttered. "Some of it anyhow."

She set the dustpan next to a small open jar. It took a second before the smell wafting from the jar registered. Coffee. Not the chicory coffee they drank every morning at breakfast, but the real thing, for which Mrs. Fletcher must have paid an outrageous amount at the market.

"Is there some special occasion?" Hattie asked, nodding at the jar.

Mrs. Fletcher picked two of the larger shards from the dustpan and set them aside. "Got notice this morning that a wounded Yank will be staying here starting tomorrow," she said, her rheumy eyes meeting Hattie's. "However they bring him in, I intend to see that he leaves in a coffin."

Hattie held back a gasp. The blue glass must have come from an apothecary bottle, she realized. "You mean to poison him," she said.

Lips pressed in a tight smile, Mrs. Fletcher nudged a bit of the white powder in the dustpan. "He'll be wanting real coffee, just like all them Yanks drink in their camps while we suffer with the chicory. Figured I'd have it at the ready, seasoned just so."

"How clever," Hattie managed to say. "But aren't you worried his death would raise suspicions?"

The landlady shrugged. "Them boys die all the time, don't they? Typhus, smallpox, dysentery." She cocked her head, studying Hattie's face. "Lost your color, girl. Don't tell me you're getting squeamish."

Hattie shook her head. "It's only that my monthlies are about to start, and I've got some cramping." She pressed her hands to her abdomen, for effect.

"Good thing." The landlady pointed a bony finger at her. "If I thought you'd changed your allegiance, I might have to mix up a brew for you too."

Hattie forced a smile. "You are a force to be reckoned with, Mrs. Fletcher."

The landlady plucked another shard of glass from the dustpan. "We must all do our part."

~ ~ ~

Hattie posted her letter, then hurried to the Army Police headquarters. Having made a show of her Secesh sympathies, she knew better than to go in the front. Instead, she waited until no one was looking, then slipped into an alleyway and entered through the back door.

John Elliott was at his desk, penning a note. Hattie rapped on his half-open door. He looked up and, seeing her, smiled warmly. "Hattie," he said, standing to greet her. "I've been wondering what had become of you. Do come in."

She entered, closing the door behind her, and sat in the chair opposite his desk. "As you instructed, I've been ingratiating myself with Felicia Ford and her Soldiers' Aid Society," she said. "I don't mind telling you it's a rather unpleasant assignment."

He tilted his chin, gazing at her with what might or might not have been concern. "How so?"

"The meetings begin with a wretched ritual involving a Union soldier's leg bone that Felicia Ford keeps on her mantle. The proceedings devolve from there into gossip."

He drummed his fingers on his desk. "Gossip can prove useful."

Her eyes flashed. "I'm well aware of that, lieutenant. But these women are hardly forthcoming."

"They don't trust you." Not a question. A statement.

"You mistake my meaning," she said sharply. "Their lack of candor is a modus operandi. For any activities that might implicate them, they rely on the less fortunate."

He leaned back in his chair. "They told you this?"

"I've been told, yes," she said, hedging.

"I don't suppose this revelation came at the price of a rhubarb tart."

She drew a sharp breath. "With so much serious work before you," she said, sweeping her hand over the papers on his desk, "I'd hardly think your interests would run to baked goods."

He folded his arms across his broad chest. "They do when those baked goods are used to defy my explicit instructions. The last time we talked, I specifically told you to stay away from those prisoners. Then I got word from a guard that the same pretty young woman who made the Jeff Davis toast at the New Allen's Theatre was handing out bribes in the form of rhubarb tarts."

Pressing her hands to her lap, Hattie met his gaze. "As I told you before, I believed the prisoner might share things with me that she wouldn't reveal to male investigators."

"And as I told you, my plan was for you to report back to me on the activities of the Soldiers' Aid Society before we had any further discussions about your visiting the prison."

Hattie's eyes narrowed. "Mildred Trident has been transferred, hasn't she?"

"That's none of your concern," he said. "Suppose you tell me why you've taken such a keen interest in her case."

"I saw an opportunity and seized it. That's the sort of thing you miss when you put too much emphasis on making plans."

He offered a twisted smile. "I'll certainly take that under advisement, Miss Thomas," he said in a tone suggesting he had no such intention. "Meanwhile, let me be clear. Much as I admire your pluck, I must insist that you abide by my orders. You must trust that your work with the Society ladies will yield results in due time. No more prison visits without my permission."

She was certain he wouldn't talk to Pauline in such a condescending way. But if she pointed this out, he might send her away altogether, before she had a chance to track down Luke Blackstone.

"Very well, sir." She rose to leave. "There's one more thing. The landlady, Mrs. Fletcher. I caught her this morning making plans to poison a Union soldier."

He stood, his brow furrowed. "What sort of plans?"

"She obtained a white powder from the apothecary. She told me it's a poison she intends to mix with coffee and serve to the wounded soldier who'll be staying at her boarding house."

"Those are serious allegations. You're sure it's not an idle threat?"

"I'm certain. I witnessed her preparations this morning."

He nodded curtly. "Very well. I'll see that no soldiers are boarded there."

"Will you have her arrested?"

He shook his head. "Some people are more valuable to us where they are."

Hattie might have argued the point, but she knew she'd be wasting her breath. John Elliott seemed intent on asserting his authority over her. From now on, she'd have to pick her battles.

~ ~ ~

By the time Hattie returned to the boardinghouse, Pauline was up. When Hattie entered their room, she was fastening her layered skirt over her crinoline.

"You have no idea how lucky you are," she complained. "You only have to dress like this on Tuesdays."

"I'll trade places with you any time," Hattie said. "Just say the word."

"As much as he fancies you, Lieutenant Elliott would never allow it."

"Fancies me?" Hattie said. "He can scarcely abide my presence."

"Because you challenge him," Pauline said.

"And you don't?"

"Not like you do. But whenever I report to him, he always comes round to asking about you. In my book, that's a sign of male interest, being overly concerned about a woman's safety."

"Overly controlling, you mean," Hattie said darkly.

"Perhaps." Pauline tugged at her corset. "I wish you'd been here when I was dressing. When Mrs. Fletcher tightens my stays, she seems intent on squeezing the life out of me."

"You wouldn't be her only victim," Hattie said, lowering her voice. "Earlier, I caught her preparing poison for the Union soldier who was to board here starting tomorrow."

Pauline gave a low whistle. "You don't say. No wonder she was feeling so feisty." She wriggled her shoulders. "Be a dear and loosen my stays a bit, would you, and tell me the details."

Hattie complied, unfastening the buttons down Pauline's back, then untying and retying her corset strings as she relayed in whispers what she'd seen that morning and what she'd done about it. "I don't see why Lieutenant Elliott doesn't have her arrested," she said.

Pauline turned her head, looking over her shoulder at Hattie. "That's your way of dealing with him, isn't it? Finding fault so you won't have to acknowledge his interest."

Hattie stiffened. "I find fault because he's wrong."

"Any other woman in Nashville would jump at the chance to return the lieutenant's attentions."

"There are no attentions," Hattie said crossly, redoing the last of the stays. "And I don't see you mooning over him."

Pauline shrugged. "Never had much use for men myself. But I'm guessing you do. A beau off fighting somewhere?"

"A casualty," Hattie said, tears filling her eyes.

Pauline turned around, gazing at her with more compassion than Hattie had ever seen from her. "I'm sorry for that," she said. "He must have meant a great deal to you."

Hattie swallowed back the lump that had formed in her throat. "He did," she said, wishing she could keep her voice from trembling.

Pauline set her hand on Hattie's shoulder, an affectionate gesture that took Hattie by surprise. "I'm sure he'd be proud of what you're doing here, continuing the fight."

More than you know, Hattie thought. "I believe he would," she said.

Pauline fastened her bodice. "Well, I'm off to the bank. If this assignment goes on much longer, I'll end up withdrawing my life's savings which, granted, isn't a lot. And you?"

Hattie groaned. "I'm supposed to report to the hospital again. I hate pandering to the wounded Rebs. If I were to so much as look at a Union soldier, Felicia's hawk would swoop in and drag me off."

"You needn't be a mouse to her hawks," Pauline said. "Choose a hospital where none of those ladies would be caught dead."

Hattie tipped her chin, puzzled. "I'm not sure I follow."

Pauline took her purse from the dressing table and hung it over her wrist. "Hospital No. 11. I guarantee you'd have the place to yourself."

"But Felicia says the Society has posted ladies in every Nashville hospital."

Pauline flashed a smile. "Every reputable hospital," she said, then let herself out the door.

This was enough to intrigue Hattie. She'd been told to report to Hospital No. 10 today. If she showed up at No. 11 instead, she could claim she'd made a mistake. At least she'd get a day's respite from the Society's agenda.

~ ~ ~

Hospital No. 11 was at the corner of Broad and Vine, housed in an old but beautiful mansion that had once been a Federal building. Before the war, medical students from Central University had studied there. Only blocks away was Nashville's infamous Smokey Row, where prostitutes plied their trade.

The day was bright and warm, and by the time Hattie reached the front door of Hospital No. 11, perspiration had dampened at her collar and hairline. She brushed back a limp curl from her forehead and went inside. At first glance, there seemed nothing disreputable about the place other than its proximity to Smokey Row. Like most hospitals, it smelled of camphor and ether. The oak floor looked as if it had been recently swept, and the windows on either side of the door let in a profusion of light, suggesting they, too, had been recently cleaned. The doors along the hallway were marked with brass numbers. All were closed, and it was so quiet that Hattie wondered for a moment if the hospital was occupied.

Stepping onto a thick rug that muffled her footsteps, she proceeded down the hall. As she passed door after door, she listened for any sign that the rooms were occupied. Behind one door, she heard a woman's laughter, and that encouraged her to go on.

Toward the end of the hall, Hattie came upon a door that was cracked open an inch or so. She paused, hearing a man's voice from beyond the cocked door. Listening, she caught snippets of what sounded like a lecture. "Incompetent...tyrannical...intolerable," the man was saying.

Hattie pressed close to the wall, not wanting to be seen as she tried to make out his words.

"You must not obey the orders of any surgeon other than myself," the man was saying. "Nor should you trust anyone but me to prescribe medications."

Hattie craned her neck, peering through the opening. The room contained six beds, each occupied not by a soldier but by a woman. Hospital No. 11 was the Pest House, she realized, where disreputable women could come for treatment. Pauline was right. Felicia Ford would not be dispatching her angels of mercy here. The only less desirable assignment would be the Colored Hospital.

Inside the room, the man who'd spoken was tall and thin, with a prominent chin and dark hair that was graying at the temples. From the stethoscope slung about his neck, Hattie assumed he was a doctor. The patient before him mumbled a response that Hattie couldn't make out.

"I intend to file a complaint with the Assistant Surgeon General to have her removed," the man said. "In the meantime, do as I've instructed."

Hattie stepped back from the door. In doing so, she nearly ran into a woman who'd come up behind her. Hattie turned, her face flushed with embarrassment. "Sorry," she said. "I didn't..." Her voice trailed off as she took in the familiar set of the woman's hazel eyes and her prim mouth. Wearing a dark waistcoat over bloomers, she was unmistakable. Dr. Edith Greenfield, who'd tended Hattie's sprained ankle and admonished her to get back to spying.

Plucking Hattie's sleeve, she tugged her away from the door. "What sort of spy pays so much attention to her eavesdropping that she fails to hear someone approaching from behind?" the doctor asked in a loud whisper.

Hattie felt her face flush. "Dr. Greenfield. I knew you were in Tennessee, but I didn't expect to find you here."

The doctor shrugged. "And yet here I am, much to the dismay of Dr. Burle." She nodded toward the door. "I expect you got an earful."

Hattie nodded. "Is there somewhere we can talk openly?"

"Follow me," Dr. Greenfield said, leading Hattie down the hall to a door with the brass number thirteen. The doctor twisted the knob and swung the door open, revealing a tidy office containing a set of bookshelves, a polished desk, and a red settee.

When they were both inside, Dr. Greenfield shut the door and turned the lock. "Can't be too careful," she said.

"That man—" Hattie began.

"Dr. Burle."

"Yes, Dr. Burle. He was telling his patient to listen to no one but him. And he said he intends to file a complaint with the Assistant Surgeon General."

Edith sighed. "I'm not surprised. I'm used to male doctors resenting my presence. But Dr. Burle has taken my being here especially hard. He simply can't accept that the general put me in charge."

"How unfortunate," Hattie said.

"Indeed." Dr. Greenfield studied her face, reminding Hattie of a bright-eyed bird. "I didn't recognize you at first, Miss Logan, with your hair dyed and cut."

"It's Miss Thomas now. General Sharpe advised me to alter my appearance and adopt a new surname. But please, call me Hattie."

"So we're to be friends now, are we?"

The bluntness of her question caught Hattie off-guard. "If you're not opposed to it. You encouraged me when I most needed it. If not for you, I wouldn't be here."

Edith nodded curtly. "That may not prove to your advantage in the end. But I'm glad to see you've chosen not to wile away your days pining for what you've lost. And your ankle has healed quite nicely, too, judging from the steadiness of your gait. But let's sit nonetheless." She gestured toward the settee. "I'm on my feet a good part of the day."

"You treat women here," Hattie said as she sat, taking one end of the settee while Edith took the other.

"Someone needs to," Edith said. "These women may have no battle wounds, but they're ill as often as men are. Is that why you've come here, seeking treatment for some malady that doesn't show in your general demeanor?"

"No," Hattie said. "I'm feeling well enough, so long as my landlady doesn't learn my actual purpose in Nashville and decide to poison me."

Edith's lips curled in a smile. "Poison you? Do tell."

Hattie explained about Mrs. Fletcher's plans for the coffee and her own frustration with Lieutenant Elliott's response. "Do you report to him too?" she asked.

Edith shook her head. "We've been introduced. Handsome young man, quite earnest. A potentially troublesome combination in my experience. But my primary purpose here is doctoring, and it wouldn't do for me to be running in and out of the Army Police Headquarters, even if I had the time. But you still haven't said why you're here at the hospital."

"It's because of Lieutenant Elliott, at least indirectly." Hattie filled her in on Pauline and the toast and Hattie's subsequent assignment with Felicia Ford's Society ladies.

"Mrs. Ford's reputation precedes her," Edith said. "And your friend is correct. She'd not for one moment think of dispatching her ladies to this institution. As you've likely heard, a fair number of our patients are public women."

Hattie recognized the polite term for prostitutes. "I'm surprised your Dr. Burle is eager to treat them."

Edith sat up straighter. "Dr. Burle is eager for his own advancement. If he can have me removed from my post, he assumes he'll be appointed director here. With that feather in his cap, I imagine he thinks he can procure a similar position at a more reputable hospital. You'd think during wartime people would set such ambitions aside, but it seems rather the opposite, with people seizing every opportunity for personal gain. One can hardly blame the public women for following suit, even if it's to the detriment of their health."

"They contract the pox?"

"That's right. The provost marshal claims Smokey Row has killed more soldiers than the war has. He'd just as soon all the women from there were rounded up and shot." She shook her head. "Vectors of disease, that's all they are to him, never mind the poverty and hardship that drove them to sell their bodies for a few coins. And of course, no one suggests punishing the men who take their amusement on the Row."

Hattie thought of the prostitute who'd befriended her at Richmond's Castle Thunder. A rough sort, but she couldn't have been kinder to Hattie.

"I know next to nothing of nursing," Hattie said. "But perhaps I could be of some help here. And I might even glean some information from your patients. I assume some have plied their trade with Rebels as well as Federal soldiers."

"Oh, they have," Edith said. "The Secesh men of Nashville make a fuss about whores by day, but after dark, you'd find a good many of them lurking about Smokey Row."

Hattie shifted in her seat, feeling ever more grateful for Pauline's sly suggestion of visiting Hospital No. 11. What a twist it would be on John Elliott's insistence on Society work if she could volunteer here with Edith and the prostitutes.

"I suspect the husbands of some of Felicia Ford's Society women visit Smokey Row too," she said. "If they thought you were helping cure the same diseases their husbands bring home, they might even approve of my coming here."

"No cure, I'm afraid," Edith said crisply. "We can contain the symptoms, but by the time most men realize they've contracted gonorrhea or syphilis, they've likely already passed the disease on to their wives."

"I could also tell the Society women that some of the women here support the Southern cause. Even Felicia Ford would have to admit those women are worthy of attention, soiled or not." Hattie rose to leave. "I'll be back. Between the two of us, perhaps we can remind Dr. Burle of his place."

Edith stood too. "That will take some doing."

Hattie started for the door, then turned. "I don't suppose you've learned anything of Luke Blackstone since you've been in Tennessee."

Edith shook her head. "It's my understanding he's somewhere in the state, but I know nothing more."

"After I made my toast, I thought I saw him standing against a wall of the theatre. But in the dim lighting, I couldn't be sure."

Edith's eyes narrowed. "It's entirely possible. I don't think I need to warn you to take care. Eager as you are to see him punished, he'd no doubt love to be rid of you for good."

Chapter Fourteen

May 5, 1863

The following Tuesday, after enduring another Soldiers' Aid Society bone-and-poem ritual, Hattie proposed the idea of her volunteering at Hospital No. 11.

To a one, the ladies looked aghast. Then Felicia's face softened, and Hattie saw pity in her eyes. "Being new to our city, you must not know the sort of clientele that frequent that hospital, dear. Women of a most disreputable sort."

Hattie straightened. "I understand that. But I'm also told that many of those women are sympathetic to our cause. I've also heard that the doctor in charge is making every attempt to curb the spread of diseases that demoralize our troops."

"Diseases that demoralize the Yanks, you mean," one of the ladies said. "The population at Smokey Row exploded after the Federals took over this town."

"Those fancy women do sap a man's vital energies," another lady remarked. "You know what they say. A night with Venus, a lifetime with mercury," she said, referring to a standard treatment for the pox.

Felicia waved her hand dismissively. "Their work is immoral, but if it's Yankee energies they sap, what do we care?"

Hattie feared she was losing the argument. "But unless we have some interaction with them, how can we convince them to stay away from our own men?"

A few of the women exchanged glances—the ones with wayward husbands, she suspected. "Hattie makes a good point," one of them said. "We can't simply ignore the problem."

Hattie seized on this small encouragement. "We are the Soldiers' Aid Society, are we not? If we're to be of any use, we must be willing to stretch ourselves a bit."

Felicia's brow furrowed, and Hattie could tell she was pondering this. "There's another point to consider, ladies," Felicia said. "Yesterday, an officer of the Army police visited here. He maintained that it was only a routine visit, but he asked a good number of questions about our society's activities."

Murmurs erupted over this bit of news. Hattie seethed inwardly. So this was Lieutenant Elliott's idea of trust, sending an officer to do the work he'd assigned her?

"Naturally, the officer left knowing as little as when he came," Felicia said. "But it would behoove us to make a show of our efforts to better the town, not just on behalf of our Confederate wounded."

"If I'm required to so much as touch a Yank, I'll leave this Society immediately," one lady said indignantly.

Felicia held out her hand, palm out. "I'm suggesting nothing of the sort. But if Hattie here has the fortitude to minister to the frail sisters at Hospital No. 11, it might prompt the authorities to look more generously on our activities." She turned to face Hattie. "That is, my dear, if you're sure you're up to the task. Your associations there might sully your reputation."

Suppressing a smile, Hattie met her gaze. "We must all make our sacrifices."

~ ~ ~

In the weeks that followed, Hattie happily spent her daytime hours under Edith Greenfield's tutelage, helping to care for the women at Hospital No. 11. Keeping busy, it was easier to avoid the waves of grief that threatened at the most inopportune moments.

Not all the women at No. 11 were prostitutes, she learned. Some were women too poor to afford private doctoring. Others were Negroes who'd fled the South, suffering injuries or falling ill along the way. Under the Fugitive Slave law, they would have no protection from their owners coming after them until they were well enough to reach Canada, so Edith and Hattie screened visitors carefully, on the lookout for bounty hunters.

Hattie had never liked the sight of blood, but she grew to tolerate small amounts of it when she changed dressings. She also assisted in some procedures, including surgeries, where she was tasked with administering the ether. She had a keen interest in how ether and other medicinals worked. Other than drama, science had been a favorite subject of hers in school. Noting her interest, Dr. Greenfield had her work in the hospital's dispensary, housed in one of the upstairs bedrooms.

Dr. Greenfield explained that when she'd first arrived at the hospital, an army steward had been in charge of the medicinals. But she soon found that more opium was being dispensed than prescribed, and she surmised that the man's shallow breathing, irritability, and shirking of his responsibilities resulted from his habitual use of the drug. She'd insisted he be reassigned, and rather than take her chances on another soldier, she'd been handling the medicinals herself in addition to her other duties.

So Edith was only too happy to make Hattie steward over the dispensary, charged with keeping records and serving as pharmacist under the doctor's direction. Hattie liked the sense of order within the dispensary's walls, the innocuous-looking bottles of pills and tinctures and powders lined up in rows, each with the potential to heal or, in the wrong doses, to harm. Dr. Greenfield was conservative in her prescribing, for even in the North, supplies were limited, and as a general rule, she believed other doctors were far too liberal in dispensing medications without understanding their full effects.

Hattie came every day except Tuesdays to sit at her work area lit by the dispensary's large window and prepare, preserve, and compound the substances Dr. Greenfield prescribed. For guidance, she consulted The American New Dispensary. From ingredients that included ferrous sulfate, calcium carbonate, and potassium nitrate, she mixed compounds such as potassium tartrate, silver nitrate, and calomel, the common name for mercurous chloride. Properly dosed, calomel was thought to purge patients of syphilis, but Dr. Greenfield had observed serious side effects from long-term use, including weight loss and intense itching. In addition to compounding, Hattie also examined premade pills for harmful adulterations, such as blue clay mixed in with certain blue-hued pills.

Dr. Greenfield was pleased with her work. "If you were a man, I'd suggested pharmaceutical school after the war. But as a woman, your chances of getting in would be as dismal as getting into medical school."

"But you managed it," Hattie said.

"Not without a good deal of difficulty."

Even if she were a man, Hattie couldn't see herself devoting her life to pharmaceuticals, but the dispensary was a good diversion while she was here. In some ways, working with the chemicals reminded her of the decoding she'd taken on while with Pinkerton's. Close attention was required, and she delighted in the work.

But she wasn't going to let her work in the dispensary keep her from tracking down Luke Blackstone. It would help if Lieutenant Elliott was on her side. He was holding her interview with Mildred Trident against her, but if she could bring him some useful bits of information, she hoped his opinion of her would shift.

She was getting little from the Society ladies, who seemed especially closelipped after the smuggling arrests. But she could try to gather information from some of the hospital's patients. She smiled to think how the good lieutenant might react if he learned she'd gotten more from public women than Society ladies. Maybe he'd finally realize his attempts to control Hattie were pointless.

So Hattie made a point of leaving the dispensary now and then to mingle with the patients. Some were sullen and despondent, the circumstances of the war and their illnesses weighing heavily upon them. The livelier patients were often the public women Dr. Greenfield was treating for syphilis. Aside from a rash, they often suffered only from a slight fever and muscle aches.

For some, their treatment couldn't end soon enough. They wanted to get back to their work, where they earned more money than they could doing anything else. Others were less enthused about returning to Smokey Row, having fallen into the shoals of vice and passion, as Felicia Ford liked to say, after being widowed or otherwise abandoned. Reluctant to go back to the brothels, these women were grateful for the respite of the hospital, and they gladly complied when Dr. Greenfield insisted they stay for the full course of their treatment.

One of Hattie's favorites was a woman who called herself Marlena. A German immigrant with lively green eyes and abundant brown hair that cascaded over her shoulders, she'd come to Nashville with a man shortly after the war broke out. Not long after their arrival, he'd abandoned her. With no other means to support herself, she'd taken up her profession at the Haystack, one of the town's more lucrative brothels.

She seemed happy for Hattie's interest, speaking to her with a flourish that might have served her well on the stage. Now and then, she interjected a word from her native tongue. She seemed unabashed about how she supported herself.

"Ach, the men can be boors," she told Hattie, eyes sparkling. "Of both types. Isn't that how you say it in English, boor and bore, the dull and the piggish?"

Laughing, Hattie assured her that her understanding was correct.

Marlena liked to reference the framed picture she kept at her bedside, a full-length photo of herself in a gown of tulle and lace. "It was that dress that convinced Adelle Hay to take me on," Marlena said, eyes sparkling. "She thought me a fine lady. The men like that, you know."

She claimed she was twenty-three, making her only three years older than Hattie. The stories she told would've shocked the Society Ladies, but Hattie found them entertaining. In one, she told of an officer who'd fallen asleep in her bed, then woke from a dream convinced a rat was chewing on the collar of his uniform. Marlena tried to convince him there was no rat, but he'd taken up his revolver and shot three holes in his uniform—and the wall—before Marlena was able to wrestle the gun from him.

"As you can imagine, Adelle was none too happy," Marlena said. "Made him pay to have the wall fixed and told him to take his business elsewhere."

"I wonder what he told his commander about the uniform," Hattie said.

Marlena shrugged. "A man with an imagination like that, he'd come up with something."

Staying at the hospital made Marlena restless, but her madam insisted that she not return to work until her syphilitic rash was gone. Dr. Greenfield was administering the usual calomel treatment, but she was puzzled by the fact that in addition to the rash, Marlena had unusually hard patches on her palms and the soles of her feet. In addition, the skin on the inside of her forearms was darkening.

"Must be from me cavorting with the devil," Marlena said, smiling slyly.

One sunny day in May, Hattie sat at the dispensary's work area, sunlight streaming over the compound she was mixing. A knock at the door interrupted her work. When she opened it, she was surprised to see Marlena, wrapped in the lavender silk dressing gown she wore when she ambled about her ward.

"Guten Tag," she said, greeting Hattie in her native tongue. "May I come in?"

Hattie hesitated. "The dispensary is a restricted area."

Laughing, Marlena charged past the threshold. "I'm no laudanum addict if that's your worry. I only need a minute of your time."

Hattie shut the door. "If you need medication, the doctor—"

"I've got the medication," Marlena said, producing a vial of powder from her dressing gown pocket. "But it needs to be mixed with rosewater." She looked around at the dispensary's shelves. "Or with wine, if you've got it."

"No wine." Hattie stretched out her hand. "May I have a look?"

Marlena handed her the vial, then padded after Hattie to her work area. Hattie opened the vial and tapped out a bit of the powder. With a stirring stick, she spread it over a piece of blotting paper, then leaned close to examine the odorless, crystalline salt.

"Where did you get this?" she asked, looking up.

"A few blocks from here."

"The apothecary on Line Street?"

Marlena shook her head. "From a doctor at a private residence. On a side street in the opposite direction of the apothecary." She waved her hand about the room. "He's got shelves and shelves of powders and tinctures, even more than you have here. And a regular laboratory too. My uncle back in Hamburg is a chemist, so I recognized much of the equipment. Glass tubes, beakers, burners."

Hattie puzzled over this. She wasn't aware of any doctors practicing near Hospital No. 11, not to mention one with a well-stocked lab. "You sought treatment from this doctor?"

Marlena nodded. "Before I came here, I had to turn away one of my regulars due to, you know, the rash. He said this doctor makes all sorts of medicinals."

"But his cure must not have worked. You still have your rash."

"The doctor said it might take a while. I took a little extra, you know, just in case. Helped myself to that while he was doing his mixing. But I need rosewater to mix it with."

"Did he say what it was?"

She scrunched her forehead, thinking. "Fowler's?"

Hattie nudged the powder toward the paper's edge. Tapping it into the vial, she held back a few grains. "I'm out of rosewater," she said. "But I'll see if I can find a suitable substitute. Does Dr. Greenfield know you've been taking this?"

Shaking her head, Marlena slipped the vial back into her pocket. "My uncle always said doctors were jealous of one another's cures. I didn't want her taking it away. Two medicines work quicker than one, yah?"

"Not necessarily," Hattie said. "There can be interactions." She nodded at the darkened skin of Marlena's forearm. "I'll check into that and let you know what I find."

~ ~ ~

By searching The American New Dispensary and The Pharmacopoeia of the United States, Hattie determined that Marlena's powder was potassium arsenite. Mixed with rosewater, it formed a solution called Fowler's, used to treat neuralgia, rheumatism, malaria, asthma, and syphilis. Used for too long or in inappropriate doses, it could cause symptoms of arsenic poisoning, including skin discoloration and thickened skin on the palms and the soles of the feet.

Dr. Greenfield frowned when Hattie brought her into the dispensary and showed her the powder, explaining what she'd learned. "I know Marlena's anxious to get out of here," the doctor said. "All the same, she shouldn't have been dosing herself without my knowledge. And I wonder about this doctor she saw. You said she mentioned a laboratory. That's highly unusual."

"Might he be doing research?"

"With war raging all around? I shouldn't think he'd have time for research. And if he's working so close to here, why haven't I heard of him?"

A doctor who worked in secret. Hattie was intrigued. That afternoon, she found Marlena at the end of a corridor, looking out a window.

"Ach, this used to be such a pretty town," she said as Hattie approached. "Now it's all cannons and soldiers."

"The war won't last forever," Hattie said. "I want to talk with you about that powder."

Marlena's face brightened. "Did you get some rosewater?"

Hattie shook her head. "No rosewater. You need to stop taking that medicine. It's causing those dark splotches on your arms."

Marlena lifted the edge of her sleeve, exposing the darkened skin. "They are unsightly, yah? But if it cures me, that's the price I'll have to pay. I could bleach them."

"It's from arsenic, Marlena. That's a poison."

Marlena's expression darkened. "The doctor never told me that."

"Is that doctor Luke Blackstone?"

"Gott in Himmel, how should I know? I only went for the medicine, and the man who sent me isn't much for introductions." Marlena smiled knowingly. "If you read the papers, you might have heard of him. Champ Farmington."

"Oh my." Hattie drew back. She'd heard of Farmington, not from the papers but from Mrs. Fletcher, who spoke of him with admiration. Hailing from East Tennessee, he led a band of a hundred guerillas that terrorized anyone who supported the Union. "Mr. Farmington recommended this doctor?"

"Right you are. Said he's never met a man with so much knowledge and so many clever ways to use it."

Like spreading smallpox and having spies put to death, Hattie thought. "I don't suppose you recall his address?"

"Not the number, no. But the house I remember well. Just a small place, but it's got a lavender door. Lavender trim around the windows too." Marlena fingered the sleeve of her dressing gown. "My favorite color, you know. Odd that a man would choose a color like that for his house. But I suppose he just rents it. Champ said he's not from around here."

"Sounds like the two of them are rather close," Hattie said.

"They've got plans, those two, if you believe Champ. Which I do, mostly. He's done some...how do you say it...outlandish things in his day."

Hattie shuddered inwardly. According to Mrs. Fletcher, Champ Farmington had shot a neighbor with Union sympathies while he was asleep in his bed.

"Plans. I wonder what those could be," Hattie said.

Marlena glanced from side to side. "Champ didn't say exactly," she said in a low voice. "He's too sly for that. But he warned me to watch myself around the doctor's powders and such. He's got things in that house that could blow this whole town up, Champ said."

"How unusual," Hattie said, trying not to sound too interested. Plenty of powders and solutions became volatile under the right conditions. But in quantities sufficient to blow up a town? That bore investigating, especially if the person in control of them happened to be Luke Blackstone.

~ ~ ~

Leaving the hospital that afternoon, Hattie strolled several blocks up Line Street in the direction opposite the apothecary. She looked down each side street but saw no houses with lavender trim. The next day, she repeated her search in the opposite direction, in case Marlena was confused. But again, her search yielded nothing.

She thought of pressing Marlena for more details but decided against it. Champ Farmington seemed a little too close to the doctor, and she didn't want word of her interest getting back to the infamous guerilla.

Instead, she paid a visit to Smokey Row the next afternoon. Many of the brothels there were in shanties and shacks. Women with heavily rouged cheeks leaned from the windows into the warm air, beckoning at men who passed by.

Partway through the Row, Hattie came upon a large green house with red trim. Above the door hung a wooden sign reading Haystack. From what Marlena had said, Line Street was five blocks to the left. Maybe the side road with the doctor's residence lay between here and there.

"Help you, ma'am?" A plump red-haired woman leaned from a second-story window, her plunging neckline revealing an ample bosom. "You look lost."

"I was," Hattie said. "But I believe I've found my way."

She followed a side street out of Smokey Row and into a modest but decidedly more respectable neighborhood. Glancing down another side street, she spotted a small house with a lavender door and lavender trim.

She knew better than to approach the house straight on. Instead, she walked around the block, formulating a plan. If Dr. Blackstone was there, she did not want to run into him. If the man at the theatre was him, he might recognize her, and then she'd lose the advantage of surprise.

Coming around the block, she studied the house from a distance, formulating a plan. She'd pose as a servant going to and from the market.

The next day, she returned after her work at the hospital. Carrying a basket, she strolled up the street as if going to the market. As she passed the lavender-trimmed house, it seemed no one was home. She hoped Blackstone hadn't moved on, if in fact he'd been there at all.

But when she returned from the market, her efforts were rewarded. Within a block of the house, she spotted a tall, middle-aged woman going out the door. Her dark hair was pulled back in a severe bun and covered with a plain gray bonnet, and worry lines marred her brow. From the woman's plain skirt and bodice, Hattie thought she must be a servant, heading home at the end of the day. So someone must occupy the house, after all, someone with the means to hire household help.

At the hospital the next day, Hattie told Edith Greenfield about finding the house and her suspicions about its occupant. When she mentioned Champ Farmington and how he'd warned Marlena about substances that could blow up the city, Edith's eyes narrowed.

"That does sound like Blackstone," she said. "Any so-called doctor who'd try to purposely infect innocent people with yellow fever wouldn't hesitate to mix chemicals that would lead to a disastrous explosion. Will you take your suspicions to Lieutenant Elliott?"

Hattie shook her head. "Not until I have proof. I just need to find a way into the house."

Edith frowned. "Too dangerous if Blackstone's there."

"He must leave now and then. I thought if I could shift the times I'm at the dispensary, I'd have a better chance of seeing him leave."

"Of course." Edith rested a hand on Hattie's shoulder. "I know how important this is to you. And from what you said, it's important to the entire war effort. An explosion at a strategic point in Nashville, like a railway station, could cripple the Union's efforts."

Chapter Fifteen

June 18, 1863

With Edith's blessing, Hattie mapped out a full surveillance plan for the lavender-trimmed house. From what she'd learned of Miss Warne's Pinkerton assignments, she knew such efforts required patience, a trait she didn't come by naturally. But as her work at the dispensary proved, Hattie could be methodical when she needed to be.

For the next several days, she strolled past the lavender-trimmed house, getting a firm grasp on the household's routines. She knew when the housekeeper arrived for work and when she left. She knew when she hung out the laundry and when she took it in, and she noticed there were no ladies' items on the line, only men's. She knew when the servant went to the market and what she bought there, in quantities that indicated she was feeding only one man.

Hattie hoped to see others coming and going, co-conspirators in whatever plots were being hatched within the house. Even more, she hoped to get a good look at the master of the house and confirm he was Blackstone. But she had yet to see anyone but the servant leaving the house.

Fortunately, the days were growing ever longer with summer's approach, so Hattie could do more of her surveillance during the evening, then hurry home as darkness fell, the streets in that part of town not being safe after dark. But the market closed at six, so she needed another reason for strolling up and down the street.

She landed on the idea of playing nursemaid. She knew little about babies, but she'd seen many women pushing buggies in the evening, presumably lulling babies to sleep. Visiting a secondhand shop, she bought a used buggy, then stuffed a blanket inside, wadding it into a shape that roughly resembled a sleeping infant. Now she had only to pray no one would stop and ask for a peek at the wee one.

Her second evening of pushing the buggy yielded results. As she neared the lavender-trimmed house, a carriage stopped in front of it. Hattie slowed her stride, fussing with the blanket while glancing now and then at the man who left the house, locked the door, then entered the carriage. Sandy-colored hair, bearded. Thin lips, pale blue eyes. Tucking the blanket around itself, she felt her heart quicken.

Luke Blackstone.

As the carriage rolled away, Hattie pushed the buggy around to the alley in back of the house. She glanced at the neighbors' windows. In all but one, the curtains were closed. She stashed her buggy out of sight of the open window, then hurried toward the lavender-trimmed back door, assuming a confident stride that she hoped would convince a curious neighbor that she had business there.

Unsurprisingly, the door was locked, so she retreated just as quickly as she'd come. She knew where Blackstone was. Now she had to find a way to prove he was up to no good.

The next morning, Hattie was dressing when Pauline woke earlier than usual. Turning to one side, the actress propped herself on an elbow. "You've got the satisfied look of a cat that's swallowed the canary."

Hattie fastened her boot. "As you did when they finally arrested your banker."

Pauline lay back, throwing her arm over her head. "And not a moment too soon. He'd gotten jumpy as a cockroach in a frypan. I told Lieutenant Elliott the next time he's got a banker on his list, I'm not interested."

"Lieutenant Elliott strikes me as a man who'd rather give direction than take it."

Rolling to her stomach, Pauline propped her chin in her hands. "I've told you before, he gives you more direction because he fancies you. He's wondering when you're going to report in, you know. Over a month, he says it's been. I assured him you're fine and going about your work with the Society. You're still attending their meetings, aren't you?"

"Most of them," Hattie said, though she'd skipped the last two so she could conduct her surveillance at the lavender-trimmed house.

"Are you going to tell him about volunteering at Hospital No. 11?"

"Only if something useful comes of it. And it very well may have. I just need to confirm a few details."

"You've been pumping the Daughters of Eve for information?"

"Not pumping, exactly. But I may have uncovered a plot to inflict widespread harm on Nashville's citizens."

Pauline's eyes widened. "And you haven't told Elliott yet?"

Hattie shook her head. "All in due time."

"You'd better hurry," Pauline said. "He's headed south soon. With me."

Hattie straightened. "You and Lieutenant Elliott are leaving Nashville together?"

Pauline laughed. "Don't go getting ideas. I'll be scouting ahead of an advance General Rosecrans is planning. Lieutenant Elliott will see me across enemy lines."

"Were you planning to tell me at some point, or would I have had to deduce this myself when I found your bed empty?"

"Don't be cross about it. It wasn't until last night that I got the final word that the plans are in place. Even so, it may be a while before I'm cleared to leave. In the meantime, I'm to go to the stables to choose a horse."

"I haven't been on a horse in ages," Hattie said wistfully. "I miss riding."

Pauline shrugged. "Maybe you should ask Elliott if you can ride along. I expect to have some fine adventures. I understand the hills are thick with guerillas."

Hattie drew back, surprised that Pauline would suggest her coming along. Perhaps her roommate no longer perceived her as a threat. "Lieutenant Elliott would never allow it. Not until I can prove I'm good for more than monitoring the Society ladies."

Pauline cocked her head. "You're up to something, aren't you?"

Hattie smiled. "Maybe."

~ ~ ~

Without knowing more, Hattie didn't think she could convince Lieutenant Elliott to go after Luke Blackstone. He didn't know Blackstone's sordid history, and while she could fill him in on the doctor's yellow fever scheme, she wasn't ready to divulge the personal reasons she wanted him apprehended. Nor did she expect the lieutenant to sound the alarm over a public woman's report. She needed evidence that what Blackstone was doing in that house posed a real danger to Nashville.

She resumed her market routine, heading out right after sunrise, figuring that if she lingered long enough at the market, she might be able to strike up a conversation with Blackstone's housekeeper. She'd learned from Thom that friendly chatter often yielded useful information.

With the sun shining and the summer roses blooming bright, she found herself missing Thom more than ever. It was hard not to think of the life they might have enjoyed together and even harder to accept that he was lost to her forever. *I miss you so much,* she thought as she strolled toward Blackstone's residence, her basket over her arm. *I'm going to do my best to make sure Blackstone pays for what he did.*

Luck was with her this morning. As she neared the house, she saw that Luke Blackstone was outside, carrying an overnight bag as he headed for a carriage parked out front. She slowed her pace. As he climbed into the carriage, she turned the corner, walking briskly away.

Her heart beating wildly, she headed for the market. There she forced herself to peruse the meager offerings, fingering the moldy onions and the scraggly carrots. Breaking her habit of only looking, she purchased two soft, sprouting potatoes. Mrs. Fletcher had been talking about digging up part of the yard to grow potatoes for winter. She'd be pleased with the offering.

When she was certain enough time had passed, Hattie left the market, turning back down Line Street and then south toward Blackstone's residence. She forced herself to assume a measured, even stride. Reaching the house, she turned up the walk. *Play your cards one by one,* she reminded herself, recalling advice Miss Warne had given her.

She wrapped on the lavender door. Footsteps sounded on the other side, and the door swung open, revealing the housekeeper, who looked sterner up close than she had from a distance.

"I've come to fetch a medicinal from Dr. Blackstone," Hattie said. "The missus sent me."

The housekeeper's gaze sharpened. "The doctor's out. You'll have to come back another day."

She started to shut the door, but Hattie stepped into the threshold. "The missus said he'd be out. She said he'd be leaving the medicinal for me back where he makes his compounds."

"The doctor allows no one in his workshop without his permission," the housekeeper said.

"But it's for the child. Only eleven years old," Hattie said, choosing an age she thought the housekeeper's own children might be. "He's come down with the typhus."

The housekeeper shook her head. "A wicked disease."

Hattie nodded vigorously. "Poor boy can't hardly sleep for the pain, and Mrs. Farmington ain't sleeping either, staying up nights with him."

The housekeeper's expression shifted, recognition in her eyes. "Farmington, you say?"

"Yes. Her husband's an associate of the doctor's, she said, so naturally, she consulted with him about her son."

The maid stiffened, her eyes signaling disapproval. "Mr. Farmington hardly strikes me as a family man."

Hattie locked her gaze on her, hoping to convey her earnestness. "It was a surprise to me as well, the first time I met him. It was the missus who'd taken me on, you see. I don't know all the circumstances, but..." She looked from side to side, as if to make sure no one else was listening, then continued in a conspiratorial tone. "I'm of the impression that the son's birth came quite shortly on the heels of their marriage. I shouldn't be telling tales out of school, but I think there's little affection between the parents. But rough as Mr. Farmington is, he dotes on the child. I hate to think of his fury if the boy should die because of a misunderstanding over the medicinals."

A look of uncertainty came over the housekeeper. "All the doctor said before leaving was to tell Mr. Farmington, should he come by, that he'd return within the week. Nothing about a medicinal."

"Ah, but you know how men are, ever forgetting the things that matter most," Hattie said. "The doctor must have been preoccupied and neglected to mention it. Surely he knows as well as anyone that without proper treatment, the child is as good as dead. It would be a shame if the blame for that fell on you. I don't know how well you know Mr. Farmington, but he's not one I'd want to cross."

"A vile excuse for a man," the housekeeper muttered. She hesitated, then gestured for Hattie to come in. "You may have a moment's look in the workshop, but no more, and only under my supervision."

"Of course," Hattie said. She followed the housekeeper past a sparsely furnished parlor to the back of the house, where she opened a door to a room opposite the kitchen. Inside it was dark as a cave, the drapes pulled tight. The housekeeper reached in her apron pocket and withdrew a lucifer match. She struck it, releasing an acrid smell that stung Hattie's nostrils, then lit a coal oil lamp.

The light was dim. "Perhaps if we open the curtains," Hattie suggested.

"Not allowed," the housekeeper said firmly. "The doctor says sunlight would damage some of the substances he keeps."

Hattie reached for the oil lamp. "I'll just carry this over to his work area then."

The housekeeper held out her hand to stop Hattie. "No. He's got explosives here too."

Hattie stepped back. So what Marlena had told her was true. In the flickering light, she scanned the shelves of bottles and vials, some filled with powders, others with liquid. She could not think of a single compound in the dispensary at Hospital No. 11 that would require such caution.

"Well, then," she said. "I'll leave the lamp be." She crossed the room to scan the beakers, pipettes, tubes, and scales on the doctor's worktable. On one end of the table were two rows of brass bottles, each fitted with a stopcock and tube. Hattie made a quick count of the bottles. Two dozen, give or take. Sniffing, she detected the faint odor of almonds.

"See what you came for?" the housekeeper asked impatiently.

"I'm looking." Hattie's heart raced. "Hard to see in the dark." Studying the work surface more closely, she spotted a slip of paper. "Ah, here's a note."

She leaned close, squinting at the paper.

100g NaOH
43g C3H3N3O3
12g C
1 hr at 600 c
Cool. Dissolve CH3OH
100g NaHCO₃
Filter and test with FeSO4
Prussian blue
EXPLOSIVE. HANDLE WITH CARE.

"You said you were after a medicinal," the housekeeper said.

"Oh, I am," Hattie said. "This note says where it is."

She turned, blocking the housekeeper's view. Did she dare slip the paper into her basket? But when Blackstone returned, he'd surely notice it was missing. Instead, she ran her finger through the air near one of the shelves while trying to commit at least a portion of the note to memory.

"Get on with it," the housekeeper said crossly.

"It should be right here." Something in the air was making her woozy. "The lighting is quite poor."

"As I said, that can't be helped," the housekeeper snapped.

Hattie would never remember the quantities. But knowing the compounds would help. NaOH—that was sodium hydroxide. C3H3N3O3 was unfamiliar. She repeated the formula over and over in her head, then moved on to CH3OH. That was menthol, wasn't it?

Her head began to pound. She ran her fingers along the edge of the second shelf while keeping one eye on the paper, committing the formulas to memory.

"It should be the third bottle from the right." Hattie pulled a vial from the shelf and examined it. "This isn't right. It must be on the next shelf."

"Lands sake, you're slow," the housekeeper muttered.

Standing on tiptoe, Hattie ran her hand along the next shelf, trying to ignore the throbbing in her head. *Ferrous sulfate. Prussian blue.*

"Ah, here it is." She withdrew a small vial from the back of the shelf. She had no idea what it contained, but with two similar vials beside it, so she hoped Luke Blackstone wouldn't notice it was gone.

She slipped the vial into her pocket and left the Blackstone residence as quickly as she could. Outside, she gulped at the fresh air, clearing her head. As she walked away, the throbbing in her head subsided.

Heading for Hospital No. 11, she whispered the contents of the note over and over until she was sure she'd committed it to memory. When she got there, she went straight to the dispensary and jotted down what she remembered. Some of the quantities eluded her. Was it one hundred grams of sodium hydroxide or sodium bicarbonate?

No matter. She only needed a general idea of what would happen when the compounds were mixed and heated. She thumbed through *The American New Dispensary*, then *The Pharmacopoeia of the United States.* Nothing in either volume told her what she needed to know.

With a sigh, she closed the books. She was putting them back on the shelf when Edith came in, looking for an ointment for treating lumbago.

"I thought you might have given up on your service here altogether," Edith said.

"I got inside Blackstone's house today," Hattie said.

Edith raised her eyebrows. "How'd you manage that?"

"I saw him leave with a travel bag. So I took a chance and approached the housekeeper with a story about him having left medication for a sick child."

Edith harumphed. "I can't see that man giving a second thought to a sick child."

"Maybe not. But the housekeeper believed me. She allowed me into the back room where the doctor works, kept under lock and key. I found a note with some ingredients."

She handed Edith the paper with her jotted notes. "This is as much as I recall. At the bottom was a warning. EXPLOSIVE. HANDLE WITH CARE. Do you have any idea what the formula is for?

Edith frowned as she studied the paper. "Not really."

"I found nothing like it in *The American New Dispensary* or the *Pharmacopoeia*. So I don't think it's for a medicinal."

"I should hope not." Edith handed the paper back to her. "Last I heard, doctors were not in the habit of exploding their patients."

"I'd like to take this information to Lieutenant Elliott, but I need to be able to prove it's dangerous."

Edith pressed her finger briefly to her lips. "There's a druggist on Market Street, not far from the Army Police Headquarters. His knowledge of the trade is extensive. He might be of help."

"Might I go there now? If it won't overly inconvenience you, I mean."

"Do as you must. You're no good here when your mind's on something else."

Hattie tucked the note into her pocket, then grabbed her purse. "I'll be back as soon as I can."

She left the hospital and caught the omnibus to Market Street. She got off a few blocks from the police headquarters, near the pharmacy Edith had mentioned. Stepping inside, she inhaled a familiar mix of medicinal smells, with camphor, eucalyptus, and menthol being the most prominent.

Behind the counter, a balding man with a thin gray beard was weighing a small mound of white powder on a scale. He looked up from his work, peering at Hattie over the top of his oval-shaped eyeglasses. "May I help you?"

"I hope so. I assist in the dispensary at Hospital No. 11."

The druggist's expression sharpened. "Instead of treating the Daughters of Eve, we'd be better off getting them out of town altogether."

She ignored this remark. Arguing the point would do nothing to further her cause. Instead, she took the paper from her pocket and handed it to him. "I'm told you're one of the better-trained druggists in the city. Might you be able to clarify what this formula is for?"

At her mention of his expertise, the druggist's expression softened. He pushed his glasses higher on his nose and studied the paper. "Prussian blue," he said. "That's an antidote to some poisons. Heavy metals, specifically. It's also an ingredient in laundry bluing."

"Oh," Hattie said. "So it's not at all dangerous?"

He returned the paper. "Not after the ferrous sulfate is added. But this preparation for Prussian blue creates cyanide salts. Those can be deadly."

"How's that?" she asked, returning the paper to her pocket.

He blinked repeatedly. "The fumes from even a small quantity can cause headache, dizziness, nausea. In large amounts, inhalation leads to convulsions and death from respiratory failure. I don't know where you got those compounding instructions, but you definitely shouldn't be experimenting with making Prussian Blue yourself."

"Oh, I wouldn't," she said. "Not now that you've explained the danger." She hesitated, choosing her words with care. "It sounds almost like cyanide salts could be used as a weapon."

"They've been used as a weapon, all right. Going back to the Romans. Nero used a naturally occurring form of cyanide to poison his enemies. If you need some Prussian Blue for your dispensary, I believe I have some in the back."

"I'll need to check with the doctor before making any acquisitions. Limited resources, you know." Hattie flashed a smile.

The druggist sighed. "Can't get half what I need either," he muttered. "Damn Yanks."

She bid him good day and left before he could offer any further opinions. Armed with definitive knowledge that Blackstone was up to no good, she headed for the Army Police Headquarters.

When she reached her destination, she was still considering the best way to tell Lieutenant Elliott about her discovery without getting into too much detail about how she'd come upon it. As before, she let herself in the back, then went straight to Elliott's office and rapped on the door. When no one answered, she knocked again, louder.

The door next to his swung open, and an officer with thick brown whiskers poked his head out. "Something I can help with, Miss?"

"I was hoping for a word with Lieutenant Elliott," she said. "He's my...superior." She supposed that was the Army's way of putting it, though it pained her to say it.

The officer shook his head. "Crinoline spies," he said. "Why the colonel takes on the likes of you women, I'll never know."

Hattie ignored the jab. "Do you expect the lieutenant back soon?"

He shrugged. "Went off to the stables with another of your ranks." He shook his head. "They say all's fair in war, but this traipsing around with you women when his wife's not a year in the grave, it's not right."

Hattie held her expression steady, not wanting to show her surprise at this revelation. When Pauline had teased Hattie about the lieutenant fancying her, had she known he was a widower? But beyond her surprise, Hattie also felt a pang of understanding, knowing how deeply a loss like that could hurt.

She squared her shoulders. "I assure you, sir, our interactions with the lieutenant are quite proper. Good day."

She turned, exiting the way she'd come in. She sniffed the air. The entire town smelled like horse manure, given how many horses tromped along the streets. But the odor was especially strong to the east, and as she followed her nose, she heard a chorus of whinnies that led her to believe she was on the right track.

Sure enough, she came upon a large set of stables. Lifting her skirts, she picked her way through straw and manure, checking each stall as she passed. Despite the difficulty walking, she loved seeing the horses as they neighed and snorted and pawed at the straw. Along with reading, riding had been her delight when she was young. She and George would go out into the countryside, following bumpy roads and galloping along the edges of cornfields, free of expectations and constraints. Then Hattie's body had changed, developing the curves of womanhood, and her mother had expressly forbidden all riding unless it was in a sidesaddle, accompanied by a chaperone.

Halfway through the stables, she came upon the lieutenant inside a stall with a fine brown mare. He had lifted the horse's front hoof and was inspecting its shoeing.

Beside him stood Pauline. She wore a riding frock, with a long train to cover a lady's legs while on a horse. Seeing Hattie, she smiled quizzically.

"Looks adequate. Now to round up a side-saddle." The lieutenant let go of the horse's hoof and looked up. "Hattie. What brings you here?"

For a moment, Hattie was tongue-tied. The officer had mentioned the lieutenant being in the company of a woman, but she hadn't expected Pauline. She had the uneasy feeling of having turned up where her presence was not only unexpected but also unwelcome.

"I need a word with you," she said. "It's important."

He frowned. "So is what we're doing here. Pauline needs to get outfitted for her assignment."

Hattie glanced at her roommate, who shrugged. "Rosecrans is preparing his troops to march south from Murfreesboro. I'm to leave in the morning so I can get out ahead of him. The lieutenant will see me off"

Hattie felt a twinge of jealousy even though she'd known about Pauline's assignment for some time. The open air, the countryside, the freedom of riding.

"I'll be back in the office the day after tomorrow," Elliott said. "You can give me your updates then, Hattie."

"I haven't come with updates. I've got information about possible sabotage. If Rosecrans is on the move, he needs to be warned."

Elliott's expression darkened. "Someone's planning to blow up a bridge? A railroad? And you heard this from Felicia Ford and her ladies?"

Hattie shook her head. "I didn't learn anything useful from the Society ladies. I learned this through volunteering at a hospital, as the Society requires."

Pauline offered a knowing smile. "A unique hospital."

"I don't know exactly what will be blown up or when," Hattie said. "But there's a doctor in Nashville who's making explosives."

Elliott's hand went to his beard, his thumb rubbing his jawline. "A doctor, you say? At the hospital where you volunteer?"

"Not at the hospital. At his residence."

"I don't follow." Elliott looked perturbed. "What were you doing at a doctor's residence?"

"I had suspicions," Hattie said. "So I found a way in."

"Suspicions you gained through another unauthorized interview with a prisoner?"

Her eyes narrowed, and she felt her temper rising. "Where I got them is irrelevant. The point is that this doctor—"

Elliott held up his hand, palm out. "Where you got your suspicions is highly relevant. So is your evidence. If you've brought some, now would be the time to produce it."

Hoping for support, Hattie glanced at Pauline. But she was brushing the horse's neck, clearly distancing herself from what was proving a contentious interaction.

Hattie produced the paper from her pocket and handed it to Elliott. "These are instructions for making cyanide salts. They give off a gas that's fatal if inhaled in sufficient quantities."

Elliott glanced at the paper, then returned it to her. "And how exactly are you proposing this compound would affect Rosecrans's advance on the enemy?"

"I – I'm not exactly sure when or how it would be used. But this doctor is not to be trusted."

Elliott locked eyes with her. "You're making several unsubstantiated claims. In general, I prefer evidence."

Hattie shoved the paper back into her pocket. "You don't seem to care about evidence from the Society ladies. You're content to waste my time and talents on gossip."

Before he could answer, she turned heel and left the stable, walking as quickly as she could manage through the muck.

~ ~ ~

Hattie had calmed down only a little by the time she returned to Mrs. Fletcher's later that afternoon. She hadn't expected Elliott to embrace her theories whole-cloth, but she'd at least expected him to hear her out. After his abrupt dismissal, she'd thought of going over his head to Colonel Truesdail but decided against it. The colonel had enough on his plate, and if forced to choose a side, she suspected he'd take Elliott's.

It was infuriating. She was so close to seeing Blackstone apprehended. She'd simply have to figure out how to make that happen without Lieutenant Elliott's help.

Upstairs in their room, she found Pauline rolling up stockings and other necessaries for her journey, a saddlebag lying across her mattress.

"You must be excited," Hattie said, flopping down on her bed. "Doing something that matters. If only Lieutenant Elliott trusted me the way he trusts you."

Pauline shook her head. "Didn't help, you going off like a half-cocked pistol today in the stables."

"Because he refused to give any credence to what I was telling him."

Pauline wedged the stockings she'd been rolling into one side of the saddlebag. "Maybe if you'd had more specifics. Like the name of that doctor you swear is up to no good."

"If he'd wanted the name, he should've asked."

Pauline lifted an eyebrow. "And you'd have told him?"

"Probably." Under the weight of Pauline's gaze, she revised her response. "Maybe."

A fresh pair of stockings in her hand, Pauline crossed the room and sat down on the bed beside Hattie. "It's fine if you're private about certain things. But you can't go around all clammed up and expect folks to trust you."

"Restraint goes with our work."

"When you're with the Society ladies, yes. But you could be more forthcoming with the lieutenant. Or for that matter, with me."

"I'm forthcoming," she said.

"Truly? Then why is it I have no idea where you came from or what exactly you did with the Pinkerton Agency or why you came to Nashville? I told you all about me not long after you arrived."

Hattie offered a wry smile. "After you chewed me up and spit me out, you mean."

"I admit I wasn't that keen on you inserting yourself in my work. Or my room."

"That wasn't my idea."

"Right. But my point is, I warmed up soon enough and told you where I'd come from and what I'm up to. You could've reciprocated."

Hattie leaned back, shoulders against the wall. "When I approached General Sharpe about coming here, he suggested I change my name and alter my appearance. Otherwise, I might be recognized. From the newspapers."

Pauline slapped her hand on her thigh. "Here I am, in the company of someone famous, and I don't even know it."

"Not famous, exactly. It's just that, out East, there was mention of my...my predicament in the press."

"You're evading," Pauline said.

Hattie sighed. "If I explain, you must promise to say nothing to Lieutenant Elliott or Colonel Truesdail. Or anyone else, for that matter."

"Do I look like one of those gossips at your Tuesday meetings?"

Hattie squinted at her. "In the right light, you bear a fair resemblance to Mrs. Hathaway."

"Never!" Pauline swatted her playfully with the stockings, and for a moment Hattie felt for her something of the affection she felt for Anne.

She proceeded to explain, in as short a form as she could manage, how she'd taken the assignment of the courier's wife, and how tragically the whole thing had ended. As she spoke of Thom's death, tears welled in her eyes.

Pauline put her arm around Hattie's shoulders. "So tragic," she said.

Wiping her eyes Hattie felt grateful for Pauline's embrace. Though speaking of Thom's death stirred her grief, it gave her some comfort to loosen her hold on the feelings she kept bottled inside.

"I vowed to hunt down Luke Blackstone," she said. "He shouldn't get off scot-free after putting Thom in his grave."

"I understand your feeling that way. But he's a spy, right? Spies catch other spies."

"But he's a doctor first. You don't pretend to help a patient and then do your utmost to see him killed. And Blackstone is also said to have masterminded a plot to cause yellow fever outbreaks in Northern cities."

Pauline's eyes widened. "But that would kill innocent people. Children, even."

"Exactly. So I know whatever he's got in mind with this cyanide business can't be good. And the timing of it, with Rosecrans moving south—that can't be good either." She squeezed Pauline's hand. "Be careful out there."

Chapter Sixteen

June 23, 1863

Hattie envied the freedom Pauline had in her new assignment, not to mention the significant information she was likely to gather while posing as a Secesh sympathizer trying to locate her brother, a Confederate soldier. She was probably already at the Confederate encampment at Shelbyville in southern Tennessee, no doubt charming soldiers with her good looks and devotion to her made-up brother.

Her search wouldn't be out of the ordinary. Both sides had their camp followers, women who hung about the troops for any number of reasons. Some were public women plying their trade, but a good number were respectable wives and sisters who couldn't bear to be apart from their husbands and brothers—or who simply seized an opportunity to escape the dull routines of their ordinary lives.

Hattie envisioned Pauline riding through the Tennessee hills, forging her own destiny, even if she'd been forced to do it riding side-saddle and wearing a proper riding habit with its annoyingly long train. While Hattie was stuck in the city, clutching that horrid bone and reciting the Society's dreadful poem in Felicia Ford's parlor every Tuesday, Pauline was aiding General Rosecrans's troops.

At today's meeting, as the Society ladies rolled bandages, they were all a-skitter over news of the Union general's advance.

"The papers say they're going right down the Lewisburg Turnpike," one woman said.

"Arrogant fools!" Felicia said. "Not enough sense to conceal their movements."

"My husband says General Bragg is moving his men from the hills toward Shelbyville. He'll have quite the reception for Rosencrans."

"Hattie, you've been quiet," Felicia said. "What are your thoughts on the impending battle?"

Hattie's true thoughts were that such an obvious march must be a ploy to draw Bragg and his men from the hills. Instead, she said, "I expect Shelbyville will hold."

"The hill country around those parts is simply dreadful," one of the larger ladies said, the skin under her chin waggling. "Forests, mountain lions, bushwhackers," she said, using the common term for guerillas.

"I thought the bushwhackers were on our side. Like Champ Farmington," Hattie said, glad for the opportunity to find out what the ladies had to say about Blackstone's associate.

"Indeed," Felicia said. "Mr. Farmington has done a good deal for our cause."

"But he's an outlaw, isn't he?" Hattie said. "Roaming the Cumberland hills with his guerillas, looting and stealing and killing whoever gets in their way. It all sounds rather ruthless."

Felicia patted her arm. "This is war, dear. Ruthlessness is to be expected."

The conversation turned from guerillas to the exorbitant price of butter. But as Hattie rolled one bandage after the other, her thoughts stayed on Champ Farmington and the Cumberland hills. She wondered what sort of scouting was being done to curb their activities. Not much, she decided. Lieutenant Elliott seemed to lack the imagination to meet a problem head-on. As he'd requested, she'd reported to his office after Pauline left. He'd said he'd take her concerns about Blackstone under advisement, which she figured was his way of dismissing them whole-cloth.

But Hattie knew Blackstone was a threat, and she didn't put anything past him. She wanted him arrested, captured, and made to pay for what he'd done. She'd thought of going back to John Elliott and divulging her history with the doctor. But dismissive as he was, she feared he'd only accuse her of more unsubstantiated claims and lack of evidence. She couldn't bear that.

She wished Pauline would come home soon. Despite their rocky start, Pauline was the only confidante she had here, and she seemed to understand the enigmatic lieutenant far better than Hattie did. In the meantime, Hattie was keeping an eye on Blackstone's house during her daily strolls. Of late, she'd seen little activity. The windows remained shuttered, and she wondered if the doctor was still away. But she only saw a sliver of what went on there each day. It would take a team of spies to observe the actual goings-on.

~ ~ ~

As the days passed, Hattie grew increasingly restless in her routines. Worried about Pauline, she followed newspaper reports on Rosecrans's advance. After occupying Nashville, the Federals had installed Union-friendly editors at most of the papers, and so the reports were colored with laudatory accounts of Rosecrans' tactics and disparaging views of Confederate General Bragg's hamhanded response.

Even the Society ladies were wringing their hands over how Rosecrans' advance into Middle Tennessee was progressing. Confederate troops had come out of the Tennessee hills to bolster General Bragg's response, and Union forces were swooping in to control what passes they could.

By July 4, the papers were reporting a Union victory. Having diverted Bragg's troops, General Rosecrans had driven the Confederates from middle Tennessee, taking over Bragg's former headquarters at Tullahoma. But East Tennessee, including Chatanooga and Knoxville, remained in Rebel hands. Could Pauline have been sent there? Hattie didn't think she'd planned on being away so long.

Nashville was an odd place to celebrate Independence Day. Buntings and flags were displayed all over the city, and the Union soldiers stationed there were raucous. In addition to Rosecrans's victory, they celebrated a Union win at Gettysburg, Pennsylvania. General Grant had finally prevailed in Vicksburg, Mississippi, too. Hattie was especially pleased with Grant's victory at Vicksburg, having passed along information before her arrest that had likely helped him prevail.

While the Union had much cause to celebrate, Southern sympathizers in Nashville were understandably subdued, and a general sullenness prevailed alongside the military's merrymaking. Hattie feared that even more of the Secesh were turning to the Sons of Liberty, an organization that operated with far more secrecy and nefarious intent than the Soldiers' Aid Society. The Sons of Liberty were the latest iteration of the Knights of the Golden Circle, a pro-slavery group Thom had told her about. While the Union victories were cause for celebration, no one expected the South to go down without a fight. Aligned with the Copperheads, the Sons of Liberty were encouraging Union desertions and blocking enlistments.

Knowing her husband was involved. Hattie's friend Anne had personal concerns about these groups, "They seem to have big plans," she'd written in response to Hattie's letter. "No good can come of it." Hattie worried for Anne, carrying this troubling burden. In a broader sense, she worried about the festering resentments such groups encouraged, whether or not they led to the big plans Anne mentioned.

All this was on Hattie's mind as she headed for her daily surveillance at the Blackstone residence. All around, guns were going off. If she hadn't known this was Independence Day, she'd have feared the shooting meant the tides of battle had turned toward Nashville. The ruckus seemed to make her especially impatient. She was tired of merely strolling past a house without being able to do anything about the harm the man inside might be plotting.

Rounding a corner, she decided to act. Playing the part of the Farmington servant, she'd go up to the house and ask for more medication. If Blackstone came to the door instead of the housekeeper, she'd have to hope he didn't recognize her.

She strode up the walk and knocked on the door, then waited for the sound of the housekeeper's footsteps. Hearing only silence, she knocked louder.

A gray-haired neighbor stuck her head out the window. "The doctor's moved on," the woman said.

Moved on. It took a second for Hattie to grasp what this meant. "When?" she asked.

"Last week," the neighbor said.

"I don't suppose you know where he's gone."

The neighbor tilted her head side to side, reminding Hattie of a sparrow. "Haven't the slightest," she said. "But if it's doctoring you're after, you're better off with Doc Brand over on Line Street. This one here had folks coming and going at the oddest hours. Didn't seem a reputable practice if you know what I mean."

Hattie thanked her for the information. Discouraged, she left the property. If she'd come at those odd hours, she might have been able to track down Blackstone's associates. Now he was gone, and his hydrogen cyanide with him. There was no telling what damage he'd do or where he'd do it.

She blamed Lieutenant Elliott for his escape. Elliott, with his protocol and his tightly controlled assignments that yielded nothing useful. He shouldn't have needed to know her history with Blackstone to understand the threat. She'd done everything the lieutenant asked and then some. He should have trusted her.

It was time to speak her mind to Elliott. He needed to know he hadn't cowed her into submission, needed to know the result of his obstinate refusal to acknowledge her concerns.

Amid the continuing gunfire of Fourth of July revelers, she hurried to the Army Police Headquarters. As usual, she approached from behind the building. Pausing in the shadow of a spreading elm, she waited for a stranger to pass. As she was about to come out of the shadows, Lieutenant Elliott emerged from the back door of the headquarters.

She hurried after him, but he was walking briskly, and she struggled to close the distance between them without attracting attention. He turned toward the City Hotel. To her surprise, he entered the Rivertown Saloon next door.

She slowed her pace. Elliott didn't seem the type to drink for pleasure. Likely he'd gone in to retrieve some wayward soldier. Instead of charging in after him, she decided to wait. She entered the hotel, then stood near a lobby window, keeping watch. The last time she'd been in this lobby, she'd witnessed Mildred Trident's arrest.

Where was Mildred now, Hattie wondered. Had her sick boy recovered? Hattie didn't regret talking with her even if it had set Lieutenant Elliott against her. Mildred had all but confirmed Blackstone as the mastermind of the quinine smuggling ring. And yet that hadn't roused Elliott to action either.

The more she considered all the information the lieutenant had ignored, the more infuriated she became with him. When was he going to emerge from the saloon? Standing at the window, her feet began to ache. Twice she had to assure hotel staff that there was nothing they could help with, she was only waiting. She must look like a jilted lover, she thought, a tragic figure waiting for a man determined to evade her.

The minutes ticked away on the lobby's grandfather clock—fifteen, then thirty. She grew more and more perturbed. What was Elliott doing in a saloon when he should be at work?

When forty minutes had passed, she left her post, pushing through the hotel doors and out onto the street. She marched toward the saloon. She wouldn't be the first woman to enter there, she told herself.

She barged through the door. Heads turned as she entered, and a few of the men smiled slyly. Reputable women didn't frequent saloons. They must think her a public woman, Hattie realized, glad for the darkness that hid the color rising in her cheeks. Looking side to side for Elliott, she proceeded through the bar, the pungent smell of cigar smoke filling her nostrils.

She was about to give up, thinking Elliott must have somehow left the saloon without her seeing him. Then she spotted the lieutenant sitting alone at a small corner table. A lantern glowed dimly from the center of the table, but it did little to brighten the corner, and she had to look twice to make sure it was him. The dress coat he'd been wearing was slung over the back of a chair beside him, and his white shirt was unbuttoned at the collar. An empty shot glass on the table in front of him, he sat with his head in his hands.

She stepped close. "Lieutenant Elliott?"

He raised his head, then shook it slightly. "Hattie." He offered a weak smile. "What a pleasant surprise."

She held her head high. "I – I need to speak with you. I saw you leaving the headquarters, and I—"

He waved his hand at an empty chair. "Have a seat."

"I'd rather not." Disgust rose in her. The lieutenant ordered her about, and yet he had no more self-control than this? "I'll come back another time when you're presumably more...approachable."

She turned to leave, dreading that she'd have to pass back through the gauntlet of leering men to exit the saloon.

Elliott plucked her sleeve. She whirled around, and he straightened. "I'm approachable now, Miss Thomas. Quite approachable."

Through the smoky darkness, she saw a man at a nearby table turn, his interest no doubt piqued by Elliott's loud pronouncement. She raised a finger to her lips. "If it's all the same to you, I'd prefer you not draw attention."

Elliott held up both hands, palms out as if to convey his innocence. "Please. Sit. I promise to mend my ways."

She glanced again at the man at the nearby table, who was still staring. If she left now, she'd only draw more attention.

"I've only got a moment." She lowered herself into the empty chair, avoiding the glow of the lantern in the center of the table.

Elliott folded his hands on the table as if it were his office desk. "What's on your mind?"

She hesitated. She could hardly go into the specifics here. "There has been an opportunity missed. A significant opportunity."

He sat a moment, staring into the lantern's light, his eyes shining. Then he looked up at her, gazing so intently that she had to force herself not to look away. "Missed opportunities are a plague upon my life."

"I don't follow your meaning, Lieutenant Elliott."

"John." His hand darted for hers. "We are friends, after all, aren't we?"

She pulled her hand from his reach. Toward the front of the saloon, a sloppy chorus of "When Johnny Comes Marching Home" broke out. "We are cordial with one another," she said. "As is necessary for our joint efforts."

John Elliott shook his head as if she'd delivered some sort of dreaded news. "Our efforts. Well, there's that. Though at the moment, I fear I'm of little use."

He'd had too much to drink. She should leave now. But the sorrow in his eyes evoked her pity. "It's only that you've overindulged, Lieutenant. You're not alone in that regard. There's much to celebrate today."

"Which makes it all the more difficult." He pushed the empty shot glass aside, then stood, offering his arm to her. "I should be leaving. Allow me?"

She stood. At the front of the saloon, the raucous singing had disintegrated into backslapping and shouted hoorahs. "I don't suppose there's another way out?"

"There's always another way out." Elliott tilted his head toward the back door.

She took his arm, and they proceeded to the door. He held it open for her, his gentlemanly manners restored. But outside, she saw how he swayed, unsteady on his feet.

"I trust you can make your way home," she said.

"A scout like me? Absolutely." Stepping toward her, he stumbled, and she caught his arm.

"Perhaps I should have someone call a carriage."

"That won't be necessary." He raised his hand, gently brushing her cheek. "But it's so kind of you to offer."

She stepped back. "You're not yourself, Lieutenant."

He shook his head. "I suppose not."

From the direction of the fort, several rounds of celebratory gunfire sounded. "I believe you've done enough celebrating for one afternoon," she said.

He gazed at her intently. "You misunderstand me," he said. "It's...it's just that I've gotten word...word that Pauline...Pauline has been captured."

Hattie's hand flew to her mouth. "When? How?"

"Days ago. Ran into trouble trying...trying to get back."

More celebratory volleys sounded. "So that's why you were...indulging."

He hung his head. "I blame myself. I never should have sent her out."

She set her hand on his shoulder. "Pauline's tough. Wily. She'll get out of this."

She very much hoped this was true.

Chapter Seventeen

July 7, 1863

The following Tuesday, as Hattie was leaving the boardinghouse to spend another tedious afternoon in the company of Felicia Ford's Society ladies, Mrs. Fletcher called to her from the kitchen.

"There you are," she said as if Hattie had spent the morning avoiding her. In Pauline's absence—called away by her mother's illness was the excuse Pauline had given—Mrs. Fletcher's mood had soured considerably. Pauline was a lively presence at meals, sharing theatre gossip and tales of growing up among the Indians. Hattie suspected a good deal of what she said was embellished if not outright fabricated, but Mrs. Fletcher didn't seem to care.

"I'm headed out for the afternoon," Hattie said.

The day was sweltering, and yet Mrs. Fletcher, ever a creature of habit, had stoked the oven for biscuits. She wiped the sweat from her brow with the back of her floury hand. "Message came for you. It's over there." She nodded at a paper on the table.

Hattie crossed the kitchen and retrieved the folded paper, addressed to Miss H. Thomas. "When did this arrive?"

"Hour ago, maybe. Lad that brought it pounded on the door like he meant to wake the dead. Surprised you didn't hear."

Hattie unfolded the paper and read the message:

Meet me 2 o'clock. J.E.

Mrs. Fletcher shoved the biscuits in the oven, then shut the door with a grunt. "Got a beau, have you?" she asked, confirming Hattie's suspicion that she'd read the message.

Hattie wished she had Pauline's olive-toned skin, so the flush she now felt creeping over her cheeks wouldn't show. "Just a...friend."

Mrs. Fletcher brushed her hands on her apron. "Don't your Society ladies meet at two?"

"That's right," Hattie said. If John Elliott were truly such a stickler for detail, he should have known that. Well, he'd have to wait. After their awkward encounter at the saloon, she didn't relish the idea of meeting with him Then again, maybe he had some news of Pauline.

She shoved the note into her skirt pocket. "I'm headed to the Society meeting now. I'd best not be late."

She hurried for the door, eager to escape any more prying questions. "Dinner's at five," Mrs. Fletcher called after Hattie, as if that were some new revelation.

~ ~ ~

It was nearly as hot in Felicia Ford's parlor as it was in the boardinghouse kitchen. The ladies sat fanning themselves, each with a painted silk fan that matched her dress. Many had even forsaken their hoops in favor of morning dresses. Hattie wished she'd thought to grab a fan from Pauline's extensive collection of accessories.

Seeing she was without a fan, Felicia arranged a seat for Hattie next to the Negro servant girl positioned in a corner of the room, waving a huge fan like the ones used every summer afternoon at Hattie's grandfather's Louisiana plantation. As usual, piles of cloth sat on the table, ready to be torn and folded into bandages. But between the heat and the recent Confederate defeat at Tullahoma, a general listlessness pervaded, and none of the ladies seemed eager to get to work.

"Such a shame about Bragg," one of them said dolefully.

"Apparently, he lost communication with his generals," another said.

"I'll bet it was Yankee spies, spoiling his plans," Felicia said.

Hattie suppressed a smile. "Surely General Bragg has scouts too."

"Of course he does," said the lady sitting next to her. "Why, they operate in plain sight. Come up to Nashville and take the oath of allegiance so they can cross the lines as often as they please."

Around the room, the ladies tittered, murmuring their pleasure at this deception. Hattie clenched her teeth. So this was the Army Police's idea of defending Union strongholds, trusting Rebels who took the oath of allegiance? No wonder a man with villainous plans like Luke Blackstone could come and go as he pleased.

Hattie reached for her lemonade, taking a long, cool sip. With market goods so diminished, she had no idea how Felicia Ford managed to get lemons. Maybe those oath-taking scouts were smugglers too.

More than ever, she felt the ridiculousness of her work with the Society ladies. And after seeing Lieutenant Elliott's sorry condition on July 4, she felt even less inclined to respect his assignments. She shared his distress over Pauline's fate, but she hadn't drowned her sorrows in whisky. Not that such options were as open to women as men, but there were plenty of medicinals mixed with alcohol that she knew women to consume in large quantities. In fact, she'd smelled it more than once on the breath of one doe-eyed Society lady who was nearly as young as Hattie. When the other women channeled their energies into complaints, this younger woman withdrew inwardly. Hattie had tried to draw her out, but all she could ascertain was that the woman despaired of her young husband returning from battle alive.

Today's chatter turned to speculation over Bragg's next move now that he'd been pushed back to Lookout Mountain near the Georgia line. Tired of sitting idly, Hattie reached for a square of cloth and began ripping it into strips. She could scarcely share her supposition that whatever Bragg did next, he'd have the advantage of a malevolent doctor's arsenal of hydrogen cyanide.

She rolled a strip and placed it on the table. "Oh, do give that up, Hattie dear," Felicia said. "This war won't be won on bandages."

"But if the Army Police come—" Hattie said.

Interrupting, Felicia waved away her concern. "The Army Police have bigger fish to fry."

"Smugglers, you mean?" Hattie said.

Felicia's eyes twinkled. "Child's play, compared to what's being planned."

The lady beside her nodded. "The next time Rosecrans comes knocking on a Rebel door, he won't like what awaits him."

"Might even be lethal." Felicia took a long draw from her lemonade.

Hattie's heart quickened. "Assassination, you mean?"

Felicity shook her head. "Assassination is bad form, dear. But there are other ways."

Hattie returned to ripping cloth into strips. At least this was something she could report to Elliot. Of course, he'd only say the information was too vague to act on. But what if the threat to Rosecrans was Blackstone and his hydrogen cyanide? She turned over and over the facts the chemist had told her, about how lethal the poison was if inhaled and how as far back as the Roman Empire, it had been deployed against enemies. What she kept coming back to were the stoppered bottles lined up on Blackstone's work table. The tubes protruding from the stoppers—if those were aimed through inconspicuous holes drilled in the walls of the general's headquarters, the entire leadership of the Army of the Cumberland might be wiped out in one fell swoop.

Rolling the strips she'd torn, Hattie only half-heard the women's banter, which had come round to one of their favorite topics, the Negroes who'd escaped the South and settled in Nashville. Lazy troublemakers—that was the consensus on these escaped slaves, an assessment that made Hattie fume. These people had suffered a lifetime of abuse, many escaping within an inch of their lives. A good number of the men were fighting for the Union. At least one woman was, too, if the rumors Hattie heard were correct, about a Negro named Harriet Tubman who scouted for the Union in southern swamps while also delivering her countrymen to freedom.

The sound of Hattie's name pulled her from her reverie. "Sorry," she said. "What was that?"

"I was asking," said Felicia, "if you think Rosecrans will make a play for Chattanooga now."

"Or Knoxville," said a heavy-set woman.

"Having been such a short time in Tennessee, I don't have an opinion," Hattie said. In truth, she wasn't even sure where Chattanooga and Knoxville were.

Felicia set a hand on her knee. "You mustn't use that excuse, dear. It behooves us all to pay attention. Otherwise, what good are we to the cause?"

"You're right," Hattie said. "I'm afraid I was lost in my thoughts. My friend, Pauline, was called home to tend to her mother, and I've been wondering how she's faring."

"The actress?" asked the youngest of the ladies, drawn from her usual sullen silence. "What a shame she had to leave."

"These are such troubling times to be ill," said a lady as she waved her pink fan.

This was her chance to mention Blackstone, Hattie realized. Before, she'd feared her inquiries would get back to him. But there was no danger of that now that he'd moved on. "Indeed," she said. "It's hard to get doctoring, what with all the wounded who need treating. But Pauline says her mother has an excellent physician whose allegiance to the South couldn't be stronger. Blackstone, I believe she said his name was."

"Good for her," Felicia said. "Dr. Blackstone is a loyal and accomplished physician. If only he'd stayed in Nashville. But I understand he's gone to Chattanooga."

Hattie's stomach fluttered at this revelation. "I do hope he's able to help Pauline's mother," she said. "I miss Pauline. And so does the theatre's management, I'm sure."

With that, the conversation shifted to the theatre. Steadying her hands, Hattie rolled another bandage. Now that Blackstone was gone, there was no reason for her to stay in Nashville. She'd just have to convince John Elliott to dispatch her to Chattanooga.

~ ~ ~

After the Society meeting, Hattie went to the Army Police Headquarters feeling both dread and anticipation. When she entered Elliott's office, she found him standing at his desk, studying a map. As he looked up at her, she saw none of the emotion he'd displayed at the saloon. His shirt was properly buttoned to the collar, and the brass buttons of his coat looked as if they'd been freshly polished.

"It's well past two o'clock, Miss Thomas," he said coolly.

Without waiting for him to offer, she sat, arranging her purse in her lap. "The Society meets on Tuesdays at two," she said, matching his icy tone. "I'd have thought you knew that."

He rubbed his jawline. "There are a good number of other details I'm managing," he said.

"At any rate, I'm here now. Why did you summon me here, Lieutenant?"

For a moment, his expression softened. Then the set of his mouth hardened again, and his gaze bore into her. "You are nothing if not direct, Miss Thomas." He cleared his throat. "I wanted to apologize for my conduct the other day. It was unbefitting my position."

"You were understandably distressed. Have you any word of Pauline?"

He shook his head. "Our scouts think she was apprehended somewhere along this road." He traced a finger west to east along a red line near the bottom of the map. "There was fighting all around. Here, here, and here." He pointed to towns whose names meant nothing to her. "Even if she were to attempt an escape, there's danger throughout Eastern Tennessee. Guerillas, all over the Cumberland."

"Surely Colonel Truesdail is working to secure Pauline's release in a prisoner exchange?"

"He will. But first, we have to verify where she's being held and who's in charge."

Hattie looked more closely at the map, locating Chattanooga to the south and Knoxville to the east of Nashville. "The ladies seem to think the next Union effort will be in Chattanooga or Knoxville. The Rebels must be fortifying their positions there. So perhaps—"

"No need to trouble yourself with such details," the lieutenant interrupted, rolling up his map. "You never have in the past."

She locked eyes with him, her hackles raised. "If you intend to criticize my work, I wish you'd just come out and say what fault you find with it. Clearly, you don't think highly of me, keeping me in my place with a meaningless assignment that any schoolgirl could take on."

His jaw tightened. "You lack experience, Miss Thomas."

She stood. Pressing her hands flat on his desk, she leaned forward. "I've had experiences you can't begin to imagine."

He offered a twisted smile. "You haven't experienced a fraction what I have in this war."

"And Pauline has? You trusted her with a challenging assignment."

"Pauline has fortitude."

"And I don't?" Her voice was rising, she knew.

"You have ample opportunity to prove yourself right where you are."

She slapped her hand on the polished wood of his desk. "Nothing I do will ever satisfy you. I spent weeks tracking a doctor whose chemicals may well be used against our troops. I got myself into his workshop and determined the compound. I reported all of this to you, and you dismissed it as farfetched."

His gaze held steady. "In this division, we do not go willy-nilly after fanciful imaginings. We assemble information. We prioritize. We proceed in an orderly fashion."

Her hands trembled. This man was exactly the wrong sort of person to be running a spy operation. The last person she wanted her fate tied to.

"All that assembling and prioritizing and order, and look where it landed Pauline."

Elliott's face clouded. He glanced away, and when he looked back at her, his gaze was even harsher than before. "I've heard enough, Miss Thomas. You may return next week, assuming you've got something of actual value to report."

~ ~ ~

Hattie was still fuming when she reported to the hospital the next day. Approaching Edith Greenfield's office with a list of supplies needed to restock the dispensary, she found the doctor, who she hadn't seen in days, in an equally foul mood.

"The provost marshal is rounding up public women," Edith said. "Even from this hospital. He's hired a steamer to take them to Louisville. Apparently, he thinks that's a grand solution to the problem of Smokey Row."

"At least that will free up some beds here," Hattie said.

The doctor shook her head. "It's the wrong tack entirely. Do you think Louisville wants our public women? They'll be shipped on to the next town and the next till the steamer runs out of river."

"But short of a cure, what other solution is there? You've said yourself that most of these women will go back to their work as soon as they're released, and their diseases will spread to more soldiers."

"Some discipline among the soldiers would help," Edith snapped. "Though I don't suppose there's any hope for that. The men are somehow never thought to be the problem. I told the provost marshal that what he needs to do is make Smokey Row respectable."

"How would he manage that? He can't just snap his fingers and turn the brothels into ice cream parlors."

Edith straightened. "He could license their activities."

"You must be joking. What those women do isn't legal."

"And why not? The same men who partake of their services beneath the sheets are the ones who most loudly voice their objections in the public sphere." Edith folded her arms at her chest. "If the activity can't be stopped, it must at least be controlled. Make it legal and issue licenses, under the condition that licensed women be examined weekly for signs of disease, and the license revoked if they're found unhealthy."

Hattie tipped her head, considering this. "You know, that does make some sense."

"Try telling that to the provost marshal," Edith said darkly. "I've talked myself blue, and instead he's gone and contracted with a steamer captain. The marshal clearly doesn't understand that these women will be back. They have fortitude."

The mention of fortitude stirred Hattie's anger anew, recalling her meeting with Elliott. How dare the lieutenant assume she lacked it, after all she'd been through?

She handed her supply list to Edith. "Be glad you're dealing with the provost marshal and not Lieutenant Elliott. The man's impossible. I told him what Blackstone was up to, and he dismissed it as speculation. Now Blackstone's left town."

Edith looked up from the supply list. Her gray eyes, always observant, looked especially keen. "You're rather single-minded, you know."

"Of course I'm single-minded. You know what Blackstone did to me, did to Thom."

"I do know. But does Lieutenant Elliott?"

Hattie's hands tightened into fists. "There's no point in telling him. If he knew how I'd failed to save Thom, he'd think even less of me than he already does. He's a hard man. Judgmental. Controlling. Everything by the book. He doesn't know the first thing about real spy work. No wonder Pauline ended up getting captured."

Edith's eyebrows lifted. "Your friend was captured?"

Hattie nodded. "I hate to think of her...enduring anything like what happened to me. I wish there was something I could do."

Edith set aside the supply list. "Perhaps the best thing you could do is to align yourself with the lieutenant."

"Surely you jest. I told you, the man's inflexible. When I went to see him today, all he did was lecture me about assembling and prioritizing and putting things in order. A fine one he is to talk. You should have seen the state he was in on Independence Day. I'd wager he drained half a bottle of whisky all by himself. I've half a mind to report him to Colonel Truesdail."

"You think that would be wise?"

Hattie's eyes flashed. The idea had only just now occurred to her, but it seemed altogether reasonable. "Why not?"

Taking up a pen, Edith rapped it on the desk. "The lieutenant may have a point, you know."

Hattie crossed her arms. "So now you're taking his side."

"I've observed you in the dispensary." Edith's calm tone irritated Hattie all the more. "You're orderly. You prioritize. You pay attention to details. But when it comes to Blackstone, you do none of that."

"I went by his house every day for weeks. That's not orderly? I memorized the formula I found. That's not paying attention to details?"

"I'm only saying that you're incredibly fixated on your pursuit of Luke Blackstone."

"You said yourself he's dangerous, trying to infect whole cities with yellow fever."

"Oh, he's dangerous, all right. Which is all the more reason you should proceed with caution." Edith leaned forward. "What can you tell me about the recent fighting at Tullahoma?"

Hattie shrugged. "What's to tell? The Union prevailed. And I don't see what that has to do with Luke Blackstone."

"Luke Blackstone isn't plotting whatever he's plotting for his own amusement. He's working on a strategy that fits in with a larger strategy. Your focus is so narrow, you see only him. Unless you take the time to truly understand the bigger picture, you shouldn't expect to succeed."

"There are plenty of people following every campaign of this war," Hattie said. *Like Anne,* she thought. Smart and informed and methodical.

Edith shrugged. "Do as you please then. You always do."

"I don't know what you mean." There was no sense in continuing this conversation. "Good day, Edith."

Hattie strode from the room, the door shuddering in its hinges as she slammed it behind her.

Chapter Eighteen

August 2, 1863

M uch as Hattie wanted to reject Edith's admonishments, she couldn't entirely dismiss them. It was true that her focus was narrow. She wanted Blackstone apprehended. Not that there was anything wrong with that. If she didn't pursue him, who would? Certainly not John Elliott, so caught up with methods and procedures that he couldn't see the forest for the trees.

And Hattie did prefer to do as she pleased. But who was Edith to talk, going about dressed in bloomers?

But then there was what Edith said about strategy. Hattie had never much bothered with understanding the context of her assignments. She believed in the Union cause, restoring the nation to wholeness and abolishing slavery once and for all. The details of battles and tactics didn't interest her except as they pertained to people she cared about.

But she had to admit that the details of the current situation in Tennessee might indeed be significant to Luke Blackstone and his guerilla associate Champ Farmington. It wouldn't hurt to deepen her understanding, and it would be a good diversion from her worry over Pauline, which grew with each passing day.

So when she wasn't in the dispensary or attending Society meetings, Hattie spent her time reading newspapers, studying maps, and talking to soldiers. Soon she knew the locations of not just Knoxville and Chattanooga but also little towns like Shelbyville, Wartrace, and Maryville. She also learned that President Lincoln himself was urging his generals to retake East Tennessee as quickly as possible, and she understood why—the region was rich in grain and livestock, plus it was a vital railroad corridor.

She paid special attention to anything involving the East Tennessee town of Knoxville since the Society ladies had mentioned it. Union soldiers were talking about Knoxville too. If action was planned there, Hattie expected Blackstone to be in the thick of it.

With her increased understanding, she picked up more from the Society ladies than she had before. She forced herself to deliver these tidbits to Lieutenant Elliott, including rumors of a local man who was nabbing free Negroes and selling them in the South. With her newfound knowledge, she was able to speak with more authority than before, and to her surprise, Elliott seemed appreciative.

Hattie shared Elliott's frustration over how little was known of Pauline's fate. At one point, he'd been told she was at General Bragg's headquarters. Then he'd gotten reports she was being held at General Forrest's compound. Another scout reported that Pauline was sick, but that General Bragg meant to see her hanged as soon as she was well.

All talk, Hattie hoped. Surely the Rebs wouldn't execute a woman. But Lieutenant Elliott seemed worried. The Confederates had rejected offers of a prisoner exchange, and he feared they meant to make an example of Pauline.

With this in mind, Hattie began to formulate a plan. While Rosecrans was said to be gearing up to drive the Rebs completely out of Chatanooga, the Union's General Burnside was pressing toward Knoxville in East Tennessee. An advance regiment was said to have already destroyed Confederate-held railroads and disrupted communications there.

At Hattie's request, Elliott had given her a map of the region, which she kept in her armoire, tucked into the long, puffy sleeve of one of the dresses Pauline had left behind. Each night, she'd lock the door to her room, unroll the map, and study it. Chattanooga or Knoxville? The ladies' idle speculations took on new importance. Blackstone could well be in one of those cities, she thought. But which one?

The key might be Farmington, Hattie thought. Blackstone wasn't the sort of man who'd soil his hands with the actual poisoning of Federal troops. As with his yellow fever plot, he'd convince some underling to do the dirty work. The notorious Rebel guerilla would be a perfect choice, with a band of men who could sneak into a Union encampment and release the poison.

If only Hattie knew Farmington's whereabouts. She thought Marlena might know. But as Edith Greenville had warned, Marlena had been forced out of Nashville. Along with a hundred or so public women, she'd been herded onto the steamer Idahoe, which took the women to Louisville. And as Edith had predicted, officials in Louisville had refused to allow the steamer to dock, forcing it to continue on to Cincinnati, where city officials had insisted it dock on the Kentucky side of the river.

At this point, the women were understandably restless, with few provisions to sustain them other than the whisky they'd reportedly smuggled aboard. A few even tried to swim for shore, but they were turned back.

Edith said the steamer was now headed back to Nashville, due to dock this evening. Hattie decided to insert herself among the curiosity seekers who would surely be there to meet it. With any luck, she'd be able to corner Marlena as she got off the boat and inquire about Champ Farmington.

The evening was hot and humid. As Hattie suspected, a crowd had gathered at the dock, among them several rough-looking men. She scanned the faces of the women as they came off the steamer. They were a lively bunch, shouting and blowing kisses to the crowd.

At last, she spotted Marlena, her long brown locks disheveled and her white dress soiled. Hattie hurried toward her. For a moment, she lost sight of her altogether, but then she saw that Marlena had stopped to banter with one of the men.

As she caught up with her, Marlena had turned from the man and was sauntering off in the direction of Smokey Row.

"Marlena," Hattie said, hoping she didn't sound too out of breath from her pursuit. "You remember me?"

Marlena flashed a smile. "Yah, of course. The girl that keeps the medicines at the hospital." She sidled close. "I don't suppose you bring me some laudanum?"

"You know Dr. Greenfield keeps a close eye on the laudanum." Hattie fished some coins from her purse. "I...we were wondering if you might come by the hospital so the doctor can see how you've fared since your release."

Eying the coins, Marlena slowed her pace. "And if I've got the pox again, she'll have me locked up there all over again. No thank you."

Hattie jangled the coins. "I understand. Perhaps you could just answer a few questions and be on your way."

Marlena raised an eyebrow. "I'd still get the money?"

"Of course." Hattie pressed the coins in Marlena's hand, then took a small notebook and pencil from her purse.

"Any fatigue?" she asked.

Marlena shook her head.

"Rash?"

Marlena showed her arms. "Gone. The black parts too."

"Good," Hattie said. She asked a few more questions, and Marlena duly answered.

"Almost finished," Hattie said, noting that Marlena was beginning to look impatient. "I just need to ask about your...um...clientele. You mentioned Champ Farmington. I don't suppose you know whether he's had symptoms?"

Marlena's lips formed a sneer. "Champ Farmington can go to hell for all I care. Ran back to Sparta, leavin' me high and dry."

"I see." Hattie slipped her notebook and pencil back in her purse. "Well, I suppose if he's feeling unwell, that doctor friend of his can treat him."

Marlena looked at her curiously. "You remember about that doctor?"

Hattie shrugged. "I remember how that powder he gave you darkened your skin."

"Didn't do me no favors, that one. Not Champ neither. Sparta can have 'em both."

An open carriage pulled up alongside where they stood. A large woman in a red silk gown leaned from the window, her face powdered and rouged. "Marlena!" she effused. "I've been looking everywhere for you."

"Adelle!" Marlena said.

So this was Adelle Hay, Hattie thought, the madam of the infamous Haystack brothel.

Adelle popped the carriage door. "Made a friend on the boat, did you?" She studied Hattie. "You've got a fresh look about you, sweetie. And as luck would have it, there's room for you at the Haystack."

"Oh, I'm not seeking employment," Hattie stammered.

"She's from the hospital, Adelle," Marlena said as she climbed into the carriage. "Look how you've made her blush."

The two of them laughed uproariously as if this was the funniest thing they'd heard in ages. Then Adelle shut the door, and the carriage rolled away.

~ ~ ~

Back in her room, the window open to let in the evening air, Hattie took her map from the sleeve of Pauline's dress. As crickets chirped, she unrolled the map across her bed and located Sparta, halfway between Nashville and Knoxville. If her hunch was correct, Knoxville must be where Blackstone intended to use his chemicals, with Farmington's help.

The only way to know for sure was to go after them. Trying to convince Elliott to send her to Sparta was pointless. But what about Colonel Truesdail? He'd want to know why Hattie was bringing her request to him instead of the lieutenant, of course. But there were ways to explain that.

Hattie rolled up the map. She had to act now. She couldn't let Blackstone slip through her fingers again.

Chapter Nineteen

August 7, 1863

B y the end of the week, Hattie had what she needed to go to Colonel Truesdail. It came in the form of a message addressed to her and delivered to Hospital No. 11.

Engagement in Knoxville. Buckner to attend. Bring wardrobe. There's a dress hanging you mustn't forget. Desperate to see you. P.

Pauline. In Knoxville.

Hattie studied what she'd written. Bring wardrobe. Not send wardrobe. Pauline was telling Hattie to come to her. Desperate to see you.

There was no time to lose. Leaving the hospital early, Hattie went to the Army Police Headquarters. Fortunately, Lieutenant Elliott had someone in his office, and though his door was only half-closed, Hattie was able to slip past without him spotting her.

She knocked on the colonel's door. "Enter!" he barked.

She let herself in. Closing the door behind her, she approached his desk. "I'm sorry to come unannounced, Colonel. It's about Pauline Carlton." She held out the message.

Truesdail took the paper, his face looking more careworn than ever. He unfolded the message and read it. Then he looked up at Hattie. "You're certain this is from her?" he asked.

"It's written in her hand. She sent it to me in care of Hospital No. 11, where she knows I help out in the dispensary."

He gestured to the empty chair near his desk, and she sat. "I'm glad for word from her," Truesdail said. "It must have taken some effort for her to get a message out."

Hattie nodded. "The theatrical references help to hide her meaning."

He drummed his fingers on his desk, studying the note. "Knoxville. With Rosecrans bearing down on Chattanooga, it makes sense that they've moved her east.

"And she mentions Buckner. He's the Confederate general in charge at Knoxville, is he not?" Hattie said, proud that she knew this.

He nodded. "But what's this about the wardrobe and the dress?"

Hattie pointed at the words. "See where she says bring the wardrobe? Under normal circumstances, an actor asks that her wardrobe be sent, not brought."

The colonel raised his dark eyebrows. "So it's a plea for rescue?"

"I think so. And then there's this part about the dress. I think she's used hanging intentionally. Combined with desperate, I fear she's in danger of execution."

"They intend to make an example of her," Truesdail muttered. "And East Tennessee would be the place to do it. There's no end to the trouble Union loyalists have caused them there. Hanging a woman for spying would certainly get their attention." He refolded the note and set it atop a pile of papers on his desk. "You were right to bring this straight to Headquarters. But why didn't you go to Lieutenant Elliott?"

Hattie straightened. "On this matter, I lack confidence in Lieutenant Elliott."

Truesdail leaned back in his chair, arms folded at his chest. "How's that?"

"He took the news of Miss Carlton's capture hard. I don't believe he can be clearheaded regarding her rescue."

"And you can?"

"I assure you, Colonel Truesdail, that I am most clearheaded. Pauline entrusted me directly with this message. She's looking to me to act. She must know that with my reputation, earned from my toast at the theatre, I can get past Rebel pickets."

"Even if you can get to Knoxville, you have no way of securing her release. With all due respect, that's a task best left to our soldiers. General Burnside is headed for Knoxville as we speak. Once he takes the city—assuming he takes it—he'll be better positioned to see to Miss Carlton."

"But Buckner will retreat as Burnside closes in." Hattie was glad she had sufficient understanding to speak with authority on this. "He'll take Pauline with him, and then who knows where she'll end up."

"We make our calculations as best we can. There are no guarantees," Truesdail said darkly. "I'll bring this to Lieutenant Elliott's attention. He knows East Tennessee. We'll make a plan."

"A plan that involves me?"

"That will be up to Lieutenant Elliott."

Hattie stood, clutching her purse. "As I've said, I lack confidence in Lieutenant Elliott, and he in me."

He studied her. "You're not aware of all the factors at play in this situation, Miss Thomas. I appreciate your concern about Miss Carlton, and should we decide to involve you, one of us will send for you. In the meantime, I urge you to put your differences aside and do as Lieutenant Elliott asks.

~ ~ ~

Three long days passed. Truesdail must have gone directly to Elliott with her news from Pauline. Had they made a plan to rescue her? Or were they content to let Burnside decide her fate, if and when he took Knoxville?

Hattie grew more and more frustrated. Pauline was in certain danger, and if Champ Farmington and Luke Blackstone had their way, General Burnside was too. If no one was going to listen to Hattie, much less trust her to go behind enemy lines, then she needed to take matters into her own hands.

Once she'd decided to act, her preparations were minimal. She let Felicia Ford know she'd miss the next meeting or two, having been called East on a family emergency. She gave the same excuse to Mrs. Fletcher, paying ahead on her room and board. With Edith Greenfield, she was more forthcoming, telling her she was headed to Knoxville, where she hoped to aid in Pauline's escape. In case her plans went awry, Hattie wanted someone to know where she'd gone.

She allowed Edith to assume that her assignment behind enemy lines had gone through the usual channels, and she didn't mention the twelve bottles of quinine she'd borrowed from the dispensary. During her time at the hospital, Hattie had only known the doctor to prescribe quinine a few times, the ailments it cured being more common on the battlefields than in the city.

She needed saddlebags, which she bought at an inflated price from a dealer in secondhand goods. Into these, she packed a single change of clothes along with biscuits she'd saved from her meals and carrots she'd dug after dark one night from the garden. She packed her map, too, with her intended route sketched in pencil.

On the day of her departure, she rose at her usual time and ate her breakfast with Mrs. Fletcher, who passed along chatter from the market about how the South's generals Bragg and Buckner were sure to turn back the North's advances on Chattanooga and Knoxville. Hattie stuffed two extra biscuits in her skirt pockets when Mrs. Fletcher had her back turned, then she said her goodbyes and went on her way.

She managed to get away without Mrs. Fletcher seeing the saddlebags—not the usual way a lady packed for a journey to the East, but these were strange times, after all, and no one on the omnibus paid her much mind. She got off a block past the Army Police Headquarters, then circled back to the stables.

"Lieutenant Elliott sent me to select a horse," she told the stable boy.

He looked at her quizzically but led her to the stalls in the back. "These ones here, they're the only ones not spoken for," he said, gesturing toward three Chesnut Morgans.

Hattie thanked him, and he went back to feeding the horses at the front of the stable. She approached the three Morgans, feeling light and free as she had when she was young, sneaking out to ride with George.

She decided on the mare with lively eyes and a white-streaked nose. She had no saddle, but she'd ridden bareback as a girl, and she was sure she could do so again.

She was just getting ready to hoist the saddlebags over the mare's back when she heard footsteps behind her. She whirled around, hoping it was the stable boy.

"Taken up horse thieving, have you, Miss Thomas?" Lieutenant Elliott asked.

She was not going to let him cow her into submission, not now that she'd gotten this far. "Colonel Truesdail allowed that I could choose a horse."

He fingered his beard. "Intriguing. The stable boy was under the impression that I'd sent you."

She lowered her arm, the saddlebags brushing the straw on the stable floor. "He must be mistaken."

"It would be in your best interest to be forthright with me," Elliott said.

"Very well," she said. "I'm going after Pauline."

"There will be no need for that," he said coolly. "In fact, I'm here to select a mount for the man I intend to send to intercept General Burnside on her behalf."

"You needn't send a man," she said. "You can send me. I'll have no trouble getting past the pickets. I'll tell them Colonel Truesdail has forced me out of Nashville because of my Secesh leanings."

"Why not?" he said grimly. "Since you've seen fit to go over my head. I suppose I should have expected it after what happened at the saloon."

"I said nothing about the saloon."

"But you told him I'd lost perspective. You'd do well to keep yourself out of my business, Miss Thomas."

"But you were upset about Pauline."

"I'm doing all I can for Pauline," he said curtly.

"You must know that there's a good chance Burnside won't reach her before Buckner withdraws."

His eyes bore into her. "I must say I'm impressed, Miss Thomas. A month ago, I doubt you'd have known which side either of those generals was on."

"I know now," she said. "And I'm prepared for this journey."

"You know nothing of the country between here and Knoxville," he said. "Nothing of the dangers there. Do you actually think you can take this horse and saunter off through enemy territory as if you're on a Sunday outing?"

She grabbed the horse's reins. "I'm tired of you coddling me, lieutenant. You can grant me permission, or I can take the horse on my own. Either way, I intend to make my way to Knoxville."

He sighed. "You are incredibly stubborn, Miss Thomas."

The mare whinnied, and she patted its nose. "So I've been told."

"You take that horse, and I can have you arrested."

"I might as well be imprisoned," she snapped, "for all the good I'm doing here."

He stepped toward her. "If you insist on making this reckless journey, I'm going with you. I lived the better part of my life in

East Tennessee. It's not easy to find your way, especially with Rebel guerrillas patrolling the forests. They'd love to get their hands on a woman traveling alone, and they won't care about your having made some bogus toast."

She started to object, then thought the better of it. She didn't relish the idea of traveling with the lieutenant, but his arresting her was a far worse alternative. And if he truly did know the countryside, he might even be useful. She could not afford to get lost, not if she was going to get to Blackstone—and Pauline—in time.

"We leave today," she said, looking him squarely in the eye. "And when we reach Knoxville, we go our separate ways."

He offered a wry smile. "I should have known you'd insist on your terms. All right, Miss Thomas. Return here at two o'clock, and we'll be on our way."

~ ~ ~

As they left Nashville on the turnpike, headed east, the August sun was warm on Hattie's back. Her mare, Nellie, kept a steady pace with Elliott's horse. Riding past swaths of purple mist flowers, breathing the country air, Hattie felt more alive than she had in weeks. Ahead lay the chance to save Pauline and also stop Blackstone.

She'd said nothing of Blackstone to Elliott, who rode stiff-backed and silent at her side. But she only had to tolerate him for a few days, and he'd already proven useful, equipping her with a side saddle which, if not her preferred way to ride, at least kept her from having to explain to every Rebel along the way why a lady was riding bareback.

They rode for an hour, the only sounds being the clapping of their horses' hooves and the wheep, wheep of flycatchers high in the trees, before they came upon their first Confederate pickets, a boyish soldier and an older one with a high forehead and bushy beard. Elliott presented his pass, which the Army Police had confiscated from a Rebel they'd recently arrested for smuggling. In black trousers and a white shirt, Elliott looked the part of an East Tennessee storekeeper as the pass claimed him to be.

He told the pickets Hattie was his cousin, and he was escorting her out of Nashville because the Yanks had expelled her due to her open Secesh sympathies.

The bearded man looked her up and down. "Can't keep your mouth shut, is that it?"

She assumed a defiant look "I'm inclined to speak my mind, sir."

The picket returned Elliott's papers. "Go on ahead," he said, waving them through.

"To Jeff Davis and the Confederacy," Hattie said, smiling sweetly as she passed. The younger man grinned.

When they'd gotten some distance from the pickets, Elliott slowed his horse, waiting for Hattie to come alongside him. "You don't need to be so blatant in your displays of loyalty," he said. "If questions are asked, they're going to remember you."

"I've played the part a good while now," she said. "I know what I'm doing."

Elliott shook his head, surveying the rolling hills that stretched before them. "We should make Watertown by nightfall."

"What's in Watertown?"

He offered a tight smile. "Not much. Just a small hamlet built around a farm and gristmill. But there are friends there."

"From your childhood?"

"No. I come from farther east, between Sparta and Nashville. I don't have..." His voice trailed off. "Not much family left, I'm afraid."

From the hard set of his jaw, Hattie knew better than to ask him to elaborate. Besides, she had more immediate concerns. She hadn't eaten since breakfast, and she was hungry. "I hope these friends in Watertown will share their supper."

"They'll treat us kindly," he said.

From the faraway look in his eyes, she could tell his thoughts weren't on Watertown. As they rode on, she considered what he'd said about not having much family left. The war might have divided them, she thought, as it had divided so many families, including her own. If she and Elliott were on friendlier terms, she might have shared something of her own family troubles. As it was, they rode on in silence.

Dusk was falling when they finally left the road, turning up a long drive toward a red barn. Dismounting to the sound of crickets chirping in the grass, they hitched their horses to a post.

"I thought we were stopping in Watertown," Hattie said.

"We are," Elliott said. "Sawmill, gristmill, post office. And this residence," he said, indicating a large white house with a covered veranda. "That's Watertown."

"So we're spending the night here?" She'd expected an inn.

"Unless you'd rather camp in the woods."

She followed him to the house. He rapped on the door. A moment later, it opened a crack.

"Who's there?" a woman asked.

Holding up his arm, Elliott pushed back his cuff, revealing a red string tied around his wrist. "Rail-Splitter's companions."

The door opened wider, revealing a light-haired woman in a green plaid skirt and a cream-colored bodice. A small boy clung to her skirt. She ushered them over the threshold, then latched the door. "I'm Beulah Waters," she said. "Welcome."

"John Elliott," the lieutenant said, not naming his rank. "And this is Hattie Thomas."

"We've just finished supper," Beulah said. "But there's a few slices of ham left, and some cornbread." She turned to the child at her side. "Go on upstairs now and tell Aunt Nancy and your sisters that I'll be up as soon as our guests are settled."

The boy looked up at her, wide-eyed, then let go of his grip on her skirt and dashed up the stairs. Beulah led Elliott and Hattie to a well-appointed kitchen thick with the smell of smoked ham. Fastening an apron about her thin waist, Beulah gestured toward a long table.

"I'm afraid we don't use the dining room anymore," she said apologetically. "Too much upkeep. With my husband off fighting, we've got the house servants doing fieldwork. My sister and the children and I help where we can."

"We appreciate your hospitality." Elliott pulled out a chair at the table. He motioned for Hattie to sit, then took the chair across from her. "I know it comes at some risk."

"It's the least we can do." Beulah served them each a plate with a single slice of ham and a square of cornbread. "Leave your plates in the sink and turn out the lantern when you're finished eating," she said, wiping her hands on her apron. "We're in the bedroom at the top of the stairs. Safer these days if we all sleep together. Take your pick of the others. Apologies if the linens aren't fresh. The laundry's another chore that's neglected these days, least till the harvest is done."

She left them to their meal. Famished, Hattie sawed off large chunks of ham, savoring the salty taste on her tongue. The cornbread was dry but delicious, even without butter.

"How do you know the Waters family?" she asked, her stomach feeling satisfied.

He swallowed a bite of ham. "I don't." He wiped his fingers on his napkin, then pulled a slip of paper from his pocket and set it in front of her. "This is a list of safe houses in East Tennessee."

"Safe for Union sympathizers?"

He nodded, his face softened by the lantern light. "A secret society to aid the Union. It started in the Carolinas, then spread to West Virginia and East Tennessee. The Heroes of America, also known as the Red String Society. They open their homes, helping Union soldiers get through Rebel territory."

"Like the Underground Railroad."

"Right. For the most part, people in East Tennessee are farmers who don't own slaves. They're a burr in the saddle to the Confederates. They know about the Red Strings but can't ever seem to catch them."

She started to hand the paper back to him, but he shook his head. "Keep it," he said. "In case we get separated."

"But we're past the pickets. We won't get separated."

"Things happen," he said.

She tucked the paper into her pocket. John Elliott had always struck her as the type to overthink things.

They finished eating and went upstairs, their way lit only by moonlight. Exhausted, Hattie gladly fell into the first bed she found. The room smelled musty, and there was a thin layer of dust on the coverlet, but Hattie was too tired to care. Her last thought before falling asleep was gratitude that she didn't have to share a room with John Elliott.

~ ~ ~

Elliott wanted to reach Sparta by nightfall, so they rode hard the next day. Halfway between along their route, Sparta would position them to reach Nashville in another day and a half. Once they'd seen to Pauline, they'd go their separate ways. It wouldn't matter whether Elliott thought Luke Blackstone a threat. Hattie knew he was, and she intended to make sure he couldn't harm anyone with his cyanide. She just had to figure out how.

The closer they got to Sparta, the grimmer John Elliott's expression grew. His mouth took on a hard, determined set, and Hattie gave up trying to make conversation. She supposed he regretted making this trip. Well, it was his own fault. He could have sent someone else as a guide if he truly thought she needed one. Mostly, she didn't, though in a few places where the road narrowed and split, both routes leading through dense thickets of oak and hackberry, she was glad he knew the way.

She was sore from riding all day. It had been years since she'd spent so much time in a saddle, and she was looking forward to dismounting and bedding down for the night. Behind them, the sun was setting, casting a pink glow.

Approaching Sparta, Elliott glanced about nervously.

"What's wrong?" Hattie asked.

"This is where Champ Farmington comes from. We're lucky there's a safe house at all." At the next intersection, he took the road to the right, spurring his horse toward a lone farmhouse. This must be the Littles' place, Hattie thought, having studied the list of safe houses. It was an unassuming residence, not half as grand as the Waters' house. Chickens scratched in the yard, and from somewhere in the barn, a donkey brayed.

They brought their horses alongside the barn, out of view of the main road. "Wait here," Elliott said. "I'll get our instructions."

He went up to the house and knocked on the door. A stoop-shouldered man opened it. He and Elliott went back and forth with words she couldn't quite make out, the man gesturing wildly.

Then the man shut the door. Shaking his head, Elliott returned to her. "He says it's too dangerous for us to stay here. We can feed and water the horses, and then he wants us to move on."

They led the horses into the barn, Hattie fighting off exhaustion. The air inside smelled grassy. Fresh-cut hay, she thought. "Couldn't we sleep up there?" she said, indicating the loft. "And then leave before dawn?"

"I suggested that," the lieutenant said as the horses began to eat. "But Mr. Little refused. There was a bit of trouble here recently. Bushwhackers thought he was hiding Yankees in the barn and threatened to set fire to it."

"There's another safe house in Sparta, isn't there?" Hattie said, remembering what she'd seen on the paper.

Elliott shook his head. "Mr. Little says they've shut down too. Too many of Farmington's men around. Six hundred in this county alone. Some even fired their guns into a church congregation last week because they suspected parishioners of being loyal to the Union

Hattie rubbed a cramp in her leg. "Then where will we sleep?"

"We've got bedrolls," he said, leading the horses from the barn. "We'll make do."

They mounted their horses and continued down the road, the hills purpled with shadows that lengthened and then dissolved into darkness. Hattie didn't much like riding at night, but Nellie seemed not to mind. As the evening's first stars popped out in the velvet sky, the road narrowed, the forest encroaching on both sides, From somewhere in the dark, an owl hooted.

Hattie felt bone-weary. "This looks like a good spot."

"It isn't," Elliott said gruffly.

So they traveled on, the half-moon casting shadows of the pine trees over the road. All at once, Elliott stopped his horse, stretching out his hand to signal that Hattie should stop too. Pressing his finger to his lips, he cocked his head, listening. "There's a noise up ahead," he whispered.

Cocking her head, she listened too. In the distance, she heard a horse's whinny. "Perhaps we should get off the road."

Nodding curtly, he dismounted, then led his horse into a thicket of trees. She followed suit, following the path he forged in the brush. On the other side of the thicket lay a meadow. Beyond it, she heard the faint sound of a burbling creek. She licked her lips, having emptied her canteen hours ago. "We could camp across the meadow," she suggested.

"I don't like the idea of crossing in the open," he said.

"But there are trees on the other side," she said. "And there's water."

He studied her face, lit by moonlight. He seemed about to speak when the clomping of horses' hooves on the road broke the silence. Hattie froze. Elliott held a finger to his lips, his eyes on the path they'd made to get here.

They both stood stock-still, listening until the horses passed. Eager to get farther from the road, Hattie started for the meadow. Holding out his arm, Elliott shook his head. "Not yet," he hissed.

Hattie grated at his caution. The riders on the road were likely just townspeople who meant them no harm. And if they were Farmington's men, what of it? They'd tell the same story they'd told the pickets, that Hattie had been forced from Nashville for supporting the Rebels, and Elliott was her cousin, guiding her home.

Tired and cold, she mounted her horse. "They're gone, whoever they are." She steered Nellie around his outstretched arm and started for the clearing.

She heard a horse coming up behind her. Elliott, she thought, but she turned to check. Yes, Elliott.

He caught up with her. "It's too risky to cross the meadow."

"It's dark," she snapped. "No one will see."

In the moonlight, his frown looked grimmer than usual. "Suit yourself." He turned his horse and started through the brush, riding roughly parallel to the road.

Hattie gazed across the meadow, listening to the welcome sound of the creek. She was so thirsty, and she thought Nellie must be too. But Elliott had the bedrolls and the hardtack. Teeth clenched, she turned and followed after him.

Without so much as glancing her direction, he stopped after going a mile or so, in the middle of a stand of pines. "This will do," he said, more to himself than to her.

He undid the bedrolls and tossed one in her direction, acknowledging her at last. She'd never slept in the open before, but weary as she was, she could have fallen asleep on a bed of nails. She secured her horse, then laid out the blankets over a cushion of fallen pine needles. The blankets were thin, and with the season so close to autumn, there was a chill in the air, but they'd have to do.

As she arranged her bed, Elliott gathered a pile of sticks, then used a flint to light a small fire. He crouched beside it, poking into the flames with a stick.

Hattie shivered in the night air. The fire looked enticing, but what was his point in lighting it when he'd wanted to stay hidden in the woods?

She wrapped her top blanket around her shoulders, then sat on a stump close enough to the flames to warm her. "I should think the smoke would attract bushwhackers."

"Quite the opposite," Elliott said, not looking up from his fire. "A fire makes people think we've nothing to hide. Surely you noticed the wisps of smoke rising here and there from the woods?"

"Of course I noticed," she said crossly. "From cottages, I assumed."

"Not around these parts." He set down his stick, then perched on a boulder a few feet from her, hands stretched toward the flames. "More likely Farmington's bushwhackers, setting up camp for the night. Maybe some Red String men too. Lots of skirmishes between them out this way."

"You seem to know a lot about Farmington and his men."

"I wish I didn't," he said darkly, staring into the fire. "Champ Farmington is a renegade of the worst sort. He'd as soon shoot you as look at you. This war is a boon to people like him. The more desperate the Rebels get, the more they embrace his wicked ways."

Hattie pulled the blanket tighter around her shoulders. She wondered if she should mention Farmington's connection to Luke Blackstone. No, she decided. Elliott would just dismiss that as more speculation. But maybe he had some useful information about Farmington, something that could help her get to Blackstone.

"You said you're from this part of Tennessee," she said. "Where, exactly?"

"East of here, just over the county line."

Somewhere in the forest, a volley of shots rang out. Instinctively, Hattie looked to her left and right but saw only the dark shapes of trees. "The guerrillas?" she asked.

"I expect so." His hand hovered near his pistol until the pop-pop-pop faded into silence. "What they shoot in the dark, I'd rather not know."

"Did Farmington make trouble even before the war?" Hattie asked.

"I expect so. He's evil to the core. Speaks poorly of the Rebs that they've allowed him into their ranks."

"But he's not a uniformed soldier, is he?"

"I doubt he wears a uniform. But he might as well. The Confederates authorized him to raise a cavalry company." Elliott fingered the pistol holstered at his side, his eyes narrowing with a hardness she'd not seen in him before. "If there's any man that deserves a bullet, it's Farmington. In these woods, I feel it all the more."

"Feel what?" she asked.

His face lit by the leaping flames, his gaze bore into her, and yet he seemed not to see her at all. "How much I despise the man."

Manifesting his hatred, Elliott's tone and the hard set of his jaw made her shiver despite the fire's warmth. She knew that sort of hatred. She felt it every time she thought of what Blackstone had done to her and Thom.

"Will you return to East Tennessee when the war's over?" she asked.

Elliott's gaze softened a bit, and there seemed more heartache than hate in his eyes. "I doubt it. Too many memories. Too much I need to forget. What about you? Have you plans for when the war ends?"

"I hope to reconnect with my brother. I'm told he's in Canada, working as an operative for Lafayette Baker's National Detective Police. But I haven't been able to verify that."

Elliott's lips turned slightly, forming a crooked smile. "Detective work must run in your family."

"Not really. George knows nothing of what I've been up to, and it was only a few months ago that I learned he might be working with Baker."

He picked up his stick and stirred the fire, sending sparks into the night. "You're lucky to have a reason to go on."

She eyed him curiously. "Surely you do as well, Lieutenant."

Lit by the fire's glow, his face took on a melancholy cast as he stirred the fire once more. Then he stood. "It's time we turned in. We've got a long ride tomorrow if we're to make Knoxville."

Whatever he was hiding, it pained him greatly, Hattie thought. She understood enough about hiding and pain to allow him both. "Goodnight, Lieutenant Elliott."

"Goodnight, Hattie."

She rose from the stump and moved to the blankets she'd laid out. On the other side of the fire, Elliott began arranging his bedroll.

One more day of riding, and they'd be in Knoxville, where she intended to head off Blackstone's plot and see what she could do to free Pauline. She wouldn't need Elliott's help, though she had to admit that here in these dark woods, it wasn't exactly unwelcome.

Falling asleep was more difficult than she'd expected. The ground was hard and damp, and though she tried to push the thought from her mind, she worried about what awaited in Knoxville. How close was Burnside to the city? Was Blackstone waiting there, ready to deploy his cyanide? What about Farmington? And Pauline?

~ ~ ~

Hattie must have fallen asleep at last, for she woke to the blue light of dawn. Somewhere in the canopy of trees, a warbler trilled. But she heard another sound, too—a rustling in the brush. She tensed, holding her breath. Whatever it was, it was drawing close from the same direction they'd come last night.

Clutching her blanket, she crept toward where Elliott slept, lightly snoring. Crouching beside him, she nudged his shoulder. "Lieutenant, wake up. There's something in the woods. A bobcat, maybe. Or a bear."

He startled awake. Sitting up, he cocked his head, listening. "That's not a bobcat. Or a bear." He scrambled to his feet. "Load up Nellie as quietly as you can. Head for the road. Ride ahead of me. I'll catch up."

Heart thumping, Hattie settled the saddlebags over Nellie's back, then reached for the bedroll.

The rustling grew close. She heard a man's voice, but she couldn't make out his words.

"Leave the bedroll," Elliott hissed as he mounted his horse. "There's no time."

Swiftly, Hattie unhitched Nellie. She started to swing onto the saddle. Then, thinking better of it, she tossed the saddle to the ground. If there was a need to ride quickly, she didn't intend to do it perched like a parakeet on a swing.

Stepping onto a fallen tree, she mounted bareback. Beneath her legs, she felt the muscles of Nellie's back tense. But someone must have trained her without a saddle because just as quickly, the horse relaxed.

"Go," Elliott urged.

Hattie pointed Nellie toward what looked like a game trail. The path was narrow and rocky, but it would have to do. She was about to flick the reins when out of the corner of her eye, she saw a man on horseback emerge from the pines. In the half-light, she saw he wore a tattered gray coat. A deserter, she thought.

But the cold glint in his dark eyes, hooded by thick brows, was not the look of a man who'd given up the fight. It was the look of a man who intended to get what he wanted no matter what it took.

With a jeering smile, the man raised his pistol, training it on Hattie. "Look who's back in White County," he growled. "Thought I'd run you out of here for good."

Though he had her in his sights, he wasn't speaking to her, Hattie realized. He was talking to Elliott.

"Champ Farmington." Elliott raised his pistol. "Let the lady go. This doesn't involve her."

Hattie's heart skipped a beat, knowing this was one of Blackstone's associates.

Farmington laughed, a grating sound. "You always was clueless, John."

A second horse poked through the trees. "By God, Champ," its rider was saying. "If this is another wild goose chase, I swear I'll..."

Spotting Hattie, he stopped mid-sentence. Her stomach turned, bile rising in her throat. "Luke Blackstone," she said as evenly as she could manage. "Just the man I'd hoped to run into."

Elliott glanced at her. Confusion clouded his eyes, then lifted as he cocked his pistol, swinging it toward Blackstone.

"Don't even think about it," Farmington said. "Or I'll do her like I did to your little lady."

Blackstone sneered. "This one's no lady. She's a spy. If it had been up to me, she'd have swung with her husband, and we wouldn't have had to worry about her snooping around in our business."

Despite the morning chill, perspiration beaded along Hattie's collar. How had he known? The housekeeper, she thought. "Your business involving cyanide, you mean?"

Blackstone looked momentarily off-guard. "I have no idea what you're talking about."

"What I'm itchin' to know is what business y'all have in Knoxville," Farmington said.

"Nothing that involves you," Elliott barked.

"Oh, but it does," Hattie said. She addressed Elliott but kept her eyes on Farmington and his pistol, wishing very much that she'd brought one of her own. Not that she knew the first thing about shooting, but if she got out of this alive, she intended to learn.

"Champ Farmington is in on the plot I told you about, Lieutenant. The one involving Luke Blackstone's cyanide. That must be why the two of them are out here in these woods. They know the Army Police are after them." A total fabrication, but these men wouldn't know it, or so she hoped.

Farmington laughed, an ugly sound. "These are my woods. Out here, I do as I please. John Elliott knows that better than most."

"I know you're as evil as they come," Elliott said. "Let her go, and we'll sort this out between us men."

"You associate with all the wrong sorts of women, Lieutenant," Farmington said. "Why, this one even goes about with public women, asking a whole lot more questions than she should."

Elliott shot her a look, and the pit Hattie felt in her stomach deepened. Public women. The Ivanhoe.

She realized her mistake, having gone to meet Marlena at the dock. Champ Farmington must have been there, too. He must have seen them together and quizzed Marlena about Hattie and her interest in the doctor.

Hattie fixed her gaze on Blackstone. "I'd rather associate with a public woman than a man who passes for a doctor while scheming to send people to their death."

Blackstone flashed a wicked grin. "Ah, but you'd love to send me to my death, wouldn't you, my dear?"

She'd never hated him more than at that moment. But that was precisely what he wanted, she realized—for the blindness of her hatred to cloud her thinking even more than it already had.

"Your death will come in due time, Dr. Blackstone," she said coolly.

"How very philosophical of you, Miss Logan," Blackstone said. "Your father would be proud."

She looked from him to Farmington and his pistol. He was counting on her fear. And she was afraid, no doubt about that. But she'd already let emotion cloud her thinking. She wasn't going to make that mistake again.

Nellie snorted, her hoof pawing the ground. Farmington and Blackstone had the element of surprise, sneaking up at the break of dawn. But if Hattie played her cards right, she could turn the tables on them. She just needed to signal her intentions to Elliott.

There was a trick she'd learned onstage, fixing her eyes straight ahead while watching for a cue in her peripheral vision. Now she trained her eyes on Blackstone. Out of the corner of her eye, she could see Elliott, jaw set, lips pressed tightly together. When he got that intense look, not much got past him. She was counting on that now.

Pay attention, John Elliott. Be ready.

She tightened her hold on the reins, leaning forward ever so slightly, allowing Elliott the smallest of openings. Offering Blackstone a nervous smile, she dipped her head demurely.

"You're a clever man, Dr. Blackstone," she said. "I'll give you that. No wonder Father sought you out."

Blackstone chuckled. Out of the corner of her eye, she saw Elliott nod slightly, signaling that he saw the opening she'd made with her slight shift in posture.

"What a little hellion that man raised," Blackstone said. "I've half a mind—"

"Now!" Elliott shouted.

Hattie jabbed her boots into Nellie's side, and the horse lunged toward the game trail.

Gunshots rang out, pop, pop, pop. Farmington shooting at her, Farmington shooting at Elliott, Elliott shooting at Farmington. She couldn't tell which. She could only ride away, away, and hope John Elliott would soon follow behind her.

Chapter Twenty

August 12, 1863

Hattie held on for dear life, pushing Nellie as hard and fast as the trail would allow. Hanging on without a saddle was harder than she remembered, especially at a full gallop. Her brother's long-ago advice came back to her. *Feel the horse beneath you. Let it feel your confidence.*

She pressed her legs tight to Nellie, feeling the ripple of her muscles carrying her through the thicket. She listened for the sound of Elliott's horse behind her. *I'll catch up,* he'd said. Where was he?

Seeing an opening in the thicket, Hattie veered the horse toward the road. She kept Nellie at a gallop, the horse seeming to understand her urgency. As the rising sun bathed the route with golden light, they passed open fields interspersed with oak and pine forests. Now and then, Hattie twisted to look behind her, thinking she heard hoofbeats. But she only saw the dust stirred by Nellie's pounding feet.

Finally, they reached Pleasant Hill, a hamlet Hattie recognized from her map. She slowed Nellie to a trot, then reached for her pocket. To her horror, the safe house list was protruding from her pocket, about to fall out. She withdrew the paper, glad not to have lost it.

The list showed a safe house on the western edge of town. In case the list fell into enemy hands, the directions were in code, but Elliott had explained the cipher. Hattie tucked the paper in her bodice for safekeeping, then proceeded to a white two-story house tucked in a grove of shortleaf pines.

She turned Nellie up the drive. Water trickled in a gully alongside the dirt. On the other side, in a small pasture, a cow and calf grazed. Reaching the house, Hattie brought Nellie around to the back, well out of sight of the road, and hitched her to a post near the shed.

Legs wobbly from her ride, Hattie climbed the back steps and knocked three short raps on the door as Elliott had when they'd stayed at the safe house. A middle-aged woman in a blue calico morning dress came to the door, her graying hair piled in a loose knot on top of her head.

"The Rail-splitter sent me." Until she spoke, Hattie hadn't realized how out of breath she was from the ride.

The woman ushered her inside, latching the door behind her. She tugged up one sleeve, revealing a red string tied around her wrist, then trained her gray-green eyes on Hattie.

She shook her head "I don't have a string. But I assure you, I'm on your side."

At the roughhewn kitchen table sat a white-haired man and a girl who couldn't have been any older than twelve. Looking up from his bowl of grits, the man eyed Hattie. "And which side would that be?" he asked.

"The rail-splitter's," the girl chirped. "Same as us."

Pushing back his chair, the man rose from the table. As he did, he thrust his hand into his trouser pocket.

Fearing he had a knife, Hattie reached for the paper she'd tucked in her bodice, a maneuver that would have horrified

Miss Whitcomb, the headmistress at Ladygrace Finishing School. But Hattie hardly looked the part of a lady anyhow, with her windblown hair, her chapped hands, and her skirt dirty and torn.

"I've been traveling with Lieutenant Elliott of the Army Police," she said. "He wears the red string. He gave me this..."

Hearing footfalls on the stairs, Hattie paused, her voice trailing off. She saw one slippered foot, then another, then a woman wearing a worn dressing gown, tied at the waist.

"Land's sakes," she said. "A girl can't get a wink of sleep around these parts."

"Pauline!" Hattie rushed for the stairs. "I thought the Rebs had you locked up."

Pauline hurried down the stairs and threw her arms around Hattie's neck. She looked thinner than Hattie remembered, but her eyes were bright as ever.

"Hattie Thomas." She pulled back, assessing Hattie's disheveled condition. "If you've come to break me out of prison, you can see that your services are no longer required. Camille here took care of that." She gestured at the girl.

"Me and the Maryville Loyal Ladies Home Guard," Camille said proudly.

"In the nick of time too," Pauline said. "The general had threatened to hang me as soon as I was well. Which I already was, of course, but I know how to play the invalid." She pressed the back of her hand to her forehead as if she felt a swoon coming on. Removing it, she said, "You've met our hosts?"

The woman who answered the door extended her hand. "Sarah Swanson," she said. "And this is my father, Michael." She gestured toward the old man, who was noisily scraping the last of the grits from his bowl.

Hattie took Sarah's hand, relishing its warmth. "Thank you for letting me in. I...I'm running from a bushwhacker."

Sarah turned to the old man. "See, Father. I told you we had to answer the door."

The old man grunted. "And now we'll have a bushwhacker on our tail."

Camille's eyes widened. "Will you have to shoot him?"

"If he pulls a gun on me," the old man said.

Pauline took Hattie's hand and led her to the table. "You look a fright," she said. "Have a bite to eat, and then we'll get you cleaned up. If Sarah's grits are half as good as the stew she served us last night, you're in for a treat."

"My horse—I mean, the Army's horse—needs tending. If possible, she should be in the barn so as not to give me away."

Michael stood. "I'll tend to the horse."

"I can't believe Lieutenant Elliott let you take a horse," Pauline said.

"It was that or steal one," Hattie said. "And he insisted on coming with me." A shiver ran down her spine. "But Champ Farmington tracked us down, along with that doctor I told you about."

Pauline whistled, long and low. "Up to no good, I'll reckon."

"Ain't been no good associated with Champ Farmington since the day his mother birthed him." Michael's eyes narrowed. "You say he's the one tailing you?"

Hattie swallowed hard. "Yes. He and Luke Blackstone surprised us this morning when we were breaking camp. The lieutenant..." She turned to Pauline. "There were gunshots. I need to go back for him."

"Better make sure Farmington's out of the picture first." Shaking his head, Michael left for the barn.

Camille brought her empty bowl to the sink. "I wouldn't mind meeting a real live bushwhacker."

"Once you've met one, you won't want to meet another." Pouring from a coffee pot, Sarah filled a mug and handed it to Hattie. "It's chicory, of course. Grits?"

"That's a yes from me," Pauline said. "I'm simply famished. Sit, would you, Hattie? You're making me nervous, and Lord knows my nerves are frayed enough as it is."

Hattie perched on a chair, the mug warm in her hands. She sipped, feeling guilty that while she sat safely in a stranger's kitchen, John Elliott might be lying wounded or dead in the woods. Sarah set a bowl of grits in front of her. But hungry as she was, the thought of eating turned her stomach.

"Pert near jumped out of my skin when I saw you," Pauline said, picking up her spoon.

"I got your message," Hattie said, toying with her spoon. "I couldn't very well ignore it."

Pauline shook her head. "And now that doctor you've been after is after you. Well, at least we found each other. I guess I shouldn't be surprised. This is the last safe house before Knoxville."

The door flew open, and Michael burst in. "There's a man on horseback coming up the drive."

"John!" Hattie said.

"On a first name basis, are we?" Pauline said.

He shook his head. "Don't look like no Army Police. Champ Farmington, I'd say."

Hattie's heart sank. She'd put all these good people in danger.

Sarah snatched the bowls of grits from the table. "The plan we made when Pauline came. You all remember what to do? Camille?"

"Yes, ma'am." Camille grabbed a pile of torn cloth from a pile near the table.

"A shame about the timing." With a sigh, Pauline stood. "Those grits truly were delicious."

Sarah steered her out of the kitchen toward a back room. Over her shoulder, she said, "Hattie, you go upstairs to my room. Climb into the armoire and hide behind the clothes. With any luck, we'll be able to keep our visitor from going up there. Michael, back to the barn."

He shook his head. "I don't like leaving you women folk here alone."

"Our plan hinges on this being no place for a man," Sarah said. "And your rifle's out there if it comes to that."

"Pigheaded from the day she was born," Michael muttered as he left.

Hattie bounded up the stairs. In the first bedroom, she found the armoire. If Farmington came up here, she feared it would be the first place he looked, but it was too late now to look for another place to hide.

Parting Sarah's clothes, she climbed inside, folding herself into the space. She pulled the door shut, then leaned back in the dark, feeling as if her pounding heart would give her away. Downstairs, someone banged at the door. "Open up!" Farmington's voice. Hattie sucked in a breath.

"Coming!" Camille said.

As the door creaked open, Pauline let out a blood-curdling scream.

"Breathe," Sarah said calmly, her voice carrying through the gaps in the upstairs floorboards. "In and out, in and out. You're almost there."

"Move aside, child," Farmington said, his boots clomping across the wooden floor. "Where's your mama?"

Pauline let out another scream. "Oh, the pain! Can I...can I..." Even from her hiding place, Hattie could hear Pauline's heaving breaths. "Can I push yet?"

"Not just yet," Sarah said evenly.

"I wouldn't go in there if I was you," Camille warned. "Mama's birthin' a baby."

A creak of hinges, followed by the sound of a door banging against a wall. "I'm after a fugitive. She's—"

Pauline's wail drowned out his voice. "AYYY...YIIII...AYYY!"

"More rags, please, Camille," Sarah said.

"Right here, ma'am."

"I can't...I can't..." Pauline panted.

"Are you the one who got her in this sorry state, sir?" Sarah snapped.

"Me? No. Never seen her before in my life. I told you, I'm after a fugitive."

Hattie imagined Sarah shaking her head. "Well, unless you've come to help with the birthing, I suggest you take your search elsewhere. As you can see, we're too busy to harbor a fugitive even if we were inclined to, which we aren't."

"Arghhhh!" Pauline yelled.

Hattie heard Sarah's soft footsteps. She must be moving to the foot of the bed, Hattie thought, to catch Pauline's non-existent baby.

"All right," Sarah said firmly. "Push."

Pauline let out another scream, then grunted loudly. Hattie heard Farmington's clomping footsteps moving away from the room.

"Long as you're here, you might carry that pot of water from the stove to the bedroom," Camille said cheerily. "Mama needs it for washing up the blood."

"Not on your life," Farmington said.

Hearing the door open and then slam shut, Hattie let out the breath she'd been holding. She sat still as a statue, her knees pulled to her chest, wanting to make sure he was truly gone. Finally, she parted the clothes, pushed open the door, and crawled out of the armoire. She stretched her cramped legs, then headed downstairs.

In the back room, Pauline stood beside a bed. Blood splotched her nightdress, which was stretched taut over her bulging belly. She lifted the nightgown, and Camille undid a string, removing the pillow around Pauline's wait. "This one's got a future in the theatre, don't you think, Hattie?"

Hattie smiled. "You all were splendid. I don't know that I've ever heard such a realistic portrayal of childbirth. I was ready to run for the boiling water myself."

Sarah shook her head. "I hate to think how much bleach we'll need to get that chicken blood out of the sheets."

"A brilliant plan, don't you think, Hattie?" Pauline asked. "Nothing like the blood and pain of a woman in childbirth to send a man running."

"That bit about the child being Farminton's was a nice touch," Hattie said.

"Thanks," Sarah said. "I just hope we chased him off for good."

Pauline dressed, and they moved to the kitchen. For the next several minutes, they waited on pins and needles. At last, Michael came in from the barn. Sarah threw her arms around his neck and hugged him. "I was beginning to think Champ Farmington recruited you for his band of outlaws."

"Gave me a good dressing down about me not having enlisted with the Rebs," Michael said. "At my age, if you can believe it." He turned to Hattie. "I imagine you're anxious to get to that young man of yours. But we need to wait till Farmington leaves town."

"How long will that take?"

Michael shrugged. "A few hours, maybe. He'll check every house."

A few hours. By then, John Elliott could be dead, if he wasn't already.

~ ~ ~

An hour passed, then another. Pauline regaled them with tales of her exploits with the Rebels, before and after her arrest. As usual, there was a good deal of exaggeration, Hattie thought, but parts of her tales rang true, especially what she said about the privations of her imprisonment.

After her arrest, she'd been moved from one county jail to the next, each one farther to the east. Eventually, she'd ended up at a fort the Confederates were building in Knoxville. When scouts confirmed Burnside's advance on Knoxville, the Confederates had abandoned the fort, moving Pauline and the other prisoners south to Maryville.

"That's when the Maryville Loyal Ladies stepped up," Camille said solemnly. "We seize every opportunity to help the Union. In secret, of course."

"As you might imagine, there was a good deal of confusion with the move to Maryville," Pauline said. "The ladies took advantage of that, some distracting the guards while others made off with the prisoners."

"I got to Pauline before anyone else," Camille said. "The Ladies said I'd best get her to a safe house before the Rebs figured out she was gone."

Pauline slung her arm around Camille's shoulder. "We traveled as sisters. No one suspected a thing. And then here comes Hattie, like clockwork."

Nothing she'd done felt like clockwork. Her actions felt imprecise and misguided, with the very real possibility that John Elliott had been gotten killed.

After what seemed an eternity, Michael ventured out. He returned with assurance from the neighbors that Champ Farmington had searched every house in town, then moved on. "Probably he'll hole up a while," Michael said. "Till his shoulder heals."

"He's wounded?" Hattie asked.

"Not all that blood's from the chicken." Sarah gestured toward drops on the kitchen floor. "Farmington was dripping blood too."

"I don't suppose they mentioned anyone else?" Hattie said. "Another stranger in town?"

Michael rubbed his chin. "Yup. Gladys Wright, she lives next to Doc Nearman's place. Says she saw Farmington ride in with another man slumped on his horse. Took some work to get him inside to the doc, Gladys said. Guess he could barely walk."

"Champ Farmington getting medical attention for Lieutenant Elliott," Pauline said. "I find that hard to believe."

"And Doc Nearman wouldn't tend a Union soldier," Sarah said. "He's a Rebel through and through."

"Then the injured man must have been Luke Blackstone," Hattie said. Strangely, she took little satisfaction in the thought. "I believe he and Farmington intend harm to Burnside and his men once they reach Knoxville."

Camille straightened. "If there's a need to warn Burnside, the Loyal Ladies of Maryville will see to it."

"That would be a great help," Hattie said. "Depending on how badly he and Blackstone are hurt, Burnside could still be in danger. And with Farmington looking for me, I'm not much help."

"You might not be the one he's after," Michael said. "Folks says he's looking for a man."

Hattie's heart swelled. "Then there's hope Lieutenant Elliott got away. When he gave me the list of safe houses, he told me he'd committed them to memory. Maybe he's already on his way back to Nashville."

Pauline raised an eyebrow. "Without you? I doubt it."

"There's one way to find out," Michael said. "I'll saddle the horses."

~ ~ ~

It was past noon when Hattie and Michael set out. Hattie whispered an apology to Nellie for not having allowed her a longer rest. But the horse trotted along with a sense of purpose, almost as if she, too, was anxious to find the lieutenant.

The sun bore down hot on Hattie's back. The sky was blue with promise, scalloped with the Cumberland's green hills that stretched out all around. Occasionally, they passed another horse, but none had Elliott at the reins. Some were farmers pulling carts loaded with fresh vegetables that Mrs. Fletcher would have given her eyeteeth for.

It was such a pleasant pastoral landscape that until they passed a soldier, it was almost easy to forget the country was at war. But Hattie's worries about the lieutenant were not so easily erased. It was her fault, she knew, that he'd been in harm's way at all.

Finally, Hattie spotted the clearing she'd seen last night. She called to Michael, and he slowed his horse. From the side of the road, they surveyed the area. "We camped about twenty minutes east of here," she said. "That's where Farmington found us."

Michael swung his horse around. "Could be anywhere in these woods. But we may as well start where you last seen him."

They trotted back the way they'd come. Hattie searched for the spot where she'd left the woods, headed for Pleasant Hill. She wasn't at all sure where the game trail came out. There had been so little light at that time of the morning.

At last, she spotted an opening. "There it is," she said, turning Nellie off the road toward the trail.

Michael looked up and down the road, then followed after her. "Can't let anyone see us," he said, catching up with her. "If your friend's the one that shot up Champ's shoulder, you can bet he's got his men out looking for him."

A swallowtail butterfly flitted past. Ducking under a low branch, Hattie entered the woods. Leaves fluttered in the breeze, and the shade felt cool and welcoming. As her eyes adjusted, she was struck by the beauty of the forest. A pang of longing seized her heart. If only Thom were here to share the moment with her.

Shaking off her sadness, she continued along the trail. It was John Elliott who needed her now, and it didn't matter whether she felt anything for him or not.

Behind her, Michael began to whistle "When Johnny Comes Marching Home." The song would let Elliott know they were friendly, Hattie thought. But it would also signal to Farmington's bushwhackers that they were foes.

On the ground ahead, she spotted something glinting in the sunlight. As she neared, she saw it was a bit of metal tubing protruding from the weeds. She stopped Nellie, then slid from the saddle Michael had provided.

She reached for the gleaming metal, a metal tube inserted into a rubber stopper that plugged the opening to a glass vial. She wrapped her fingers around the glass. Straightening, she held the stoppered bottle up to a ray of sunlight streaming through the branches. The light glinted off it. Innocuous. But if filled with cyanide, the gas released through the tube could kill.

Michael came alongside her. "What you got there?"

"That man who was with Farmington, the one needing medical attention—he must have dropped this. Part of his plan to harm Burnside's troops."

Michael shook his head. "Seen a lot of strange things in this war, but never heard of no one getting hurt by a bottle."

"He's a devious man." She fingered the bottle, wondering whether she should keep it as evidence. But it proved nothing. It was only a stoppered vial that could have been used for any number of purposes.

She tossed the vial back where she'd found it. Blackstone had been sidelined. Burnside would be warned. It wasn't the revenge she'd sought, but for now, it would have to do.

Michael took up his whistling again as they continued along the trail. The uncertainty of what lay ahead jangled Hattie's nerves. To quiet them, she hummed along with the tune.

When Johnny comes marching home again, Hurrah, hurrah!
We'll give him a hearty welcome then, Hurrah, hurrah!
The men will cheer, the boys will shout,
The ladies, they will all turn out.

The glory of war. Did anyone truly believe it? She supposed she had at first. Then she'd witnessed the wounded, the dying, the dead. She'd seen what lengths men like Blackstone would go to in pursuit of victory.

The faint smell of campfire smoke wafted in the breeze. Ahead, she saw a break in the trees. Filled with anticipation and dread, she urged Nellie forward.

"Here." Elliott's voice, faint but discernable. "Over here."

"John? Is that you?"

She couldn't make out his reply, barely more than a gurgle carried on the wind. Her name, maybe.

She tugged the reins, then dismounted. Ahead she saw the ashes from last night's fire. Beyond that was her blanket in a heap on the ground. She turned a circle, searching. Several yards away, she spotted him, leaning against the thick trunk of a spreading oak tree.

She ran to him. Her skirt snagged on a bramble. Tugging it free, she heard the fabric rip. She reached the oak, then knelt beside him. She touched his forehead, smoothing back a lock of hair. His eyes were listless, but she saw a flicker of recognition.

"Hattie," he said, his voice barely more than a whisper. He closed his eyes, his lips moving as if he was trying to say more.

"Shhhh," she said. "Just rest. I've brought help."

His lips quit moving, and his face seemed to relax. She pressed her hand to his neck. His skin was clammy and his pulse was weak. Leaves and twigs littered his chest. He must have crawled some distance to get to this spot.

The worst of it was his right leg. Stretched out in front of him, it was drenched in so much blood that for a second, she had to look away. At the top of his thigh, he'd tied a strip of fabric torn from his shirt. Trying to staunch the flow of blood, she thought.

She scarcely noticed Michael, dismounting his horse and kneeling at her side. "He don't look good."

"Can we...get him out of here somehow?"

"Might be we could drag him. But if the bleeding starts up again—"

"There's a bedroll over where we camped," she said. "We could make a stretcher with a blanket and carry him out."

"Won't hurt to try," Michael said, but he sounded doubtful. "I'll fetch the blanket."

As he went back for the blanket, she took Elliott's hand. The day was warm, but his fingers were cold.

"Hang on, John. You've made it this far. We're going to get you out of here."

His eyelids fluttered open. "So...so thirsty," he whispered.

She reached for his canteen and unscrewed the cap. Gently, she lifted his head and put the canteen to his parched lips. "Don't gulp," she warned, the advice she'd heard Edith Greenfield give injured patients.

Sipping the water, he struggled to keep his head up. With a loss of blood, Edith always said it was important to lower the patient's head.

"Let's get you more comfortable," Hattie said when Elliott had finished drinking. "You need to lie down."

He nodded. She could see him trying to shift his position but to little effect.

"Let me help." She hoisted his shoulders away from the tree trunk. His torso was heavy, and it took all her strength to lower his head to her lap. She moved him as gently as she could, but even so, she saw him wince.

"Hattie," he whispered as if he'd only now noticed she was there.

She shushed him. "Save your strength."

Michael returned with the blanket. Though Elliott grimaced in pain, they managed to lift him onto it. With much effort, they heaved him from the ground. For his age, Michael was stronger than he looked. Hattie's arms burned with the effort as they started slowly down the trail, the horses following behind.

The effort exhausted Hattie. It was all she could do to keep her end off the ground. Now and then, she asked Michael to stop so she could catch her breath. Each time, it took more out of her to lift Elliott from the ground and move him further along the trail. His head lolled side to side, and she checked time and again for the rising of his chest, a sign that he was still breathing.

Finally, they reached the road. They lay Elliott in a patch of tall weeds and considered what to do next. Getting him astride a horse would be next to impossible, Michael said. And Hattie pointed out that even if they were able to manage it, they might run into Rebel soldiers who'd arrest them all, and that would be a death sentence for Elliott.

As they were considering what to do, a man with a cart approached. Thankfully, he was one of Michael's neighbors, friendly to the Union cause. He stopped, and when they explained the situation, he rearranged the hay bales in his cart to make room for Elliott, then helped Michael hoist him inside.

While Michael and the driver tied their horses behind the wagon, Hattie climbed in the back and covered Elliott with loose hay, hoping to disguise him in case Rebel soldiers stopped them. When the horses were secure, Michael offered his hand to help her down, but she refused, saying she wanted to stay in the back with Elliott. Withdrawing his hand, Michael shook his head, then climbed up front with the driver.

As they drove off, Hattie murmured encouragement though she doubted Elliott could hear her. As best she could, she also tried to cushion his leg from the worst of the road's bumps. It seemed to take forever to reach Pleasant Hill. *Hurry, hurry,* she silently urged the horses.

She and Michael had agreed there was no point in taking Elliott to the Reb-friendly Doc Nearman. Instead, they brought him to Sarah, who from her midwifery knew a good deal about treating patients who'd lost a lot of blood.

Feeling worse than useless, Hattie wrung her hands. Pauline slung her arm over her shoulder, trying to reassure her. Sarah managed to rouse Elliott enough that he could down some whisky. Camille helped her wash his leg so she could find the wound. Hattie averted her eyes while Sarah cut into his flesh. Elliott groaned as she fished the bullet from his leg, then tied off a severed vein and stitched up the wound.

"The best we can do under the circumstances," Sarah said as she washed the blood from her hands. "Now we wait and see."

~ ~ ~

Camille returned to Maryville the next day, riding in the same cart that had transported Elliott, the farmer having a load of muskmelons to take to town. She took with her a note Hattie had penned to General Burnside:

I write to you as an operative with Colonel Truesdail in Nashville. There is reason to believe that you and your men may face sabotage of an unusual type at the hands of Confederate guerillas operating in the eastern part of the state. Be especially wary in closed spaces.

H. Thomas

Hattie stayed at Elliott's bedside in the room off the kitchen, leaving only when Pauline insisted on spelling her so she could get some rest herself. Two days after they'd found him, he opened his eyes briefly. Holding his head as she had in the forest, Hattie offered water, which he sipped greedily. Laying his head back down, he smiled faintly, then drifted back to sleep.

On the third day, Hattie came downstairs after a few hours of fitful sleep to find Elliott propped up on pillows. Pauline rose from the chair at his bedside. "Our patient's on the mend." She smiled knowingly. "He's been asking for you."

Pauline slipped out the door, and Hattie took her seat, elated and yet awkward, too, as if Elliott were a stranger.

"You're a sight for sore eyes," he said weakly.

Thom had said the same to her once. She shook her head slightly, pushing the memory from her mind. "It's good to see you awake."

"I feel like hell," he said. "I only hope those bastards got the worst of it. Please tell me they're dead."

She shook her head. "You slowed them down though. A local doctor treated them both for gunshot wounds. Word is that they've moved on."

"You wanted to see Blackstone captured," he said.

"I did." She hated that Blackstone had slipped from her reach. "But I was able to warn General Burnside of the plot I suspected."

He shook his head though she could see the effort pained him. "I should've listened to you."

Sarah came in then, carrying a bowl of her bone broth. She greeted Elliott cheerfully, as if he'd been awake the whole while. Hattie had seen Edith do the same with a seriously ill patient, the idea being that a dire assessment could encourage dire outcomes owing to the patient's state of mind.

Sarah left the soup with Hattie. She spooned broth from the bowl, and Elliott swallowed it. Despite his weakened state, she saw a glint in his eyes like she'd seen that night at the campfire. "It's Farmington I wanted dead," he said, leaning back on the pillows. "Blackstone just got in the way."

She sat back, spoon in hand, a realization forming in her mind. "Champ Farmington hurt you," she said.

Elliott turned his face to the wall. A moment later, he turned back to her, his lips pressed firmly together, his eyes glistening with tears.

She set the bowl and spoon aside, then took his hand. "I understand that sort of hurt. The kind that makes you want to hurt back harder even though you know that's impossible. It's why I was so intent on cornering Luke Blackstone. I wanted to get even for a wrong he did to me. My desire for vengeance put you in harm's way. I'm sorry for that."

His gaze softened. "There was no way I'd have let you go after him alone. And if I'd known Farmington was involved...I couldn't have lived with myself if he'd taken you from me too."

Taken you from me too. Her heart ached for him.

She let go of his hand. "I owe you an explanation. I am...I was...with the Pinkerton Agency. I took an assignment as a courier's wife. Thom Welton was the courier."

Recognition lit Elliott's eyes. "The spy Rebels hanged in Richmond. It was in all the papers."

She nodded. "I...we...had fallen in love. We made plans together for when the fighting was over. Then Blackstone turned us in. I escaped, but Thom was killed. Ever since, I've wanted to get back at Blackstone. I heard he'd gone to Tennessee. So instead of returning to Pinkerton's, I went to General Sharpe and asked for a posting here, hoping I'd find him."

"And you did." He shook his head. "But I ignored your concerns."

"I don't blame you. You and I got off to a rocky start, and I wasn't exactly forthcoming about my motives."

He reached for her hand. "You should know my motives too. Two years ago last spring, when the war was just getting underway, I let it be known that I intended to serve on the Union side. I knew there'd be people around these parts who'd disagree. What I didn't know was that a man like Champ Farmington would come after me. A man evil enough to know that I'd have preferred death over being forced to watch..." He choked on his words. "Forced to watch him kill my wife and our baby girl."

"Oh, John." She squeezed his hand. "I'm so sorry."

The glint she'd seen earlier returned to his eyes. "We can go after them, Hattie, just as soon as I'm well. Track down Farmington and Blackstone both, and see that justice is served. There's no one I'd rather have at my side."

She hesitated, unsure how to respond. Elliott's need to control, his lack of trust, his desire to protect her—it all went back to the horror of Farmington's ruthless murder of the people he loved most in the world. She understood all too well the depths to which grief and the desire for revenge could take a person. But she also knew, looking into his eyes, how those things could cloud a person's thinking.

She set her hand on his cheek. "You're a good man, John Elliott. But much as I despise Blackstone, I've learned that revenge is a darker path than I want to follow."

The glint was still in his eyes, but she detected sadness there too. "You're a better person than I am, Hattie."

She rose from her chair, then bent to kiss his forehead. "Not better. But having come so close, I see now that even if I succeeded in getting back at Blackstone, it wouldn't bring Thom back. I'd rather honor his memory, and I can better do that looking forward, not back."

Epilogue

November 11, 1863

Anne gave birth to her daughter on a blustery November day. She arrived two weeks early, right after Hattie returned to Indianapolis in anticipation of her birth. Hattie was glad she'd arrived in time to sit with Anne through her labor.

Pressing a cool rag to her forehead, she could see the pain Anne endured, though there were none of the histrionics of Pauline's feigned childbirth. But the pain was forgotten when the midwife lifted the child, still waxy and red from the birthing, and placed her in Anne's arms. The adoration in Anne's eyes was like nothing Hattie had ever seen, the feeling of love so thick in the room that it seemed something she could reach out and touch. Anne called the child Josephine, after her beloved grandmother who'd died near the start of the war.

Now, two days after Jo's birth, Anne's husband Franklin had yet to meet his daughter. While his wife was having their baby, he'd been in southern Indiana's Gibson County. Anne was vague about his business there.

But the day after Jo's birth, Hattie had come across a clue. While searching for a pen in Franklin's desk drawer, she'd come across a stash of Knights of the Golden Circle tickets. The Knights were a radical arm of the Copperheads, the self-termed Peace Democrats who were trying to take over the Indiana legislature. Hattie tried to get Anne to elaborate on Franklin's political activity, but she seemed reluctant to talk about it. Hattie hoped for that little Jo's sake, her parents would be able to mend their differences.

Though Hattie knew next to nothing about cooking, Sarah had shown her how to make bone broth and biscuits while Lieutenant Elliott was recovering. Now she fixed these for Anne, though Anne's mother brought meals too. When Anne rested Hattie held the baby, surprised at how warm and soft she felt in her arms. Anne's mother warned that they'd spoil the child by holding her so much, but Hattie noticed that she, too, seemed reluctant to let go of her first grandchild.

Mrs. Duncan hovered about a good deal during the day, but when the two friends were alone at night, Hattie entertained Anne with details of the adventures she'd had in Tennessee. Anne insisted on knowing all about Pauline and Edith Greenfield, who'd doctored Henry Duncan back in Washington. She teased Hattie about John Elliott's interest, but Hattie assured her that while there was much about the lieutenant she admired, she still felt loyal to Thom.

"You have to let go," Anne said. "He'd have wanted you to be happy."

Hattie rocked forward and back in her chair, the baby on her shoulder. She had only a precious few more hours with Anne and the baby. Franklin was due back tomorrow, and Hattie intended to be gone by then.

"I'm happy enough." Saying this, Hattie felt as if she was trying to convince herself as much as she was Anne. "I've gotten better at spying."

"You were good from the start," Anne said. "Breaking those codes when we worked in Pinkerton's mailroom. Delivering letters when Thom was sick."

A lump rose in Hattie's throat at the mention of Thom. She'd go days thinking she'd gotten past her grief, and then all at once, her feelings would rush over her.

"I made mistakes." She touched the chain where Thom's watch hung.

Anne studied her face. "You miss him still"

Hattie nodded. "I've been thinking lately about him being buried in Richmond. He'd have hated that. Maybe I can convince Mr. Pinkerton to get him moved north."

"That's kind of you," Anne said. "And Mr. Pinkerton might try to persuade you to work for him again. Would you do it?"

Stirring, the baby lifted her head. Her gray eyes seemed to fix a moment on Hattie. She patted Jo's back softly, and the child relaxed.

"I'm not sure. I want to be useful to the cause. I'd also like to find George, but I'd rather not deal with Lafayette Baker."

"You won't be writing a book like your friend?" Anne teased.

"Pauline's got a much more vivid imagination than I do. Whatever she ends up writing, it will have people turning pages. How much of it will be true is anyone's guess."

Jo stirred again, then started to whimper. Anne reached for her, and Hattie set the small bundle on her chest to nurse. "Might make for good bedtime reading for this one when she's older," Anne said. "She'll be impressed with all that her Aunt Hattie's done."

Hattie laughed. "I expect the only hero of that book will be Pauline. She intends to go on the lecture circuit too. She's asked me to go with her."

"Then you should," Anne said. "Travel while you're young."

And not tied down with a family, Hattie thought. They fell silent a moment, the only sound Jo's greedy suckling.

Anne reached for Hattie's hand. "I'll miss you, you know. If it wasn't for this little one, I'd want to go with you, whatever you do. I can't wait to hear about your next adventure."

Hattie squeezed her hand. "You'll be the first to know."

THE END

**Thank you for reading *Enemy Lines*,
Book Two in the Secrets of the Blue and Gray series.
If you enjoyed this book,
please take a moment to share your thoughts with a review.**

**MORE BOOKS IN VANESSA LIND'S CIVIL WAR SERIES
Prequel *Lady in Disguise (exclusive to newsletter subscribers)*
Book One *The Courier's Wife*
Book Three *Gray Waters***

**Be the first to know about new books and giveaways—
sign up for Vanessa Lind's newsletter and get a free copy
of *Lady in Disguise*, the prequel to *The Courier's Wife*.**

Author's Note

This is a work of fiction, but real women who spied during the Civil War inspired the story. Hattie Logan (Thomas) is based on Hattie Lawson (Lewis), a Pinkerton operative who posed as the wife of courier Timothy Webster, who inspired the character Thom Welton.

Hattie and Timothy spied for the Union, posing as Confederate sympathizers in Baltimore and Richmond. When Timothy fell ill with rheumatoid arthritis and was confined to bed in their Richmond hotel, Hattie took care of him. They were arrested there and imprisoned. Timothy was sentenced to death. Grief-stricken, Hattie did all she could to save him, even making a personal appeal to the wife of Confederate president Jefferson Davis, but to no avail.

The scant accounts of Hattie's life end with her release in a prisoner exchange. From there, she disappears from the annals of history. I chose to have her escape from Libby Prison instead, drawing on the historical record for some details of Hattie and Richard's escape. Elizabeth Van Lew and her Black servant Mary Bowser (Mary Richards Denman) aided the Union prisoners, and Abigail Green helped orchestrate the Libby Prison break.

Dr. Luke Blackstone is a wholly imagined character, though I drew the smallpox plot from an actual incident later in the war instigated by a doctor with Confederate sympathies. Doctors on both sides often worked as spies, passing along information as they crossed enemy lines to tend to patients. It was actually the Confederate Assistant Surgeon General who proposed using cyanide gas to poison Union troops, but his plan was never put in motion.

The inspiration for Edith Greenfield comes from Dr. Mary Walker, a Union doctor who was also a spy. A controversial figure because she dressed in bloomers, convinced that the fashions of the era constrained women, she received a Medal of Honor for her service during the war.

Pauline's character is inspired by actress Pauline Cushman, who spied for the Army of the Cumberland. Pauline's toast to Jefferson Davis endeared her to Rebel sympathizers in the border states of Kentucky and Tennessee. I've attributed Pauline's toast to Hattie, drawing details from Cushman's biography, *Spy of the Cumberland*. Like many biographies of the day, this account of Pauline's adventures is exaggerated, but she was in fact captured and threatened with hanging. She became a popular figure in the North, touring with P.T. Barnum near the war's end.

Colonel Truesdail of the Army Police was an actual person. He directed the activities of spies who worked out of Nashville, including Pauline Cushman. Terrorizing East Tennessee, real-life Confederate guerrilla (bushwhacker) Champ Ferguson inspired the character of Champ Farmington in this book.

The Copperheads that Anne's husband got involved with were a force to be reckoned with in the North, especially after Lincoln's Emancipation Proclamation. Though aligned with the Democratic Party, the most extreme Copperheads also joined groups like the Knights of the Golden Circle and the Sons of Liberty, precursors to the Ku Klux Klan.

Women's societies also played a significant role in the Civil War, including some that were organized in Nashville. Though their primary function was to provide relief to soldiers, there is evidence that at least one of the Nashville societies was involved in smuggling and spying for the South. In this book, the Nashville society's oath comes from a poem allegedly written by an anonymous Civil War woman. Also, a Nashville woman did allegedly keep a Union soldier's leg bone on her mantel.

The Loyal Ladies Home Guard of Maryville was an actual group too. Six women banded together to spy for the Union in their Confederate-controlled hometown, south of Knoxville, Tennessee. Camille's character in this book is based on the real-life Camelia Jane McTeer, the youngest member of the Loyal Ladies.

Tennessee was a significant battleground during the war. It was the last state to secede from the Union, and loyalties there were divided throughout the conflict, especially in Nashville, where Southern sympathizers decried the Union Army's operations in the city, and also in Eastern Tennessee, where the Union-leaning populace resented Confederate occupation.

A significant sidenote to Tennessee's Civil War history involves the town's attempts to deal with the problem of prostitution and venereal disease, which crippled many soldiers. After an unsuccessful effort to relocate prostitutes by sending them to Louisville on a steamship, city officials took the bold move of legalizing prostitution. They required sex workers to be licensed, a process that involved weekly health checks.

Part of my delight in telling this story is to show the profound impact women had on the war and how it was waged. For more heart-rending adventures of women spies in the Civil War, check out all the books in the series SECRETS OF THE BLUE AND GRAY. A sneak peek at Book Three follows here.

Excerpt from Gray Waters

Book Three of the SECRETS OF THE BLUE AND GRAY series
featuring women spies in the American Civil War

C louds hung low over New York Harbor, the waters
mirroring the overcast sky. Hattie Logan huddled under the
eaves of the ferry terminal, her damp hair curling around her face.
There was a chill in the air, and she felt as if it was getting colder by
the minute. March was a fickle month, even back in Indiana where
she'd grown up. But she wasn't accustomed to this sort of damp.

Despite the dismal weather, Hattie felt bright with anticipation.
The Governor's Island ferry was due to dock any minute. Aboard
was Kate Warne, the Pinkerton operative who'd overseen Hattie's
spy work when she'd first come East. Hattie was ready for a change,
and Miss Warne, she hoped, would provide the opportunity.

This was Hattie's first time in New York, and the city amazed
her. Nowhere had she ever seen so much excitement and activity
concentrated in a small area. She'd been told more than 800,000
people lived on Manhattan Island alone, many of them recent
immigrants crowded into the tenements of the Five Points district.

In three years of spying for the Union, Hattie had traveled to Washington City, Richmond, and Nashville. She'd decoded messages, posed as a courier's wife, and used her acting talents to endear herself to the enemy. She'd escaped prison and thwarted a Rebel attack. She'd found and lost love. This was far more adventure than she'd have known if not for the war, and parts of it she could have done without. Yet at the same time, she wanted more. Not excitement for its own sake, but a sense that she was truly making a difference.

The rain that had fallen in sheets only moments ago was now a steady drizzle. A bank of fog rolled in, obscuring Hattie's view of the boats plying the harbor's waters. Ships blew their horns, signaling their locations with sounds that might have come from a crazed calliope. As hard as the war had been on the nation these past three years, commerce appeared to be thriving.

Then the mist lifted, and Hattie saw the ferry pulling up to the dock. Her fingers chilled to the bone, she clutched the edges of her cloak, keeping it warm about her shoulders as she scanned the faces of disembarking passengers for Miss Warne. When at last Hattie spotted her, she had to look twice. Usually, Miss Warne dressed plainly. Today she looked as if she'd stepped from the pages of Godey's Lady's Book. Beneath her velvet cloak, she wore a black grenadine dress with a standing collar and a fashionable black silk bow at the neck, the edges of a white braided sacque peeking out beneath her cloak.

Other than her manner of dress, Kate Warne looked much as Hattie remembered, her features becoming and yet unremarkable, her gaze soft and unassuming, inspiring trust. This served her well in her work, Hattie knew.

Spotting Hattie, Miss Warne's lips turned in a rare smile, and her pace quickened. Approaching, she held out her arms. "My dear," she said, pressing her cheek to Hattie's. "So good to see you,"

From the generally reserved woman, the greeting was effusive. Hattie knew it was an act, a show of affection to suggest they were longtime friends or family. Still, her heart warmed, Kate Warne being someone whose trust she coveted.

"A delight to see you as well," Hattie said. "You're looking well."

"As are you," Miss Warne said. "Though I fear you'll catch your death if you stay out in this chill a moment longer."

They linked arms, and Miss Warne led her at a brisk pace toward a carriage. Acknowledging the operative with a nod, the driver helped them inside. To fend off the chill, they arranged a robe over their laps, and the horses set off, hooves clomping, toward Broadway, the main thoroughfare.

"Thank you for meeting the ferry." Miss Warne removed her hat and brushed raindrops from its brim. "There's a chance I'm being followed, and an encounter at the ferry terminal seemed least likely to arouse suspicions. I wouldn't want you to be drawn into my current operation."

"Unless I want to be drawn in," Hattie said.

Miss Warne tilted her head slightly, taking this is. "You'd like to return to Pinkerton's?"

"Perhaps," Hattie said, holding her gaze. She looked up to her former supervisor, but at the same time, Kate Warne could unnerve her. While with the Pinkerton agency, Miss Warne had befriended bank robbers and nabbed Confederate spies. She'd feigned injury to gain access to a suspect's home, and she'd posed as a fortuneteller to extract information about a murder. She'd even helped uncover and thwart a plot to save President Lincoln from possible assassination.

By comparison, Hattie felt like a failure. In her first real assignment with Pinkerton's, she'd been arrested and imprisoned, as had her companion, Thom Welton, the love of her young life. Unable to save Thom, she'd gone after Dr. Luke Blackstone, the man who'd betrayed them. But she'd ended up risking another man's life, and in the end, Blackstone had gotten away.

In light of these failures, Hattie had gladly stepped away from spying, accepting an offer to travel with her friend Pauline Carlton.

Now she was restless. She knew she could do more. Not just for the Union cause, but for herself.

Miss Warne's eyes softened, and she patted Hattie's hand. "Mr. Pinkerton feels terrible about what happened to you and Thom, you know. He tried everything to get you out of prison. Only..." Her voice trailed off.

"Only what?" Hattie couldn't hide the edge in her voice.

"Only he wonders why you didn't come to him when you first escape instead of going to General Sharpe."

Hattie suppressed a sigh. Three agencies, with three men in charge, each claiming to be the nation's "Secret Service." No wonder Allen Pinkerton resented her having taken a position with one of his competitors.

"I intended no slight," she said. "But I couldn't find you in Washington, Miss Warne."

"Call me Kate. I'm no longer your supervisor, after all."

"Kate," Hattie said, trying out the name, but it felt odd on her tongue. "I went to the house where you'd kept your office in Washington, but you were no longer there."

Kate offered a rueful smile. "You're a spy, Hattie. If you'd truly wanted to, you could have found me."

Color rose in Hattie's cheeks. "I had something specific in mind, and I didn't think Mr. Pinkerton would go along with it. An assignment in Tennessee, where I'd been told I might find Luke Blackstone."

Kate's lips turned in a slight frown. "You wanted revenge."

Hattie nodded slowly. Stated so bluntly, the error of her pursuit now seemed obvious, especially since she'd nearly gotten her Army Police supervisor killed in the process. "I wanted to stop Blackstone from harming anyone else. I discovered he was plotting to use a chemical gas to harm Union soldiers."

"So you had him arrested?"

Hattie jutted her chin. "I made sure the generals knew of his plans. That's the best I could do."

"I've always known you to do your best, Hattie. At times I've wondered what you're trying to prove."

That I'm competent, Hattie might have said. *That I'm worthy.*

She sat up straighter. "Does that mean you'd give me another chance at Pinkerton's?"

"Of course. I take it you're no longer on assignment with General Sharpe?"

Hattie shook her head. "There were complications. I reported to the Army Police in Nashville. But the lieutenant there..." Her voice trailed off. How to explain John Elliott's troubled past, his desire to protect her, his affection for her, when she'd vowed to stay to Thom Welton's memory? She cleared her throat. "The lieutenant is a good man. But I want to do more than what he'll allow."

Miss Warne nodded. "I see," she said, committing to nothing.

That's her nature, Hattie told herself. *She's not passing judgment.* "I thought I might be able to do something more meaningful at Pinkerton's. Something that would truly make a difference."

Miss Warne offered a crooked smile. "We like to think that every case we pursue makes a difference. Currently, our focus is on exposing corruption and grift. The Army's quartermasters are uniquely positioned to profit from the war, and some are doing so quite handsomely. At Governor's Island today, I presented myself as the wife of a businessman who proposed to sell camp stoves to the army at inflated prices with the understanding that the quartermaster who approved the purchase would receive a share of the profits. Sadly, the gentleman readily agreed." Her gaze seemed to deepen. "Is that the sort of making a difference you have in mind?"

Hattie glanced out the window. To the east, she saw the tenements that housed some of New York's poorest working-class residents. They were the city's lifeblood, and yet she knew how they suffered as wartime prices rose and wages stagnated. For the wealthy to profit in such circumstances was egregious. But could she truly distinguish herself, exposing their corruption?

"It sounds like an important effort," she said.

"But not a glamorous one," Miss Warne said. "Nor is it especially exciting. I suspect you want something more."

Hattie smiled. "Your powers of observation are acute."

"An occupational hazard." Kate nodded at the window. "There's your hotel,"

The carriage slowed, the driver steering deftly among the other carriages to the curb. A pang of sadness struck Hattie. For all she'd anticipated this reunion, it was ending all too soon, with Hattie having gained no real clarity about her future.

"It's been good to see you, Miss Warne. You've always..." Her voice caught in her throat. "Always believed in me. I appreciate that."

"Kate." She smiled. "There's always a place for you at Pinkerton's, Hattie, should you decide you want it. I trust you to choose the best course for yourself going forward."

"Thank you." She wished she shared Kate Warne's confidence. "If I may, there's another matter that's been weighing on me heavily. Thom Welton." She blinked back tears. "What became of him after his death? His body, I mean."

"The Confederates say they've buried him outside Richmond. An inglorious end, I'm afraid."

"I'd like to see him properly buried on northern soil," Hattie said. "I know it will take some effort, but I think we could convince the Rebels to allow his body to be moved. I could make some overtures in Washington. General Sharpe might be of help. Perhaps I could even get an audience with Mr. Lincoln. But I'll need Mr. Pinkerton's help in procuring a proper resting place in the North."

Miss Warne clasped Hattie's hand, an unexpectedly warm gesture. "That's kind of you, Hattie. Thom would have appreciated your concern. But there's something you should know."

Visit www.vanessalind.com to order *Gray Waters*, Book Three in the historical fiction series Secrets of the Blue and Gray.

Want to be the first to know about Vanessa Lind's latest books? Sign up for her Passion for the Past newsletter and receive a free copy of *Lady in Disguise*, prequel to *The Courier's Wife*.